THE
BLACK
WOLF

Louise Penny is the number one *New York Times* bestselling author of the Chief Inspector Gamache series. *Still Life*, the first of the series, won the CWA John Creasey Dagger in 2006. A recipient of virtually every existing award for crime fiction, Louise was also granted the Order of Canada in 2014 and received an honorary doctorate of literature from Carleton University and the Ordre Nationale du Québec in 2017. She lives in a small village south of Montreal.

The Chief Inspector Gamache Series

Still Life
A Fatal Grace
The Cruellest Month
A Rule Against Murder
The Brutal Telling
Bury Your Dead
A Trick of the Light
The Beautiful Mystery
How the Light Gets In
The Long Way Home
The Nature of the Beast
A Great Reckoning
Glass Houses
Kingdom of the Blind
A Better Man
All the Devils Are Here
The Madness of Crowds
A World of Curiosities
The Grey Wolf

LOUISE PENNY

THE
BLACK
WOLF

HODDER &
STOUGHTON

First published in the United States in 2025 by Minotaur,
a division of St Martin's Publishing Group
First published in Great Britain in 2025 by Hodder & Stoughton Limited
An Hachette UK company

The authorised representative in the EEA is Hachette Ireland, 8 Castlecourt
Centre, Dublin 15, D15 XTP3, Ireland (email: info@hbgi.ie)

1

Map by Rhys Davies

Quotes from *Billy Bishop Goes to War* © 1981, 2012 by John MacLachlan Gray
with Eric Peterson, Talonbooks, used with permission of the publisher.

A CIP catalogue record for this title is available from the British Library

Hardback ISBN 9781399730570
Trade Paperback ISBN 9781399730587
ebook ISBN 9781399730594

Printed and bound in Great Britain by Clays Ltd, Elcograf S.p.A.

Hodder & Stoughton policy is to use papers that are natural, renewable
and recyclable products and made from wood grown in sustainable
forests. The logging and manufacturing processes are expected to
conform to the environmental regulations of the country of origin.

Hodder & Stoughton Limited
Carmelite House
50 Victoria Embankment
London EC4Y 0DZ

www.hodder.co.uk

*For Andy Martin, my longtime publisher and,
more importantly, my longtime friend.
Thank you for climbing the mountain with me.*

Du Moulin

AUTHOR'S NOTE

I wrote this book over the course of 2024, and turned in the final draft to my publisher in September 2024. Imagine my surprise in January 2025 when I started spotting headlines that could have been ripped right from the book...

CHAPTER 1

We have a problem."

Now, weeks later, Chief Inspector Armand Gamache could not overstate what a huge understatement that had been. Though at the time, while it was clear something was off, it had seemed only that.

A slight odor. A scent, a sense of something going bad.

A problem.

Not a crisis. Not a looming catastrophe that put the poisoning plot, if not to shame, then into perspective.

Jean-Guy Beauvoir and Isabelle Lacoste, his dual seconds-in-command at the Sûreté du Québec, had joined him in Three Pines in the small hours of that August morning, and together they'd reread and reread the second notebook, the one they'd underestimated, even dismissed.

The one they'd, he'd, assumed contained preliminary notes. Not the final, the fatal one, that had already killed so many.

When they'd arrived, Armand hadn't told Jean-Guy and Isabelle what he thought. He wanted to see if they saw what he did. He knew the blast in Montréal's water-treatment plant had severely affected his hearing. Maybe his other senses had also been jarred. So that he could no longer see and think clearly. Could no longer trust what his eyes, his common sense, his sixth sense, the tingling in his scalp told him.

But both Beauvoir and Lacoste, his best and brightest, had looked up and nodded.

"We have a problem," they'd agreed.

He couldn't actually hear the words over the scream of the millions of cicadas nesting in his head since the explosion, but he'd become adept at lip-reading. And if their mouths hadn't told him, their eyes, their expressions, the sudden tension in their bodies did.

But still it was far from clear what they were now facing. What they'd missed, dismissed.

They only knew they'd been wrong about the order of the books the young biologist had hidden. They'd assumed the one outlining the poisoning plot was the second. The conclusion. The end.

But they were wrong. It was just the beginning.

Even now, weeks later, the exact threat was still concealed inside the words, the notations, the cryptic drawings and numbers that Charles Langlois had left behind. Before he'd been murdered. Mowed down within sight, within reach of Armand himself.

He'd died holding Armand's hand. Clinging to his eyes. A young man, barely more than a boy, about to die.

When Armand had begged him for some clue, some idea, of what was happening, Charles had coughed up one blood-spattered word.

"Family."

Nothing more.

Charles had been the first of many to die, some colluding in the poisoning plot, some trying to stop it, including the Grey Wolf himself. Giving his life to stop a catastrophe.

Dom Philippe was the one who'd first, years earlier on the shores of a pristine lake, told Armand the tale of the grey and black wolves, engaged in battle. The one advocating for decency, for peace, for civility and the courage to be kind. To forgive.

The other pressing forward with an agenda of hate, of aggression. Of retribution. Of a quest for power and domination, through fear. Through twisting the truth into a great lie, a great grievance.

Which one would win?

The Grey Wolf was gone. Murdered.

They'd thought the Black Wolf had been captured. But now, as Armand stepped out of the shower this early October morning, he was far from sure.

It was still dark outside when the head of homicide for the Sûreté wiped the condensation off the bathroom mirror and a man in his late fifties appeared, half his face covered in shaving cream. Though it happened each and every morning, the face that looked back could still surprise him.

Away from any reflection, he was in his early forties. But each morning he was reminded that was not actually true. And getting less true by the moment, he thought as he brushed grey hair, damp and askew from the shower, off his forehead, then continued to shave.

The creases that appeared with each stroke of the razor were more pronounced, etching deeper into his face with every year, every month, each day and concern.

He wondered what his father would have looked like, had he reached this age.

Almost every working day Armand Gamache knelt beside people who would grow no older; many would never brush grey hair from their foreheads or see lines down their faces. Would never meet children or grandchildren.

And so he did not begrudge these signs of age, they just slightly surprised him.

Behind him in the reflection, Armand saw their bedroom in the village of Three Pines. Worn oriental rugs were scattered on the wide-plank pine floors. The walls were covered in bookcases and paintings inherited when parents and grandparents died. Eclectic and not, perhaps, great art, but comforting in their familiarity. And the more appreciated for it.

A large armchair in the corner held the clothes they'd taken off the night before and tossed there, his on top of hers because he'd crawled into bed later. Though Reine-Marie had remained reading after he'd already fallen asleep, the book splayed on his chest and his reading glasses slipping down his nose.

Each morning he found both placed safely on the bedside table.

A cold breeze through the slightly open windows fluttered the curtains and brought in fresh morning air, lightly scented with pine and musky autumn leaves.

The dogs, Henri and Fred, were asleep at the foot of the queen bed, while Gracie, who might or might not be a chipmunk, or a ferret, had made a nest of their clothes and now lay half buried in them.

But while Armand took all this in, his eyes sought only one thing. They came to rest, like a homing instinct, on Reine-Marie. She was curled under the duvet, asleep. Her grey hair lay on the pillow. Her mouth was open slightly, no doubt snoring softly. A sound he'd never thought about but now missed.

He smiled, and as he did, the lines in his face deepened. His pleasure cut through and broke up those etched there by stress, by worry, by pain and sorrow.

His smile overpowered them. Though one remained. The deep scar at his temple that spoke of a sorrow that would never, could never, should never go away completely. He would carry it, Armand knew, into the next life and the next. Until he could make amends. For that terrible failure.

Now, in early October, the sun was rising later and later, though Armand himself was getting up earlier and earlier, propelled out of bed by the siren in his head and the agonizing feeling, the dread, that he'd made a mistake.

We have a problem.

The words, spoken in unison by Jean-Guy and Isabelle as they'd sat in the living room and read that second notebook weeks ago, were getting louder and louder.

We have a problem.

He shaved off the rest of the stubble and wiped his face with the moist cloth. Then, holding on to the edges of the sink, he leaned in and took a good, hard look in the mirror. He had to be brutally honest with himself.

He'd been over and over Charles Langlois's second notebook. He'd practically memorized all the strange entries the young biologist had made.

They had a problem, and the problem was that they still didn't know what the problem was. Only that one existed. Something dreadful was about to happen. Langlois, before he'd been murdered, had stumbled onto something that involved poisoning the drinking water of Montréal but did not stop there. That one terrible act of domestic terrorism was simply a prelude, perhaps even misdirection. Meant to mask what was really happening.

And Armand had fallen for it.

True, he and his team had stopped the poisoning, but they hadn't seen that there was something else he should have given equal weight to. Another tranche, a deeper, darker level. Now Armand went to bed later and later and was woken up earlier and earlier by the howl in his head and the sickening feeling he'd made another terrible, terrible mistake. In focusing on the one plot, he'd given the other time to grow, to fester, to march toward completion.

Somewhere out there, in the darkness, a black wolf was feeding, being fed. Growing.

The creature was becoming immense, grotesque. Powerful. Looming over them. Perhaps so close it was unrecognizable for what it was.

Watching and waiting.

We wait. We wait.

The problem, Armand was beginning to believe, wasn't just out there, but in here. In the mirror. The problem was him. But maybe, maybe, so was the solution.

Some malady is coming upon us. We wait. We wait.

"Not a problem."

"How can you know that? You underestimated him once."

As she listened to Joseph Moretti's warm voice down the phone line, she felt the thin ice crack beneath her.

She'd come close, so close, to solid ground. To safety. After years out in the wilderness, she'd finally been able to see the shore. Even smell it. That sweet pine scent that had always signaled happy times. The Christmas tree, with its playful lights and ornaments and presents. That first walk in the forest after the winter melt when the air finally held some warmth, and the evergreen needles released their scent.

Ever green. What a concept. Nature was resilient. Even optimistic.

Humankind less so.

After years of skating, of balancing, of slipping and sliding, she thought she could finally pull herself to safety. Finally.

And then, at the last moment, disaster. Thanks to Gamache. That fucker. She could not afford another mistake. Another misjudgment. Another moment of weakness.

Though they were miles apart on this Saturday morning in early October, she in her office in downtown Montréal and Moretti in the north end of Montréal at the Jean-Talon farmers' market, she could feel his eyes on her. Intense, penetrating. Strip-searching her. Removing layers, not just of her clothing but of her skin, tearing it off in strips as he searched for any lie she might be hiding in her flesh, in her bones, in her marrow.

After all these years, he still did not trust her. Despite all she'd done. He was like some predator that relied on instinct. Sniffing the air for the stench of betrayal, of approaching danger.

She wished she could stop there. Dismiss him as a wild creature, but the fact was, over the years, as she'd watched him closely, she'd seen not just the mafia boss's cunning, his guile, his charm and brutality, but also his intelligence.

This was no madman, careering from crime to hideous crime. This was a man who could have been anything.

Had Joseph been born into any family other than the Morettis, any other dynasty, his life would have been different.

But now she wondered if that was true.

For all his education and intelligence, something was off. A screw was loose. Whether it was loosened by his upbringing or by genetics, she didn't know. What she did know was that something rancid, something corrosive, was seeping through that opening.

"You say Gamache isn't a problem," said Moretti. "But he and his people managed to fuck up the first part of the plan. Killing six of my soldiers, including two made men, in the process. It would be over by now if he hadn't interfered. The Five Families are getting worried. How much does he know? He found the notebooks, right?"

"*Oui.* He gave them to the prosecutors."

"Did he read them?"

She was about to snap, *How would I know?* But pulled herself back.

"I suspect he did." Her voice was calm. "But so did I. I don't think he could tell much from that second book, even if he realizes it's the one that matters."

"You don't think? You don't think?" Moretti's voice had risen, then suddenly dropped to a growl. "You should've had him killed in the church."

"I wanted him to be the one to sound the alarm. They'd have believed him. He's trusted."

"Yeah, well, if he begins to suspect there's more—"

"He won't. Look, the investigation's wrapped. No one is paying any attention. Especially not Gamache. As far as they're concerned, it's over."

She was tired of his paranoia. It was exhausting. She was exhausted. So close to the shore, to the end, she could not afford a mistake now. Another one. Moretti was right. She should have had Gamache killed in the church.

She had to shut this down.

"The biologist is dead—" she began.

"I know that." He was getting snippy.

You should, she thought. *You're the one who had him killed.*

"He's the only one who came close to figuring out what's happening," she continued. "But even he didn't know it all. If he had, he'd have told Gamache when they met at Open Da Night. And even if Charles Langlois had worked it out, no one would have listened to him. Would you, if someone came to you with that story?"

She waited for the laughter, but none came.

"*Non,*" she answered her own question. "You'd have dismissed what he said as unbelievable, and Charles Langlois as crazy, delusional. Paranoid. He had a history of addiction, of mental illness. He'd be seen as a pathetic young man from a homeless shelter who was clearly out of his mind and had bought into one too many conspiracy theories. Ironically, the truth would have proven how crazy he was. No. He knew nothing of the plan."

"He knew enough to contact Gamache," Moretti pointed out. "Gamache listened to him, believed him."

"True, but only about the lesser target. *Voyons,* his notebook is pretty much gibberish unless you know what to look for."

"And Gamache doesn't?"

"He hasn't a clue. He's on leave and recovering in that little village of his. He's been silent since all this happened."

"Silent doesn't mean inactive. You underestimated him once. That can't happen again."

She sighed. "If you're that worried, why not just kill him now? The first snowfall is in the forecast. He probably doesn't have his snow tires on yet. Just run him off the road. *Fini.*"

She waited. *We wait. We wait.*

Moretti was considering it.

"*Non*. If he'd died in the church or the water-treatment plant, that would've been fine. Line of duty and all that. But now? Kill a senior Sûreté du Québec officer? Can you imagine the blowback? Even if it looked like an accident, the timing would be suspicious. There'd be questions. His people would never stop digging and God knows what they'd find. *Non*. We just need to make sure he's not a problem."

"He's not."

"You keep saying that, but how can you be so sure?"

"Because if he has any suspicions, I'll be the first one he comes to."

"He trusts you? Still?"

"Of course. Why not? As far as he knows, I helped end the poison plot."

"You aren't lying to me, are you?"

"I wouldn't do that, Don Moretti. If nothing else, it wouldn't be prudent."

There was a pause, and then soft laughter. "You are many things, but prudent isn't one."

He was probably right, she thought. Otherwise she'd never have found herself this far from shore.

"*Bon*," he finally said. Good. "It'll be over soon."

The thing about psychopaths, and she'd met her fair share, was that they knew they were the sun around which everything moved. They were the light, the dark, the gravity, the rational. The reason and the reason why. Joseph Moretti knew he was the sun, the son, the grandson. The grand sun. That nothing happened without his approval. He was all-seeing, all-knowing.

He was wrong.

This was bigger than even he knew. There was another celestial body that eclipsed even the boss of bosses. She just had to keep skating, keep her equilibrium. Keep him happy and onside. And looking in one direction, and not the other.

"*C'est vrai*," she laughed. "We're safe. Don't worry."

"Oh, I'm not the one who should be worried."

There was a pause, and in that moment she saw her mistake. She'd dared think that she might yet make it to safety.

That was how mistakes were made, how cracks formed. Hope lured people closer to the edge, to the shore. Not realizing that was where the ice melted first. Just feet from solid ground, it gave way, and they plunged into the icy water, their breaths taken away, their hearts spasming, their last view that of the pine trees overhead, almost within reach as they sank.

"And the map?" he asked. Down the phone line she could hear voices raised, calling to each other. Friendly voices.

"We don't know for sure there is one. If Charles Langlois had a map, it's well hidden. If it exists at all, we'll find it. No one else has it, otherwise I'd have heard."

"I think it would be a good idea if you joined me here, Evelyn."

"Now, today? At the market?" She felt her anxiety rise along with the hairs on her forearms.

Was he serious? Was this a test? Or had she already flunked the test? Was it a trap? "But we might be seen together."

"I'm sure you can come up with a believable explanation. You're allowed to shop for dinner."

Into the silence, she sighed. "I'm on my way."

She hung up and looked at the small, slightly disheveled young woman standing at the door to her office.

"You're not going, are you, *patron?*"

"No choice." She put on her fall coat and large hat. "Besides, I do need Brussels sprouts."

"Can't you get them at the grocery store?"

"I was kidding."

They were walking briskly down the long, deserted corridor toward the elevators.

"Stop!"

"What is it?"

Her assistant now hesitated. "I heard what Moretti said. He's right. You should have had Gamache killed."

She nodded. They both knew that was true. That was her mistake, the chink in her armor through which Joseph Moretti was peering. And did he see the big lie?

"Should I get you a car?"

"*Non.* I'll take the Métro."

Just as the elevator doors closed, she heard, "*Fais attention.*"

Be careful.

As she searched her handbag for her subway pass, Chief Inspector Evelyn Tardiff knew they were well beyond careful. It was now just degrees of reckless. Her skates had slid out from under her. Her arms were pinwheeling. She was suspended in midair, and the only question was how bad, how hard, would the fall be? How much would this hurt?

On the station platform, her back pressed against the tile wall, she heard the singsong of an approaching subway train. And sighed. She'd been at this too long. She was getting too old, too tired, too sloppy. She had no idea how to regain her balance, never mind get to the shore.

Survival was not guaranteed.

You should have had Gamache killed.

There was nothing vindictive in it. It was simply true. And might still be necessary. Her only way to shore might be over his body.

Don Moretti slid his phone into his pocket. Picking a plump beefsteak tomato off a neat pile, he caressed its flesh for firmness in a gesture that managed to be sensual. Bringing it to his nose, he inhaled and smiled as he caught his wife's eye, one aisle over. Then he cocked his arm and pretended to throw the tomato at his young daughter, who squealed with laughter and ducked.

Moretti then carefully replaced the tomato. Its thin skin undamaged.

It was a few minutes to seven on this autumn morning, the market not yet open. The farmers still putting out their produce.

The sky was a deep velvety blue at the horizon. The day would dawn bright and fresh and filled with promise. Anything might happen.

CHAPTER 2

⌣

Clara Morrow brought the mug of tepid coffee to her mouth, forgetting that she had a paintbrush clasped between her teeth, like some gunslinger preparing to have a bullet removed.

The analogy wasn't that far off. This stage in her creations was always painful, wracked as she was with insecurities. The bleeding was internal. The wound worse than it appeared.

Survival was not guaranteed.

Through the window of her small home in the Québec village of Three Pines she could see a light at the rambling white clapboard house across the village green, and smoke rising from the chimney.

Someone was up and functioning at the Gamache home. And so early.

Then she noticed a soft glow over the forests and hills that surrounded the village. The sun was rising.

What time was it? Last time she looked, it was 2:17 in the morning, when That Familiar Voice had screamed that she was a fraud. That she was fucked.

It had propelled her out of bed, down the narrow stairs, and into her studio to stare at the canvas and the *merde* that someone, surely not her, had put there.

This was to be the centerpiece of her solo show at Montréal's Musée d'art contemporain.

Fuck. Fuckity, fuck, fuck!

The only comfort was that the bistro would open soon and she could escape into the company of toasted cinnamon buns, dripping butter. And maple-smoked bacon. And, and...

Myrna.

The two women would drink strong café au lait in front of the muttering fire, and for those few minutes Clara could forget the six-shooter pointed at her heart. The trigger being pulled. Pulled...

Putting down the mug and spitting out her brush, Clara Morrow turned her back on the easel and the series she'd been working on for two years.

It was called *Just before something happens*...

"Mario!" Joseph Moretti put his hand on the elderly man's shoulder. "How're your plums?"

"As juicy as ever, Don Moretti."

Both men laughed.

This was an old joke started decades ago when Mario had been a virile young man, and Joseph a child trailing his grandfather around the Marché Jean-Talon. At the time, the boy had thought his grandfather's question was literal, which confused him since Mario was a butcher and did not sell plums.

The joke had been passed down to son and now grandson, who'd finally understood it about the time his own plums appeared. It was clear that the old joke, never clever or even funny, was now distressing to the dignified older man. And always had been. Which was why Moretti, like his father and grandfather, repeated it. Each and every weekend.

Joe Moretti had been coming, man and boy, to this farmers' market in Little Italy every Saturday morning since he was younger than his daughter. Before the market opened, he'd hold his father's hand and walk the aisles a few steps behind his grandfather, amid the hubbub of farmers unloading their produce. Setting up their stalls of bright gourds and multicolored peppers, of fragrant apples and earthy potatoes and assorted onions.

The men and women called to each other. Some singing, some arguing over a football match. A miscalled penalty. Groaning over a free kick that hit the crossbar.

It was good-natured, and young Joe had envied them. Their comradery. The ease with which they laughed and even argued. The apparent simplicity of their lives. The certainty and predictability. What to do. How to do it. While crops might sometimes fail, it was through no fault of their own. They were blameless.

Even as a child, he'd envied that and understood the difference between them.

Young Joseph had also noticed that as his grandfather approached, as his father and even he approached, the farmers fell silent, the laughter stopped. The jocularity dying on their lips, they touched their caps and nodded. Each hoping Don Moretti would stop. Would admire their produce and give them a chance to offer the family the best they had.

And now, decades later, the place looked, sounded, even smelled the same. It was still buzzing. Still fragrant with the scent of fresh-picked autumn fruits and vegetables. Even the blood from the slaughtered animals smelled good to Moretti. Or at least familiar. Now.

As a child, as a teen, as a young man, he'd taken it all in, just as his daughter did now. The young Joe had noted, subconsciously, the respect, the reverence, in which his grandfather and father, his entire family was held. It was their due, his birthright.

Or so it seemed.

A decade later, in his late teens, he'd watched it seep away when the old man had been arrested for running guns into the States and the leadership had passed to Joe Jr.'s father. A man ill-suited to the job. He was too nice, too willing to forgive, too ready to compromise and collaborate with other Québec crime families. To make alliances with the biker gangs, the East End gang. The Irish and Jewish crime families. Too willing to give up territory to preserve peace.

He was weak.

Joe Jr. knew it. And had known from a young age what would have to be done to guarantee survival.

The signs of disrespect when the grandfather had been arrested and the son took over were subtle but immediate and unmistakable. The pies held out to Joe Sr. were charred on the edges. They were ones that could only be given away. To the poor, or the Morettis.

Produce was still offered, but perhaps not the best cuts of meat. Not the choicest of fruit or vegetable. Bruises were evident. As was the message.

But still Joe Sr., the new Don, took the offerings and even thanked the farmers, while Joe Jr.'s lips curled and his emotions curdled, and he took note of names as the Moretti empire crumbled.

But the satisfaction, bordering on glee, of those who enjoyed the downfall was short-lived. As were they.

With the death in prison of the grandfather, the grandson had moved swiftly to establish himself, leapfrogging over his own father. A bold, some said foolish move that threatened all-out war. Until Joseph Moretti Sr. had been killed in Sainte-Émiline, north of Montréal, in a fire at the country home of his mistress. A fire ruled accidental by a young investigator in the Sûreté's Arson division.

Then the reprisals, swift, relentless, merciless, had begun.

And when it was over, Joe Moretti the younger emerged as the new capo di tutti capi. The head of the Sixth Family. The most powerful mob boss in Canada and one of the most powerful in North America, behind the five New York–based mafia families.

On this bright Saturday in early October, while Don Moretti strolled the aisles of the Marché Jean-Talon, collecting gifts and signs of respect, "*Bonjour*, Don Moretti," enjoying the fruits of others' labors, the former arson investigator sat looking at her reflection in the window of the Métro car as it careered through another tunnel.

Jean-Guy Beauvoir stood just inside the church and looked around for his father-in-law.

He'd woken early to the smell of fresh-brewed coffee and a cold breeze scraping his face. He opened his eyes and stared with rancor at the curtains puffing out at the open window.

Fuck. Fuckity, fuck, fuck.

He snuggled deeper into the bed, spooning Annie and feeling her body heat combined with his own warming the duvet around them. He pulled it tighter and pretended the cold air wasn't rushing into the room.

He nudged Annie gently, hoping she'd wake up and shut the window. But she didn't move.

Getting up, he ran to the window with every intention of shutting it, then hopping back into bed. But as he reached it, he saw his father-in-law walking through the soft predawn light along the dirt road that led out of the village. Followed, Dr. Dolittle–like, by the small parade of animals. Henri, the ears that walked like a dog; old Fred; and little Gracie.

Jean-Guy looked back at his warm bed, where Annie was snoring, then returned to the window, but Armand had disappeared.

Closing the window, he kissed Annie and whispered, "I know you're awake, awful woman."

Her snoring grew slightly louder.

After checking on Honoré and Idola, he quickly showered, shaved, put on his heavy fall sweater that smelled of the cedar closet, and his cords. Following the scent of fresh-brewed coffee to the kitchen, he poured two mugs; then he too left the quiet house.

The sun was barely visible through the forest. There was a hint of light, rather than light itself. A promise of things to come. It was a few minutes past seven and the day glistened, bright and fresh and filled with promise. Anything might happen.

A mist hung over the village nestled in the valley as the cooler autumn air mingled with the warm earth. The vapor rose thicker over the Riv-ière Bella Bella, creating a sinewy ribbon over the forest as it followed the freshwater spring through Three Pines and out the other side.

All this gave a village already steeped in mystery an almost mystical feel, heightened even further by the near impossible fall colors of the sur-rounding forest.

The vapor from the mugs joined the mist, adding coffee to the fragrance of fresh grass and mud and the musky fallen leaves. Jean-Guy took a big breath and inhaled a deep sense of peace.

He knew it was temporary, perhaps even illusionary, but he welcomed it as he followed in Armand's footsteps up the hill to St. Thomas's.

Once at the church, he climbed the stairs and paused to look back at the fieldstone and rose brick and white clapboard homes that circled the village green. Three immense pines stood in the middle of the Québec village, tow-ering over the homes and shops, as though sentinels. In fact, as Jean-Guy had learned, three pines planted in formation was an old code, meant to tell those fleeing for their lives that they were finally safe. They had found sanctuary.

People still got sick, still died in Three Pines. Were still hurt, wounded. Terrible things still happened here, as elsewhere. The village did not, could never, guarantee safety from the blows life dealt. That would be ridiculous. The safety they found in the village wasn't physical but emotional.

Whatever happened, they were not alone. There was help and company, and finally, at the end, there was comfort. A hand to hold.

Jean-Guy saw Olivier leave the Bed-and-Brunch he shared with Gabri and walk across the village green to their bistro. Light soon appeared through the mullioned windows. Before long a thin line of smoke would rise from the bistro chimneys, and villagers would take it as a sign far more important in their lives than any papal election.

Breakfast was ready.

Their Saturday would begin in front of the large open fires, with strong coffee and crêpes, or French toast sprinkled with fresh fruit and doused in maple syrup drawn from trees Jean-Guy could see from where he stood.

There'd be scrambled eggs with melted Brie and maple-smoked bacon, flaky croissants and warm cinnamon buns from Sarah's Boulangerie next door.

Most of all, the villagers would start their day with each other. While Armand walked up to the church alone. He sat in the same pew each morning, under the stained-glass image of the boys, the brothers who'd left Three Pines more than a century earlier for the Great War and never returned.

It was an image that haunted not for its heroism, though there was that, but for the fear etched deep and forever into the faces of two of the boys while the third, the youngest brother, looked out at the congregation. Not with accusation, though that would have been understandable, but with something more terrifying. Almost unfathomable.

At the age of seventeen he marched with his brothers to certain death in a futile battle that only presaged the next slaughter. And then he spent the next century staring out at the congregation, at those who'd let this happen, who'd let them go. He wanted them to know one thing.

That he forgave them.

Sneak home and pray you never know / the hell where youth and laughter go.

Each morning Armand sat in that fear and forgiveness and pulled the copy he'd made of Charles's notebook from his pocket, struggling to see what he was missing. Fighting to understand what was written in those pages by another young man who'd also given his life for others.

Armand knew if he got it wrong, it would be unforgivable.

All this Jean-Guy also knew as he turned away from the peaceful view and entered the church.

The lines between Armand's brows deepened.

There was still so much they did not know, but what was clear to the head of homicide for the Sûreté du Québec was that something else was planned. Which meant there were others still out there. Those who had avoided arrest. And to do that, their influence must extend to the highest levels of government, the judiciary, industry. Organized crime.

The police.

Even, he feared, within the Sûreté. He didn't know who, though he had suspicions. Some officers had been arrested in that first sweep, but where there were bad apples, the rot spread. Which was why Armand kept the fact he had not stopped investigating to his tight circle. Only a few knew. Very few. A carefully chosen few.

"There must be more," Armand had whispered that morning as he'd gripped the side of the sink and stared at his reflection.

There must, he'd thought as he'd entered the quiet church, followed by the small parade of creatures. And the ghosts that never left.

"There must," he muttered as he stood very still and stared straight ahead. As he fought to understand what was happening. What was about to happen.

If anything.

A part of him still hoped he was wrong. Hoped he was reading far too much into a dead man's indecipherable notes. Had the screaming in his ear, in his head, made him deaf to reason?

Everyone else was convinced the danger was over. The plotters had been arrested. Were in prison. Including the man behind it all.

The former Deputy Prime Minister of Canada.

Marcus Lauzon denied he was involved, but the evidence against him was overwhelming. While the evidence against Don Moretti had evaporated. Disappeared.

How could that be? How could that man, that murderer, not even be arrested?

The answer was, of course, clear. Someone high up had corrupted the process.

But following that train of thought brought Gamache to an even more troubling question: Why had Moretti gotten off while Marcus Lauzon had been convicted? Would Lauzon, as the Black Wolf, not make sure the evidence against him disappeared, and Moretti fell?

Why the other way around? Why?

There were, of course, two possible answers.

Lauzon preferred to be in prison, beyond suspicion, when something else happened.

Or…

Armand closed his eyes and, teetering on the edge, he took a deep breath, then took the plunge.

Or… he'd been wrong. Marcus Lauzon was not the Black Wolf.

After the inquiry wrapped a few weeks earlier, Armand had called the head of the Sûreté's Organized Crime division. In person was always better, but for now, video and virtual would have to do.

"I have the same questions, Armand." Evelyn Tardiff's words were transcribed at the bottom of the screen for him to read. "It seems incredible that Moretti got off. Who else is involved? And why did the head of the crime family even agree to work with anyone? He's notorious for killing rivals, not partnering with them."

"*Oui.* He murdered his own father for doing the same thing."

"Unfortunately, that could never be proven. God knows I tried. As you know, I was the arson investigator on that case."

"*Oui.*"

There was something else he knew. At the time of the fire that killed Moretti's father, then Agent Tardiff had been approached by the head of the Sûreté to let young Moretti know she'd be open to a bribe. To make the investigation go away.

She did. And slowly over the years she'd gained more and more access to the head of the Montréal mob, even as she rose through the Sûreté ranks.

But what worried him now was that Evelyn Tardiff might have known about the poisoning plot and said nothing. What really worried him now was that he no longer knew whose side she was on.

"I'll see what I can find out," she said. "Though the question is now moot, thankfully. It's over."

Armand left it at that. He wasn't ready to tell her about the suspicions that propelled him out of his warm bed, to sit within the light of the luminous boys and ponder the unimaginable. The unforgivable.

"Morning, numbnuts."

Jean-Guy started, spilling a bit of coffee out of each mug. For a moment a trick of the young light made it look as though one of the stained-glass boys had spoken. And called him numbnuts. That could not be good.

Though Jean-Guy quickly realized who it must be. It was not much better.

Ruth Zardo, the elderly poet, popped up in the pew where she'd apparently been napping.

"Sleeping it off, you old hag?" He slipped onto the bench beside her. Rosa the duck looked at him, clearly pissed off at having been woken up. But then ducks were often pissed off. At least, this one was.

"Fuck, fuck, fuck," Rosa muttered before once again burying her beak between her chest and wing.

"Looking for Clouseau?" Ruth took one of the mugs from Jean-Guy. "For me?"

"Actually—"

Before he could stop her, she took a long sip. "Just coffee. Blech. Why would you bring me that?"

"I—"

"He's in the basement. No doubt hiding from you. Can't say I blame him."

Jean-Guy stared at the mug and wondered how to get it away from her. Armand needn't know she'd taken a sip. "How does he seem to you?"

Ruth considered the question. "Perhaps a bit better. Hard to tell. He seems worried." Now she looked at Jean-Guy more closely. "What's going on? What's he worried about? Why's he down there?"

"Hiding from you, I suspect. Can't say I blame him."

"Shit-head."

"Witch."

He looked at the warm mug cupped in her cold hands and decided not to wrestle her for it. She'd probably win.

As he walked to the stairs, he heard, "Say hi to your boss."

Though on leave from the Sûreté, Armand Gamache was still, and would always be, Beauvoir's mentor and boss. His Chief Inspector. No matter what happened.

And a lot had.

"*Bonjour,* Jean-Guy."

Beauvoir stopped dead at the bottom of the basement stairs, his eyes wide with surprise. "Did you hear me coming?"

Armand's back remained to him, his hands clasped together behind him. Jean-Guy could see the red slashes, scars where the zip ties had bitten into Armand's wrists.

Then the older man turned, and his face broke into a smile of genuine pleasure. At over six feet tall, he was solidly built. His face was worn from days and nights in windswept fields, trudging through forests, kneeling in deep snow beside some unfortunate who had become a corpse, but never just a case.

And yet, if met by chance at a party, Chief Inspector Gamache would easily be mistaken for a professor of ancient history at the Université de Montréal. Someone who studied the lives of those long dead instead of the head of homicide, hunting those who dealt out fresh death.

Jean-Guy had watched him at social events, listening closely as strangers told Armand the minutiae of their lives. He listened and nodded, asking questions. He let whoever he was with know they were not just fascinating, they were precious. Their stories heard and valued.

Though Armand did not go to many parties anymore, and the listening part had changed, after what had happened.

Perhaps the biggest reason Armand would never be taken for a homicide cop was what Jean-Guy saw now. The smile. Radiant, it radiated from the corners of his eyes and mouth, cutting across the worry lines.

Here was a clearly happy man despite, or perhaps because of, all that he'd knelt beside. All that he'd seen.

And he'd seen the worst. But Armand Gamache had also seen the best, and insisted his people see it too and not get mired in the all-too-obvious darkness.

"How else are we going to survive," he told them, "unless we also see the kindness, the courage, the decency in people? There's more goodness than cruelty in this world."

And he believed it.

"I smelled coffee and thought it must be you," Armand explained, his voice only slightly louder than it should have been. He'd become good at modulating it. "Ruth has a whole other smell. Besides, when you and Annie and the children spend the weekend, you always join me here."

"Upstairs, yes, but not down here." Jean-Guy spoke slowly, making sure he faced his father-in-law. "Why're you here?"

The basement, with its low, acoustic-tiled ceiling and florescent lights, wasn't just gloomy, it was cold. Jean-Guy looked at his untouched mug of warm coffee, then held it out.

"For you."

"Me? Isn't it yours?"

"No. I've had mine. I brought it for you."

Armand studied him, then took the mug.

Like Ruth upstairs, Armand held the warm mug in his cold hands for a moment. He knew perfectly well the coffee was Jean-Guy's. But he also knew to refuse the kind gesture would have been much worse than accepting.

He took a long sip and exhaled. "*Merci.*" He saw the pleasure on Jean-Guy's face, then turned and gestured at the wall of the church basement.

"That's why I'm here."

Evelyn Tardiff's breath came out in puffs as she walked through the chilly morning. The streets of north end Montréal were quiet. It was going to be one of those picture-perfect autumn days. Bright and fresh, the air crisp and clean.

As she made her way to the farmers' market, she wondered how many of the people she passed would be dead now, had the plot to poison the drinking water succeeded. At least half was the official estimate, maybe more.

Maybe that child across the street. Probably that elderly couple walking arm in arm toward the bagel place.

Don Moretti blamed her, probably rightly, for Gamache managing to stop the plot. But there was an advantage to what had happened. Or didn't happen.

Not only were the investigations and postmortems focused elsewhere, but everyone now believed those responsible were behind bars and the water supply safe.

But water security had all sorts of meaning. The danger to it was not simply from pollution or even deliberate poisoning. A whole new threat was emerging globally, and Canada was about to demonstrate to the rest of the world how insecure a water-rich country could be.

It surprised her that no one saw it. It seemed so obvious.

Yes, Moretti and the others were home free as long as no one thought to dig deeper into the notebooks. As long as they were the only things Gamache had found.

As long as Joe Moretti hadn't seen, hadn't sensed, the one who was really in charge. Far more powerful than him. Far viler. Vastly more dangerous.

Some malady is coming upon us. We wait. We wait.

And the head of Organized Crime for the Sûreté knew that wait was almost over.

Armand had pinned a creased and marked-up map of the province of Québec to the wall of the church basement and was staring at it. He swayed slightly, in contemplation. Or perhaps exhaustion.

Jean-Guy had seen this map before. In fact, he'd been the one to find it in the monastery on the shores of that remote lake. They'd studied it closely, knowing if the biologist and the Abbot had hidden it, it must be important.

But try as they might, the map had yielded precious little.

When the poison plot had been uncovered and the perpetrators arrested, Armand had rolled up the map and hidden it in a cylinder under his desk at home. Telling no one except his closest confidants about the find. After all, he'd told himself, he wasn't concealing evidence. The map had nothing to do with the poison plot.

And yet the young biologist and the elderly Abbot had taken great pains to hide it. Which was another reason Armand suspected there was more coming.

This was the first time since the arrests that the map had seen the light of day.

It was a risk. But all they had left was risk.

CHAPTER 3

"*Merci.*" Myrna accepted the bowl of café au lait just as Gabri threw himself into the armchair beside the hearth.

"So how's the painting going?" asked Gabri.

Clara moaned.

"Let's talk about something more cheerful," said Myrna. "Like the frost warning."

"Why did I call it *Just before something happens?*" Clara asked. "How do you paint nothing? Why didn't I call it *Something happened?*"

"Or *Just as something happens,*" suggested Gabri. Which was not helpful.

"But isn't that life?" Myrna asked, moving her pain au chocolat away from Gabri's reach. "We're sitting here calmly. But I'm sure something's about to happen. It always is. For instance, Gabri was about to take my pastry."

"Oh, dear God," muttered Clara. "I really am fucked."

"Or," said Gabri, "are you about to be fucked?"

Jean-Guy stepped closer until his nose was practically pressed against the map. Then he turned to Armand.

"We still don't know why Charles visited this specific lake. There're hundreds to choose from. Why this one? There's nothing there."

The two men stared, willing the map to cough up one, just one more, of its secrets.

Jean-Guy was right, and yet wrong. There was nothing at the lake itself. They'd looked. But something had been written on the lake. Numbers and symbols. In Charles's hand. There were also numbers scrawled on other lakes, but they'd realized those were dossier numbers. Approvals for the illegal sale of primary industries to foreign investors, given by Marcus Lauzon, the former Deputy Prime Minister, in exchange for massive payoffs.

Though illegal, it had nothing to do with the poisoning plot.

So what did those other numbers mean, on that one lake. The last one Charles Langlois visited before he was murdered. But stare as they might, the figures still held on to their secret.

Jean-Guy now pointed to the bottom of the paper. "It looks like he crossed into Vermont, but there're no lakes or rivers marked up."

Eager to make his point, he forgot to turn toward Armand, and now had to repeat himself.

"True." Armand looked at the faint line the biologist had drawn leading from Canada into the States.

"What is it?" Jean-Guy asked.

Armand's expression had become dissatisfied, even frustrated. "We still haven't found Charles's laptop. It's possible the conspirators didn't know about it and the map. I was only asked about the notebooks."

"Asked"? thought Jean-Guy. Could putting a gun to Armand's head really be called "asking"? The deputy commissioner of the RCMP was beyond being questioned. He'd been killed in the water-treatment plant. The fact the second most powerful Mountie was involved in the plot had caused a national scandal and all but paralyzed the RCMP. They were still sorting out the mess.

"We need to find that laptop," said Armand.

"Agreed. We're trying. But if it was that important, wouldn't Charles have told you where to find it? We found his map in the monastery and the notebooks where he hid them with his family. But no laptop. We've looked everywhere." Beauvoir hesitated, hating to say what he suspected. "Is it possible, *patron*, that they found the laptop and destroyed it? Maybe that's why they didn't ask."

Armand was quiet. That was a disconcerting thought.

He'd stared at Jean-Guy as the younger man spoke, but like most people talking to the deaf, Jean-Guy had started off slowly, clearly, then picked up speed, so that lip-reading became more and more difficult.

But the truth was, Armand only picked up a fraction of what was said that way. The rest he read in the raised brow, the slightly furrowed forehead, the narrowed eyes. The uncontrollable blush or pallor. The hands. The smile. Their body language spoke volumes.

As the head of homicide, Armand Gamache had interviewed enough witnesses, enough suspects, to not rely solely on what people said.

And now he'd become like the monks of the monastery of Saint-Gilbert-Entre-les-Loups. Saint Gilbert Between the Wolves. Who'd taken a vow of silence and yet communicated volumes with a raised brow, a frown, a grin. A gesture. Though unlike the monks, the silence in Armand's world was not a vow, not voluntary.

And he didn't live in silence—that would have been a blessing. He lived with a permanent shriek. Like tinnitus on steroids.

At first Armand thought, feared, the screaming in his head would drive him mad. Brought on by the report of the gun right next to his head, it meant he struggled to sleep, to read, to think. He often felt off-balance, nauseous. There was now a buffer between himself and his family. His friends. His colleagues.

Reine-Marie.

It was lonely. He was lonely.

But with time, and help, he found himself more at peace with the shriek. He tried to think of it as a constant companion. Granted, one that seemed perpetually angry at him, but still, the perception seemed to help.

He wasn't sure if it was that, or just time, but it seemed to Armand that the cicadas were leaving. The siren seemed to have diminished.

He still could not hear what was being said, but he had hope that one day he'd wake up to the soft sound of Reine-Marie's breath on the pillow next to him.

It surprised him what he missed. The voices of family and friends were obvious. As was music. But who knew he'd miss the sound of sizzling bacon? Milk pouring into a glass for the children. The shuffle of leaves. The rustle of paper. The click of a light going on or off. A door opening.

Henri's snore.

The minutiae. The soundscape of a life.

But for now, he had his other senses. And they all told him the same thing. Something was approaching. Something dreadful was about to happen.

He looked at his watch and was surprised by the time.

"Isabelle will be here soon," he said.

"I hope she brings doughnuts," said Jean-Guy.

"I hope she brings doughnuts," said Armand.

As she approached the market, Evelyn saw the trucks being loaded. She knew that they'd soon be heading toward the border with Ontario and the Maritime Provinces. But most would cross, unchallenged, into the United States with loads of weapons, booze, drugs. Some would stop on the way to take on human cargo.

And then they'd return, laden with contraband.

She couldn't stop the trucks even if she wanted to, so she turned her back and scanned the stalls looking for Moretti.

There was his daughter, in her cheerful amber coat, and there was Moretti's wife. A helpmate to her mobster husband. She too came from a crime family and understood the rules. As their daughter would one day. Already unwittingly being groomed for the family business.

And there was Don Moretti, looking especially benign that Saturday morning in his canvas field coat, his peaked cap. His black Lab on a leash and choke collar beside him.

Slender, athletic, in his mid-forties, dark hair greying just at the temples, Joe Moretti looked like a country gentleman.

Though no one was fooled. Everyone in Little Italy knew him. And knew him for what he was.

"Evelyn." The shout came from two aisles over as he spotted her and nodded to the large men to let her pass. "Thank you for coming."

Moretti greeted her with a kiss on each cheek. She wasn't fooled.

If he chose to have her shot right then and there, no one would stop him. And no one would see or say anything. She would end up in a crate, then a field, feeding the next crop of gourds to be sold at market.

"Come." He took her arm. "Whisper in my ear. Tell me everything it was not wise to say over the phone. Hold nothing back."

The hand on her arm tightened until it was almost painful.

As she spoke, Don Moretti watched her, his gaze intense. Taking in not just her words but her tone. Her body language. Her pupils, the color in her cheeks, any furrows in her brow. Searching for the crack, the lie that lay beneath the words. The one he knew must be there.

As they strolled down aisles lined with pumpkins and leering jack-o'-lanterns, inhaling the scent of fresh produce and the musky undercurrent of incipient rot, Evelyn Tardiff, the head of the Sûreté's Organized Crime division, told Joseph Moretti, the head of the Montréal mafia, everything she knew about her friend and colleague Armand Gamache. The head of homicide for the Sûreté du Québec. The one she should have had killed.

Back at Sûreté headquarters, Agent Yvette Nichol sat at her desk just outside Chief Inspector Tardiff's office and thought for a long moment. Then she typed a text over Signal, the encoded messenger.

Armand Gamache's phone vibrated. Taking it out, he read the message.

"Is that Isabelle?" asked Jean-Guy. "Tell her I want the raspberry jelly doughnuts this time."

Armand smiled. "Raspberry it is."

"Oh, and a double double."

"Goes without saying, but I will anyway."

He typed out a reply, then went back to contemplating the map.

Moretti checked the message that had just come in on his phone.

"Anything important?" asked Chief Inspector Tardiff, studying him.

"Nothing for you to worry about, Evelyn," he said.

But she was always worried now.

CHAPTER 4

⁓

The three of them sat in plastic garden chairs all in a row in the basement of St. Thomas's Church and stared at the map.

Raspberry jelly squirted from Jean-Guy's doughnut, and Armand absently handed him yet another napkin.

Isabelle went to the map and turned toward Armand. To help him out, she also mimed. It was intentionally helpful, and unintentionally funny.

"We know what these mean, *patron*." She swept her right arm, with unnecessary exaggeration, over certain lakes, like a weather forecaster on MétéoMédia demonstrating an incoming storm system.

Gamache nodded, trying not to smile.

"The numbers are dates when Charles Langlois visited the lakes," she continued, "but he also wrote down those approval numbers."

"The ones given by Marcus Lauzon to foreign buyers."

The former Deputy Prime Minister, as it turned out, wasn't just a terrorist; he was also a climate criminal, allowing certain industries to exceed the pollution limit by thirty times.

Chief Inspector Gamache had taken great personal pleasure in watching Marcus Lauzon being led off in cuffs. As he'd stood in the crowd on Parliament Hill, Armand had unconsciously rubbed his wrists where the zip ties had bitten into his flesh as he'd knelt on the concrete floor of the water-treatment plant, waiting to be executed. On the word of this man. The former Deputy Prime Minister of Canada. A man poised to become the nation's next leader.

Armand could still feel the meaty hand of the hitman shoving his head forward. Then the muzzle of the gun pressed into the base of his skull.

He'd closed his eyes.

We wait. We wait.

As he waited, Armand repeated one thing over and over: *Reine-Marie.*
Reine-Maire.

Reine—

Lauzon's accomplice pulled the trigger.

Armand had survived thanks to an unlikely intervention, and lived to stand in the crowd watching as Lauzon was led away. The Chief Inspector had been offered special dispensation to arrest and escort the man himself, but he preferred to stand in the crowd, surrounded by the men and women whom the former Deputy Prime Minister had tried to kill in exchange for unlimited power.

Lauzon was far from the first politician whose reins of power were around the necks of their citizenry.

It had been a profoundly satisfying moment when the two men had, through the crowd, locked eyes.

And then it was over.

Or not.

"We need to speak to him," said Gamache, his face grim as Lacoste handed him a napkin.

"Lauzon? Why?" she asked, watching as Armand absently brushed icing sugar off his sweater. "He just keeps denying everything."

"Still, we need to try. And—"

"Dear God, I'm begging you," said Jean-Guy, handing Isabelle a napkin and indicating a smear of chocolate from her glazed doughnut on her cheek. "Don't say it."

"—we need to go back to this lake. The last one Charles visited. See why he was there."

"Easy for you, your doctor forbids you to fly." Jean-Guy turned to Isabelle. "I guess he means you."

Beauvoir would rather sit with Ruth in her rat's nest of a living room, listening to her recite her own poetry—

> *You were a moth*
> *brushing against my cheek*
> *in the dark*

I killed you
not knowing
you were only a moth,
with no sting.

—than get back into another float plane, after what had happened last time.

"There aren't any settlements on the lake," said Armand. "No industry, nothing. As far as we can tell, it's pristine. So what was Charles's interest in it? Why did he return there several times, including just days before he was killed?"

He tapped the map and stared at the body of water. He wished he could sit on the shore and stare across the lake to the untouched forests. He'd take off his boots, roll up his slacks, and dangle his bare feet in the fresh cold water, and try to figure out what Charles Langlois saw in that peaceful setting that might have cost him his life.

Instead, he looked at Isabelle, who nodded.

"*D'accord, patron,*" she said.

She was looking forward to going, though she would never tell Jean-Guy that. To land on some remote body of water, like a dragonfly. To see something as yet unspoiled. She wished she could take her children. To show them what the world had been like. Should still be like. If not for the plague that was humanity.

"It's getting cold down here," said Gamache. "Let's go."

It had, in fact, never been warm in the church basement, but now the cold had crept into his bones, magnified by uncertainty and fear.

They had a problem.

"Where to?" asked Isabelle as they followed the Chief out of St. Thomas's.

While he didn't hear her question, Jean-Guy did. "Guess."

The three investigators sat in armchairs by the large open fire of the bistro, feeling the chill slide off them. They hadn't realized how cold they were until they came into the warmth.

Though the mist had long since burned off, revealing a bright blue sky, there was indeed a nip, even a bite, in the air.

Winter was fast approaching. The trees on the surrounding mountains were already naked. Their branches grey, like old bones left out in the elements. Soon the maples and apples and oaks in the village would also be bare. Many of their red and amber and yellow leaves had already fallen.

The first snow was expected in the coming week. A killing frost was on the way.

But for now, the villagers were snug and warm in their heavy sweaters. Their scarves and hats and boots and gloves were at the ready by the front door.

The firewood was cut and stacked.

Shovels leaned against veranda walls and snow brushes had been placed in vehicles along with booster cables and emergency kits.

This was a time to prepare. To build the defenses.

Though far from building a defense, these three sat in front of the muttering fire and planned an offense.

"I wonder what they're talking about," said Clara.

Myrna had placed herself where she could see the three Sûreté officers. Though she was unable to hear what they said, she too was adept at reading body language. Now she tried out her lip-reading skills.

Jean-Guy and Isabelle's faces were intense as they listened to their Chief. Nodding every now and then.

Armand's back was to Myrna and Clara, but it was still eloquent. His shoulders were slightly raised, in tension. Then, as Myrna watched, he rolled them, then lowered his head a bit, and much of the stress fell away. Though not, Myrna could see, the burden. But it was now shared.

As she watched her friends, she thought of the power of three. It had long ago struck her, in her practice as a psychologist, what could happen, for better or worse, when three people found a common goal.

One person alone could have a great idea, but it was unlikely to thrive until someone came along who agreed. At that point, life was breathed into that idea. It was animated.

But what happened when a third person was invited in?

It was a tricky number. *Three's a crowd. Three on a match. The third wheel.* There were all sorts of warnings about the number three. But at the same time, it was considered by many cultures and beliefs as the most powerful number. The perfect number.

The Three Graces. The Holy Trinity.

For Pythagoras, three was the number of harmony, wisdom, and understanding. Three words to describe the number three.

Philosophy aside, it was the first number that could form a pattern.

Three people in agreement, working together toward a common goal, could feed each other, encourage and support each other, bring different strengths to the project, and send their common idea out, healthy and strong, into the world.

For better or worse.

And Myrna Landers, in her work in the Special Handling Unit, had looked into the eyes of "worse." People who might have led normal, even exemplary lives had they not met that other one. And then the final one.

Dr. Myrna Landers watched Armand and Jean-Guy and Isabelle.

When the rule of three worked, its power was nearly immeasurable.

"The sooner you get to that lake, the better, Isabelle," said Armand.

He was trying to catch the eye of the new server in the bistro, who seemed determined not to serve them.

"I'm ready now. Just have to let my husband know and pack a few things in case the pilot and I need to camp. Do you think we can get a hot chocolate?"

"I'm trying," said Armand, raising his arm, but to no effect.

Brother Simon, the wayward Gilbertine monk, still had not forgiven Gamache for taking him out of the monastery. For his own safety, Armand had explained.

And while Simon pretended to hate his new life, the fact was he'd grown fond of the villagers and the village. To serving. It was a different sort of service, but the former acting Abbot was realizing he could serve God and serve coffee at the same time.

Just not to Armand.

"Isabelle is saying, 'Hot choking,'" said Myrna. "Now why would she say that?"

"Maybe she didn't," said Gabri.

"Shhhh. Well, now I've lost it."

Clara made a guttural sound and focused on her bowl of café au lait.

"I have a close friend who's a biologist," said Armand, giving up on Simon. It had actually become a sort of game between them. One the former monk was winning. "Someone I trust. I'll see if she can go with you. She might be able to see what you can't."

"Good idea," said Jean-Guy.

"Wait. Jean-Guy is speaking. He's saying, 'Bunny day.'"

"What?" said Clara. "Dear God, you're worse than autocorrect."

Myrna turned back to her friend. Lip-reading was harder than it looked, and exhausting.

Ruth, Rosa, and Olivier joined them. Myrna continued to shoot glances at the Sûreté officers. It might be near impossible to pick up the specifics of their conversation, but the gist was clear to anyone watching. Even Rosa could figure out that something was wrong.

"Did Isabelle just say, 'Giraffes can't swim'?" Gabri asked.

"I think it was 'Gyroscopes cancel soap,'" said Olivier.

"You're morons," said Ruth. "She said she'll be happy to fly to the lake."

"Well, that doesn't make sense, does it?" said Gabri, turning to Clara.

But she wasn't paying attention. She was staring at the investigators around the fire. All three, in unison, had turned so that their faces were in profile, staring into the flames.

Something was about to happen.

CHAPTER 5

Can you tell me more?

Vivienne LaPierre understandably wanted to know why she was being asked to accompany a senior Sûreté officer, a stranger, to a remote lake.

They were communicating over secure text, but still Armand hesitated. He was so accustomed to keeping secrets, especially this one, that it took a force of will to let it out. Even to one of their best friends.

Dr. LaPierre was an environmental biologist, the head of the department at the Université de Montréal. A full professor and leader in the field, Dr. LaPierre was one of the first scientists to warn about the changes in algae levels in remote lakes.

She was brutally mocked for it. Who cared about algae? It was green and slimy. Not exactly a great "poster child" for an impending environmental disaster.

But she persisted. It took her decades to get it through their thick heads that algae was the DEW Line, the early warning. The canary in the mine.

But more worrisome, besides the sudden thickness of human skulls, was why algae was disappearing. Dr. LaPierre had finally convinced regulators to turn their attention to acid rain.

That was decades ago. She'd since focused her study on the Arctic and the changes, no longer subtle, she'd detected there. But the icebreaker research ship wasn't scheduled to sail for a few weeks, and so Armand found her at home this Saturday morning enjoying a late breakfast with her husband.

After she'd replied to his text, there was a silence so long that she wondered if the connection had been lost.

Armand? she typed.

When his reply finally did come, she stared at it, uncomprehending. *So this,* she thought, *is what a thick skull feels like.* It was not pleasant.

His words seemed to be knocking against her head, for admittance. Had the message come from anyone other than Armand, she'd have hit the red end icon and blocked the lunatic.

Vivienne? he typed, after a disconcertingly long pause.

He could imagine her sitting at the kitchen table, beside her husband. They were his and Reine-Marie's best friends. The Gamaches had followed the ups and downs of her career as she'd fought the system from her tiny office without a view. Such had been the respect given to anyone who studied the environment when offices at the university were assigned decades ago.

But now biologists were the superheroes. The ones who could see what others would not. Who understood that even the smallest change in the ecosystem could be catastrophic.

They were also the ones who could prevent the catastrophe. Biologists led the way, and Vivienne LaPierre was at the sharp end of that stick.

But even she struggled to absorb what Armand had written.

Go over your text pls. Are there any typos? Did you mean to write "thirty times"? Maybe it's "thirty percent."

Which would, she knew, be bad enough. That whole tar sands fiasco was a case in point, the government allowing it to pollute well beyond acceptable or admitted levels. It was unconscionable. But now to allow mines and pulp mills and oil refineries and other processing plants across the country to exceed the pollution limits, already weak, by thirty times would be a disaster. Criminal.

Unforgivable.

No typos.

"*Merde,*" she muttered and reread what Armand had written.

Marcus Lauzon was not just behind the poisoning plot. Part of his plan involved agreeing to sell controlling interest in primary industries to Americans, and allowing certain industries to exceed pollution limits by thirty times. The young biologist who was murdered was investigating. He visited one lake in particular, several times. We need to know why. There's something up there. We need someone we can trust. We need you.

Dr. Vivienne LaPierre typed her reply, then told her husband she would not be home for dinner. Or probably breakfast. And that the avocados were becoming overripe and should be eaten.

Reine-Marie stared at the map, and Armand stared at her staring.

And waited.

They were very alike in many ways and quite different in others, which made for a strong partnership. Each filled in the other's gaps. Each saw what the other missed.

He hoped and prayed that was true now.

Finally, she turned around. "Where did you find this?"

He'd realized soon after his return from the hospital that he could read Reine-Marie's lips better than anyone else's. No doubt because he knew them best.

"It was hidden in the monastery among a collection of old documents. Jean-Guy found it."

"How did you know it was there?"

"We didn't. We were looking for something, anything, that could tell us where the Abbot had gone. The biologist's map was a surprise."

"But this has nothing to do with the plot to poison the drinking water. There's something else. Something important in the map itself."

It was a shame, and then some, that they could not ask either the Abbot or the biologist. Young Langlois had been mowed down by a vehicle, which narrowly missed Armand.

Armand tilted his head back and stared at the mottled acoustic tiles of the basement ceiling. Above them was the church itself. They were almost directly under the spot where Dom Philippe, the Abbot, had been murdered.

Not in the cathedral, like Thomas à Becket, but close enough.

Some malady. Dom Philippe had scrawled that quote from T. S. Eliot on the back of a scrap of paper and left it in this little village church for Armand to find, knowing he'd connect the quote to the person who had left it, and make the connection with the Abbot's monastery of Saint-Gilbert-Entre-les-Loups.

When the dignified old Abbot had sat upstairs in the pew by the soldier boys and written those two simple words from *Murder in the Cathedral*, he could not have known that just a few days later he himself would be murdered. In the church.

37

"Agreed. Both Dom Philippe and Charles Langlois wanted us to find it. And they both wanted to make sure no one else found this map. But what does it contain? We've stared at it, studied it. Nothing. Isabelle is flying to the lake today. I asked Vivienne to go with her."

"LaPierre?"

"*Oui.*"

Reine-Marie, though surprised, considered. Then nodded. "Smart. We can trust her."

Armand smiled. Reine-Marie'd said "we." He liked that.

"Did she agree?"

"She did. They'll arrive early this afternoon."

They stared at the wall, and silence fell once again over the room, though the shriek persisted in Armand's head.

Then Reine-Marie stepped closer to the wall and peered at the very bottom of the map, where it ran out. She turned back to Armand.

"Have you seen this?"

The Archambault penitentiary in Sainte-Anne-des-Plaines was not where even hardened criminals wanted to serve out their sentences.

It formed a sort of doughnut, with the outer layer being medium security, with some maximum security prisoners mixed in. That was bad enough, but what was really scary was what was in the jam in the middle.

It was a prison within a prison and was considered "supermax," which always sounded to Jean-Guy like a McDonald's meal option. One that would, over time, kill you.

The men in supermax would not take so long.

And if, like the jelly still staining his sweater, any of them squeezed out, escaped, they were all fucked.

Jean-Guy was headed there to speak to the man behind what would have been the mass murder of tens of thousands.

It should have, would have, taken Jean-Guy just over two hours to reach Sainte-Anne-des-Plaines from Three Pines, if not for the traffic through Montréal and then the cop who'd pulled him over on the autoroute.

"I'm on SQ business," said Jean-Guy, showing him his ID.

"You were still going one forty in a hundred-kilometer-an-hour zone, sir. Is there an emergency I don't know about?"

"Do we run everything by you first?" demanded Beauvoir, making note of the agent's name. "Let me go."

"I can escort you. Where are you going?"

While he bristled at being questioned by such a junior officer, Jean-Guy did admit an escort would be much faster.

"Archambault."

"The prison? Great. I hear Lauzon's there."

"*Oui.* I'm going to speak to him."

"Really, can I come? Those fuckers," said the SQ officer.

"Agreed."

"Treating him like a criminal." The officer leaned closer and lowered his voice. "They want us to believe the bullshit about the water."

"What bullshit?" Beauvoir was trying to grasp what he was hearing. The young man leaning into his window looked intelligent and yet...

"The poisoning plot. It's not real. They think we're stupid. Look it up. It never happened."

Beauvoir could feel the blood rush to his face and was just about to blast this ignorant young man when he hesitated. Some instinct told him to go another route.

"Why do you say that?"

The officer looked at Beauvoir as though at a child. Jean-Guy clenched his fists but said nothing.

"Because it's true. There's proof. Photographs of them staging it. They're brainwashing us into thinking poison was about to be put in the drinking water. Do you know what the government is putting in the drinking water? Drugs to tranquilize us. So that we don't care, don't question. Bad enough that they put tracking devices in vaccines, but we can at least avoid that. We can't stop drinking water. Lauzon was about to expose them, so they had to do something. He's lucky to be alive."

At this point, the young SQ agent was lucky to be alive. Or at least conscious.

Once again Inspector Beauvoir swallowed what he really wanted to say, and instead asked, "How do you know all this?"

"It's all over the internet. Look it up, sir. And don't get me started on Gamache. Did you know he abandoned the rest of us and saved himself and his family, then faked an injury so no one would suspect him?"

That finally crossed the line.

"You have no fucking idea what you're talking about. I don't know what shit you're reading, but you need to stop. Use your head, use your intelligence."

But he could see his words had just bounced off this officer.

Beauvoir took his ID back, and, declining the offer of an escort, drove off.

A line formed between Jean-Guy's brows. It would be there for the rest of his life.

"What are you seeing?" Armand asked.

"This line," said Reine-Marie. "Your young biologist must've drawn it."

"Yes, we did see it," said Armand. He was slightly disappointed. He'd hoped she'd noticed something they hadn't. "I've ordered a map of New England, to see where he might have gone."

"It's funny, I have the opposite impression."

"What do you mean?"

"I thought it was the other way around."

"Go on."

"Well, look there." She pointed to a mark along the perforated line.

Armand's face opened in surprise. What she'd seen, and he'd missed, looked like a circumflex, though it was over a printed letter that should not have the little cap. It was actually a very small arrow. Pointing up.

Armand stood back and drew his brows together. Was it possible they were wrong? Was the movement Charles had drawn not south after all, not from Québec into Vermont, but the other way around?

Was something moving, or going to move, north, into Canada from the States?

Was something headed their way?

"Dr. LaPierre?"

"Vivienne, s'il vous plaît."

"Isabelle Lacoste. Thank you for doing this, and at such short notice."

They were at the Port de Montréal, standing on a quay. "I'm not sure if you remember, but we've met before."

"I do remember." The image of the young, grim officer in slow march behind Armand, who was leading the cortège with the coffins of his agents, would stay with Vivienne forever. "Armand speaks highly of you."

"And you," said Isabelle as they made their way toward the float plane. "There aren't many he'd trust with this information."

"Such as it is." Vivienne tossed her satchel into the hold of the small craft. She'd brought testing equipment, a tent, a sleeping bag, some tools, some food. She'd considered bringing water, despite the fact they'd be camping on the shores of a lake. She'd seen enough pollution to be wary.

Still, this time she left it behind in favor of thermal underwear.

"He didn't tell me much."

"He told you as much as any of us knows," said Isabelle.

Also a habituée of making camp, Isabelle had brought her own kit, which included not just the usual but also flares and a fishing pole. You never knew when you could get stranded. The Canadian wilderness forgave little. And always punished stupidity.

The pilot double-checked the destination, not totally believing they wanted to go to such a remote location.

Once in the air, the two women stared out the windows at the vast expanse of forest and lakes and rivers that stretched on for hours.

"Dear God," whispered Lacoste. It was beautiful. Majestic.

Though as they headed farther north, she was reminded of flying over the wildfire-ravaged forests, with mile after mile of charcoal stumps. Some still smoldering months later.

Finally, they began their descent.

CHAPTER 6

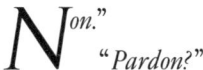*on."*

"*Pardon?*"

"You heard me. No. I'm not going to speak to you or anyone else. Only Gamache."

"That's not going to happen, Monsieur Lauzon. The Chief Inspector is still recovering from wounds inflicted on your orders—"

Beauvoir held up his hand to forestall Marcus Lauzon's objections.

"I was wrong. Apologies. You ordered your man to kill the Chief Inspector, not wound him. It was only thanks to the presence of your own Chief of Staff that that didn't happen."

"Jeanne Caron is a traitor," snapped the former Deputy Prime Minister of Canada.

"And lucky for you, for all of us, that she betrayed you."

"Not me, you piece of shit. She's a traitor to this country."

"Right. And you're the hero." Though Beauvoir was still smarting from what that officer had said. He apparently did think Lauzon was a hero. And if a Sûreté officer could believe it, how many others did too? What lies were being spread?

Beauvoir studied the man across the table from him. He was almost unrecognizable now. Once composed and dignified, refined and yet managing to also seem a man of the people, Marcus Lauzon had rocketed up the party ladder, from backbencher to cabinet minister, his portfolios and power increasing, until finally he'd been made the second most powerful person in the nation. Behind the Prime Minister. His fetid breath on the PM's neck.

Now the man's cheeks were sunken, his eyes bright with what looked like a leering madness. His face was irregularly shaven, with patches of grey stubble.

If met on the street, Marcus Lauzon would be taken for indigent. Destitute.

And in many ways, thought Beauvoir, he was. He was morally bankrupt, bereft of normal human emotions. Missing empathy and any moral guardrails.

"Caron set me up. None of what was said in court was true. All those documents used against me were faked. By her. Who else had access to them?"

"Well, sir, you did. They were in your handwriting, and in your private and protected computer files. You—" Jean-Guy stopped himself and gave a small laugh. He'd almost fallen for it. Fallen down that deep dark hole where this man kept his tangled lies.

Beauvoir stared at the former politician for so long, the man grew uncomfortable.

"*Quoi?*" What?

"We know."

"Know what?"

It was hard for Jean-Guy to decide if Lauzon was really interested or was simply trying to prolong this visit, before being returned to the prison within a prison. Within a prison. Where he would almost certainly eventually, despite precautions, be killed.

It was the one thing Beauvoir and that young Sûreté agent agreed on. It was surprising that Marcus Lauzon had lasted this long. The only reason he had was that Gamache had requested that Lauzon be placed in solitary. It appeared to be added punishment. It was actually to protect him.

It was not, Beauvoir knew, compassion on the part of the Chief Inspector that led him to put a cordon around Lauzon. It was realpolitik. He needed the former politician alive until all their questions were answered.

Sitting in front of Jean-Guy Beauvoir was one of the only people who knew what was about to happen. Knew what they'd missed.

"We know that the second notebook is the one that matters," said Beauvoir. He watched Lauzon for a reaction. There was none.

"I will only speak to Gamache. I deserve that."

"What you deserve, sir"—Beauvoir lowered his voice and leaned across the table—"is what we both know you are going to get, one night after lights out. If you do not answer me now, Chief Inspector Gamache will ask the warden to return you to the general population."

That struck home. Lauzon clearly did not realize that the only reason he was alive was because of the man he'd tried to murder.

And now the time had come for the former politician to prove he had worth alive.

Lauzon knew this was the last time he'd be visited. The last time he'd be asked. But there was, alongside the fear, an animal cunning. And for a moment Jean-Guy Beauvoir had a sense of the creature he was locked in with. He felt the hairs on his forearms involuntarily raise.

Lauzon's mouth curled into what might have been a smile. More like a leer, a sneer.

"Tell your boss that he's the only one I will talk to. If he won't come here, then take me to him. Or kill me. But the truth dies with me. As you so eloquently said, it's just a matter of time."

Marcus Lauzon got up so quickly his chair scraped the floor and startled Beauvoir. His show of nerves annoyed him and amused the former Deputy Prime Minister of Canada, who seemed to have filled out, feeding on Jean-Guy's fear.

Evelyn, do you think you can come down to Three Pines and join us for Sunday lunch tomorrow?

Chief Inspector Tardiff sat in her office staring at the message.

"What is it, *patronne?*" Agent Yvette Nichol asked.

"Gamache wants me to go to Three Pines for lunch tomorrow."

Nichol stepped closer and read the message over her boss's shoulder. "Why?"

"He doesn't say, and if I ask, it would seem suspicious. It might be just social. Sunday lunch with the family."

"Has he ever asked you before?"

Silence answered that question.

"Will you go?"

Armand was back home in his study, and Reine-Marie had driven off to the Pinnacle Peddler gas station in Richford, Vermont, to find a map of the state.

Isabelle had reported in. They'd arrived at the lake and had asked the pilot to motor around its perimeter, to see if anything stood out, before finding a likely spot to inflate the raft and row to shore.

She sent a few photos. Once again Armand could almost hear the soft lap of water on rock and the splash of plump fish that saw, as yet, no reason to be afraid of people.

If there was a heaven on earth, this was it.

And yet the head of homicide for the Sûreté du Québec was pretty sure visiting that lake was what had gotten Charles Langlois killed. Or had, at least, been the final push over the edge. Even Paradise had its edges, its limits.

Jean-Guy had also written. His meeting with Lauzon had gone nowhere. *He says he'll only speak to you, patron.*

It was not the first time Lauzon had made that demand, but this time Gamache sat back in his chair and considered it as he looked out the window at the village green and the gardens surrounding it. Neighbors were busy cutting back the perennials, the rose bushes and daylilies and hostas, for the winter.

The bee balm would be left, only cut down at the last minute. But the last minute was getting close.

He could feel it in his bones.

One more thing, patron.

Jean-Guy sat in his car in the long shadow of Archambault penitentiary and wrote. He'd been unsure how much to say to the Chief but decided on everything.

This was clearly no time to be diplomatic or practice restraint. And he did not want Armand to come across it by accident.

Armand sat in the peaceful study and read the message, while outside his window villagers knelt in their gardens and children ran and leaped and no doubt shrieked with delight as they scattered the carefully collected autumn leaves.

He read what the young highways agent had said. About him. About abandoning his agents and saving only his own family. Leaving the rest to possibly die.

This was no lie spread by conspiracy theorists on marginal sites.

It was true. It was true.

Even as he knew it was not the whole story, it was still enough of the truth to make him lightheaded. He was followed day and night by the image of himself, standing on the threshold of his office, watching his senior inspectors, his junior agents, the men and women whom he led. Who followed him. Who trusted him with their lives.

He'd wanted to shout, *Leave! Get your families and leave the city! The drinking water is about to be poisoned!*

Even now he felt those words burn his throat.

But he'd swallowed the warning, not willing to risk triggering the attack by alerting the terrorists with an exodus.

And so he'd kept quiet and felt part of his own humanity die.

The fact that decision was almost certainly the right one didn't matter. The fact that he'd gotten his own children and grandchildren quietly out of Montréal and down to Three Pines also followed him every day. Haunting and taunting, and whispering that he'd been a hypocrite and a coward. A traitor to his team.

But really, how could he not save his own family? If he had to do it again, would he?

Yes. In a heartbeat. He'd sacrifice his own life—it was his to give—but not those of his family.

Once the crisis had passed and he'd left the hospital, his first stop was to Sûreté headquarters and a meeting with his department. As he'd entered, they'd stood and applauded, and Armand could feel his cheeks burning.

Stepping onto a chair, then up onto a desk, so all could see him, he'd thanked them, and then . . .

"There's something you need to know."

He'd steeled himself for this moment, practicing what he'd say. Words mattered, these words mattered. But finally, as he stood there and looked into their upturned faces, his mind went blank.

"We know, *patron*," one of his senior inspectors spoke.

But Armand couldn't hear. The shriek in his head was at a fever pitch. It was all he could do not to lose his equilibrium and tumble off the desk. He stared at the inspector, whom he'd worked with for decades, who also had children and grandchildren. He'd gone to their weddings and bat mitzvahs. But Armand could not decipher what he'd just said.

The man's eyes, though, were kind, and there was a gentle smile that created lines down his familiar face.

Clearly he didn't know what his Chief Inspector was going to say. Otherwise he would not be smiling.

Armand held up his hand, and the smile vanished. They all looked worried now. What was their Chief about to tell them?

And then he began to speak, his voice much louder than it normally would have been. He wasn't yet practiced in modulating it, so he was unintentionally, unknowingly shouting at them over the noise only he could hear.

When he'd finished, there was silence. He swayed slightly but caught his balance. And looked out at the dozens of faces. Of men and women who'd trusted him. And who he'd abandoned.

Then one of the agents stepped forward. The youngest. The newest recruit. Mélanie Fontaine. Just out of the academy, she had her whole life ahead of her. The agent who knew him least, and who had the most reason to despise him.

"I understand." She'd spoken slowly, her actions managing to also convey meaning. "You had no choice. My own father would have done the same. As would I."

Others around the room were nodding. Not all, perhaps, but the vast majority.

He did not catch every word the young agent said, and yet he'd understood her meaning more clearly than anything else that had been said to him practically his whole life. Except that first time Reine-Marie had whispered, "I love you."

This young woman had, in effect, said, *I forgive you.*

He felt himself losing his balance. As he swayed almost to the point of no return, Armand felt hands reach out and hold him steady. Hold him up. Hold him safe.

All this Armand remembered as he stared out the window at Honoré and Idola and Annie. At Rosa and mad Ruth, who was perhaps the sanest of them all.

And now it is now
and the dark thing is here,

The lines that drifted into Armand's mind were from Ruth's poem "Waiting."

and after all it is nothing new;
it is only a memory after all:
a memory of a fear . . .
you have long since forgotten
and that has now come true.

Now there was a new fear. One the young Sûreté highways agent had inadvertently alerted Beauvoir to. Not about Armand himself and what he'd done, but what had been found hiding in plain sight on the internet.

If a trained Sûreté agent could believe the lies, believe the poisoning plot never happened, then how many others had been manipulated too?

How many others now believed Lauzon was a hero. Railroaded. Wrongly convicted and soon to be martyred.

And the most pressing question: Who was behind those posts? And why do it? Was it just to stir the pot, or was there another reason?

Merci, he wrote.

What do you want me to do now? replied Jean-Guy.

Armand wrote, *Nothing. Come back.* But then he erased it and wrote, *Find Jeanne Caron. Bring her down here.*

In his car, Jean-Guy looked at the text and frowned.

And don't make a face, wrote Armand. *I'll meet her in the church, not at home.*

They both knew Reine-Marie would never allow that woman in her home. Or the bistro. Or the bench. The church was okay. It could be cleansed.

Armand could imagine the women, led by Myrna with her smoldering stick, smudging the space in an ancient and powerful ritual.

D'accord, wrote Jean-Guy. *And what do we do about Lauzon?*

We need to speak to Caron before deciding.

Jeanne Caron had been Marcus Lauzon's assistant, then Chief of Staff, and chief architect of his ascent and wrongdoings since the early days in their small Québec town.

Caron had also been the instigator of the attacks on Chief Inspector Gamache when, years ago, he'd refused to let Lauzon's daughter off a manslaughter charge.

The charges had ultimately been dropped, thanks to the first in what would be a long series of dirty dealings by Caron on her boss's behalf. But Gamache had still gone to the ethics commissioner to report the then junior member of Parliament.

It did no good. The daughter remained free, and the attacks on Gamache only escalated. When those didn't work, Caron and Lauzon turned their attention to the Chief Inspector's teenage son, Daniel, who was struggling with drug addiction.

Their attacks, the lies and insinuations, had been so brutal, so aggressive, Daniel had relapsed and tried to overdose, in a suicide attempt.

Straight now for decades, neither son nor parents would ever forget.

And yet, when the gun had been pressed against Armand's skull as he'd knelt on the concrete floor, handcuffed and helpless in that water-treatment plant, it had been Jeanne Caron who had saved his life. And almost certainly the lives of thousands, perhaps millions, of others.

She'd tried, since that day, to make amends. Apologizing to Daniel. To Armand. Trying to apologize to Reine-Marie. But Daniel's mother would not listen. Would never believe there was any genuine remorse. Or that Caron wouldn't attack again, if need be.

So, no. Jeanne Caron was not invited to Sunday lunch. But Armand still needed to meet with her. And there was someone else he needed to contact, urgently.

"Have you told Moretti that you're going to see Gamache?" Yvette Nichol asked, and got an angry glare from Chief Inspector Tardiff.

"Don't tell me what to do."

"*Désolée, patronne.* I'm not telling, just asking."

"We both know it comes to the same thing," Tardiff snapped. "I'm going home. You should too."

Yvette Nichol knew she should, and she would. But she waited until the Chief Inspector had left, then fired off a message.

Joseph Moretti was enjoying a meal with his family in the same hole-in-the-wall diner he'd visited every Saturday since he could remember. His phone buzzed, and he read the flagged message.

Merci, he tapped out. *Good to know.*

Then he went back to his croque-monsieur, the thick sliced ham under melted Gruyère and béchamel, on the fresh croissant, while his daughter struggled with a large cannoli. Off to the side, the owner of the small restaurant in north end Montréal watched, wiping her moist palms on her dirty apron.

CHAPTER 7

Reine-Marie tacked the crisp new map of Vermont below Charles Langlois's worn map.

Then they stepped back.

"What do you see?" Armand asked.

Reine-Marie was adept at reading maps, especially hand-drawn curiosities or those containing oddities. It stemmed from her time working in the archives of Québec. Old explorers' and mariners' maps and charts had been a large part of her job, and her interest.

Though these mass-produced maps were on the border of also becoming oddities. Still to be found in gas stations but fast disappearing, these particular maps had something else in common with their ancestors. The consequences of a misread could be disastrous.

"Charles's dotted line would come out here. May I?" She held up the pencil she'd brought with her. He nodded and watched as she consulted the young biologist's markings, then drew a line from Québec, across the frontier, into Vermont.

"It's impossible to tell where it went from here," she said, tapping the eraser head against her lips.

"And where he went," said Armand. "I have a query in to see when and where Langlois crossed into Vermont and back into Canada. Of course he might have gone in illegally. Maybe by boat down here."

Armand pointed to Lake Champlain, that huge expanse of water that spanned the US-Canada border and stretched from Venise-en-Québec to the city of Burlington, Vermont, and beyond.

"It would be easy enough, at night, to paddle across," he said and got an amused look from her.

"Easy, *monsieur*? I dare you to try."

He laughed. "Well, for a twenty-five-year-old, maybe." He paused, contemplating the map. "Though the lake is heavily patrolled on both sides. It would be a risk. One I'm not sure he'd take."

"Why not? If he was investigating something possibly criminal, wouldn't he want to sneak across?"

"True, but if caught, he could end up in the hands of the very people he was trying to avoid."

She nodded and went back to studying the map. The pencil was now in her mouth, being nibbled. How many bright yellow HB pencils had he found throughout their lives, throughout their homes, with teeth marks? Daniel did the same thing, though not with the same vigor and appetite as his mother.

"If we draw a line straight down, it heads off into the Green Mountains." She looked at her husband. "What's there?"

He frowned. "Well, there's Jay Peak. We've skied there."

"True. And the Appalachian Trail, *non*?"

"I've heard of the Green Mountain Boys," said Armand. "It's the nickname for the Air National Guard out of the Burlington airport. But Langlois's line doesn't go through the airport."

"We need to follow it, at least partway into the Green Mountains. See what's there."

"Though we don't know how far down Langlois went. Still, it's a start. I'll send Jean-Guy." Then, remembering the imminent arrival of his visitor, he said, "Unless you'd like to—"

She was about to agree when she read the look on his face. "What haven't you told me?"

He took a deep breath but didn't have to actually say it. Only one thing could explain his expression.

"You haven't," Reine-Marie said. "My God, you have. You've invited her here, haven't you."

"Yes. I need to talk to her." Neither used Jeanne Caron's name. "She'll meet me here in the church."

Reine-Marie looked at him as though he'd raised his fist to her. It shocked and hurt him. But he understood. He had, in her view, invited what might as well have been their son's murderer into their safe place. For a chat.

Reine-Marie sighed. "I hate this. I hate her. And at this moment I don't much like you. But I understand." She looked around. "And at least it'll be easy to perform the exorcism."

She gave him a cursory kiss on the cheek, then left. And for the first time in months, he wished he hadn't understood what had been said to him.

"Over there."

Isabelle Lacoste's keen eyes had picked out not just a small clearing by the water's edge, but also what looked like a stone circle. It was either a very, very small megalith, a minilith, or—

"Looks like an encampment," said Vivienne LaPierre.

Once the seaplane got as close as the pilot dared, Lacoste inflated the raft and the two women paddled to shore.

They wore their heaviest sweaters under thick wax coats. This far north they were on the cusp of winter. It was certainly cold enough to sleet, if not snow.

"This is fairly recent," said Vivienne, kneeling beside the campfire and examining the black muck in the middle that had been charred firewood.

"Agreed. Looks like a tent was pitched over there, but the grass and underbrush has had time to grow back."

"We make camp?" asked Vivienne.

"We make camp, but first I need to go over the area to make sure we don't destroy any evidence."

"*Bon.* While you look, I'll get our stuff onshore. Good to keep moving."

The chill had seeped through her coat and was menacing her thick sweater. The last line of defense before her skin.

By the time Isabelle had been over the campsite and even into the surrounding woods, Vivienne had brought everything over from the plane.

Puffing from the exertion, she said, "The pilot says he'll come back for us tomorrow at this time. Is that okay?"

Isabelle saw the pilot watching them from the cockpit. She gave him the thumbs-up, he returned it, and within minutes he'd gathered speed, bumping down the lake; then he lifted off in a graceful arc over the trees. And disappeared.

It took a while for the sound of the plane to die in the distance, for the waves the plane created to stop slapping against the rocky shore and the startled birds to return. But eventually peace and tranquility had been restored, except for the grunting as Vivienne lugged another large backpack farther ashore.

"Hope your work isn't too much for you," she said as she dropped the heavy satchel with a thud and watched Isabelle sitting at the base of a large tree. "Really, don't worry about me." She wiped her brow, inadvertently putting a streak of muck there, and walked over. "What're you looking at?"

Isabelle pointed to a smooth stone nestled against the tree trunk. "That didn't get there on its own. It's a river rock."

Vivienne automatically reached for it, but Isabelle stopped her. "Don't touch."

The biologist knelt beside the Sûreté officer and together they studied it. The stone was completely smooth.

"You think someone put it there?" asked Vivienne.

"I think Charles Langlois put it there."

It seemed a leap of logic. And yet the biologist had to agree, a river rock didn't get this far from the shore without help.

Isabelle put on latex gloves and now carefully picked it up, brushing dirt off its underside.

But the rock was just that. A rock. Not a message from a dead young man.

Could they be wrong? If this place was so important, why didn't Charles tell Chief Inspector Gamache about it when they'd met at Open Da Night?

After taking a photo of the stone and the area where it was found, Isabelle placed it in an evidence bag, then into her knapsack.

"Great," muttered Vivienne. "Now we're putting rocks in them."

While she set up camp, Isabelle walked an ever-widening perimeter around the site, looking for whatever the young biologist might have found. And might have left behind.

There must, Isabelle thought, be something.

But she found nothing. It might not even be his campsite. For all they knew it could have been hunters, or fishers, or tourists on a wilderness adventure.

Isabelle picked up a rock by the shore and skipped it across the calm water while in the distance a loon called.

W*elcome to Jericho.*

Reine-Marie sat in her car and stared at the sign.

Charles Langlois's dotted line, if it had continued, would have gone straight through this small Vermont town.

Population 5,101.

It seemed oddly precise. She liked that. It felt as though the townspeople valued each and every person, young and old. They were all counted. They all counted.

And yet, as she stared at the pockmarked sign, she was reluctant to enter Jericho. The only thing she could remember, from her days studying to be confirmed, was that it was on the road between Jericho and Jerusalem where the parable of the Good Samaritan occurred.

The traveler who helped his fellow, despite their differences.

Reine-Marie looked back down the road she'd just traveled. And she thought of Armand, meeting with that woman.

"Jeanne Caron." She said the name aloud for the first time in decades.

Jeanne Caron. Who'd almost killed Daniel, and who had saved Armand.

Reine-Marie took a deep breath; then, turning the car around, she headed home along the road between Jericho and Three Pines.

"T hank you for coming."

"Last time I was here…" Jeanne Caron glanced up to the ceiling. To the altar above them, where her uncle had been killed and she herself had been wounded.

Then she turned back to Gamache. "How are you?"

He seemed older. And there was that strained look on his face as he fought to understand what was being said. Was it just his hearing, or had more been blown away by that explosion?

He looked unsure. Perplexed. Slightly lost.

"I'm doing well. You?"

"To be honest, I'm a bit confused. Why did you bring me here?"

Armand motioned to one of the plastic garden chairs, but Caron had seen the map on the wall and was walking toward it.

She stood studying it, while Jean-Guy and Armand studied her.

Armand was far from certain having his former adversary see Langlois's map was wise. But something had to be shaken loose, and this was one way.

Finally, she turned and said, "What's all this?"

She swept her arm in an arc to indicate the maps, in a movement reminiscent of Isabelle Lacoste's television meteorologist.

"*S'il vous plaît.*" Armand again indicated a chair. This time she took it, while both he and Jean-Guy dragged theirs over so that they now formed a tight circle. Of three.

"We have a problem."

She cocked her head. "How so?"

Jean-Guy wondered how far Armand would go. He had his answer almost immediately.

"Something else is about to happen. Something much worse."

"Than killing most of the population of Montréal and setting off a global panic?" She seemed almost amused.

As Jean-Guy watched, her amusement slid away and was replaced by something close to pity. It was obvious to him, and probably Armand, exactly what she was thinking, if not saying.

That Chief Inspector Gamache had fabricated some crisis to make himself important. Again. Give himself purpose again.

Did she really think he was that pathetic? Apparently so. Though Jeanne Caron's opinion of him did not seem to bother Armand one bit. Instead of explaining or defending himself, he persevered.

"Where's your assistant?" he asked.

There was silence as Caron stared from one to the other, her rapid mind trying to catch up to this change of direction.

"Frederick? Castonguay? Him?"

"*Oui.*"

"Why in the world would you suddenly be asking about him?"

"Because he's disappeared," said Beauvoir.

"So? He's no longer my assistant. I'm unemployed. Unemployable.

Frederick Castonguay is the least of my worries. Who cares where he is?" Though even as she said it, she was examining them. "You care. Which means you've been looking for him. Which means..." Now she stopped and stared in open astonishment. "You're investigating. Still. Good God, you really do believe this isn't over. Have you lost your minds?"

She seemed to be trying to figure out who was the most unhinged, Gamache or his number two. She settled on the Chief Inspector.

"Okay, let's say you are investigating." She did not add, but it was clear she wanted to say, *the mythical second plot.* "Why would you be looking for Frederick?"

Though she spoke to Gamache, it was Beauvoir who answered, clearly covering for his Chief.

"He was here that night. You were wounded but managed to get into the car with Frederick. What happened then?"

"You know what happened. I'd been shot and needed to stop the bleeding." By instinct, she brought her left elbow closer to her side, as though protecting it. "I had him pull over at a pharmacy and get painkillers, antiseptic, bandages. When Frederick came back, he tossed the bag into the car and ran away. I got as far as Montréal before I pulled over and passed out. I came to just in time to get to the water-treatment plant."

It was unsaid but implied, and never forgotten: *And save your life, Armand.*

"Have you seen Castonguay since?"

"*Non.* I've looked, but not too hard. Honestly, I have nothing to say to him except good luck and goodbye, you cowardly shit."

Beauvoir barely suppressed a grin. He and Honoré had been watching *The Wizard of Oz.* Over and over. The Cowardly Shit would make a good character in an alternative production. He'd watch that.

"We've looked for him since the events in the plant," said Beauvoir. "He wasn't initially a priority, just a loose end. But we can't find him. It's actually quite difficult for people to disappear completely. Unless..."

"Unless he's dead." Caron studied their faces, remaining on Gamache's, who'd been silent. "You think he's dead?" She spoke the words clearly.

Armand nodded, understanding. "If he is, it means he knew enough to be dangerous to someone still out there."

"Funny how people around you get killed," said Beauvoir.

"I could say the same about you." She threw him an angry glance before her eyes drifted slowly, meaningfully, back to Gamache, as though she could see the ghosts that surrounded him.

Ignoring that gibe, Armand walked over to the wall. "This map belonged to Charles Langlois, the biologist who alerted me—"

"Yes, I know who he was." She'd joined him. "I was the one who recruited him. Remember?"

"What I remember, Jeanne, is that you hired Charles Langlois to quietly investigate what was happening at the water-treatment plants. What you didn't assign him to do, what you didn't even know he was doing, was visiting remote lakes."

As he spoke, Armand's tone was growing harder, harsher. "He hid this map." His glare was now icy. Glare ice. "From you."

The air crackled between them. By instinct, Jean-Guy stepped closer to Armand.

Jeanne Caron shifted her attention from Gamache to the map. Her ire forgotten.

"Why did Charles Langlois go to these lakes?" Then a thought struck her. "He was working part-time for that environmental agency. What's it called? Agence Québec Bleu."

"Action Québec Bleu," Beauvoir corrected, while Gamache continued to watch Caron.

"Right. Maybe it has something to do with his work there. Maybe it's meaningless."

"Then why hide it?" asked Beauvoir.

She turned to look squarely at them. "You really think there's more going on? Something else?" She watched their faces. "Something worse?"

"*Oui*," said Beauvoir. "We think the poisoning of the water was the first step."

"But if we stopped that, then maybe there is no second step."

"Why did Marcus Lauzon, the Deputy Prime Minister, approve the sales of primary industries to Americans?" Jean-Guy asked, in what appeared to be another ninety-degree turn. "He knew it was illegal. He must've known if it came out, his political career would be in ruins."

"Why do you think? He got huge kickbacks, that's why. And thought he could cover it up."

"With your help," said Beauvoir.

"*Oui.*" There was no use denying it. She'd been given immunity in exchange for her testimony against her former boss and in light of her actions in stopping the poison attack.

"But these lakes that Langlois visited," she said, looking again at the map, "aren't the ones with industry. They have nothing to do with those agreements or the poisoning plot."

They waited for her to say more, which she finally did. "Charles Langlois wrote on some of them. I recognize approval numbers, but what are the others?"

"Dates when he visited. This"—Beauvoir tapped the paper—"is the last lake he went to before he was killed."

"But there are other numbers and symbols on it. What's that about?"

"No idea," admitted Armand, speaking at last.

Caron dropped her eyes to the bottom of the map. "What does this mean? This line."

She was pointing to the dotted line that bled into Vermont.

"We don't know," said Beauvoir.

"Where does it go?" asked Caron.

"Jericho."

They turned and saw Reine-Marie standing at the foot of the stairs.

"It goes to Jericho," she said, looking straight at Jeanne Caron.

CHAPTER 8

⁓

Vivienne LaPierre held the litmus paper up against the sky. The color matched the fading blue to the east.

"Anything?" called Isabelle from the clearing where she was setting up their tent. When there was silence, she looked over. "Vivienne?"

It was a perfect early evening. Any breeze had disappeared, as often happened as the sun began to set. The air and water became perfectly still except where the biologist had dipped another vial into the shallows. This time, instead of the litmus paper, she brought out an eyedropper with solution.

"What is it?" asked Isabelle. "Did you find something?"

"I'm not sure."

Though her fingers were numb from the frigid water, she continued to work, trembling slightly as she tried to squeeze liquid from the dropper into the small tube. She missed a couple of times before finally getting a few drops in.

After some moments the testing agent reacted, and the water changed color. Vivienne sat back on her haunches. "It seems to be at acceptable levels, but borderline."

"Levels of what?"

Isabelle had just noticed the shifting colors of the evening sky, undulating shades of soft pink, reflected in the mirror-calm lake.

Red sky at night, she automatically thought. *Sailor's delight.*

It wasn't quite red, nor was it quite night. It was more like late afternoon, but the sun was going down earlier and earlier, especially there in the north. While the sun would still be up in Three Pines, here the light was already fading.

Two birds flew over the water, their wingtips just touching the surface, and far offshore Isabelle heard a plop as a fish leaped for an insect.

Vivienne showed Isabelle the litmus paper and the second vial. "In a healthy, pristine freshwater lake these would stay purple and the pH level should be at seven. This lake is at nine point five, perhaps ten."

"Which means?"

"Something's caused an increase in alkaline. Not dangerous." She looked around. "At least not yet. Still looks like a healthy ecosystem. Of course that's how it happens."

Almost afraid to ask, Isabelle did anyway. "What happens?"

"The sudden collapse. A system looks just fine, and then, almost overnight…"

"But we're not there yet." Isabelle tried to keep her voice neutral, though even she could hear the disquiet. She looked past the biologist, across the water to the far shore.

"I don't think so. But the lake is more out of balance than I'd have expected this far north. If it continues…" Vivienne pondered, then spoke almost to herself: "If anything, I'd have expected this"—she looked down at her tests—"to either stay the same or turn pink."

"Why? What would that mean?"

"Acid rain. We know most lakes are at least slightly affected by it. But this shows the opposite."

"What could be causing it?"

Now Vivienne spoke to herself. "I don't know how enough of it could get into this lake."

"Enough of what?"

"Phosphorous could upset the balance, raise the pH. Or maybe potassium. But still…"

"And this is a big lake," said Isabelle. "It would take a lot to affect it. Are you worried?"

"Worried? No, not really. Perplexed."

While Isabelle lit the fire, Vivienne retreated to their small tent, emerging a minute or so later wearing a tuque and gloves. And carrying a nice Pinot Noir and two tumblers.

"Please tell me you remembered the corkscrew," said Isabelle.

"I did." She fished it out of her coat pocket. "Only forgot it once." She poured them both liberal quantities. "Fortunately, I know how to open a wine bottle without one."

"You unscrew the top?" Isabelle heard Vivienne's full-throated laugh.

"*Non.* A cork. I'll show you sometime."

"When needs must…," said Isabelle, tipping her tumbler toward Vivienne.

"…the devil drives." Vivienne touched the plastic cups and finished the old saying. The second half of which Lacoste had never heard.

They sat quietly on the stones warmed by the fire. Embers drifted lazily into the darkening sky before dying and landing in the lake. They'd been careful to build their fire by the shore and not risk a forest fire. There had been more than enough of those.

The two women watched the sunset, drank red wine, and huddled close to the crackling campfire on the shores of the remote lake, their faces illuminated by the burning logs.

"Are you okay?"

Armand and Reine-Marie were at the basement door. He'd taken both her hands in his and could feel her tremble. It wasn't from the cold, it was barely contained rage.

She nodded and looked behind him at the woman standing beside the map. It was all she could do not to scream at her.

For her part, Jeanne Caron was smart enough to just say, "I am sorry, Madame Gamache, for what I did. But I won't ask forgiveness."

Then she accepted the cookie and mug of tea Reine-Marie held out to her. Almost as though Daniel's mother were offering her a wafer and chalice. If Jeanne Caron noticed that Madame Gamache's hands shook, she didn't show it.

Now Armand and Reine-Marie stood at the exit. He stroked her hands with his thumb.

Reine-Marie brought her gaze back to her husband's face. She could not imagine, though she'd tried, what those minutes that must've felt like hours and nanoseconds were like as he'd knelt on the floor, waiting to be killed. And then to be saved. By this woman. By that woman.

How that moment must have bonded them, bound them. In some strange connection.

"Are you sure about her, Armand?"

He smiled. "She didn't have to do what she did. Do I think she's suddenly an exemplary human? No. I know her for what she is. But we also need her."

"When needs must?" Reine-Marie kissed him on the lips and left.

He watched her walk down the hill toward Myrna's bookshop. One of Reine-Marie's many havens.

Once there she helped Myrna shelve the latest consignment of used books, picking out a few for herself. Reine-Marie suspected they were ones she and Armand had donated to the library sale. And would again. And buy them again. The life cycle of a book.

Armand turned back to the room and Jeanne Caron.

When needs must, the devil drives . . .

"You have an extraordinary wife, Armand."

"*Oui*," he said, though the less time Caron spent thinking about his family, the better. He needed this woman. He was grateful to her for saving his life. But he did not like her.

And he suspected it was mutual.

"Okay, out with it. Why did you bring me down here? Why do you think there's more going on? Not because of some numbers on an old map, and the fact my shit of an assistant has run away and is probably making piña coladas for tourists in Saint Lucia."

"Do you know the code we used to describe the poisoning plot?" Armand asked.

"The Grey Wolf and the Black Wolf. *Oui*," said Jeanne Caron.

"Well, the Grey Wolf is dead. And I'm afraid the Black Wolf is still out there."

That was met with stony silence.

Finally, her voice patient, kindly even, she said, "He's in Archambault, Armand. Your testimony helped put him there."

"I don't think so."

Caron's expressive face changed again. She was no longer amused. And no longer sympathetic. "What're you saying?"

"Isn't it clear? I'm saying that I don't think Marcus Lauzon is the Black Wolf."

"Are you sick? You're certainly delusional. He's been tried and convicted. You yourself made sure of that."

"I'm not saying he's innocent."

"Then what are you saying?"

"That it's possible he's not guilty of this particular crime. It's possible he was a pawn in the poisoning plot."

Now it was Beauvoir's turn to stare at Gamache. It was the first he'd heard of this. He couldn't believe what he had just heard. Though he remained silent.

Caron did not. "Why in the world would you suddenly think that?"

"Has it occurred to you that the evidence against him, once we began to look, was too perfect. Too much? It was an avalanche of damnation."

"Are you kidding me?" Her voice had risen in disbelief. "You're worried about too much evidence? I was the one who helped you find it. I can guarantee you it's real."

"How do you know?"

"Because I know the man. I know his handwriting. I know his methods and his thinking. I know what propels him. What the fuck are you thinking? Wait a minute. You haven't been reading that crazy conspiracy shit."

"You've seen it?" said Beauvoir.

"Of course I've seen it. People keep sending me links. Like I want to see it. So far the posts are all in the fetid swamp of the internet, those marginal sites. But they're seeping out." She looked at the two officers. "You can't tell me you believe that crap. That Lauzon's been railroaded, is some sort of martyr for the people."

"Is it so unbelievable?" asked Gamache.

"Yes, yes, it is. In the same posts they say the poisoning plot never happened. Do you believe that too?"

Now Gamache smiled. "No. We all know the truth."

"So, one statement is true, the other a lie?"

"Isn't that the best way to misdirect? To hide the lie inside a truth?"

Her eyes were wide, certain she was in a basement with at least one lunatic. And his apprentice.

"The trail back to Lauzon is just too direct," said Armand. "It's like a superhighway of damning evidence. Is he really that stupid?"

Beauvoir was looking from one to the other, barely believing the conversation had taken this turn.

"Listen, I worked for the guy for decades, since his first election to town council. He's not stupid, but he's driven by ego and insecurity, and a need to prove something to the world. Which makes him unpredictable at times. It was my job to keep the guardrails up."

"The lane was pretty wide," said Beauvoir.

"The guardrails were to keep other people out," she said, glaring at him. "To keep him safe. Marcus Lauzon is, in many ways, quite extraordinary. A real tactician. Smart, he sees many steps ahead. He just doesn't always choose the best way to get there."

That did not sound like much of a tactician to Gamache. Surely the best way forward was an integral part of tactics.

"That's where you came in," said Beauvoir.

She ignored him. "He has something very rare in my experience. A well-honed animal instinct. He can always find the weak spot. He can smell fear."

Beauvoir knew that to be true.

"Do you mean a killer instinct?" Armand asked.

"Of sorts. He will go for the jugular." Too late she remembered whose jugular Lauzon had gripped. Daniel Gamache's.

Jean-Guy saw the color rise so quickly in Armand's face he feared the man might pass out. But he stood stock-still, fighting to regain control. He needed Caron. But Daniel's father had clearly not forgiven her.

Beauvoir remained silent but watchful, in case that rage broke free. As a father now, he completely understood. What wouldn't he do to someone who'd tried to kill Honoré and little Idola? He suspected his own restraints would be breached in no time.

Standing close to Armand, he saw something Caron probably could not. His lips were moving very, very slightly. In prayer? Armand was repeating some phrase that was helping to keep him from lashing out.

"The current Prime Minister is young and popular," said Caron. "Marcus Lauzon is neither. People admired, even respected, him, but they did not like him. A successful politician must be liked. He knew he'd never get to the top job legitimately."

"And so he planned to wipe out hundreds of thousands of his own citizens?" asked Gamache, having regained control of himself.

"Well, someone did," she said. "Why not a man driven mad by insecurity and thwarted ambition?

"All those damning documents you found," said Beauvoir. "His trips to Sainte-Émiline. His links with the Moretti family. His accepting bribes to sell off Canada's resources and allow clear-cut catastrophic pollution—"

"But he actually did all those things," said Caron, trying to make them see reason.

"Did he? All of that could be faked." Beauvoir was beginning to see Gamache's reasoning. "Or at least planted."

Caron's eyes widened. She looked at Gamache, who was peering at her closely.

"Frederick Castonguay?" She said it slowly, enunciating clearly so he could not mistake what she said. "That's what you're thinking?"

Gamache nodded. "*Oui.* It's a possibility. He had access not just to your computer and office and files, but Lauzon's."

"You think he planted the evidence? Wait." She put up her hand and studied the large, quiet man in front of her. "You think my assistant was, is, behind whatever is happening?"

"Not necessarily. But I do think he knows who it is. Is, in fact, working for him. Or her."

His last words seemed lost on Jeanne Caron as she put down her mug of tea and stared at the map, then turned back to the two senior officers.

"So what's this all about? What's going to happen?"

"We don't know," admitted Gamache.

Caron looked at her phone. "It's getting late. If you don't have anything else you need from me, I'll head home."

"You'll keep this to yourself," said Gamache as they walked to the door.

"You really think I want a butterfly net over my head? Believe me, this is going no further. But you'll keep me posted?"

"*Oui.* Let us know if Castonguay gets in touch."

"I will. You think he's either dead or the one in charge. Seems quite a difference."

"And we're either brilliant or crazy," said Gamache.

Caron stared at him, not expecting humor. "For what it's worth, I'm pretty sure you've lost your minds." She looked around. "I need a bathroom."

While she was away, Armand turned to Jean-Guy and whispered, "I need to speak to Marcus Lauzon. We'll invite him to Sunday lunch."

"You are crazy. Who's going to tell Reine-Marie?"

"I'll give you five dollars to do it."

"Not even for ten." He glanced at the bathroom door, still closed. "What were you saying?"

Armand raised his brows. "What do you mean? I thought I was the one with the hearing problem."

"No, I mean when Caron talked about…" Jean-Guy didn't want to bring it up again, so he ended up just waving his hand. "You know."

"Daniel."

"*Oui.* You were repeating something to yourself. What was it?"

Armand paused and lowered his eyes to the worn linoleum floor before raising them again. "Do you remember the Vaslov case?"

"Of course. The girl murdered by her classmates for being transgender."

It had been a horrific crime. A hate crime by a gang of teenagers. It was a shock, and a wake-up.

Armand and Isabelle had spent a lot of time with Katie's parents. Trying to answer questions. Preparing them for the onslaught of press, and the court cases. And the online bile and hate. Aimed, incredibly, at their daughter, and them.

"Her parents are staunch Christians. Born-again. They couldn't accept Katie as transgender. After she was killed, they went to the trial every day, then in the evenings they volunteered at the LGBTQIA+ help line."

"I didn't know that."

"*Non.* Not many do. They wanted to turn their ignorance into understanding. To help others like Katie. To help other parents, like themselves. To turn hate into love."

"So that was what you were repeating? 'Hate into love.'"

"*Non.* I was saying, 'Katie Vaslov. Katie Vaslov.' It's what I always say when tempted to put more hate into the world."

"Is there no one you hate?"

Again, the smile, though now without the tinge of sadness. "I wouldn't say that. If you took the last éclair …"

"I would never dare, *patron.* Now, off to let Reine-Marie know who else is coming for Sunday lunch." Jean-Guy motioned to the door. "You first."

CHAPTER 9

⌐⌐

Shona Dorion looked around the dingy room in the dingy office building, in the dingiest *quartier* of Montréal. Real estate agents had rebranded it Vieux-Montréal, the more honest among them adding "adjacent," in an effort to align the neighborhood with the charm of the cobblestoned Old Montréal next door. And increase property values. But with a view of a cement plant on the shores of the St. Lawrence River on one side and railway tracks on the other, it was a hopeless cause.

Shona liked hopeless causes. As, clearly, did the rest of the dingy people in the room.

Now that the end-of-day briefing was over, and next-day assignments were handed out, Shona bent over her phone. Its face was cracked, but it still worked. Most of the time. She tapped out a message.

I have something. Meet me tomorrow for breakfast. The Ritz.

She hit send and waited.

"Shona, can you join me please?" The boss was hanging half out of her office.

"*Oui, d'accord.*" She slipped her phone into her pocket.

"I read your story on our work."

Shona had, unusually, given it to the head of the organization to read over before posting it on her site. She was anxious to get on the woman's good side. This sort of obsequious behavior went against the grain, unless there was a higher purpose.

Action Québec Bleu was formed to study and promote water security. Though that was not the higher purpose Shona Dorion had in mind.

"It's wonderful, very powerful. Though there is an error in the second

69

paragraph. Our funding was dropped by the provincial government, not the federal. We never did get money from the feds."

"Damn, I'm sorry. A stupid mistake. I knew that. *Merci*. I'll make the change, Margaux."

Back at her desk she checked the reply.

8 a.m. The Ritz.

Outside the filthy windows she could see the streetlights had come on. Another day was ending.

Armand sat on the bench on the village green and stared at the message he'd just received and replied to.

The Ritz.

That was amusing, but what was making him smile was Shona's profile shot. Most people had their face, or that of their child, or pet, or a pretty scene. But not this young journalist. Hers was a raised middle finger.

"You're in my place."

Ruth began to sit, and had Armand not moved, she and Rosa would have ended up on his lap.

Ruth pulled her moth-eaten sweater tight around her, while Rosa was magnificent in her cashmere coat, probably meant for spoiled cats or dogs. Shockingly few clothes were designed for ducks. Though ducks did end up in quite a few garments.

"I just heard that Honoré and Idola are heading back to the city after dinner. What did you do to drive them away?"

Though she was absolutely right, he had no intention of telling her about the guests coming for Sunday lunch, and the need for Annie and the children not to be there.

He'd told Reine-Marie about their guests, of course. She already knew about Evelyn Tardiff, but Evelyn was a friend. The man convicted of plotting mass murder was not.

"Are you mad?" had been her reply. "Marcus Lauzon?" she repeated, just to make sure she'd heard right. When he braced and nodded, she added, "I'll set an extra place in case you run into Satan and invite him too."

Though he'd pretty much already done that.

Armand had then gone over to Monsieur Béliveau's General Store to pick up the chicken and vegetables they always ordered for Sunday lunch. On the way back he paused to sit on the bench and ponder. A few minutes later he was joined by the mad poet and her equally mad, though more stylish, duck.

Instead of answering her question about what he'd done to drive away his daughter and grandchildren, he stared at Ruth. For so long she grew uncomfortable.

"Are you having a stroke? For God's sake, don't fall on me."

Still, she looked concerned, so intense were his eyes, so unyielding his stare.

"Armand?"

The phrase "drive away" had reminded him of the inconvenient fact that he was barred from driving, even short distances, until his hearing returned. He opened his mouth, but before committing himself, he looked once more at his phone, and the text that had come in from Shona Dorion. Not the words, but the image. The raised finger. Then he committed himself.

"I need to get into Montréal tomorrow morning, for a breakfast meeting."

"So?"

"Will you drive me?"

Now it was her turn to stare. "Are you mad?"

It was not the first time that day he'd been asked that question. Or even the third. And perhaps not the last. And, as with the other times, it was a legitimate question. So legitimate, Armand wondered if perhaps he had lost his mind.

Maybe the cicadas had finally drilled so deep into his brain his marbles had rolled out.

"Mad?" He looked into her wizened face. "Maybe."

"Then yes, absolutely. Sane people bore me. You normally bore me, but I find you suddenly interesting."

For some reason, this pleased Armand.

The light that was draining from the sky seemed to be absorbed into the homes and businesses around the village green. Amber light appeared in windows, spilling onto lawns and gardens. It was twilight. A near-magical time in Three Pines, the transition from day to night. As the torch was passed.

Myrna waved to them as she made her way over to Clara's. She was carrying a book and a bottle.

The bistro was lit up and filling up.

Ruth and Rosa sat on this bench every day, at dawn and dusk, as though the very day depended on them seeing it safely in and out.

"What time do you need to be there?"

"Eight o'clock." He paused, waiting for the protest, though he knew that Ruth, and therefore Rosa, rose early. With the light. But Ruth just waited, while Rosa nodded. Though ducks often did.

"Breakfast is at the Ritz," he added. "Please, join us."

That was a vital part of his half-baked plan.

"Too fucking right I will. Can Rosa come?"

He looked at the soignée duck. Why not. "Of course."

He got up, and they followed him into the home, into the kitchen. Into the liquor cabinet.

Armand watched Ruth pour a vat of "scotch" from a bottle they kept specially for her. One that contained only tea. Which he suspected she knew.

Getting her to drive was a good idea, he repeated as he poured himself a stiff drink. This was the right decision. This was not crazy at all.

The elderly poet joining their breakfast would serve many purposes, including convincing anyone watching that this could not possibly be a serious meeting. Not with a duck in attendance.

It was social. Nothing more. And barely that...

Yes, he thought as he put an ice cube into his drink, it was the right decision.

Ruth tipped her glass, which they both knew was a vase, toward him and winked. Narrowing his eyes, Armand walked over to the sideboard and sniffed the bottle he and Reine-Marie had rigged. Then he gave a single snort of laughter.

There was indeed scotch in it. Ruth had switched it back.

He sniffed his drink. It was tea.

She caught his eye and raised her brows. She would have raised a finger, but she needed both hands to grip the vat.

Eight a.m. The Ritz. When he produced for the young journalist the older version of herself, he might even go up in Shona's eyes.

God knew it was impossible to get lower.

"What else have you got in there, Ms. Poppins?" Isabelle asked.

After many years conducting investigations in the most remote parts of Québec, the senior Sûreté officer considered herself mighty adept at camping. But now Isabelle realized she was a rank amateur next to the biologist.

"A lamppost, of course," said Vivienne, smiling. "And a golden retriever. A flat-screen TV and this." She pulled out a collapsible pot and opened it with the same flick and flare Fred Astaire had used to open countless top hats.

Isabelle heard a "ta-da," though no one spoke. Then, looking closer, she gasped and thought maybe she had a small crush on Vivienne LaPierre, who was now holding up a grill in one hand and a cold pack with a large filet of marinating salmon in the other.

This beat her dehydrated beef stew, which, by her own admission, looked like something the golden retriever might throw up.

A few minutes later the two women were sitting by the campfire, drinking fine red wine and eating grilled Atlantic salmon and tiny baby potatoes.

And studying the map on her laptop, annotated by a murder victim.

"So what did Charles mean by these?" Isabelle asked.

She used her fork, speared with a potato dripping butter, to indicate the series of numbers and symbols the dead biologist had written on only this lake.

Vivienne shook her head. They'd both hoped that, once there, the sequence might make more sense. Some sense. But still they were baffled.

The fire was crackling and throwing nice heat, warming their fronts, though their backs, like the dark side of the moon, were chilled. Isabelle ran over to the tent and brought back their sleeping bags, handing one to Vivienne.

"*Merci.*"

Now wrapped up warmly, Isabelle poured them each another tumbler of wine while Vivienne placed another piece of driftwood on the fire and looked out across the still lake. Above them the sky was strewn with stars. Great swaths of them, their light millions of years old.

Both women were solemn now. Isabelle had never actually met Charles. Had only seen him across the crowded café when he'd had the rendezvous with Gamache at Open Da Night.

And she'd seen, a few minutes later, Armand's torn and bloody jacket placed over the young man's broken body as he lay in the middle of the road.

Vivienne knew even less about Charles Langlois. Had never seen him, not even a photo. All she knew was what she'd been told. He'd been a drug addict in recovery, a biologist, who'd stumbled onto a conspiracy and been murdered. But over the course of the day, she'd begun to feel a closeness to him. He could have been one of her students.

What she did know, had been told, was that he was a lost young man who'd found himself, found a passion, found a direction and purpose. And was killed when he'd found something else. And now they were trying to retrace his steps.

They were, it seemed, camping on the same site he'd chosen. Sitting around the very same campfire, on stones he'd rolled into place. Were looking out at the same view. At the same ancient light in the sky. So what had he seen that they could not?

Vivienne looked at the map again, then out across the lake. The moon had risen, its silver light reflected in the dark water. "It's beautiful. But really? It's like every other remote lake I've visited. There's nothing unusual about this place. Not that I can see."

Silence again enveloped them. Except for the far-off bark of a coyote, and the howl, even farther away, of a wolf.

"I wonder if it's what we can't see," Vivienne said at last.

"I can understand why you and the Chief are friends," said Isabelle, with a laugh. "He can also say some pretty vague things. Turns out they're just train of thought, but they can sure sound odd."

"Did I sound odd? I didn't mean to, and I wasn't being vague." She'd turned to look at Isabelle. "I'm serious. Maybe that's what's different about this lake, and why we haven't found it yet. Because what Charles found isn't on the shores of the lake, it's in it."

Isabelle had a sudden vision of a submarine. Surely not. Then her thoughts, lubricated by wine, slid over to the Chief Inspector telling her that as a unilingual Francophone about to go to university in England, he'd watched reruns of the old TV series *Voyage to the Bottom of the Sea*, to learn some English.

"You'd be surprised," he'd said in all earnestness, "how little use 'Aye, aye, Captain,' 'There's a monster from outer space, Admiral,' and 'Fire all missiles' are at Cambridge."

"Or anywhere, I hope."

"*Il y a un monstre*," she now muttered and got such a strange look from Vivienne that she put down her tumbler, suspecting the wine was doing her no favors.

In vino babbling . . .

"What do you mean by in the water?" Isabelle asked, drawing herself up and trying to look completely sober.

"The elevated pH."

"Could that be what he wrote? A chemical sequence?"

Vivienne returned to the photo of Charles's map on the laptop while Isabelle held her breath. This could be the breakthrough they were looking for.

But Vivienne was shaking her head. "*Désolée*. It's not that. I'd have recognized that. Still, he must've thought we'd understand."

"Or at least another biologist would." Isabelle hated to say it, but it was the truth, and honestly the main reason, the only reason, Gamache had asked Dr. LaPierre to come along.

Vivienne knew it too. And knew she was failing in her assignment.

Come on, come on, Charles. What're you saying?

The unidentified sequence of numbers and symbols was on the map for a reason. The map was hidden for a reason. In case . . .

Vivienne looked behind her. The light from their fire did not extend into the forest, so she could not actually see the base of the tree where Isabelle had found the rock.

The young man had probably sat exactly where she was.

Had he reached out and picked up the flat stone, maybe intending to skip it over the water?

She imagined him sitting there, looking down at the river rock. And then something had changed his mind. Instead of tossing it into the lake, he'd placed it at the base of the tree. Carefully. Deliberately.

Vivienne had been to the Arctic many times. Had seen the stone cairns erected over the graves of explorers who'd ignored the advice of the Inuit. And died. With the last of their strength, the dying men had scratched names on the stones. Dates. To let people know they'd been there. Had once lived. And perhaps as a warning to those who followed.

"Can I see the stone again?"

Isabelle dug it out of her knapsack.

Vivienne rubbed the hard dirty surface through the protective plastic baggie.

"Careful," said Isabelle, reaching out to take it back. But the deed was done.

Vivienne shook her head. Nothing.

Still, the rock itself was odd. It should not have been that far from the shore. She looked up at Isabelle.

"What?" asked Isabelle. "What're you thinking?"

"I'm thinking," said Vivienne, getting up with a groan and walking away from the lake, away from the warmth and light of the fire. Into the darkness. "Of the cairns in the Arctic. What doomed explorers left behind. I'm thinking what Charles wanted us to find wasn't the rock but—" Now she had her flashlight app on and was kneeling by the base of the tree. "This."

She leaned away and pointed.

There, cut into the bark at the base of the tree, hidden under some rotting leaves was etched a very small arrow and beside it an even smaller *cl*.

"Oh, my God," whispered Isabelle. She raised her stare from the tree into Vivienne's eyes. Her own wide with wonder. "You found it."

Vivienne reached out. Some mothering instinct wanted to caress the letters, as though to comfort. But Isabelle stopped her.

"The arrow's pointing into the woods." Isabelle's own phone was out, flashlight on. She was snapping photos as she spoke. "He wants us to go into the woods. That's where he hid it."

At last. At last.

"We'll have to look tomorrow, right? Too dark tonight." Vivienne was clearly hoping Isabelle would disagree and they could wander, drunk and lost, in the cold, dark forest.

"Yes," said Isabelle, not without regret. "Tomorrow."

Both women remained kneeling and staring into the woods. Then they walked slowly back to the campfire.

As they sat down on the warm rocks, Vivienne returned her gaze to the lake. A bat flapped overhead and disappeared into the darkness, and a loon called. It was hard to believe that not much farther north the disaster had occurred.

Wildfires had burned through millions of hectares of forest, sending plumes of ash into the atmosphere before falling to earth, coating American cities, large and small. Smothering them. The images had been apocalyptic. The events unimaginable. The fires unstoppable.

They'd broken out across Canada, all at once. As though nature had pulled a trigger.

And now there were fears the fires had heralded a new age. An annual calamity that would continue, in biblical fashion, until there was nothing left. No trees, no forest. No habitable cities. Just ash. A sort of nuclear bomb made of wood. And stupidity.

Vivienne stopped herself. The wine was making her maudlin. Surely she was overstating it. Besides, in a twist of fate, the worst of the ash had not actually landed on Canada. Such were the atmospheric conditions at the time.

A very bad thing for the United States but, it must be quietly admitted, a good thing for Canada. If you looked beyond the millions of acres of destroyed forest.

Vivienne turned around. If there was another disastrous season, this forest would be the next to go. These magnificent trees, which had been saplings when the Magna Carta was written, would go up in smoke to once again bury American cities.

How many times could that happen before too much damage was done? And what would be the American reaction if this became an annual catastrophe? How long before they tired of it and decided to do something about it? To defend themselves.

It was an unsettling thought. Not just the horrific destruction of millions of acres of vital forest, not just the environmental disaster, but how Americans might react to another onslaught. At least they'd know it was not done on purpose.

But was it? They'd been warned about climate change for decades. It was clear to any rational person that human activity was to blame. The fixes had been obvious and achievable. And yet governments and industry had—

"Huh. I'm an idiot."

"What?" asked Isabelle.

"I know why the lake has elevated pH."

"Why?"

"Potassium. I bet when I get the samples back from the lab they'll show there's potassium in the water. That will raise the pH, make it more alkaline."

"I'm assuming you don't mean that someone dumped a load of bananas into the lake."

It took Vivienne a moment to figure out why Isabelle would have said something that ludicrous, then she smiled. "*Non.* Follow me. Potassium is potash, and potash is—"

Isabelle realized she might be more than a little tipsy, which explained the banana comment, but now she was suddenly stone-cold sober. "Ash."

"And ash comes from—"

"Forest fires."

Vivienne shrugged off her sleeping bag, picked up the pot that had been used to boil the potatoes, and went to the lake while Isabelle, guessing what she was doing, broke up the smoldering logs with the tip of her boot.

Vivienne splashed water onto the embers, and there was a great hissing. The dying embers enraged.

A few more trips and the fire was out, though a plume of smoke drifted across the lake, then finally settled.

"Damn," said Vivienne. "I forgot. I have s'mores in my knapsack."

"Well, the golden retriever probably ate them."

"Hope not, there's chocolate."

This absurd conversation functioned to lighten the mood, to stop the shrieking in their heads. Telling them they had to hurry. Had to follow

Charles's arrow. Had to find whatever he'd hidden. And they had to get the results of the water tests.

Had to, had to, had to. Hurry. Hurry. Hurry.

Vivienne reached for the dirty dishes, but Isabelle stopped her.

"You cooked. I'll clean up."

She took the dishes and pans to the lake. The last thing Isabelle did, though she was bone weary, was carry their food and garbage, now in a sturdy bag, into the woods, away from their campsite. And hoist it into a tree. If bears or wolves were attracted by the scent, they would not come knocking on their tent.

As she returned to the clearing, Isabelle could feel a slight breeze. There was a definite bite to it, and something else. Something she recognized.

She tried to dismiss it. After all, hadn't the sky been red? And didn't that mean it would be clear the next day? Not the rain or sleet or snow she could sense approaching.

But nature was changing, she thought as she crawled into her sleeping bag next to Vivienne, who was already asleep.

The world was becoming less predictable, the signs less readable. And why wouldn't nature, at this point, lie to them? Turn on them?

CHAPTER 10

⌒

"This isn't the Ritz, you fuck-wit."

Rosa might as well have said it, given the expression on her duck face. But it was, of course, Ruth who was glaring at Armand.

"Did I say the Ritz? I meant this—"

"Shithole?"

Ruth and Rosa peered through the grimy window into the empty diner. Though it was not totally empty. A thin, almost emaciated older woman was leaning against a Formica counter next to a stand of doughnuts. Even from a distance they could see the fuzz on them.

"I'm not going in there."

"Suit yourself, but remember, I've seen your kitchen."

Now Rosa nodded, though ducks often did.

"It's cleaner than that," said Ruth, jerking her head toward the restaurant. "Sewers are cleaner than that. I was looking forward to eggs Benedict, not Legionnaires' disease."

"I'm sorry. Look, I'll take you to the Ritz when we've finished here. You can have whatever you like."

"Too right." Now her rheumy eyes narrowed. "What do you mean, 'when we've finished here'? Why're we here?"

Rosa's beady eyes were on Armand. He and the duck never really saw eye to eye and today was no exception.

"We're meeting someone." He opened the door. Reluctantly, and not without a touch of drama, the woman and duck walked in. Ruth's feet made a Velcro sound on the linoleum floor.

"Charming."

"Again, I've been in your kitchen."

"That happened only once, when someone flew onto the table and knocked a can of maple syrup onto the floor."

Rosa looked at Armand as though he were the one who'd flown into the syrup.

They had their choice of tables, and Armand indicated one far from the window.

"Close to the bathrooms," said Ruth. "Wise."

"What do you want?" the server demanded.

Armand recognized her from the last time he'd been there. She did not recognize him. Of course, to do that, she'd have to actually look at him.

"A bottled water, please."

"And your date?"

She'd turned to Ruth, who clearly thought she'd died and been gifted that question. But her delight changed with the next thing the server said.

"Ducks aren't allowed. Health hazard."

"I'm sorry," said Ruth. "Ducks are a health hazard, but the *E. coli* you use as condiments isn't?"

"Not my policy. The duck leaves."

Armand handed her a twenty-dollar bill and said something he never thought would come out of his mouth.

"The duck stays."

"Fine." She squeaked away.

They were still waiting fifteen, twenty, twenty-five minutes later. But there was no bottled water and no Shona.

"This is the worst date ever," said Ruth.

"Not a date," muttered Armand as he checked his phone again.

He was getting worried that maybe "the Ritz" wasn't code. Wasn't an in-joke after their last meeting here. That Shona really did mean the Ritz.

He'd messaged her but got no answer.

Now he was worried that she had meant to meet him here, but something had happened to her.

Isabelle lay face up, staring at the peak of the tent not that far above her runny nose.

She had to go to the bathroom, a.k.a. the log, badly, but was loath to get out of her toasty warm sleeping bag. And, to make matters worse, she could hear the rapid tapping of something against the canvas.

Ever since her grandparents had taken her camping as a child, Isabelle had loved the smell of a canvas tent. But that soothing scent did not outweigh the sound, and her dread of what she'd find when she opened the flap.

"Red sky at night, my ass," she muttered.

Beside her, Vivienne was still asleep. Clearly she'd chosen, intentionally or not, the side that did not have a tree root sticking up.

Desperately trying to get out of her sleeping bag without touching the sides of the tent and breaking the seal that would allow whatever was hitting the outside in, Isabelle twisted and turned and finally kicked the sleeping bag away. Unzipping the tent flap, she looked out.

It was worse than she thought. Rain wasn't hitting the canvas. It was snow. Sleet. Ice.

"Fuck, fuck, fuck, fuck," she muttered as she ran barefoot across the campsite, to the designated log. "Fuck."

But finally the relief was so great, she didn't even feel the ice and snow on her legs and under her feet.

"May I?" Vivienne plunked down beside her, not waiting for permission.

After her own deep sigh, Vivienne asked, "Okay, what do we do first?"

It reminded Isabelle of Jean-Guy's claim that he and the Chief had once, in desperation, used a two-holer outhouse as a situation room. She had never believed him. But this topped even that.

"We go into the woods, see if we can find what Charles was pointing to. I'm really hoping he left other signs."

Isabelle looked at the snow and sleet, the leaden sky and lake. Even the woods seemed drained.

And yet, for all that, what she felt was glee. They were close. Today was the day they'd break this open and stop whatever was going to happen. Or at least find out what it was. Then they'd have a fighting chance.

She looked at Vivienne, who was also staring at the lake.

"What are you thinking?"

"I'm thinking that next summer I'd like to bring my grandchildren here."

"I'll bring my kids and we can camp together. This time we won't forget the s'mores."

Neither said, as they ran back to the tent, that they hoped "here" would still be there next summer.

A few minutes later they were wearing every piece of clothing they'd brought with them. By mutual agreement they skipped breakfast. Though they ate the chocolate bars that had been intended for the s'mores.

Isabelle walked to the base of the tree and replaced the stone exactly where and how she'd found it.

"Why did you do that?" asked Vivienne.

"To hide Charles's markings We might not be the only ones looking."

They hitched their backpacks further up and headed into the woods.

"*Bonjour,* Julian—"

"Is that you, Chief Inspector?"

"*Oui.*" Armand had put on the auto-transcription function so he could read what was being said. "I'm wondering if a young woman is there, perhaps waiting for me?"

"No one has asked for you. Can you describe her?"

"Twenty-three years old, a woman of color. Probably looks annoyed."

The maître d' at the Ritz laughed. "Most young women these days seem to—"

"Oh, it's okay, Julian. *Merci.* She's just arrived."

"Who the fuck's this?" was the first thing out of Shona's mouth. She stood across the diner, glaring at Ruth, then at Rosa. Then she turned to Gamache, who'd stood up. "You brought a date?"

Armand hoped to God he'd misheard, but the laugh of delight from Ruth said differently.

What he did realize was that he'd actually heard. While the cicadas were still screaming in his ears, the noise had dropped. This was no delusion, no wishful thinking.

He'd heard Shona. And, better still, he'd heard Ruth's laugh.

How he missed laughter.

"Really, who the fuck is this?" Shona demanded. "You brought a vagrant? And a duck?"

"I heard you the first time," he said.

Ruth caught his eye, her smile widening, before she looked at Shona and demanded, "Who the fuck is this?"

Armand began to grasp what might be the enormity of his misjudgment in having these two women in the same room. Then something happened.

"*And in my heart, her anger smolders still,*" Shona quoted. "*Amid the ashes of residual guilt.*"

"Forest fires," said Vivienne.

They'd walked half a kilometer into the woods, marking the trail, then fanned out. But had found nothing. There was no evidence of anything buried or hidden.

They were now sitting on a fallen tree, resting. It had been a slog, and they still had to get back to the shore. The snow was accumulating. On the trees, the ground. Them. It tap-tap-tippity-tapped onto their rain gear, dripping under their collars and down their backs.

"What about the fires?" asked Isabelle, pulling her jacket tighter.

"Maybe that's what Charles meant by the arrow. Not something he'd hidden close by, in these woods, but something further north. Maybe he wanted to bring our attention to the wildfires."

"But the fires were news around the world. Hardly secret. And hardly a reason to be murdered."

They were now retracing their steps. Both had come to the realization that if Charles Langlois did hide something in these woods, their chances of finding it were tiny.

They were almost back at the clearing when Isabelle stopped. She put her arm across Vivienne's body to also stop her.

"What is it?"

"My God," said Shona. "You're Ruth Zardo."

"And you are?"

"Shona Dorion."

"You're not..." Ruth raised her middle finger, and so did Shona. "Ha. You're the one who's always taking a run at Armand."

"You follow her?" he said.

"Not just follow, I think I love her." Ruth, forgetting to be ornery, turned back to Shona. "No one ever quotes the middle of my poems."

"No." Shona's eyes were bright, her voice light as she leaned across the sticky table toward Ruth. "It's only the beginning and end that most people remember. I do too, but the guts, the heart of your works, that's what I love best. *From the Public school to the private hell / of the family masquerade / where could a boy on a bicycle go—*"

"*When the straight road splayed.*" Ruth finished the quote from her own poem, stroking the feathers on Rosa's small head as she spoke.

"How do you know him?" Shona jerked her head toward Armand.

"He's a neighbor." Ruth looked at him to make sure he understood what she said next, suspecting rightly that while his hearing had improved, it was far from perfect. "And a friend. How do you know him?"

"He killed my mother."

Ruth's brows shot up. It took her a moment to realize this young woman was not kidding. And Armand was not denying it.

"Well, that explains most of your posts," said Ruth.

"I've spent my adult life trying to get back at him."

"Choosing to meet here is a good step," said Ruth.

Shona smiled.

Armand realized he'd never seen her smile. Well, that was not totally true. The very first time he'd laid eyes on her, when he'd entered their squalid home with a warrant, the little girl was holding her mother's hand. And smiling up at him.

Her face, her whole being, radiated happiness and trust. This was a child raised in a crack house, by a prostitute who'd murdered her dealer. But, more than that, this was a child raised with love. Profound, all-encompassing love. And, with it, trust. She knew if she was holding her mother's hand, she was safe.

Until...

In that moment, when he'd arrested her mother for murder and gently broken that grip, the smile had been wiped off Shona's face, to be replaced by confusion. Then fear. And then, later, rage. And hatred. And finally contempt.

Shona Dorion had become a journalist. And a very good one. An investigative journalist, she was relentless in pursuit of the entitled, the bullies, those who took advantage of the vulnerable and broken. She had her own site, with hundreds of thousands of followers. Her emblem was the raised finger. And her main targets were those in power. Her favorite target was the man who'd arrested her mother. The senior Sûreté officer she held responsible for her mother's suicide in detention just days later.

Here was an old white cop who held so much power she felt in her bones he must be corrupt, though she hadn't been able to find anything on Chief Inspector Gamache. But that hadn't stopped her from hurling insulting, bordering-on-abusive questions at him in news conferences. Ones that always had some margin of truth. Like calling him a coward because he'd survived the hit-and-run, and Charles Langlois had not.

"You saved yourself," she'd shouted from the back of the hastily called conference. "How can we trust the Sûreté when its senior officers protect themselves first?"

It was in that moment, when Armand had seen the rage and satisfaction in Shona Dorion's eyes, and the discomfort of his colleagues and even the other journalists, that he'd made up his mind.

He needed an ally outside the Sûreté. Someone smart, connected, courageous, unrelenting, who could dig into things without setting off alarms. He needed someone no one would suspect could possibly be working with him.

He needed Shona Dorion.

And so, months ago, before the events in the water-treatment plant, he'd invited her to this very café to ask for her help. She'd agreed, volunteering at Action Québec Bleu, the organization where Charles Langlois had worked, to find out what she could.

Though she made it clear it was a limited truce. Once their work together was over, he was again in her crosshairs.

"So, what're you doing here?" Ruth asked. "Why did you agree to meet him?"

The old poet looked from one to the other. It was clear that if there was an *entente* between them, it was not exactly *cordiale*. Once it was over, they would return to where they had been.

Hunter and hunted.

"What do you know about FEDS?" Shona asked.

"Feds?" said Ruth. "Can't say—"

"I was asking him."

"Right."

"I take it you mean the federal government," said Gamache.

"I think so, but I'm not sure. And if so, which one?"

"What do you mean?"

"In the Action Québec Bleu files, the ones in Madame Chalifoux's office, I've found repeated references to FEDS and DC."

"Washington?"

"I don't think it's the comics, do you?"

Both Ruth and Rosa snorted.

"It didn't make sense since AQB never got money from the federal government," Shona continued. "And certainly not from the Americans."

"When Americans say 'Feds,'" said Armand, "don't they mean the FBI?"

"That's my understanding," said Ruth.

"I was talking to her."

"Right."

"Or the Federal Reserve," added Armand. He leaned across the table, forgetting how filthy it was. Until his hand touched it.

But it was too late.

"The thing is, it's not '*the* Feds,' just 'FEDS,'" said Shona. "And every reference to it is spelled with all caps."

"You've obviously looked it up online," said Armand.

"Obviously. Just what we've already said, but nothing with all caps."

Armand sat back and, deep in thought, he reached for a thin paper napkin. As he tried to wipe the sticky stuff off his hands, all he managed to do was glue the paper to his palms.

"Are you done? Can we go to the Ritz?" asked Ruth.

"*Non*," said Armand, studying the young woman across from him. "I think there's more. Why did you want to meet?"

"Because of this."

Shona placed a piece of paper in front of Gamache. He put on his reading glasses.

"What am I looking at?"

"Bank accounts. I said I wanted to write a piece on the lack of funding for AQB. Chalifoux gave me access to her applications for government funding and requests for private donations. I don't think she realized that from there I could get deeper."

"To see the funding and donations themselves," said Gamache.

"Exactly. Look at the amounts. They're huge. I can guarantee you none of this ever came to AQB. I think the organization is being used to launder money."

Armand shook his head and gave one gruff laugh, though there was little actual amusement. Removing his glasses, he rubbed his eyes. "Incredible. I think you've found it. We've been looking into this."

"What?" said Shona and Ruth in unison.

"How the bribes got to Marcus Lauzon. This must be it. They were funneled through AQB. And Charles Langlois found out."

"And 'DC'? What does that mean?" asked Shona.

"It must mean where the money came from. Washington, DC," said Ruth. "And 'FEDS' means the Federal Reserve."

"Which means not just American corporations, but the American government's involved," said Shona.

"Which means the American government's involved," Armand said, not realizing he was repeating what Shona had just said. But neither woman pointed that out.

It seemed to bear repeating.

"What is it?" whispered Vivienne, edging closer.

Isabelle Lacoste had spotted a lump, a bit of ground higher than it naturally would be, should be.

"Maybe nothing," she said, kneeling beside it. From her knapsack she took out gloves and a small shovel.

"Please," she muttered to herself, "let it be Langlois's laptop. Please..."

Several inches down she found something promising. A heavy-duty green bag. The type you'd wrap something in to keep it safe from the elements.

But as she worked the earth around it, Isabelle Lacoste grew wary. It was much larger than a normal garbage bag, and certainly larger than a laptop would be, should be. Could be.

Completely oblivious now to the sleet hitting her face and the rivulets of cold water dribbling through her scalp as she bent over, Isabelle carefully dug around the edges of the plastic. Then stopped.

"What?" asked Vivienne, sensing the change. She was no longer with Isabelle. Her companion had become Inspector Lacoste.

Vivienne leaned in to get a closer look, then took a step back. The green garbage bag was outlining what could only be a boot.

For the first time in decades, Vivienne LaPierre crossed herself.

CHAPTER 11

⌒

R uth finished her eggs Benedict at about the same time Rosa polished off the small bowl of frozen peas and sliced grapes the Ritz in Montréal had provided for her.

"Did you really kill her mother?"

He nodded. Then shook his head. It was complicated.

As Shona had left the dingy diner, she'd said to Ruth, "*Having been hanged for something / I never said, / I can now say anything I can say.*" Then she turned to Armand and said, with a glacial stare, "*Before I was not a witch, / but now I am one.*"

At the door Shona Dorion had turned and raised her middle finger. Ruth raised hers back. And, behind the counter, the emaciated server raised hers.

Armand lowered his eyes in the face of this private message between the women, a power of three that even the most obtuse man could not fail to understand.

Before I was . . .

Now, sitting in the grandeur of the Ritz, he gave his credit card to the server and said to Ruth, "I arrested her mother for killing her dealer, and asked that she be placed in the infirmary, for observation and help in coming off crack. She hanged herself."

Ruth took a deep breath in and pushed away her plate.

"I later learned that she'd killed the man when he'd tried to rape Shona, who was eight."

"Dear God," sighed Ruth.

"I don't think God had anything to do with what happened. It was a travesty from beginning to end."

"*Before I was not a witch,*" said Ruth, softly, "*but now I am one.*"

90

He nodded.

In the car on the way home Armand tried to ignore the duck on his lap. Staring at him. Her beak almost touching his nose. Had it been a gun, he would not have been more disconcerted.

"You're in her spot," Ruth explained.

He turned to look outside as city turned to countryside, though Armand barely noticed. His thoughts were on what Shona had said. About Action Québec Bleu. They'd investigated its Executive Director, Margaux Chalifoux, but found nothing against her. The environmental organization appeared to run not just on a shoestring, it would be lucky to have even that. It ran on vapors and wishful thinking and, mostly, the goodwill and passion of its workers who were, in essence, involuntary volunteers.

Isabelle had investigated their funding and found nothing irregular, beyond its lack of support from any level of government, which was in itself odd.

She'd planned to look more closely, but then the plot exploded, and was resolved, and the investigation ended.

But now . . .

But now Shona had found tens of millions of dollars had been funneled through AQB to . . . Lauzon? They'd have their forensic accountants check the accounts, to be sure.

Ruth, who was a surprisingly good driver, had gotten them almost home before she quietly said, without turning to him, "I know."

"What do you know?"

"That you heard what I just said. That your hearing is better than you let on." She glanced at him. "Why would you hide that?"

"Why do you hide that you are, in fact, a kind and decent and loving person?"

It looked as though she was not going to answer. It wasn't until they crested the hill that led down into Three Pines that she said, "Because it's dangerous to expose myself."

"Even to friends?"

"They don't have to be told, they know." She peered at him. "I'm presuming your family knows too."

He smiled. "I didn't know until you laughed." It did seem unfair that the first sound he heard clearly was out of Ruth. Though how perfect that it was a laugh. "Please don't tell anyone. Leave that to me."

"You want people to think you're not up to the job? Believe me, it's not a hard sell."

It was his turn to laugh. But she had it right. It was vital that he be un-derestimated.

There were still far too many cicadas screaming in his head, but he now had confidence they too would leave. And he found he could now think more clearly.

"It's not always obvious who our friends are," Ruth said, pulling her car partway onto her lawn.

He was not the only one who wanted to be underestimated.

"True enough. Thank you for the drive."

"And the distraction? That is why we were there, no? So that no one would figure out the real reason for your visit to Montréal?"

He smiled. "You are a witch." At which she cackled. "I'm afraid you and Rosa can't come over for Sunday lunch today."

"That's okay. I've had my fill of you."

"I'm sorry, I didn't hear that." And heard her laugh. "Thank you, Ruth. You're a good friend."

"I'm sorry, I didn't hear that," said Ruth, and heard him laugh as he got out of the car.

As he walked along the path to the house, their front door opened and Henri, Fred, and Gracie bounded out, and with them came the scent of roasting chicken.

"Evelyn's here," said Reine-Marie, giving him a hug. "She's waiting for you in the bistro. Jean-Guy isn't back yet."

He could see that. No car.

"I'm going over to Clara's before he gets here." The "he" she meant was not Jean-Guy. "Take the chicken out in half an hour and let it rest, and for God's sake, don't let Henri get it."

That had only happened once, and they suspected it wasn't Henri but Ruth who'd dragged the carcass away.

They walked together across the village green before separating. It was a brilliant fall day, crisp and cold. Though there was a warning in the wind. A growl through the trees that would soon, they knew, become a bite. Something was coming at them from the north.

Something was about to happen.

When he entered the bistro, he stood at the door to let his eyes adjust. He saw Evelyn waving from an armchair and indicated he'd be with her in a moment, then went over to the new server.

"*Salut, mon frère,*" he said quietly. "Everything okay?"

"If you call being held here against my will okay, then yes, splendid."

"There are worse prisons, and you know you can leave. But…"

"But thanks to you, if I poke my head up, I might be murdered. Like the Abbot. Like Brother Robert."

For a long time, Armand had believed this unhappy monk, the former acting Abbot of Saint-Gilbert-Entre-les-Loups, knew more. In fact, knew where Charles's missing laptop was hidden. Since they'd found the map in the monastery, why wouldn't Charles or the Abbot also send the laptop there?

But the monastery had been searched many times over, and nothing. And slowly Armand had come to the conclusion that this monk who'd opened mail and snooped into all his *confrères'* private lives was, in fact, telling the truth.

He didn't know where that elusive laptop might be.

Still, Armand had hidden Frère Simon in this hidden village, to keep him safe from the Black Wolf. As days turned to weeks and months, he had watched as Brother Simon, a Gilbertine who'd taken a vow of silence, had begun to open up. To speak. To make friends. To actually know the daily specials and master the complicated espresso machine. Had begun to fit in.

Simon had found his place. Not behind an altar but behind a counter, in service.

"Let me know if anything odd happens," said Armand.

"Ruth hasn't been in for her morning toddy. Does that count?"

"Close. I'll keep it in mind."

And Brother Simon actually smiled.

Evelyn stood as he approached, and kissing her on both cheeks, he asked why she was waiting for him in the bistro and not their home.

"I arrived early and was frankly starving. I didn't want to trouble Reine-Marie. I did offer to help her prepare lunch, but she had it all under control. You married up, Armand."

He was peering at her in the way she recognized but still hadn't gotten used to. Once such a brilliant man, such a brilliant mind, now his expression more often than not was perplexed. Even blank.

Evelyn realized she should speak in short, declarative sentences. She also realized she had not lied to Moretti on their stroll through the Jean-Talon market the day before. Armand Gamache was clearly no longer the force he once was. Not a threat. By the time he realized something was happening, it would be long over.

This was the real reason she'd accepted his invitation to Sunday lunch. To make sure. Now she could go home. Except she was committed to what promised to be a long and tedious lunch.

At least she'd had a delicious brioche here in the bistro while she'd waited.

"*Excusez-moi*," said Armand, taking out his phone. "I need to set my alarm, to remember to take out the chicken."

"Of course." Though her heart ached a little, to see this once great leader reduced to anxiety over roast chicken.

She watched as his brow furrowed, and wondered if even that simple task, of setting the timer, was proving too much. How much damage had that explosion done?

But now he got up and, "*Désolé*," took a few steps away from the table before turning his back on her.

At that moment she was distracted by another vehicle arriving.

"Fucking hell," she whispered as she recognized the man getting out.

"Anything?" asked Vivienne.

"*Rien*." Nothing.

Inspector Lacoste had sent a photo and message to Chief Inspector Gamache and Inspector Beauvoir. Now she waited.

And waited.

Finally, a few long minutes later, her phone rang.

"Chief?"

"What've you got?" His voice was low, clearly trying to keep others from overhearing.

Armand had put on the text function since he still did not trust that the cicadas would not eat a few vital words.

"Looks like a body. I stopped digging as soon as I realized. I've sent for a forensics team to get up here as soon as possible, but it'll take a while. Dr. LaPierre and I will stay by the body until they arrive."

"What equipment do you have?"

"Gloves, evidence vials, and bags. But no testing kits. I didn't think—"

"Of course you didn't." He thought for a moment, looking out the window at Marcus Lauzon. At the smug smile on that reviled face. Then he noticed Jean-Guy's face opening up into astonishment as he too read Lacoste's message and saw the photo.

Armand walked deeper into the bistro as Evelyn Tardiff returned her attention to her colleague, the head of homicide.

What the hell is he up to? What's Lauzon doing here?

Something had happened. Marcus Lauzon had obviously been taken out of maximum security, supermax, and brought here for Sunday lunch. Along with her.

Why?

Alarms began to go off, and she wondered if Armand Gamache, that wily strategist, really was as feeble, as diminished, as he seemed. She glanced out the window and inadvertently caught Marcus Lauzon's eye.

Both looked quickly away.

"Isabelle, you have to open that bag. We need to know who and what is in there."

She knew what he was asking. That they run the risk of contaminating evidence. But the need to know now outweighed the risks.

"Agreed. Stay on the line, *patron.*"

Inspector Lacoste switched her phone to camera and turned the view around so Gamache could watch. Hitting record, she handed it to her companion.

"Vivienne, can you hold this? It's recording."

"Of course." The biologist took the phone and pointed it at the partially exposed bag.

From the warmth and comfort of the bistro in Three Pines, Armand watched as Isabelle worked quickly and expertly, uncovering what was clearly now a corpse wrapped in layers of heavy plastic. Cutting the plastic open at the head, she was immediately repelled backward.

Even after years of doing this, she never got used to the sight, or smell, of a decomposing body.

Vivienne had dropped the phone. Armand could hear gagging.

"What is it?" he asked, his voice muffled, his face face down in the slush and muck. "Who is it?"

Isabelle picked up the phone, wiped the mud away on her jacket, and pointed. She heard the long sigh of someone who realized he'd been wrong. Very wrong.

Clara spotted Ruth coming down her path. "Quick, everyone, pretend you're dead."

"Everyone" was Myrna and Reine-Marie.

"Who is it?" asked Myrna.

"Who do you think?"

They crouched down and fell silent. The doorknob jiggled.

"There's a slight flaw to this strategy," whispered Reine-Marie, hiding behind Myrna, as was Clara.

"Hello?? *Bonjour?*" could be heard from the front hall. Then, "Fuck, fuck, fuck."

"You never lock your door," said Myrna, standing up from where she'd been taking refuge behind the exuberant arrangement of autumn flowers and branches and weeds she'd cut down that morning and brought with her.

"There you are," said Ruth. "I thought for a moment I'd have to make new friends."

"Out of what?" asked Clara.

"What did she make us out of?" asked Reine-Marie.

"Stone and wishful thinking," said Ruth, whose hearing was startlingly acute. "Your husband said I wasn't invited to Sunday lunch. Been replaced by a mass murderer."

"Sounds like a fair trade," said Clara. Her smile froze when she looked out the window and realized the mad poet was, for once, telling the truth.

"What's happened, Armand?" demanded Evelyn, when he'd hung up and rejoined her. "And what the hell is that man doing here?"

They were two separate questions, though Gamache knew they intersected. Somehow. The dead man and the luncheon guest.

The former political leader was walking down the path to the Gamache home, to join them for Sunday lunch. He was still in handcuffs, and Jean-Guy had a firm grip on his arm.

While Beauvoir did not think his prisoner would make a run for it, he knew that people did strange things. And this man's actions in the past went far beyond predictable.

Armand chose to focus on the second of Evelyn's questions. The one he was prepared for.

"I don't think Marcus Lauzon is the Black Wolf."

The look on Chief Inspector Tardiff's face was exactly the same as Jeanne Caron's had been the day before, when he'd dropped the same bomb on her.

"Of course he is. For fuck's sake, it was proven in court, beyond any doubt." Her voice was rising, so that others in the bistro, including the former monk turned server, turned to look. "And now you release him from prison? Have you lost your mind?"

She knew she should rein it in, but the shock had shaken her. What had this silent, still, still silent man found out?

Armand tilted his head to one side, his brows together. His expression puzzled.

"*Désolé*, Evelyn. I didn't catch it all. But you seem angry."

She was, in fact, incandescent. If her hair could have burst into flames, it would have.

"Why the fuck did you bring him down here? This is a huge mistake, Armand."

Armand shrugged and shook his head. Not in boredom, not because he disagreed, but in apparent incomprehension.

"Oh, fuck it," she muttered.

Turned out the lunch might not be as tedious as she'd thought.

As they left the bistro and made their way across the village green, Armand's mind was not on Tardiff's reaction to Lauzon, which was predictable, nor on the confrontation to come, but on the unexpected. The unpredicted.

The body in the bag.

How did Frederick Castonguay, who'd worked closely with their prisoner, their luncheon guest, the former Deputy Prime Minister, end up dead and buried beside that remote lake?

CHAPTER 12

⌒

"F rederick Castonguay."

Armand had taken Jean-Guy aside as soon as they'd entered the house and whispered those words.

Beauvoir, who had not seen the bag being opened by Isabelle, stared, then gave a curt nod. Absorbing the news. They had other priorities at the moment, and Lacoste was more than capable of doing what was necessary with the body.

Still, it was unexpected, and Beauvoir struggled to keep his expression neutral.

He and Gamache were obviously thinking the same thing: How had the young assistant to Jeanne Caron ended up in a green garbage bag in a forest?

At one time, indeed until a few minutes ago, Gamache had wondered if Frederick Castonguay wasn't deeply involved in the plots. Might he even be the one behind it all? It was unlikely, though wasn't that often the way?

But Armand now knew he'd been at least partially mistaken. And partly right. Castonguay was not the leader, but he was obviously in-volved somehow and considered so dangerous that he needed to be silenced.

Frederick Castonguay had had access to all of Jeanne Caron's docu-ments, and she, in turn, as Lauzon's Chief of Staff, had access to all the former Deputy Prime Minister's papers and emails. She had control over his movements and even his finances. Or so she'd thought.

And Castonguay, as her assistant, had access to all of that.

Could he have sidestepped his immediate boss and been working directly with Lauzon? Was he the conduit for the money? Was Frederick Castonguay, that nondescript young man, one of the main conspirators?

By the same token, it would be equally easy for Frederick Castonguay to plant evidence. To plant that money. To set up Marcus Lauzon. To make it look like the Deputy PM was the one behind the plots. And leave the real conspirators free to finish what they started.

So, thought Armand as he slowly removed his coat and put on the old cardigan, so far there was a possibility Marcus Lauzon was, or was not, behind the plots. There was a possibility the dead man was, or was not, working with him. There was a possibility the dead man was, or was not, working against him.

They did not seem further ahead.

What he did know was that there was a direct line from the man now standing in the heart of their home in Three Pines, looking around with interest, and the young man dead and decomposing hundreds of kilometers north. From Lauzon to Caron to Castonguay.

Quite a lineage.

Too many things led back to the former politician for Gamache not to wonder if Lauzon wasn't the Black Wolf after all. The one who fed people's fears, paranoia, greed, rage. He fed them and, in turn, was fed on them.

And few knew better than Armand Gamache what a bloated ruin this man was.

So why, why, he wondered as he watched Marcus Lauzon, did he harbor doubts? He was clearly the only one who did. Even his own team thought him mad to think Lauzon might have been wrongly convicted.

He put on the ragged old slippers and was aware everyone was looking at him. Waiting for him to take the lead. He glanced at Beauvoir, who also seemed distracted. Clearly struggling with the questions that emanated from that putrid find at the northern lake.

What was Frederick Castonguay looking for at the lake? How did he know that lake was of interest? Unless... was there some connection between the two young men?

Whose side was Frederick Castonguay on?

Who had followed, found, and killed him?

Who—

Armand's phone alarm went off, startling everyone in the room. And just like that, the questions retreated, and his attention was brought sharply back home.

He turned to Marcus Lauzon. "That's the chicken. It's ready to be taken out. Let's go into the kitchen."

Beauvoir and Evelyn Tardiff exchanged glances. Were they mistaken, or did this sound like two friends about to prepare a meal together?

"I'm very good at gravy," said Lauzon as he followed his host. "Should you need it."

"As it turns out, that's my specialty too," said Armand, "but I'll hand that duty over to you today. Perhaps best I carve."

Lauzon actually laughed.

The kitchen smelled of tradition and safety and comfort. Of childhood dinners with family around the table. And yet Jean-Guy found that his stomach had soured. Probably because while the scent was of safety, this reeked of danger.

There was nothing normal, nothing comforting, about it.

The long pine table, worn and patinaed by more than a century of gatherings, was ready for them. Cutlery out, linen napkins folded at each place. Glasses waiting for drinks. A cheery arrangement of late fall flowers sat in a vase in the middle of the table.

The stage was set. Armand and Jean-Guy just had to make sure they did not fall off it.

"Smells good, Armand," said Lauzon.

The use of Gamache's first name shocked Jean-Guy. Said so casually, as though the two men were friends, equals, and not enemies. He watched to see how hearing his name come out of the mouth of this vile man had affected the Chief. But he seemed not to notice, or perhaps he hadn't heard.

Armand put on oven mitts covered in hearts and rainbows, a birthday gift from his granddaughters Florence and Zora, and placed the roasting pan on top of the stove.

"Our friend Rocky gave us the secret. She always puts a couple of sprigs of tarragon and half a lemon in the cavity."

"I'll remember that," said the prisoner.

This was, thought Beauvoir, getting weirder and weirder. Clearly he and Armand weren't the only ones putting on an act. Only Chief Inspector Tardiff seemed to be without a script. Or apparent role. She was staring openly. More than a little lost.

"My wife and I used to host colleagues," Lauzon continued, "from both sides of the aisle, for Sunday lunch. It was a good way to establish a rapport and put people at their ease." He paused and held Armand's eyes. "And perhaps even make them say more than they intended, or was wise." The former politician looked down at the handcuffs. "Tough to make gravy like this."

"*Désolé.*" Armand turned to Jean-Guy. "Would you please take the restraints off our guest?"

As Lauzon held his hands out, he dropped his eyes to the angry red scars around Armand's wrists, from the zip ties.

"How often in Parliament I've felt unnecessarily restrained from being able to pass legislation, especially on the environment. But I had no idea what real restraint felt like."

He smiled slightly and rubbed his wrists. Somehow that smile, the action, those words, the surprisingly wistful tone snuck past Armand's defenses and touched him. It was so unexpected, he wondered if the monthslong battle with the swarms of cicadas hadn't drained him. Lowered his defenses.

If so, he'd better rebuild them fast. He could not allow this contemptable man, Black Wolf or not, into his head, and certainly nowhere near his heart. Bad enough he was in his home.

While the roast chicken rested under a tent of foil, Jean-Guy was put to work mashing the potatoes and Evelyn was asked to watch the Brussels sprouts, roasting in the oven amid sliced garlic and Parmesan and small dabs of red currant jelly.

"And maybe stir them a couple of times," Armand suggested.

Raising her brows and picking up a wooden spoon, she bent over and looked through the oven window, her reflection superimposed on the caramelizing Brussels sprouts.

Really? What is happening?

Lauzon was making gravy, using the potato water and pan drippings and flour, while Armand opened a bottle of Pouilly-Fuissé. Once done, he picked up a sharp carving knife and balanced it in his open palm. Then he closed his fingers around the handle.

Only Jean-Guy noticed the momentary white knuckles and thinning lips, and the sound, low and deep in his throat. Almost a snarl.

Armand claimed, believed, that Dom Philippe, the murdered Abbot of Saint-Gilbert-Entre-les-Loups, had been the Grey Wolf. The benign presence. The one you wanted on your side. The one who could defeat the other. But anyone who knew the fable knew that the Grey Wolf was standing in the kitchen, clutching a carving knife. Struggling to feed decency and not rage.

The familiar scents, the comfortable room, the jubilant sunshine streaming in only seemed to heighten the contrast between the physical world and the private thoughts. Between the apparent calm of the guests for Sunday lunch, and the inner turmoil.

"Jericho?" said Clara. "I know it well. I go down at least once a year. It's where Snowflake Bentley lived."

"Oh, of course," said Reine-Marie. She metaphorically slapped her forehead. "That's why it sounded familiar."

"Who the hell was Snowflake Bentley?" demanded Ruth. She was into her second helping of the pasta traybake that Myrna had brought over, with roast tomatoes, the ubiquitous eggplant, and melted cheese.

Clara tore off another hunk of the crispy baguette. "Snowflake Bentley? You don't know him?"

"Would I ask if I did? Okay, never mind. I'm already bored."

"We should go down," said Clara. "I haven't been yet this year, and the museum shuts soon for the winter."

"Ironic, for a place celebrating a man named Snowflake," said Myrna. "But I'm game. When?"

"Why not now?" said Reine-Marie, suddenly curious to go deeper into Jericho. Where that young biologist might have been. Where the line he drew almost certainly passed through. Doing it with friends, visiting a museum, would not arouse suspicion should anyone be watching.

She felt ridiculous even thinking that. As though visiting a museum dedicated to a man named "Snowflake" could be dangerous. Still, Reine-Marie knew there was a difference between what things appeared to be and what they actually were. Best to be careful.

She sent off a quick text to Armand, letting him know; then they headed off.

Despite her predictable protests, Ruth joined them, though she left Rosa at home in case the Customs people decided ducks could fly into the country but not be driven.

They were through the border with Reine-Marie driving when Myrna looked up from her phone. "Seems Jericho excels at odd names. Snowflake isn't the only one. It was founded by a guy named Remember."

"You're kidding." Clara sat forward from the back seat.

"No, look." Myrna passed her phone over.

Sure enough, one of the first European surveyors back in 1773 was named Remember Baker. Clara scanned the rest of the history. There was a guffaw next to her.

"What's so funny?" she asked Ruth, who was leaning on her shoulder and reading the entry.

"Look at that passage. Seems the good folks of Jericho lived in terror of invasion from Canada."

"How times have changed," said Reine-Marie.

"Well, you say that, but…"

"But what?" said Reine-Marie as they turned off the main road and reached the outskirts of the town.

"You haven't seen the posts?" asked Ruth.

Of everyone in Three Pines, Ruth Zardo was the most connected on social media. It was, they figured, one of the reasons her wits were addled.

"Some people on social media are crazy," said Ruth.

"Some people in this car are crazy," murmured Clara, and got no argument.

"Here we are." Reine-Marie turned into the Old Red Mill.

Even Ruth was reduced to silence as the four women, the only people in the museum, moved from photograph to tiny photograph, marveling at the images of snowflakes that Wilson Bentley managed to capture using an old, though state-of-the-art in the 1880s, camera and microscope. At a time when photography was in its infancy, this rugged farmer, with almost no education, had developed a fascination bordering on, and occasionally crossing into, obsession with capturing the image of a single flake.

Eventually, on January 15, 1885, he did it.

Wilson Bentley became the first person in the world to photograph a snowflake. But that wasn't the only surprise. The biggest was yet to come. Bentley discovered that no two were exactly alike.

When he announced his findings in the local paper, he was ignored. Those who did pay attention roundly mocked him. But when he showed them hundreds, then thousands of images of the stunning crystalline shapes, all different, he was finally believed.

Then forgotten.

Like his subjects, Snowflake Bentley melted away, disappearing as though he'd never existed. Until, decades later, his work was rediscovered. And now, more than a century on, four Canadian women stood in his former home, and marveled.

"They're beautiful," whispered Ruth. "I wish Rosa could see them."

"He captured a moment, a split second, before the flake melted," said Myrna. "My God, it's incredible. He essentially froze the snowflakes in time."

"Huh," said Clara. "That's true."

It was a museum dedicated not just to the remarkable man's life's work, but to that moment just before something happened.

They each bought a poster reproducing the flakes. When it was Reine-Marie's turn to pay, she casually asked the cashier if a young man, Québécois, had visited sometime in the summer.

"Kaybek?"

"French."

"Oh." She thought for a moment. "Don't know. Maybe."

As they walked to the car, Myrna used her rolled-up poster to point to a metal sign, dented by buckshot. "Look, Ethan Allen Camp. I wonder if that's where the furniture comes from."

Clara laughed. "Can you imagine sending your kid to furniture camp?"

"Can you imagine being that kid?" asked Myrna. "Maybe they have a showroom. Let's look."

A few minutes later the car stopped in front of a gate with a high fence, and barbed wire, and a sign that shouted, *Restricted. Stay Out.*

"Wow, those Ethan Allen people are a little paranoid," said Clara. "Do you think they're afraid Ikea will come snooping?"

"I think it's Camp Ethan Allen," said Myrna, looking out the car window. "Not Ethan Allen Camp. It's a military base."

"Not just any military base." Reine-Marie had her phone out and was looking it up. "Listen to this: *Camp Ethan Allen provides elite training unlike anywhere else in the nation.*" She lowered the phone. "It's a commando base."

"Jeez," said Clara. "I hope the Swedes know that."

Reine-Marie now pulled up Charles's map and was going between it and the GPS. If continued, his line would go straight through Camp Ethan Allen.

Ruth, who could see what she was doing and was familiar with the original map hanging in the basement of the Three Pines church, brought out her own phone, then said, "Go further."

"Who are you talking to?" said Clara. "We can't go further, there's a gate, and barbed wire."

But Ruth didn't answer. Instead, she held Reine-Marie's eyes in the rearview mirror.

Reine-Marie dropped her gaze back to her phone and widened the GPS map, and continued to draw the imaginary line, the one Charles Langlois might have drawn, might have followed. From Québec, into Vermont, and . . .

"Further," said Ruth.

Reine-Marie followed it down, down, down until it could go no further. Until it hit the Atlantic Ocean. But just before it did, the young biologist's line went straight through the heart of Washington, DC.

Then back up. From DC, to the commando camp, and into Québec.

"*From the Public school to the private hell / of the family masquerade,*" whispered Ruth as she stared at the line. "*Where could a boy on a bicycle go / when the straight road splayed?*"

"Oh, shit," muttered Lacoste.

"What now?" asked Vivienne.

The biologist had left Inspector Lacoste behind. Recoiling from the find, she'd slipped and slid through the muck and slush and made it to the lake, where she'd splashed cold, fresh water on her face and brushed her teeth. Then, after taking a few deep breaths and steeling herself, she'd returned to the kneeling homicide officer and the poor boy in the bag.

"His hands are zip-tied behind his back," said Isabelle.

"Which means?"

There was silence, and a squelching sound that Vivienne tried not to think about. She blocked it out by humming, *Hooray for Captain Spaulding, the African explorer* …

Isabelle, breathing through her mouth, sat up straight and turned to Vivienne. "He's been executed. Single bullet to the back of the head. Then another to be sure."

This was what they'd planned for Gamache.

What those last few moments must have been like … for both of them. The terror …

Armand had survived. This young man had no one to save him.

"This was a mob hit," she said.

"Here? In the middle of nowhere?" The biologist looked around. She'd always thought of organized crime as an urban scourge, when she thought of it at all. Though she now remembered that gruesome scene from *Goodfellas* where De Niro and Pesci dig up the body in the woods.

When she'd agreed to Armand's request to accompany Inspector Lacoste, she thought she'd be testing lakes, not re-creating that scene. And playing the part of Ray Liotta.

Isabelle went through Castonguay's pockets without expecting to find anything. And sure enough, there was nothing. No ID. No phone. No money. Nothing.

She sat back on her heels and looked around.

Why was he here? How would Frederick Castonguay even know about this lake?

Why are you here?

Why are you here?

Why were you killed, here?

Then there was the most important question. Not *Who did this to you?* but—

"Who were you working for?" she asked, looking into that wretched face.

CHAPTER 13

⁓

D elicious," said Marcus Lauzon. "It's been a while."

"No Sunday roast in prison?" asked Evelyn Tardiff.

"*Non,*" he said and smiled, as though her question had been serious. "But I didn't mean that. It's been a while since I was treated like a human being." He carefully folded his linen napkin and placed it beside his clean plate, smoothing it gently. Then he looked at his host. "I know you have an ulterior motive, and I can guess what it is. Still, I'm grateful."

Armand was trying not to leap across the table and strangle the man who'd almost killed his son. A man who was clearly unrepentant. It was a temptation that had been growing since Lauzon had arrived.

He'd wondered if the former Deputy Prime Minister would take this opportunity to apologize, as Jeanne Caron had done.

Part of him hoped he would, and that it would help sever the ties between them. Gamache knew, better than most, that hate bound a person to the one they hated. They were taken prisoner by that loathing, while the one they despised went merrily about their life, often oblivious.

He was tired of being tied to this man. And yet he was so used to it, part of him did not want to be unbound. And a big part of him did not want to be in the position of having to say, I forgive you. And then work toward making that true.

But it seemed, this sunny Sunday afternoon in October, it would not come to that.

Over warm apple crisp, made from fruit picked in the orchard in their back garden, and Coaticook vanilla ice cream, Armand finally asked the question. The one that had hung over them, creating an almost unbearable tension. Though Lauzon seemed the least tense and Chief Inspector Tardiff appeared the most.

"You've claimed all along not to be the one behind the plot to poison Montréal's water, despite all the evidence against you—" Lauzon had opened his mouth, but Gamache shut him down with a look. "If not you, then who?"

"I've waited a long time for you to ask that question."

The Sûreté officers around the table waited for the answer. Had it been a movie, this would be, Jean-Guy knew, the time when a shot would ring out and Lauzon would slump to the table, face down in his apple crisp.

But nothing happened. Though beside him, Jean-Guy noticed Armand's hands slip below the table and grip his knees so tightly they would, Jean-Guy knew, leave a mark.

But Chief Inspector Gamache's face was placid, almost blank.

"I'm tempted to ask you who you think it could be," Lauzon continued, taunting the man across from him. Teasing him. But Gamache would not rise to it.

Though he did stand up. "Coffee?"

Beauvoir lowered his gaze and fought to suppress a grin at the look of surprise, degenerating into annoyance, on Lauzon's face.

He thought he was toying with Gamache. Now the Deputy PM looked puzzled, no longer sure what was happening. And who was playing with whom.

When Lauzon didn't answer, Armand turned to Evelyn. "Café? Or perhaps tea?"

"What the hell is going on, Armand," she snapped. "What're we doing here?"

"Oh, dear lady," said Lauzon, in a purr that made Beauvoir's skin crawl and brought a flush of outrage so forceful into Tardiff's face it looked like she might burst into flames after all. "Surely, as head of Organized Crime for the Sûreté…" He paused and studied the woman sitting beside him. "That is what you are, *non*? Though, as enjoyable as your company is, I'm not sure why you're here. Nevertheless, you must recognize what this is. Don Moretti must've conducted his fair share, though not, perhaps, in as pleasant an atmosphere. I'm sure your informant within his organization has told you about them. You do have someone close to Joseph Moretti?"

Chief Inspector Tardiff was far too disciplined, too practiced at artifice, to show any reaction. Lauzon's gaze lingered on her, his nostrils flaring slightly, as though picking up a scent. He turned to Gamache, who was standing beside the dented and gurgling percolator. Coffee vapor rose from it.

"It's a 'come to Jesus' meeting, isn't it, Armand? You're offering me redemption. A last chance to save my soul, in exchange for the name of the one you've charmingly named the Black Wolf. I suppose you also expect me, as part of my salvation, to apologize for what happened to your son years ago."

"If you're not the one behind the plot, as you claim," Gamache repeated, "then who is?"

Jean-Guy, who had cleared away the dessert plates, could see that while Gamache's voice was steady, his hands were now gripping the edge of the kitchen island.

"If you knew how power works, Chief Inspector," said Lauzon, "you would not need to ask."

"I know how power works, *merci*." There was an abruptness in the tone, a rare fraying, Jean-Guy could hear, of that tight control. "And I know what happens to trumped-up little people who abuse what power they have. How the need for more and more hollows them out, eats away at them. Until they appear human but have lost all humanity."

Beauvoir took a step closer, afraid Armand would lose his grip, in every way. Then Gamache suddenly released the edge of the counter and splayed his hands on top of it.

"There was only one way"—Armand's voice became calm once again, his bearing composed, though there was the slightest tremor in his right hand—"that you ... sir ... were going to get that power, and it was not by being elected."

"That might be true, my friend. I'm not especially liked. I know that. And your description of power is apt. *Between the idea / And the reality / Between the motion / And the act / Falls the Shadow.* Or maybe, in your parlance, falls the Black Wolf. Unfortunately for you, it's not me. You are, Armand, the boy who cried wolf."

Lauzon was smiling. Quietly mocking Armand with a quote from T. S. Eliot's "The Hollow Men." Content to hold the floor, his belly full of roast chicken and gravy, of fine white wine and confidence. Of sweet apples and rich ice cream.

And Beauvoir suddenly saw this for what it was.

It had seemed foolish, bordering on insane, to bring this man into this place. Where Armand and his loved ones lived. Surrounded by their private effects.

But now Jean-Guy noticed that the most personal photos had been put away. Even Reine-Marie and Armand's favorite books had been switched out for some predictable classics. The music in the background was soft jazz, the modern equivalent of Muzak, which Armand and Reine-Marie never played.

There were children's toys, but they were not ones Jean-Guy, or his children, or Daniel's daughters had ever touched.

This was a shell around a hollow world, a life in appearance only. They were in the space between idea and reality. Even Armand's old cardigan and worn slippers were part of the act. Jean-Guy had never seen them before. They were a costume.

Then there was Armand's slightly perplexed look, trying to keep up with the conversation, though Jean-Guy, who knew him well, could tell the Chief could hear, if not perfectly, then far better than he made out.

Knowing that, and that all this was staged, choreographed, made Jean-Guy almost giddy with relief.

And Marcus Lauzon was falling for it. Under the impression he was deep into Armand Gamache's home, his real life. Deep into his broken mind. And so, free to mind-fuck a once formidable foe.

The only thing that worried Jean-Guy, as he followed Armand back to the table carrying the coffee mugs and milk jug and sugar, was the very slight tremble in that right hand. A tell. A sign of fatigue, of stress. Of barely contained rage. A warning that Armand was dangerously close to the edge of the stage.

As he once again took his seat beside the Chief, Beauvoir looked across the table at their other guest. Was the head of the Sûreté's Organized Crime division in on the ruse, or another target?

When Armand had given that out-of-character speech about "trumped-up little people," was Jean-Guy mistaken, or had Armand glanced at Chief Inspector Tardiff? Was that message about power, and the abuse of it, also meant for her?

"You've missed one important thing," said Marcus Lauzon.

"I don't think so." Armand looked at the table. "We have milk and sugar." He turned to Jean-Guy. "Have I forgotten something? Biscuits maybe?"

It was on the verge of, but not quite spilling over into, pathetic. Armand would have to be careful not to overdo it.

"I don't mean the lunch," snapped Lauzon. "We were talking about power. In accusing me of being monomaniacal in my climb to the top, I think you haven't taken into account one important thing. What happens at a banquet of the power-hungry?"

"I think you mean 'power-mad,'" said Beauvoir.

"I say what I mean." Lauzon lashed out, then turned back to Gamache, who was staring across the table into that smug face. But said nothing.

"No one reaches deputy without wanting to be the actual thing," Lauzon admitted, when faced with that silence. "To grab it all for themselves. To climb that last rung. Including me. Including you, Armand. No use denying it. You know how power works because you yourself had so much. At least for a while. But you discovered ultimate leadership isn't for everyone. I seem to remember you're afraid of heights."

"That's true," said Gamache. "It terrifies me."

Lauzon seemed surprised by this admission and briefly thrown off balance.

"You were Chief Superintendent of the Sûreté for a while. You were even offered the top job at the RCMP but turned it down. I long wondered why, but now I think I have the answer. Power is for the brave. Those who not only want to lead but are not afraid to lead. Who are not afraid of heights."

Lauzon watched to see how much damage that just did.

Tardiff was trying not to look at Gamache but finally gave in. It was like approaching a car wreck and looking inside. How bad would it be?

There weren't many things worse than being called a coward. And for a cop, a senior cop? Even if not true, an accusation like that would still sting.

Yes, Armand had led the Sûreté during an especially tumultuous time and been fired. But not for cowardice or incompetence. It was for illegally chasing a drug lord into the United States.

The Chief Inspector Gamache she saw now was not the same man who'd literally dragged the head of the cartel back across the border, to face trial in Québec.

Armand was gazing at Lauzon, perplexed. And what happened next was worse.

"*Désolé*," he said. "But could you repeat that? You were talking too fast."

It was Jean-Guy Beauvoir's turn to grip his knees. He could almost feel the blood vessels bursting under his fingers. Would Lauzon see through the ruse? And was it part of the act, or was Armand serious?

Marcus Lauzon opened his mouth, then shut it again in frustration.

"You were talking about power, I believe," said Gamache. "And heights. Then something about leadership. I caught that much. You would've given a lot, I think, to be Prime Minister. But you knew you could never be elected, so your only route to the top was in a coup. Though it couldn't be seen to be that."

"Yes, I heard that said at my trial." Lauzon was still smarting from having his *coup de grâce*, his thrust into Gamache's heart, miss. Worse, ignored. "Your own testimony, in fact, Armand. That I plotted to poison the drinking water, creating a national catastrophe that would be blamed on the incompetence of the current Prime Minister. He'd be ousted, and I would rise, heroically, selflessly even, taking charge in the face of great personal danger. I'd bring in the Emergencies Act, to head off future attacks, thereby giving myself unlimited power. All approved and even applauded by a terrified and cowed citizenry."

Gamache lifted his hands in an eloquent *That's it.*

"You despise me"—Lauzon leaned forward slightly—"and yet you have doubts."

"If not you," Gamache repeated for the third time, "then who?"

Lauzon leaned back again and studied the large, contained man before him. A man he'd rarely met in person—both had avoided it—but whom he'd hated from a distance. For decades. Far from diminishing the hate, time had only deepened that loathing.

It was all he could do now not to leap across the table and strangle the man who'd arrested his daughter for manslaughter. Who'd tried to ruin her young life.

That hit-and-run years ago had been an accident. Nothing more. She was his only child. Young and foolish, certainly, but she did not deserve to pay for one mistake for the rest of her life. The fact she'd left that grocery clerk to die alone in a ditch was a shame, but the boy probably would have died anyway.

Getting his daughter off had cost the newly elected MP decades of IOUs.

When the charges had been dropped, Gamache had lodged a complaint and requested an investigation. Nothing came of it except a mutual vendetta.

In return for Gamache's actions against Manon, Lauzon had gone after Daniel Gamache. An eye for an eye. A child for a child.

The Chief Inspector had brought it on himself. Was solely responsible, including for his son's suicide attempt. Lauzon did not feel the least bit guilty, was not the least bit sorry. Not then. Not now.

Over the years, over the distance from Ottawa to Québec City, he'd studied Gamache, watching his career and influence grow. Every time he appeared on television, in interviews and news conferences, Lauzon had watched. Smiling with satisfaction when that young journalist had appeared on the scene and begun harassing Gamache, hurling insulting accusations at him in the form of questions.

It would have been more satisfying had she managed to land a few blows. If Gamache had lost his temper and shown his true self. A large, powerful, older white cop lashing out at a young woman of color. How perfect that would have been. But instead, he'd answered each insult with a calm and reasoned explanation. Meeting rudeness with the same courtesy he showed all the journalists.

But while others might've been fooled, the former Deputy Prime Minister was not.

Lauzon had even recorded some of Gamache's appearances, sitting in his study at night after dinner, hearing his wife and daughter and grandchildren talking and laughing in the next room. He drank cognac and played and replayed the recordings. Over the years he'd watched the man age. Seen his hair turn grey. Seen that deep scar appear at his temple. Seen that familiar face become heavier, weatherworn. Careworn. Seen the lines appear. Surely more than a man his age should have.

But what struck Lauzon now, and what he'd missed from the television and the courtroom, was the look in Chief Inspector Gamache's eyes. Intelligence, yes. You'd expect that. Even now, through the slightly perplexed look, they were thoughtful. Determined even.

Despite the fact Gamache was clearly diminished, it was best, Lauzon warned himself, not to underestimate this man. There was still, in those eyes, a cunning. And yet. And yet. He narrowed his own eyes, and as he did, he saw what Gamache was clearly trying to keep secret.

Most people, Lauzon knew, hid their cruel thoughts below the surface. But if you had the wherewithal to look, and he did, then deep down, you could see. There lived, there lurked, the worst of them. Lauzon had used what he saw against friends, colleagues, competitors. It was how he got ahead, by not being afraid to step in the piles of *merde* other people made and tried to hide. By understanding their true nature.

But today, on this sunny autumn afternoon, in this cheerful home, what Lauzon saw deep in Armand Gamache's eyes wasn't shit. It was worse than that.

It was decency.

Even, God help Gamache, kindness.

In a word, weakness. And perhaps a slight gullibility, a desire to believe the best.

Lauzon saw within that deep brown stare an Achilles' heel in the form of a desire to believe that people really could be saved, salvaged from the wreckage of their lives.

Perhaps even a belief that Lauzon himself could be saved. That this come-to-Jesus meeting over roast chicken would work.

Had that belief always been there, or had it appeared to the head of homicide as he'd knelt on that cold concrete floor, the gun to the back of his skull? As he'd prayed. For what? Salvation.

And it had come. He'd been saved. And now did he feel his contract with God was to try to save others? It wasn't just an Achilles' heel. This was a superhighway of folly that led in only one direction.

"What could be worse, Armand, than a person not getting what they most want?"

The float plane had landed, and the forensics team had paddled ashore lugging their equipment, including a body bag.

While they got to work on the corpse and surrounding area, Isabelle and Vivienne packed up their campsite, remembering at the last minute to take the food and garbage out of the tree where it had been hung the night before.

"Do we still need to explore the rest of this lake?" asked Vivienne, telegraphing what she hoped and prayed would be the answer. She was wet and cold and would sell her firstborn for a coffee.

"*Non.* We'll fly back to Montréal with the body."

The first thing Isabelle needed to do was tell Frederick Castonguay's family. She knew from their initial research into the young man that while he'd worked in Ottawa as assistant to Jeanne Caron, he was originally from Montréal.

The plane took off and circled the site where the team was searching the undergrowth for evidence. Perhaps the gun, though they all knew it would be at the bottom of the lake. Still, they needed to look.

The plane rose higher, and the three of them, and Frederick Castonguay, headed for home.

Marcus Lauzon had asked to use the washroom, and while Jean-Guy accompanied him, Evelyn Tardiff saw her chance for a quiet word.

But Gamache got there first.

Taking her quickly aside, he said, "We've found the body of Frederick Castonguay."

He was looking at her with an intensity she found disconcerting. If she didn't know it was because he needed to read her lips, she'd have thought there was another reason for that scrutiny.

"Jeanne Caron's assistant? You're kidding. What's he doing dead?"

It was such a strange way of putting it that Armand almost smiled, though the situation was far from humorous.

"I take it it was not an accident," she continued.

117

"*Non.* Bullet to the back of the head. Hands tied."

"Moretti." She looked puzzled. "Now why would the mafia want Caron's assistant dead? Where was he found?"

"That's also strange." Gamache glanced at the kitchen door to make sure Lauzon wasn't returning. "Castonguay's body was found at the last lake that Charles Langlois investigated before his own murder. Up north."

"What was he doing there?" When Gamache gave her a look, she shook her head. "Sorry. I know you don't yet know. So, Jeanne Caron's assistant is dead. I've told you all along, Armand, that the Caron woman can't be trusted. Yes, she saved your life, but probably because she knew the plot had failed and they'd been exposed. She needed to do something dramatic to make herself look heroic. To place herself on the right side of the law. Saving you was that grand gesture."

That had also occurred to him. But unlike everyone else involved, Jeanne Caron hadn't tried to hide her complicity, at least in some of Marcus Lauzon's illegal activities. But there was no evidence that she was involved in the poisoning plot. Just the opposite. It all pointed to her working with her uncle the Abbot to stop it. Even approaching Gamache himself for help.

"Why didn't you know about this, Evelyn?"

"What? That Moretti put out a hit on that kid? How'm I supposed to know?"

"Your informant?"

"You think Moretti tells my informant everything?"

"I think Moretti tells you everything."

That sucked the air out of the room.

"What do you mean?" she finally managed to say.

He dropped his voice. "I know you're the informant. You infiltrated Moretti's organization during that arson investigation."

She glared at him, suddenly afraid. She'd spent years hiding, and now she stood in this country kitchen, exposed.

"As Lauzon just reminded us, I was, briefly, the head of the Sûreté," he explained. "I'd already guessed that you must have placed someone in the Moretti organization, but I wanted it confirmed. Being the Superintendent gave me access to certain files. I found the evidence."

"There's evidence?" she asked, forgetting to dodge the question.

"I destroyed it."

Now she heaved a deep sigh. "Is that why I'm here?"

"I need to know what you know about what's happening next. Moretti's involved. You met him yesterday morning at the Jean-Talon market. What did he tell you?"

"Nothing. I haven't heard anything. And why in the world would you think anything else is happening? It's been wrapped up. Lauzon's in prison." She looked toward the doorway. "Or should be."

"Why would they murder Frederick Castonguay unless it was to shut him up?" asked Gamache, choosing not to directly answer her question.

"They're just cleaning up. Moretti's a tidy man, hates loose ends. You do too, obviously. Castonguay must've been a loose end."

"Exactly. But what did he know?"

"It can't matter now. It's over, Armand." She looked at him more closely. "How did you know about my visit to the market?" When he didn't answer, her eyes opened wide. "My own assistant? Nichol? She's spying on me? For you?"

"I assigned her there, yes."

"You say that like it's reasonable to spy on a colleague, a friend." She was staring at him in disbelief.

"If the murder of thousands of citizens was a prelude, what the hell's next? I'll do whatever's necessary, including placing my own people in your department, to find out."

"Fuck you, Armand. How dare you lecture me about duty. I've risked my life every day for decades to get close to that psychopath Moretti, and you're on the verge of blowing it and getting me killed. Over some self-aggrandizing fantasy."

Gamache glanced again at the door. They didn't have much more time.

"Look, I'll protect you any way I can—"

"I don't need you to protect me, Armand. Just back off."

"—and for what it's worth, Nichol seems devoted to you. I think she instinctively trusts you."

"You say she's your agent?"

"Yes."

"That didn't stop her from saying you should've been killed in the treatment plant." It was vindictive of her to tell him that. But she was angry and frightened and needed to spread the pain.

To her surprise he gave a gruff laugh. She wondered if he'd heard her right.

"Well, she's not wrong. I think there've been times she would've happily pulled the trigger. But I suspect she said it to gauge your reaction. And that was . . . ?"

"I agreed with her, of course. If anyone is playing by a rule book, they'll be dead and buried with it."

There was a pause as both took deep breaths, literally and figuratively.

"Okay, Armand. I'll look into Moretti's connection to Castonguay and see what I can find out."

"Find out what?"

Lauzon was at the kitchen door, watching them. Beauvoir, standing behind him, had tried to make enough noise to warn Gamache and Tardiff, but they were too deep in conversation.

"The recipe for the apple crisp," said Evelyn, without missing a beat. "Armand won't tell me."

"It's an old family secret," said Armand, making for the door. "Reine-Marie would kill me if I told you."

"She'd have to take a number," said Evelyn.

"Are we leaving?" asked Lauzon, stepping aside to let Gamache pass.

Gamache could hear the fear in his voice. For all his haughtiness, Lauzon was afraid to go back to prison. And once again, against his will, Gamache found he sympathized.

"Not quite yet. I suggest we get some fresh air. Walk off some of our lunch. Perhaps through the woods."

"Where no one can see us, Armand?"

"Do you want the world to know you're out of prison and here?" Beauvoir asked.

"It would be more damaging to you than me. Imagine what the papers would say. What that young journalist whose purpose in life seems to be harassing you would say?"

Armand immediately felt alarms go off. What did this man know about Shona Dorion? Did he know that they'd met? That Shona was gathering information for him?

Having had Marcus Lauzon closer than ever before, having had a chance to study him, Armand Gamache found he was beginning to lean toward believing that Evelyn Tardiff was right. Beauvoir was right. Everyone he knew was right. Marcus Lauzon really was the Black Wolf.

Of course that would be good news. It would mean that maybe nothing else was planned. That he could go back to picking apples with Reine-Marie. To watching her tilt her head back and stretch her hand out and go up on tippy-toes for that perfect rosy apple, always just out of reach.

They could stroll around the village green, or go into Montréal and have dinner with the LaPierres. Or a quiet meal just the two of them. Talking about... nothing, as they walked back to their small apartment in the Outremont *quartier*.

He could feel her hand in his, even now. But then he always did.

If it was all over, he could exhale. For an instant he let himself believe it. And yet, and yet...

As he hung up his father's old cardigan and took off his godfather Stephen's ratty old slippers, he glanced at Evelyn Tardiff.

Her insistence that nothing else was happening, even in the face of the murder of Frederick Castonguay, was worrisome. She did not seem willing to even entertain the other possibility.

He'd placed Agent Yvette Nichol in Chief Inspector Tardiff's department to watch and report. To effectively spy on a fellow senior officer. And he'd just told Tardiff why Nichol was there.

How big a mistake that was, he wasn't sure, but suspected he'd soon find out.

He scanned his messages, then put on his field coat, called the dogs and Gracie to his side, and headed out with the others into the autumn day.

CHAPTER 14

⌒

Reine-Marie dropped Myrna and Clara off, then parked in front of Ruth's home.

"Have you seen the map?" she asked.

"The one in the basement?" Ruth nodded toward St. Thomas's Church. "Yes. I was there when Armand put it up. He's obviously shown you too. I didn't think he was that bright."

Reine-Marie smiled. An insult from Ruth was the equivalent of an embrace. A declaration of profound friendship and, perhaps more important for the wizened old poet, trust.

"Well, he bumbles along," she said, and saw Ruth smile. "I think we should talk."

"Your place or mine?"

"The church."

They picked up Rosa, then walked up the hill. For the first time since moving to Three Pines, Reine-Marie did not want to go home. Clearly their "guests" were still there. The last thing she wanted to do was run into "that man." She'd called him that for years, not wanting to humanize him by saying his name. A name his parents had given him. A name repeated by godparents and the priest at his christening.

Was holy water sprinkled on that head? Did it scald?

It was strange to think of that man having parents. A wife. A daughter. A personal life.

She knew that in refusing to name him, she was giving him more power than he deserved. More power over her. He'd become, inadvertently, not less than human but, in his anonymity, superhuman.

But her heart overruled her head, and she still did not name the man who'd almost killed their son. And who'd almost certainly ordered her husband murdered.

As she walked up the hill toward the church, Reine-Marie wondered how Armand was getting on. Would she return to find fresh-turned soil in their back garden?

If so, she would plant digitalis over it, a perennial that could kill but also heal, and get on with life.

The body of Frederick Castonguay was delivered to the forensic pathologist in Montréal.

"Would you like to stay?" she asked Isabelle.

"*Non.* I need to speak to his family. Can you let me know as soon as possible how long ago you think he was killed?

Dr. Harris looked down at the body on the table. "It won't be easy, but I'll give you my best guess. Won't be for a while though." Now she studied Isabelle. They'd worked together for years, often in the worst of conditions. Rarely had she seen the senior homicide officer so stressed. "Everything all right? I've been following the fallout from the poisoning plot. Horrific. Can you imagine—?"

She stopped. Of course Inspector Lacoste could imagine what would have happened if . . .

"But at least it's over now."

"*Oui.*"

"What?"

"Nothing. Just please let me know what you find, as soon as possible."

"Should I copy Chief Inspector Gamache and Beauvoir?"

Lacoste nodded, distracted by her next task.

The team at Sûreté HQ had reported that Frederick Castonguay's family lived on rue de Bullion, just off boulevard Saint-Laurent, the long artery that bisected Montréal. Not geographically but culturally. For decades the Anglos lived to the west of what was called "the Main," and the Francophones lived to the *est.* And never the twain, on the Main, shall meet.

That was no longer the case, and yet the sensibility was still there, of the Two Solitudes.

Isabelle stood outside the Castonguay home and tilted her head back.

It was an old town house, restored. The door, painted a glossy and cheery cherry red, opened right onto the sidewalk. It was attached to other houses on both sides, the homes marching up and down the block, undivided, as though locking arms for support. For company. For security.

Once a neighborhood of immigrants, the homes were now bought up by creatives and academics. Though here and there were still the old working-class families. Homes kept in the same family for generations. You could tell them by their slightly weary but dignified exteriors, and the lace curtains.

The Castonguays' was not one of those. Their place was immaculately restored and renovated. The stone re-pointed, the windows new, and not a hint of lace at any of them.

Her team had informed her that Frederick was one of four children. Two boys, two girls. He was the second oldest.

His father taught at the Université de Montréal in the economics department. His mother was a senior organizer for the Parti québécois, the separatist political party in Québec, and had a PhD in sociology. Frederick himself was a poli-sci grad from Laval in Québec City.

Isabelle wondered how his *souverainistes* parents felt about their son working for a federal and federalist party. Though as a civil servant it was possible to harbor different political views from your bosses. Politicians came and went. The civil service was the constant, providing memory and stability.

Unless you worked for Marcus Lauzon.

Frederick came from an intellectual, well-connected, almost certainly comfortable family. Who were about to be exploded.

Isabelle had walked around the block a couple of times, stopping to look in the windows of a few Portuguese bakeries and small restaurants specializing in roast chicken.

She never got used to the task ahead. If she ever did, that would be the day to quit. The Chief mostly took it upon himself to tell families their loved one was not just dead but murdered. But today it fell to her.

It was getting late in the day. A Sunday. She hoped they were home. She hoped they were not.

She rang the bell and heard a buzzing. A cheerful voice sang out, "I'll get it."

The door opened, and a girl no more than twelve stood there, her face friendly and curious. "*Oui?*"

All four strolled, two by two, in silence for some minutes along the path through the leaf-strewn forest, instinctively kicking the musky leaves ahead of them.

Armand held his hands loosely behind his back. His head was bowed in thought, lifting now and then to gaze at the familiar surroundings. Beside him, Evelyn Tardiff was in his peripheral vision. Where he'd had her for a number of years.

They'd left the sunshine of the village and entered twilight in the forest. It was peaceful. Calm. Not day, not yet night.

Beside Beauvoir, Marcus Lauzon was taking everything in. He stopped once to pick up a particularly perfect red maple leaf, placing it in his pocket.

They finally emerged onto the dirt road that led down into Three Pines.

"*S'il vous plaît.*" Armand indicated the bench on the hill overlooking the village.

Lauzon sat on the warm wooden slats and closed his eyes, instinctively turning his face toward the sun, now just touching the horizon.

"Do you not think it's too obvious?" asked Armand, taking a seat and staring out across the valley, to the Green Mountains of Vermont.

"What do you mean?"

"That Prime Minister Woodford is the Black Wolf."

"I never said that."

"True, but you've been hinting at it all afternoon. If not you, then who? There's only one answer to that."

"Isn't the obvious often the answer?"

"You were, and still are, the most obvious answer, Monsieur Lauzon," said Gamache, turning to look at him. "All evidence points to you. It's a firehose of damnation."

Lauzon laughed at that last word. "Are you still offering me salvation?"

"*Non.* I'm not the one who damned you. I'm not the one who can save you. But I am the one offering you a path forward. You've been convicted of leading a terrorist plot to murder tens of thousands. You've been convicted of ordering the killing of Charles Langlois." Armand faced the only person in the world he actually, actively hated. "If you really aren't guilty of all those things, why won't you save yourself? All you have to do is tell me who is really behind all this. You know."

Even at his trial, while protesting his innocence but putting up a feeble defense, Lauzon had refused to say who, if not him, was behind the terrorist plot.

Lauzon's eyes were still closed, his face turned away from Gamache. "But I've told you."

Gamache shook his head in frustration. There was only one answer to Lauzon's question. What was worse than not getting what you most want?

Losing what you had.

In this case, tasting power, holding it. Finally possessing it. Wielding it.

Then having it taken away. Or facing that possibility.

Who held the most power in the nation? And therefore had the most to lose?

The Prime Minister of Canada.

Marcus Lauzon had all but named James Woodford as the Black Wolf.

Raised in poverty, working menial jobs to support a mentally unstable single mother and two siblings, Woodford had left school early and grown into an angry, disenfranchised young man. To escape the grinding poverty, he'd enlisted, rising through the ranks, getting an education, becoming an officer. Leading troops in conflict and peacekeeping, which had proved much more difficult than war.

Once a civilian again, he'd found an outlet for his skills in community organizing, which led, naturally, to politics. All this was widely known.

Smart, inspirational, charismatic. A natural leader. Woodford spoke perfect French and English and was, by his own admission, left of center in a party that itself leaned left.

Elected on a platform of social justice, of human rights and reform, promising to increase environmental protection and refugee targets, to bring big industry to heel, he'd shot up the ladder, quickly surpassing more seasoned colleagues.

Including Marcus Lauzon.

When they stood side by side, Lauzon looked sallow, shifty, old. The poster boy for a decaying establishment.

Woodford had won the party leadership in a landslide that had effectively, and permanently, buried Lauzon's chances of getting the top job. Though not, it seemed, his ambitions.

There was one other thing Prime Minister Woodford was. An accomplished strategist. Something he learned on the backstreets of Montréal and honed as a peacekeeper. He was certainly canny enough to give his scheming Deputy PM the job hitting those net-zero environmental targets, while also making him head of the committee assigned to oversee international investments.

Prime Minister Woodford had, in effect, placed Marcus Lauzon not just on a hot seat, but on a political electric chair.

"Woodford isn't behind the plots," said Gamache.

"How do you know?" Lauzon's eyes were closed, his face turned toward the setting sun.

"Because he has all the power he needs. Not just the support of his party, but the overwhelming support of the electorate. His approval numbers remain the highest of any Prime Minister in a generation. Of all the politicians in Canada, he's the least likely to enter into a devil's bargain. His power is not threatened, and there's no more to be had."

"Are you so sure?" Lauzon opened his eyes and locked onto Armand's. The village below was bathed in golden light, precious for being the last of the day. In this light, the former Deputy PM's face looked almost angelic.

It was fleeting.

After a long moment, as the shadows reached toward them, Gamache asked, "What do you know?"

"I know what you've missed. I know that there're no boundaries when it comes to greed. To those addicted to power, there are no borders. There's always more to grab. There are new territories, new worlds, to conquer. Look at the Caesars. Alexander. Look at Genghis Khan. Napoleon. Look at Hitler and Putin. Wolves know no boundaries, respect no borders."

Lauzon's stare was so intense, Armand could feel cold creeping over him, and though he knew it was almost certainly the approaching night, he sensed it was far more than that.

Between the motion / And the act / Falls the Shadow.

"What are you saying?"

"You know what I'm saying, you're just refusing to hear it."

Behind them Beauvoir and Tardiff exchanged glances. They too had heard the accusation against Prime Minister Woodford. Jean-Guy did not believe it. He knew this was more misdirection by a man desperate to throw blame elsewhere. And crafty enough to make them beg for the lie.

It was, at least, a relief to see that Gamache clearly did not believe Lauzon either. And he was, with luck, beginning to see what was all too obvious. That the man greedily grabbing the last of the light was the Black Wolf.

"You're saying that Prime Minister Woodford is planning to, what? Make himself into a dictator? Rule Canada as a despot?"

"Isn't that what I've been accused of wanting to do? Why me and not him?"

"Because he's a decent man?" said Gamache.

Behind them there was a small snort of amusement. Lauzon turned and glared, unsure if it was Beauvoir or Tardiff. Then turned back to Gamache.

"You're thinking too small, Armand. Far too parochially." He moved his hands to indicate more. More.

"This's ridiculous." Gamache stood up. "There's no way Woodford, or any Prime Minister, could make a power grab. Even if his party would stand for it, the premiers would never allow it. Neither would the electorate. You don't give the people enough credit."

"You don't give fear enough credit."

"You're desperate. Making up conspiracies, throwing a good man—"

"To the wolves?" said Lauzon with a smile.

"You're wasting our time. When I invited you down here, I actually thought you might've been telling the truth. That you were set up. That the person behind the plots is still out there and active. But now I see I was wrong. Get up. You're going back. And this time not into solitary."

They all knew what that meant. Gamache might as well have pulled out a gun and shot Lauzon between those steady eyes.

The former politician paled, though it might've just been the dying of the light. Getting to his feet, Lauzon stepped toward Gamache but stumbled over a rock. Instinctively Gamache reached out and grabbed him to keep him from falling. As he did, Lauzon whispered directly into his ear, "FEDS."

Armand righted the man, but before he let him go, he said, quietly, "What does that mean?"

But instead of answering, Lauzon simply straightened his clothing and said, audibly, "*Merci*, Armand. I think you know the truth when you hear it."

He gave Gamache a warning look.

"If it's the truth, and you've apparently known it all along," said Gamache, taking that warning onboard, "why not say something before now? Why suddenly tell us that Prime Minister Woodford is the Black Wolf?"

"Did I say that?"

Gamache turned and began walking away.

"I was waiting for you to ask, Armand," Lauzon called after him, a very slight whiff of desperation in his voice.

It was such an extraordinary thing to say, such an unlikely thing to say, that it arrested Armand. He turned and for a moment the two men, the two combatants, stared at each other.

"Why me?"

"Because you hate me, and with reason. Just as I hate you, with reason. Still, in the face of all my attacks, you wouldn't yield. You held your ground. You're the only one I can trust with the information. To do what's necessary. To not yield."

It was, Armand and Jean-Guy both knew, exactly the same reasoning Jeanne Caron had given for approaching Gamache about the poisoning plot.

It proved true then. Could this also be true? Could this rancid man be telling the truth about the Prime Minister?

"Why the code 'Black Wolf'?" asked Lauzon. "What's it supposed to mean?"

Gamache considered not telling him, but thought it would be interesting to see Lauzon's reaction to the story.

"It's an old Cree legend about a chief who had two wolves fighting inside him, tearing him apart. The grey wolf wanted the chief to be compassionate, to lead with fairness and be forgiving of his enemies. To strive for peace. For reconciliation. The other, the black wolf, warned him that he'd lose everything, would be slaughtered, if he did that. It would be weakness. He needed to make examples of his enemies, to exact revenge. To make examples of anyone who crossed, who even questioned him. To forgive nothing. To be brutal and rule with terror."

Armand stared at Lauzon, who seemed to have lost interest. It was Evelyn Tardiff who spoke, quietly asking Beauvoir, "Which one won?"

When he was silent, she answered it herself. "The black wolf."

"Not necessarily." Lauzon was listening after all. "It's not over yet, is it. No one has won. Yet."

At the car, the cuffs were put back on Lauzon, and Armand held the back door open.

"*Merci.*" He held Armand's eyes, and in them he still saw kindness. And knew who he was actually seeing. "Maybe this meeting did serve its purpose. I wonder if salvation is possible."

"That wasn't the purpose of the meeting."

"Are you so sure? What other purpose could there possibly be? If not for me, then maybe for you."

Before getting into the vehicle that would return him to prison, Marcus Lauzon had stopped to look around, buying precious moments of freedom. Though he knew, as did Armand, that no one was completely free. There were always limits.

The former Deputy Prime Minister, the second most powerful man in the nation, stared at the modest homes and shops of Three Pines; then his gaze went further.

"We're very close to the United States here, aren't we? We could probably walk right across. And vice versa."

Just as the door was swinging shut, he said, "The one that's fed. That's the wolf that wins, isn't it."

And then the door closed, and automatically locked. He was on his way back to prison, and Armand was on his way back home.

"You mentioned social media."

"Did I?"

"You know you did, Ruth," said Reine-Marie. The three of them, including Rosa, were in the church basement. "You said we obviously hadn't seen the posts. What posts?"

"About Canada invading the States."

"Yes, you said the people of Jericho were afraid that would happen. Back in 1812, I'm assuming. You read that on some site on American-Canadian history?"

Reine-Marie, as a librarian but especially from her work in the Archives nationales du Québec, was very aware of that history. The two nations had not always been close allies. That was fairly recent. Most of the relationship in the early years had been acrimonious at best, often combative. And much of the fighting had been along the Québec-Vermont border.

In fact, Three Pines was created as a place of refuge for those Americans fleeing the fighting.

That was a long time ago.

"No," said Ruth. "These people who are posting have no idea of the history, and probably don't care about the past any more than they care about facts."

"What do they care about?"

"Hard to tell. Most are shit disturbers."

"Your people," said Reine-Marie and expected to hear the elderly poet cackle. But there was silence.

"No. There's crazy and then there's crazy. These people are crazy."

"Then why are you reading it?"

"Because if you pile up enough shit and leave it long enough, it has a way of combusting. And then you're in trouble."

Reine-Marie wanted to get away from that analogy. "What're they saying?"

"Among other things, that during the pandemic Canada sent infected vaccines to the US that, when triggered, will turn the person into a zombie—"

"Oh, come on." Reine-Marie laughed. "No one would believe that."

"There are millions who believe the vaccines contained tracking devices."

"Still, that's pretty marginal stuff. And to what end? Why would we want zombies on our doorstep?"

"To finish what was started."

"And that is?" Even as she asked it, she regretted the question. The answer would be crazy, and they had more important things to talk about.

The overhead florescent lights not only illuminated the map on the wall, they made both women look sallow.

"Canada's plan to attack the US."

"Of course. Our long-range plan, begun on July 5, 1776." Reine-Marie actually snorted with laughter. "Even you can't believe that."

"I didn't say I believe it. Of course I don't. But many do. You should look at the site. And there are more like it appearing every day, the shit is spreading, not helped by AI and fabricated 'evidence.'"

They were back there. In the *merde*.

"I have better things to do than listen to this nonsense, and honestly, Ruth, I'd have thought you'd have better things to do than read it."

She stepped closer to the map Charles Langlois had marked up and hidden and that was now tacked to the wall of the church basement. A pretty good hiding place too since few entered the church and fewer still went into the basement. Those who did would not look twice at a tattered map of the province.

Churches and maps had one thing in common. Both were becoming obsolete.

After a moment, Reine-Marie turned back to Ruth, bothered, despite herself, by what she'd heard. Mostly bothered that Ruth felt it was important enough to mention.

"Who's going to believe that nonsense? Just a few marginal people. Why are you talking about it?"

"And why are you so upset?" Ruth glared at her. "I know why. It's because you're an archivist, which makes you an historian. Which means you are very aware of what's happened in the past. The power of words. All wars start with words. All conflicts start with early warnings that are ignored." She glared at Reine-Marie before continuing. "What happened on Kristallnacht to the Jews? What happened on St. Bartholomew's Day in Paris to the Protestants? What happened to the Tutsis in Rwanda? What happened to wisewomen, healers, in the witch hunts? Ask yourself, how did that happen? How did perfectly peaceful people come in for slaughter? How did perfectly reasonable people a short time earlier take part in those atrocities?"

"Wait a minute. You've just gone from a marginal internet site to war and slaughter? Come on."

"What was in your canvas shopping bag two days ago at the market?"

"What do you mean?"

"How do you choose what to buy? Past experience, yes, but originally? It's advertising, and what's that? Propaganda, often spread through word of mouth. Someone you know tells you it's good. This's no different. How did hundreds of millions of people believe Iraq was behind the 9/11 attacks when it patently was not? How did millions believe a perfectly legitimate election was stolen and almost cause a coup? The power of persuasion. And few places are more persuasive, more influential, than the internet. Social media. Eventually a critical mass is hit. A tipping point. Shit catches fire."

Reine-Marie held up her hand. "Enough. You're not saying that people actually believe Canada is on the verge of invading the US. And has a chance of winning? It's ludicrous."

"The ludicrous happens every day. The unthinkable is made real not through rational thought, but feelings. We'll follow a charismatic leader if they tell us that we have a legitimate grievance. That they'll give us back our dignity. Our threatened way of life. If we follow them, our enemies will be vanquished and we will be heroes. Who doesn't want to be part of something bigger than ourselves? Who doesn't want to be a hero? Even if it's all fabricated. When was the last time you read *Animal Farm*?"

"Never."

"What? Not even at school?" Reine-Marie could see she'd slipped a rung, or ten, in the elderly poet's estimation.

"Right, and did you read *La Peau de chagrin*, by Balzac, or *L'Étranger*, by Camus, in school?"

"No, but I did later." Ruth closed her eyes and quoted, "*I often thought that if I had had to live in the trunk of a dead tree, little by little I would have gotten used to it.*" Then she looked straight at Reine-Marie. "We can normalize anything. Surely that much is obvious."

Then, in an instant, Ruth's face broke into a smile. "*Désolée.* I didn't mean to upset you. You're probably right. We have more important things to do." She pointed to the wall, and with that a delicate peace was restored.

Both turned to study the map. Still, it worried Reine-Marie that Ruth had given up so easily.

"We don't know that the line Charles drew was straight," said Ruth. "It could go anywhere from here. Down into Vermont, yes, but from there? It could veer into Connecticut. Or head over here, into Upstate New York."

She pointed to the perforated line Charles Langlois had drawn across the Québec-Vermont border. "It could also be completely meaningless."

"You don't believe that," said Reine-Marie. "Nothing on this map is meaningless. And we do know where it's going. Not down into New England but up into Québec. What we don't know is where it starts."

Before they left, Reine-Marie peered out the door of the church to make sure the vehicles were gone.

Sure enough, no more Lauzon. Even Evelyn Tardiff's car was gone.

As they separated on the village green, Ruth said, "Remember, *Napoleon is always right.*"

Even for Ruth it was cryptic.

CHAPTER 15

⌒

Isabelle placed a photograph on the worn pine table in front of the open fire.

Both Armand and Jean-Guy leaned forward.

She'd arrived down in Three Pines at about the same time Beauvoir returned from driving Lauzon back to the penitentiary. Chief Inspector Gamache had called ahead and asked that the inmate be placed, once again, in protective custody.

The three now sat on the sofa and comfortable armchairs, warming themselves by the hearth. The bistro was never more inviting than on a cold night as winter approached. The open fires on both ends of the intimate room were lit, sending the subtle scent of maple woodsmoke to join the aroma of rich coffee and coq au vin and boeuf bourguignon and fresh baguette.

Into that pleasant atmosphere Isabelle told her colleagues about breaking the news of Frederick's murder to his parents. One of the worst parts was that she could not leave them to their grief. She needed information.

"He texted a number of weeks ago to say he was going away for a while. When the news broke about Marcus Lauzon, they understood why, but didn't understand why he hadn't been in touch since."

"So his message to them was before Lauzon was arrested?" Beauvoir asked.

Putting his Coke down, he spread a thick smear of pâté on a slice of baguette and popped the entire thing in his mouth.

"He sent it the night it all came to a head at the church," she said, and glanced out the window toward St. Thomas's. "And the water-treatment plant."

"When he drove Jeanne Caron from here into Montréal and left her there," said Beauvoir, after managing to swallow. "His family hasn't heard from him since?"

"No."

"You're sure?"

"Well, that's what they told me, and I don't think they're lying."

"Do we know when he was killed?" asked Gamache.

"Dr. Harris hasn't reported yet. I called again and left a message, stressing that we need to know not just when but also where. It seems obvious it must be where he was buried, but we need it confirmed."

"His killers couldn't have snuck up on him," said Beauvoir. "You can only get to that lake by float plane. He'd have heard and seen them arrive. I think they must've flown up together."

"That's what I think," said Isabelle. "It's possible he was kidnapped and taken up there, but if the purpose was to kill him, why not just do it in the Montréal landfill, like they normally do? No, I think he knew and trusted his killers. And if they were mob, he must've also been working with Moretti."

"Do you have that last message he sent his family?" Gamache asked.

After those tense hours with Lauzon, he was finally able to relax. He'd been watching Jean-Guy demolish the cheese and pâté. It was oddly compelling, almost rhythmic. A famished metronome.

Now Armand took a sip of his scotch and, replacing it on the table in front of the fire, he was momentarily mesmerized by the warm amber hue and the dancing light through the cut crystal.

"The text to his . . . ," he said, then paused. "His what?"

"Mother. They were in almost daily contact, before—"

Before. There would now, for the Castonguays, always be a "before" and "after."

"I have it here." Isabelle turned her phone around for them to see.

"Who's Lapin?" asked Armand. "He says to give her his love and to tell her not to mess with the stuff he left in the closet."

"His youngest sister. She's twelve. Rabbit is her nickname. She moved into his old bedroom when he left for Ottawa."

"So they're sure it's from him?" Beauvoir asked. Lacoste nodded. "Why didn't they report him missing?"

"They didn't want to get him into trouble. If they hadn't heard by end of this week, they were going to go to the Ottawa police."

"Did they approach Jeanne Caron?" asked Beauvoir. "She was his boss after all."

"I asked. They said they didn't. I asked why not. They didn't say it in so many words, but I got the impression they don't like or trust her. His mother went to his apartment in Ottawa two weeks ago but found nothing."

"She wouldn't necessarily know what to look for," said Jean-Guy, reaching for another slice of baguette. By now Lacoste was also staring.

"True," she said, watching him put a slab of Brie on the bread, then a delicate dab of red pepper jelly. "I have the address and keys and permission from the Castonguays and local cops to search. I've sent a team."

"*Bon*," said Gamache.

"But I did find something." Isabelle reached into the satchel on the floor beside her armchair. It was warmed by the fire. "After some persuasion, the girl brought out the box with the things Frederick left behind. Most of it's junk. Old trophies. Souvenirs from concerts and family vacations. A few photographs. Including..."

That was when she placed the picture on the pine table. Its corners were curled, and there was a small puncture in the top where it had probably been pinned to a corkboard at one time.

Armand picked it up. "It's a class photo."

"From fourth grade," said Jean-Guy, reading the sign at the sneakered feet of those in the first row.

He looked up at Isabelle, his brows raised in a *So?*

"I didn't get it either, until I turned it over." She did so now and handed it back to the Chief.

It took just a moment for his own brows to rise. He passed the picture to Jean-Guy.

There in the back row was nine-year-old Frederick, grinning mischievously. Unrecognizable as the arrogant young man Jean-Guy had met. Frederick's arm was slung lazily over the shoulder of the boy next to him.

Buddies.

It was, according to the chart on the back—

"Charles Langlois," said Armand.

"Fucking hell," Jean-Guy whispered into the mound of Saint André cheese almost at his lips.

"As soon as I saw this, I asked the Castonguays about Langlois. They looked blank at first, but when I showed them the photo, Frederick's mother remembered him, but not his name. The boys were best friends for a while, but there was a falling-out over something when they were still kids. But then the daughter—"

"Lapin," said Beauvoir.

His daughter had her own nickname. When she was born, Honoré couldn't get his mouth around "Idola" so had taken to calling her "Lala."

Idola did not yet speak, though they had hopes that with her therapy she would one day. And maybe even, one day, be able to correct her epically lazy brother.

Most children with Down syndrome, he and Annie had learned from doctors and other parents, did eventually speak. Though the older Idola got, the less they worried or noticed. The little girl communicated clearly in every other way. Mostly through laughter.

"*Oui*, Lapin," confirmed Isabelle. "She remembered that over Sunday dinner a while ago Frederick mentioned he'd run into an old friend from school. One who wasn't doing so well."

"He didn't give a name?" Beauvoir asked. Incredibly he held another piece of bread, this one with a crumbly Bleu bénédictin cheese on it.

"If he did, none of them could remember. It didn't seem a big deal, just a passing comment."

The class photo was back on the pine table, the flickering light of the wood fire playing over the children's faces. Almost animating them. Armand was reminded of the stained-glass young men in the church window. Also frozen in time. Forever young.

But each year, on a precise day, as the very first rays of the sun hit the window just so, the boys appeared to move, for a moment. It was, of course, an optical illusion. One not many had witnessed. But Armand had.

He'd woken early that day, troubled by a homicide that he could not seem to get a handle on. He'd gone to the church, not to pray, but to commune with his thoughts.

It had been September 18 of that first year he and Reine-Marie had moved to Three Pines. A day that was no longer summer. Not yet fall.

He'd walked up to the church in darkness, past the homes with sleeping friends and new neighbors. Past the three tall pines. As he climbed the wooden steps and reached for the door of the white clapboard church, he turned and looked over the village. There was a softening of the sky just at the tree line.

As he watched, the elderly poet was making her way to the bench, to help in the birthing of a new day.

Then he went into the church. Soon he'd drive into Montréal and meet again with the parents of Katie Vaslov, the young girl who'd been killed. He'd listen to their pain. He'd absorb, again, their sorrow. Their rage, now directed at him. And he'd have to admit he and his team were still searching for her killer. He'd reassure them he would find whoever had done it. However long it took.

But for that moment he'd sat in the pew beneath the boys and closed his eyes. Hoping for clarity. Hoping to see what had so far eluded him.

A movement, a slight shimmering of light across his lids, made him open his eyes. The blues and greens and bright brittle reds were undulating across the polished wood, moving toward him. And when the light reached him, it rested warm and bright on his hands. As though holding them.

He looked up and could have sworn the boys were watching him. Just for an instant. And then they'd frozen again.

It was then that he'd read the plaque. Learned their names. Learned they were brothers who'd died on the same day in the infamous slaughter of the Somme.

They'd perished on September 18, 1916. Three among twenty-four thousand Canadians who were killed in that one battle. A number hauntingly imprecise.

He'd gone back the next morning, just before dawn, but it didn't happen again until the next year, on September 18.

Armand was there. To greet them. Each and every September 18 since.

He thought of that now as he looked at the school photo. Here were two more dead boys. But unlike the stained-glass brothers, there was no fear in these faces. No indication they knew their lives would be limited. Their fates intertwined.

Where little Frederick looked like the class cutup, young Charles looked almost painfully earnest.

It was, Armand knew, often the way. His own best friend growing up, Michel, had been the class clown, clever but a mischief-maker. He loved to get the uber-earnest little Armand into all sorts of trouble.

Sitting in the bistro, between Jean-Guy and Isabelle, Armand smiled and chose not to pull up the memory of what happened later in their lives.

But another memory floated into his mind. Of Frederick Castonguay in the nest of green garbage bags.

"We were wondering how Castonguay knew about the lake. Charles must've been the old friend—" Gamache stopped and looked at Isabelle, his eyes widening. "The homeless shelter, The Mission. That's where they must've met up. When Charles was either a resident there or volunteering, and Frederick was on an official visit with Jeanne Caron."

"I think so," said Lacoste, not able to hide her excitement. "I've asked them to bring up the security tapes, to see if I can find the two together."

Armand nodded approval. "*Bon. Bon.*"

"Frederick must've introduced him to Jeanne Caron, who saw that, as a biologist, Charles could be helpful," said Jean-Guy.

"Right," said Isabelle. "Caron got him to look into her suspicions about some vague plot against the drinking water. References she'd found hidden in Lauzon's files."

"And when Charles realized he was in danger, he must've told Frederick that if anything happened to him, he should go to the lake. To look there," said Jean-Guy.

"But for what? Why tell him where to look, but not what for?" asked Gamache.

"Maybe he did. And maybe Frederick found it," said Lacoste. "And was killed."

"Which means whoever he was with now has it," said Jean-Guy.

The sudden excitement had just as suddenly evaporated.

Armand gazed once more into the dancing fire. Thinking. Thinking. *Did this make sense? Did it track? And if so, where did it lead?*

"We don't know that whatever Charles left behind was found," he said. "We need to go back up to the lake. Look again. We have to be sure, one way or another."

"Do you think it's the laptop?" asked Isabelle. When Gamache gave a small, almost imperceptible nod, she added, "I'll head back first thing in the morning."

"*Bon.*"

"How did it go with Lauzon?" she asked.

She listened, not interrupting until the end. Only then did she ask, "Do you believe him, *patron*? About the Prime Minister?"

It was obvious that she did not.

"I think since Lauzon can't actually murder the Prime Minister, he's doing the next best thing."

"Character assassination," said Jean-Guy. It was his read as well.

"There is one more thing," said Armand. "You remember when he tripped over that rock—"

"And you caught him, *oui*," said Jean-Guy.

"I don't think he actually stumbled. I think he did it on purpose."

"Why?" asked Lacoste.

"To whisper something to me. He said, 'Feds.'"

"What does that mean?" asked Lacoste.

Armand raised his hands to indicate he didn't know. "But this's the second time it's been mentioned today. Shona Dorion ran into references to 'FEDS' as well."

"It must mean the federal government," said Isabelle.

"Or when people say 'the Fed,' don't they mean the Federal Reserve in the States?" said Beauvoir.

"Or the FBI," said Isabelle. "The Feds."

"But it's not 'the Feds,'" said Armand. "Both Shona and Lauzon said simply 'Feds.' And Shona said it was in all caps."

"An acronym." Beauvoir brought out his phone to look it up. "Nope, nothing. Why...?" he began, then stopped. They gave him the space and time he needed to marshal his thoughts.

Just then Ruth arrived, but at a look from Isabelle she veered off to the bar.

"Why," Jean-Guy began again, "would he need to whisper?"

Gamache had been wondering the same thing. Why not just say it out loud?

There was only one answer.

"He didn't want Chief Inspector Tardiff to hear," said Beauvoir.

"But why not?" asked Lacoste.

"He doesn't trust her," said Beauvoir. "Between us? I know she's a friend and a senior officer, *patron*, but I'm not sure I trust her either."

"Why not?"

"Chief Inspector Tardiff's the head of Organized Crime for the Sûreté. She had one job in the investigations. And yet Moretti was the only one who got off."

"And isn't she supposed to have an informant on the inside, close to him?" asked Isabelle.

"Evelyn Tardiff is the informant."

They stared at him as though he'd just produced a camel from under the table. Something recognizable but highly unlikely.

"What?" said Jean-Guy.

"Chief Inspector Tardiff has spent years gaining the trust of Joe Moretti, getting close to him. He thinks she's working for him. That's how he got off on the charges. I can't prove it, but I think she buried the evidence."

"Why would she do that?" asked Isabelle.

"I think she knew that if Moretti was tried, never mind convicted, we'd lose that line of investigation. We'd lose the connection. Though she denies it, I think she does know that something bigger's about to happen and needs Moretti to tell her. But now I'm worried that Moretti's on to her. Keeping information from her. Maybe feeding her misinformation."

"Is it possible, *patron*"—now Isabelle spoke slowly, choosing her words carefully—"that Chief Inspector Tardiff has turned? Is infiltrating the Sûreté, not the Montréal mafia? She's informing on us. Is it possible she knows what's going to happen next and is part of it?"

"And," said Beauvoir, hating to pile on, but needing to, "if Castonguay's murder was an execution, a hit, then Moretti's people were behind it. Shouldn't she have known?"

Instead of answering, Armand picked up the class picture. He looked down at the bright-eyed boys and girls. And the two buddies in the back row.

"Was this the only class photo in Frederick's box?"

"*Oui.*"

"Why?"

"*Pardon?*"

"Where are all the others? Why would he keep only this one? Especially if there'd been a falling-out and they hadn't seen each other in years?"

Isabelle and Jean-Guy considered the question, then Isabelle's eyes opened. "He got rid of them because he wanted us to focus on only this one. He wanted us to see him and Charles together and to let us know they knew each other. Were once friends—"

"Best friends," murmured Gamache.

"And make the connection. He told his sister in his last communication to essentially guard the box."

"He wanted to warn us, and to tell us whose side he really was on," said Jean-Guy. "But when you first met him, *patron*, on Parliament Hill, when you went to confront Caron, why didn't he say something then?"

Gamache nodded, remembering that encounter. "It's possible he didn't know whose side we were on. We now know there were plotters inside the Sûreté. High up. Castonguay must've been terrified when we showed up and pretty much kidnapped him. Put him in the car and drove him out into the country."

He looked down at that mischievous face.

Frederick Castonguay was caught up in something far beyond his understanding. And yet he'd persevered, long after he could have just walked away and gotten on with his life. Done nothing.

Instead, he'd done something. Frederick had gone to that remote lake, almost certainly because his friend Charles had directed him there. And, like his friend, Frederick had been murdered.

Before or after he'd found what Charles had hidden?

"*Animal House?*" asked Myrna.

"*Oui*, that's what Ruth suggested. She seemed amazed I hadn't yet read it."

"*Animal House?*" Myrna repeated.

"Yes. Why? You seem surprised too."

"For a whole other reason. I'm not at all surprised you haven't read *Animal House*. Ruth must've been pulling your leg."

"She seemed in earnest, even annoyed I didn't know it."

"How can you tell if Ruth's annoyed?" Myrna picked up the phone to call the cranky old poet, but had barely hit the icon when she hung up, with a hearty laugh, having figured it out.

A minute later, after disappearing down one of the aisles of her book-shop, she reappeared and handed a slim worn volume, essentially a no-vella, to Reine-Marie.

"You've never read this? I guess when it comes to literature there really are Two Solitudes."

Reine-Marie looked at the title and let out a roar of laughter. "Damn it, of course this's what Ruth said. Am I blushing?"

"You are and should be."

She paid for the used book and went into the bistro, catching Armand's eyes but not joining them. Instead, she found a comfortable armchair, or-dered a white wine, and began to read about Snowball and Boxer, Old Major and—she put it on her lap and stared out the window—Napoleon.

Then, once again, Reine-Marie picked it up and lost herself in the story of revolution and tyranny and the creation of a common enemy.

"What're you reading?"

Reine-Marie looked over her glasses at her husband as he took the chair opposite her in the bistro.

"*Animal House.*"

"*Animal House?* Are all students created equal, but some more equal than others?"

Reine-Marie, who hadn't quite gotten that far in the book, looked puz-zled. "What are you talking about?"

Armand laughed. "You said *Animal House.*"

Now she looked appalled. "Argh. I have that lodged in my brain. *Animal Farm, Animal Farm.* Have you read it?"

"Years ago, in Cambridge. It was a question in the debating society. 'Are all animals created equal?' Why're you reading it now?"

"Ruth suggested it. We were talking about…" Reine-Marie paused to remember their conversation. It had been so wide-ranging. "Oh, I know. Propaganda. *Napoleon is always right.*"

Armand nodded, recognizing another famous and chilling quote from the book.

"A tyrant posing as a strong leader, manipulating public opinion," he said. "But why were you talking about that? When last I heard, you and the others were heading to Jericho to the Snowflake Bentley museum."

Knowing he was preoccupied with Marcus Lauzon and Evelyn Tardiff, she hadn't updated him. It would have been, she knew, a long email. Now she told him about their outing. Including Camp Ethan Allen.

"A commando training center?" he said, leaning back and crossing his legs. "And you say Charles's line goes right through it?"

"Well, if it doesn't turn anywhere," she said. "It seems far-fetched. Why would a biologist be concerned about a commando camp?"

Armand shook his head.

"How was lunch?" she asked.

"Chicken was delicious, *merci.*"

"And the rest?"

He took a deep breath, moving his body as though to express uncertainty. Then he sat forward.

"Lauzon still maintains his innocence. Says he wasn't involved in the poisoning plot. Even denies knowing about the payoffs. Claims the money was planted."

"Nothing we didn't hear in his trial. Did he say anything new? Give you any evidence?" But even as she asked, she knew this was far too public a place to discuss it.

Jean-Guy and Isabelle had both returned to Montréal and their families. Jean-Guy to have a shower and wash off the slime from too-close contact with Marcus Lauzon. Isabelle to finally have that long, hot bubble bath she'd dreamed of since the night before in that tent. On that root. She hated that root.

Armand and Reine-Marie ordered dinner at the bistro, arctic char for him with a mild orange sauce, while she ordered the pasta in herb butter, grated Romano, and lemon zest. A particular favorite.

They were eventually joined by Clara and Myrna, who both had the grilled shrimp. Ruth came over to report that there wasn't enough roast chicken in their fridge for her dinner. They were about to order her the pasta too when Armand noticed she'd eaten half his arctic char.

Finally, Olivier and Gabri sat down with an exhausted plunk. "Dinner service is almost over. The kids can look after the rest."

Armand looked up and saw Frère Simon helping the youngsters, even though he was off shift.

"Would you like anything more?" Gabri asked.

They all wanted the crème brûlée, but no one except Ruth had the heart to ask them to get up again. The guys ignored her, and eventually she satisfied herself by taking Myrna's half-drunk glass of red wine.

Armand excused himself, and once back home in his study, he placed a call.

"Bert?"

"Armand, good to hear from you. How's Reine-Marie?"

"Knitting sweaters for winter."

It was, of course, not true. "Knitting" was the code the two old comrades had created to tell the other that what they had to say was confidential.

"Oh, someone's at the door," said General Whitehead. "I'll call you back."

He'd obviously understood, and a minute later Armand's phone rang again. This time the head of the US Joint Chiefs of Staff had used the secure line.

"How can I help, Armand?" When he didn't answer, the General's tone changed. "What is it? Something's wrong. It's not over?"

"I don't think so. I think the poisoning plot you helped us with was the first volley, maybe even meant to distract."

"A Napoleonic strategy," said Whitehead, a student of tactics.

"And *Napoleon is always right*." Even as he said it, Armand was taken aback. Where had that come from? And just as quickly he remembered. His conversation with Reine-Marie about *Animal Farm*.

"Not always," said the General. "In an effort to strangle the British, Napoleon brought in the Continental—" On hearing Armand clear his throat, he stopped and even chuckled. "Sorry. You didn't call to talk about a long-dead French emperor."

"*Non*, riveting as the Continental System is. Bert, a phrase, really a single word, keeps appearing, but I don't know what it means. What does 'FEDS' say to you?"

"'Feds'? As in federal government? Or the Feds? The FBI? Or—"

"No, we thought of all that. It's not 'the Feds,' just 'FEDS.' And seems to be in caps. Maybe an acronym."

There was a pause. "Nope, Armand. Sorry. It means nothing to me. Please give my love to Reine-Marie. Ask her to bring her knitting pattern down next time you visit. Soon, I hope, old friend."

"I'll pass it along. We both know what an enthusiastic knitter you are. One of Napoleon's hobbies too, to relieve stress, I believe."

"Really?"

"*Non*."

And with that, both men hung up. And both, unseen by the other, leaned back in their chairs and stared ahead.

Armand thought for a moment, then put in a call to Jean-Guy.

In Washington, Bert Whitehead was placing his own call.

CHAPTER 16

At the same time next morning that Jean-Guy was boarding a flight to DC, Isabelle was tossing gear into a float plane.

Armand had spent much of the night before lying in bed staring at the ceiling. Debating. He finally got up and, going downstairs, he sat in an armchair and put on music.

Music. Music. How he'd missed music.

In the quietude, he listened to Bach's Concerto for Two Violins. Calm. Calming. Restful. As he listened, he let his mind drift.

Isabelle would soon be heading back up north. To see again the lake where Charles had last visited. Where Frederick had been killed. Study again the arrow carved into the tree.

That remote body of water had produced at least one body. And he knew it had more to cough up. Something else was hiding there.

He'd woken Reine-Marie before dawn with a mug of coffee. Sitting on the side of their bed, he'd leaned down and kissed her forehead. Startled, she'd sat up so quickly she'd almost broken his nose.

"What is it?"

He'd laughed. "*Désolé.* I didn't mean to scare you. I have to go out."

She focused and saw what he was wearing. A heavy coat over a turtleneck sweater. Looking down, she saw he had on thick woolen socks and by the bedroom door was a satchel.

Reine-Marie narrowed her eyes. "I'm assuming you aren't heading to the bistro."

"*Non.* I need to go to the lake where Frederick Castonguay was found."

She pulled herself up in the bed. "You're going to fly there?"

He nodded.

"You know what the doctor said. The pressure changes could redamage your eardrums, your hearing. Maybe do permanent damage. Just when—"

She stopped when she felt a fizzing in her throat and her eyes beginning to burn.

He nodded again. Just when he almost had it all back. Just when he could once again hear her voice. Just when they could have an actual conversation, about those details of life no one else could possibly care about.

And now he was putting it all at risk.

"I am sorry," he said, softly. He placed his large hands on either side of her face and held them gently there for a moment, before leaning in and giving her a deep, long kiss. And felt her kiss him back.

Whatever happened, they would still have that. Always have that. Into eternity. There was no need for words to understand that.

As he pulled away, she reached out and held his face. Pulling him close, she whispered in his ear. "I love you."

"And I love you. I'll be back for dinner."

After she'd heard the front door close, Reine-Marie got out of bed and, wrapping the comforter around her shoulders, she stood at the window. The dogs and Gracie joined her, and all four watched his headlights illuminate the bench on the hill, before disappearing.

He'd told her the evening before what "that man" had said about Prime Minister Woodford. It was patently ridiculous. Meant to smear.

She hoped. Because if Lauzon was actually telling the truth...

"We're all in trouble," she whispered and saw Henri's satellite ears swing toward her, his face turned up to her. His eyes clearly communicating.

Breakfast.

As soon as Jean-Guy's flight landed at Reagan National in DC, he grabbed a cab.

Twenty minutes later he walked into a diner about as far from the White House as he could be. Not geographically but socially.

The diner was populated, sparsely, by the disoriented, the disenfranchised. Those without power. Without income, without jobs. Without hope.

Though there was one person, sitting at the back, wearing a Washington Mystics cap. He had on cords and a T-shirt under an old grubby and torn combat jacket, without insignia.

"Coffee, please," said Beauvoir, pausing at the counter, though he was far from sure the server heard him. Or cared.

General Whitehead nodded but didn't get up.

"Good morning. Not to be rude, but I expected Armand."

Jean-Guy sat and was grateful, though admittedly surprised, when a hand put down a mug of coffee, along with creams and sugars.

"Thank you. I'm sorry. Just me again." He popped open the creamer, then tore a little sugar packet and stirred. "What happened to Off the Record?"

It was the swank bar in the basement of the Hay-Adams hotel, across the street from the White House, where they met last time.

"For one thing, it's eight thirty in the morning and the bar isn't open. And it's too close to—"

Bert Whitehead stopped. It was clear what he meant.

"Besides," said the General, "I like it here. Sam's an old friend. We served together in the Gulf War. We're safe."

On hearing the last word, Jean-Guy stopped stirring his coffee, carefully placed the spoon on the table, and leaned forward. "Tell me about FEDS."

Though Isabelle said nothing, she noticed Armand wincing as the plane gained altitude.

They'd asked the Sûreté pilot to fly low, to lessen the pressure.

"This's a plane," said the pilot, "not a boat. If you want to fly, you have to go—" He pointed up.

Now Isabelle leaned forward and, placing her hand on the pilot's shoulder, she spoke directly into his ear.

"Take it down or I'll—"

She tightened her grip in a gesture far more eloquent than words. They descended so that they were essentially skimming the tops of the waves.

When the pressure eased and Armand opened his eyes again, they widened. He was practically making eye contact with equally surprised trout. An hour later, after almost clipping the trees, the plane made a steep turn and landed on a lake, bouncing along the tops of the waves.

Lacoste guided the pilot to the site. He stayed with his plane while Armand and Isabelle paddled the small dinghy to the pebble shore, stepping into the water and dragging the boat onto land.

It was far colder that far north. There was a light layer of snow on the ground. Their breaths came out in puffs of warm vapor. Gamache paused on the rocky shore and stared out across the lake, taking in the beauty. Absorbing the peace of the unspoiled landscape.

He drew his elbows tighter into his sides and hunched his shoulders to conserve warmth. Looking out at the lake, he brought his hand up to his brow to cut out the glare from the dazzling sun bouncing off the water. It looked to Isabelle as though he was saluting Mother Nature. And he might have been.

"It's over here, *patron*."

Isabelle had walked a short distance into the forest and now pointed to the base of the tree.

"How in the world did you find it?" Armand looked around.

The forest was dense, untouched, uncut. Filled with old growth, mostly evergreens that only died of extreme old age. Or, he thought, a fire.

He knew if they flew a little farther north, they'd see the charred remains of millions of trees. It was a national tragedy. An epic failure.

Canada's great good fortune was in being rich in natural resources. Its shame was in not being better custodians.

And it was now obvious to the entire world that Canada had failed in its responsibility. Any moral superiority, any higher ground Canada might claim, had been burned to a crisp.

The results of the water samples Vivienne had taken had come back. The biologist was right. The pH levels of this lake, and no doubt others, were affected by potassium. Potash. Ash. From those wildfires.

Many more fires, and the lake would die. And, with it, all the wildlife that depended on it.

And if it was this bad here, God only knew what lasting damage was done farther south, when the plume of ash had descended on American soil and water. On American cities and citizens.

"I was searching," said Lacoste, answering his question, "and noticed the rock looked odd, up against the tree like that. When I looked closer, it was a river rock, smooth. There's no way it could get from there"—she pointed to the shore—"to here without help. We lifted partial prints from it. They look like Charles's."

Armand picked up the stone and leaned down to examine the arrow Charles had carved into the tree along with his initials.

"Vivienne and I followed the arrow into the forest"—she pointed—"in that direction."

"And where was Frederick's body?"

"Over there." She pointed in a whole other direction.

"Huh," he grunted. "Odd. I wonder what Frederick was doing over there?"

He followed her about fifty meters in, to the crime scene tape. Armand again knelt.

They'd heard from Dr. Harris that Frederick Castonguay had almost certainly been killed where he'd been buried, and it had happened less than two months earlier, though she couldn't be more precise.

He stood up, and after brushing dirt from his slacks, he looked around, then behind them toward the tree and the stone. Both were invisible, hidden by the thick forest in between. Still . . .

Armand turned full circle, then walked back and looked down at the base of the tree. Then over to where the body had been.

"So if the arrow points in one direction, why did Frederick go in the other?"

"It's possible Frederick didn't find the arrow, otherwise he'd have followed it, *non?*" said Isabelle.

"That's possible. I guess. But if Charles told Frederick about the lake, why not tell him where to find the stone?" Armand was all but muttering to himself, and again peering around, his thoughtful gaze landing back on Lacoste.

"It doesn't make sense," Armand finally said. "Why tell Frederick about the lake but not the stone and what was under it? And how to find whatever he'd hidden. He'd tell him all or nothing, wouldn't he? Since Frederick knew about the lake, it's sensible to assume he also knew about the carving."

"And what he was looking for. So why didn't he follow the arrow?"

"There is one explanation. He realized, too late, that he was in trouble, and wanted to make sure whoever he was with didn't find the stone and whatever Charles had hidden."

"Are you saying that, knowing he was going to be murdered, he led them off in the wrong direction?"

"It's possible."

"That would mean when he got in the plane, he didn't realize his companions were dangerous. But something happened either in the flight or once they'd landed. Someone said or did something to alert him to the danger."

Armand nodded. "They might not have been Moretti's soldiers, but someone else. Someone he trusted. Otherwise he'd never have gotten in the plane."

He looked around, from the sparkling lake to the dark forest. "Whatever Charles hid here must be important."

"And dangerous, for someone to kill for it. I'm a little afraid that they did find it, despite Frederick trying to fool them. Maybe that's why we can't. It's no longer here."

"That would be a shame," he said, in a vast understatement. "They must think by killing Frederick they've covered their tracks. They obviously don't know we have Charles's map."

"But what good is it, *patron*, if whatever he hid here is gone?"

"We don't know that for sure. Besides, Charles wrote other things on the map."

"Which we don't understand."

"But we will. What we can say with some certainty is that Charles believed that Frederick was on his side, or he'd never have confided in him."

"And maybe he was. And maybe Frederick thought the people he was with were too."

The Chief spent a moment staring at the base of the tree, then he turned and walked in the direction that arrow indicated.

After another hour of searching, he shook his head. "We need more people."

But both senior officers knew they could not risk calling in a team to search since they did not know who to trust. Except themselves.

"We can only hope that if we can't find it, neither did they," he said as they walked back to the shore.

"If only we knew who 'they' were."

"That would help," he agreed.

While they paddled back to the float plane, Armand looked out across the vast expanse of fresh water. Isabelle was right. The map hadn't yet given up all its secrets. Charles had written a series of numbers and symbols on this lake.

Armand had hoped they could decode it themselves. He hated the idea of letting that information out of their tight circle, but it seemed the time had come.

When they got to the plane, Armand asked the pilot to fly north, so he could see the damage from the recent fires. He'd seen many in his life, from the air and on the ground. He'd fought a few. A brutal, at times terrifying, experience as the winds created by the fire itself whipped around. Making its path impossible to predict. Just hoping and praying he and his team weren't suddenly surrounded by the flames.

But what he saw now was on a scale he could not imagine. It took his breath away. Mile after mile of devastation, as though some nuclear bomb had been set off. It was an end-of-the-world vision.

He remembered those apocalyptic photos of New York and Chicago and other American cities and towns, almost disappearing into the ash. The sky orange as though the atmosphere itself was on fire. The sun all but blotted out. It was what a nuclear winter would look like. Horrific. Horrifying. A warning.

Please, God, he thought, *don't let it happen again.*

Though he knew it almost certainly would. Nothing could stop another wildfire now. He also knew that where they'd just stood was now the front line, next in line to be burned to the ground.

The plane was flying low over the charred remains of what had been an ancient woodland. Armand leaned forward and tapped the pilot's shoulder.

"Okay, we can go," he shouted.

He'd seen enough. He'd seen shame and sorrow made manifest. Now all he wanted was to go home.

The pilot made an A-OK sign with his fingers, then pointed up as the plane climbed. Armand opened his mouth to relieve the sudden pressure and watched as Lacoste hit the pilot on the shoulder and pointed down.

Seeing this, Armand sat back in the tiny float plane. His brow furrowed in what Lacoste assumed was pain but was, in fact, thought. He stared at the pilot's back, then suddenly leaned forward again.

"Take us back to the lake."

"*Pardon?*" the pilot shouted.

"The lake. Take us back."

The pilot repeated what the Chief Inspector said, to confirm; then, with a shrug, he turned the plane around.

Isabelle cocked her head inquiringly at Gamache, but he was staring out the window looking down as the charred stumps slowly turned to healthy evergreens as they crossed the border between hell and heaven.

"'Feds' stands for Fire Event Detection Suite," said Whitehead, his voice low. The chair of the Joint Chiefs of Staff was obviously unhappy about needing to share this information, but was prepared to do so.

Jean-Guy had to lean across the Formica table to hear. When he went to write it down, Whitehead stopped him.

"Best to just remember it. It's a new technology that tracks megafires."

"I've never heard that term."

"'Megafire'? Not surprising. We had no words to describe what happened with those forest fires in Canada. There are now. I'm not sure if you can appreciate just how shocking, how horrifying it was for the millions of people in the path of those ash clouds."

"I saw the news reports, those photos of New York—"

"Yes, that's what people saw because that's where the reporters live. New York. Washington, Minneapolis. But other places were hit even worse by the toxic clouds from Canada. Reservoirs for drinking water were poisoned. Fertile fields ruined. Crops failed. Lives were ruined. Health was ruined. The elderly. Babies with health conditions."

Whitehead suddenly stopped. After a long pause, in which he studied Beauvoir so intently the younger man felt stripped, he continued.

"It was different on the ground. In war it always is. The videos and photographs can never capture the horror. It's being called, in some quarters, the worst assault on America since 9/11."

"Now wait a minute, sir. I appreciate your job is to protect Americans and American soil, but this isn't a war, and we didn't attack you. There was nothing deliberate about it."

"Perhaps not, but if you run down someone in an accident, they're still dead."

"There's no 'perhaps' about it. Canada would never deliberately do that to the US."

For some reason the Chair of the Joint Chiefs of Staff seemed almost amused.

"Look, you and I both know that, but that's not how it's seen in many quarters, and not just by the crazy conspiracy theorists and the far-right lunatics. There's a growing sentiment here, even among policymakers. They're looking for an excuse."

"To do what?"

"The Fire Event Detection Suite can tell us how and when and where the ash from the next megafire will land. And there will be a next. FEDS is predictive."

His eyes again bore into Jean-Guy's, asking him, begging him, to understand. But Jean-Guy was lost.

Finally, Whitehead decided to help him out. "What happens, son, if you can predict the future?"

Beauvoir took a deep breath and considered. "If you actually knew what was going to happen? That would be pretty powerful."

"Not pretty powerful, it would make that person omnipotent. And then let's take it another step. Suppose in knowing the future, you could also control it?"

Jean-Guy looked at the head of the most powerful military on earth and wondered if he was a madman. Because what he'd just said was lunacy.

"We're in the real world, sir. What you're describing is science fiction."

"You think? The future is shaped every day by men and women who invent technologies. Often ones whose potential they don't understand. Often ones used far differently than their creators intended. Technologies which to our grandparents would have been science fiction. And what

156

happens when that technology—AI, for instance, with its voice and image cloning—is fed to social media? Public opinion is influenced, manipulated, changed, shaped. Governments are elected, policies formed and implemented. The future is created."

Jean-Guy was now trying to decide when the next flight back to a somewhat sane land might be. But General Whitehead was still talking.

"That plot to contaminate Montréal's drinking water was about water security, right?"

"Right."

"Have you been paying attention to that issue? Not how vulnerable cities might be to a terrorist attack like the one you almost had in Montréal, that's certainly one thing. But there's a larger issue. One facing almost every nation."

"What larger issue?"

Despite himself, Jean-Guy found he was drawn into what the General was saying. He could see that this man—who had been in wars, directed battles, had had to make terrible decisions with horrific consequences affecting tens of thousands under his command—was stressed. And with that Jean-Guy felt his own anxiety rising.

"Listen, sir, please. Just tell me. What's happening? What's about to happen? You know something."

"I don't know, not for sure. But I am afraid."

"Of what?"

Whitehead stood up and placed a hundred-dollar bill on the table, even though Beauvoir had only had a coffee and the General, from what Jean-Guy could see, had had nothing.

"Of what happens when this"—he held up his untouched glass of water—"runs out."

Armand was so anxious to get to the shore he stepped out of the dinghy before it reached the shallows and went thigh-deep into the frigid water.

But he didn't seem to notice the cold. He was completely focused on one thing.

Chief Inspector Gamache was, essentially, storming the beach. Plowing through the water. Eyes forward, desperate to get to land.

Once on the rocky shore, he sprinted to the tree line, with Lacoste close behind. It was as though the Chief was being pursued by all the demons in hell.

He made straight for the tree. Dropping to his knees, he grabbed up the stone and looked again at the etching in the tree bark.

His teeth were beginning to chatter, and his body tremble. The brutally cold water had quickly penetrated to his bones and was advancing on the marrow. Isabelle took off her pink tuque with the pom-pom and held it out, but he didn't seem to notice.

Armand's sole focus was on the arrow. He was bending over, studying it. Then something happened.

He started to laugh, with a slight edge of hysteria.

"What is it, *patron*?" She'd never heard him make quite this sound before.

He tipped his head back, and the laughing stopped. Now he almost sobbed. "Oh, dear God, thank you."

"What?"

"The arrow isn't pointing north, it's pointing up. Like the pilot did. Up." He pointed, and she followed his gaze.

There, high up and all but hidden among the branches and fragrant needles of the evergreen, was a sack. A green garbage bag. It was strung up, as campers did, as Lacoste herself had done, to keep food and dirty dishes out of reach of bears.

But what was far above them was not, they knew, food. And it wasn't bears Charles Langlois was afraid of. But a wolf.

Lacoste dropped her astonished gaze to Gamache. The Chief Inspector was sitting back on his heels, his head now lowered into his trembling hands.

CHAPTER 17

A gent Yvette Nichol was at her desk outside Chief Inspector Tardiff's office. Considering.

Her boss had just hung up from a call and was working on reports.

Going to the cabinet, Nichol chose a file, then put on her coat and knocked on the boss's door.

"*Oui?*" Tardiff looked over her reading glasses at her assistant.

"I'm not really feeling all that well, *patronne*. Would you mind if I went home?"

"No, that's fine. A cold?"

"Must be. Change of seasons. And I went for a walk last night without a coat."

"Why?"

Oh, God, why? "I didn't realize it was that cold." *Oh, for fuck's sake, stop talking*, she begged herself. *You sound like a fool.* "Sinuses are now acting up. Giving me a migraine."

"Absolutely, you need to go home." Tardiff returned to her computer screen. "Don't give it to me."

"The migraine upsets my stomach." *Stop talking. You have the win.* "Or maybe it's food poisoning."

By now Chief Inspector Tardiff's expression had gone from sympathy to boredom to annoyance. Nichol finally stopped herself, before her boss hit disbelief.

"I'll just take this file down to records and leave."

Tardiff held out her hand. "Don't bother. Give it to me and I'll have someone else take it. What is it?"

Fuck, fuck, fuckity, fuck, fuck.

"Just something they asked for."

Tardiff's hand was still out. And now the Chief opened and closed her fingers in the signal to hurry up and bring it to her.

Nichol did.

"These are requisitions for printer paper." Tardiff looked at her. "Why would records need them?"

"Did I say records? *Désolée*. Must be the meds I just took. Clouding my mind. I meant supply and services, for reimbursement." *Stop talking*.

Fortunately, what she said was so mind-numbing, the head of Organized Crime for the Sûreté stopped caring.

"Fine. Take them down and leave." Then, as an afterthought: "Feel better."

"*Merci*." As she left Yvette attempted a dry cough. It at least sounded pathetic.

Armand's head was tipped back, his arms out to catch Isabelle, should she fall.

He barely noticed his soaked slacks clinging to his legs, numbing them. His hands shook from the cold.

Still, he kept his arms out and strained to see her. The sack had been hung so far up, she had to climb from branch to branch, at times disappearing into the foliage before reappearing.

At one point a branch broke and fell. For an instant Gamache braced, thinking the woman would follow. She did not. He sidestepped the limb, never taking his eyes off Isabelle.

This was pretty much his nightmare, having to climb that high. He was endlessly grateful that while Isabelle had other fears, heights was not one.

"I'm there, *patron*." He waited for more, his eyes peeled, his arms still out. Then he heard her say, "*Mon Dieu*."

"What?" he called.

"I'm leaving it in the bag, but—"

"What is it?" Rarely had he heard such a plea in his own voice. *Please God, please God, please God*.

"You're right. It's a laptop. Either that or a pizza box." She waited for his laugh, and after a long moment it drifted up to her. Not a robust guffaw, but a sort of relieved chuckle, almost a moan.

Months, months they'd been looking for it. They'd had the monastery of Saint-Gilbert-Entre-les-Loups searched by the monks, multiple times.

They'd had The Mission, the homeless shelter where Charles had once lived and volunteered, turned upside down.

They'd searched Charles's parents' place. They'd searched the remote village of Blanc-Sablon in case Dom Philippe had hidden it there.

But it had been here all along.

Within minutes she was down again, the garbage bag clasped to her chest. "Are you going to open it?"

"*Non.*" Though every cell in his body wanted to rip the coverings off and look at their discovery. "This needs to be done properly. We need to get it back to—"

To where? The Sûreté had been compromised. He still wasn't sure of Chief Inspector Tardiff, despite what he'd said to Lacoste and Beauvoir the day before. And there were almost certainly other Sûreté officers involved in the plot and not caught in the earlier arrests.

"—Three Pines."

Once back in the float plane, the pilot put the small heater on full blast and slowly their shivering subsided. Armand's legs and hands felt pins and needles. As the craft rose and fell in the air currents, Armand clutched Charles's laptop to his chest.

He'd failed to keep the young biologist safe, he would not make the same mistake with this.

A few hours later, as Jean-Guy drove down the hill into Three Pines from the Montréal airport, he noticed Gamache's vehicle just parking.

He also noticed a stranger's car in front of the bistro.

Though it was not unheard of to have visitors to the village, it was unusual enough to be noted. And given what was happening, anything unusual was now cause for caution.

As Jean-Guy watched, he saw Isabelle reversing until her vehicle was touching the front fender of the stranger's.

Getting out quickly, she stood tense, staring at it. Gamache was also out of the car, protecting something behind his body.

Isabelle's hand was now on her hip holster. Ready.

The car appeared empty, though that didn't mean it really was. As he got closer, Jean-Guy could see the dent on the door, the rust in the wheel well, the crack in the windshield. It was missing two hubcaps. This was an old model Honda Civic. A rust bucket.

It didn't belong to anyone in the village. Even Ruth's car was in better shape.

On hearing Jean-Guy's familiar vehicle arriving, Gamache's eyes flicked briefly over to him. Then back again. Jean-Guy could now see what he was protecting. It seemed to be a sack of garbage. But as he looked closer, Jean-Guy could see by its shape that it was either a laptop or a small pizza box. Since Armand never ordered a small, that left only one option.

Holy shit, they did it. They found it.

He felt the slight nudge as his front fender touched the rear of the other vehicle. It was trapped.

"What the fuck are you doing?" came the unpleasantly familiar voice. "That's my father's car. If you've scratched it..."

Beauvoir and Lacoste turned quickly to the door of the bistro. Then back to Gamache, who was smiling.

"You remember Yvette Nichol. Agent Nichol is here to help."

"That'll be a first," muttered Beauvoir.

They all had news, big news.

All were anxious to tell the others what they'd learned. But they knew that the lede was sitting on the desk in front of them in the study.

Armand and Isabelle had both grabbed quick showers and changed into warm, dry clothes. Isabelle borrowed some from Reine-Marie, who'd put on a pot of tea.

Now they were crowded into the small study, holding mugs and staring at the laptop.

They had to wait for it to charge up.

We wait. We wait.

Isabelle had lifted three sets of prints off the computer.

"The majority belong to Charles Langlois. These here are Jeanne Caron's."

"The third?" asked Gamache.

"Marcus Lauzon?" asked Jean-Guy. "Castonguay?"

"Tardiff?" asked Nichol.

"*Non*," said Isabelle. "Whoever it is isn't in the records."

But someone else had touched Charles's laptop. Someone without a record. Someone who had never been arrested.

No longer able to hold it in, Nichol blurted out, "Tardiff's going to have Lauzon killed."

That got their attention.

"*Pardon?*" said Lacoste, looking up from the keyboard.

"I heard her on the phone. That's why I came here. She thinks I'm sick. I told her—"

"Lauzon," said Gamache, refocusing the excited young agent.

"Chief Inspector Tardiff was talking to someone. I think it was Moretti, but I only heard her side of the conversation. It was on her personal phone, so I couldn't listen in or trace it. She argued a bit, saying it would be almost impossible, and if it succeeded, it could expose her, but finally she agreed."

"When?" asked Gamache.

"I don't know. She didn't say, only that it would take time, and Moretti must've said they don't have it. What does this mean?"

"It means Marcus Lauzon has more to say," said Lacoste. "And they know it. They need to shut him up."

"Bringing him down here yesterday must've triggered something," said Gamache.

"Wait a minute," said Nichol. "You took the former Deputy Prime Minister out of supermax and brought him here?"

She stared at Gamache. She'd known that he was powerful, but she had no idea he wielded that much.

Ignoring her, Beauvoir said, "If Tardiff told Moretti about the visit, that means she really is working for him."

"Not necessarily," said Gamache. His mind was moving quickly over the options. "If I was in her place, I'd have told him too. The only way to prove loyalty is to provide important information. Accurate, verifiable information."

Beauvoir looked less than convinced. "So what do we do? Let them kill Lauzon?"

Gamache was staring at Yvette Nichol. Silence descended.

"She knows," he finally said.

"I know nothing," said Nichol, coloring furiously.

"Not you. Evelyn Tardiff knows that you were placed in her department to watch her and report to me."

"What?" demanded Nichol. "How?"

"I told her."

Now it was Nichol's turn to stare, but Chief Inspector Gamache didn't drop his eyes. He held hers until she finally found her voice.

"You told her? You blew my cover? You shit-head."

"Agent Nichol—" Beauvoir began.

"This's between Gamache and me, so fuck off."

Gamache had his hand up and once again the room fell silent, though the air sizzled.

"Agent Nichol has a right to be angry," he finally said. "And to express it, though you do not"—he stared at her—"have the right to disrespect your superiors."

"Respect? You expect respect? You betrayed me. I trusted you to keep me safe."

"You were, are, right to trust me."

Slowly, slowly the mulish scowl on Yvette Nichol's face disappeared, and she smiled. "My God, you sly dog—"

"Nichol...," Beauvoir warned.

"You used me," she said to Gamache. "You both used me. Chief Inspector Tardiff couldn't risk communicating directly with you, so she made sure I overheard the conversation. She could have gone somewhere private to have it, but chose to speak to Moretti in her office, with the door open. Where I could overhear. She wanted me to. And she wanted me to tell you. Does this mean she's working for us?"

"I think it does," said Gamache, and saw Nichol light up. He also saw the look on Beauvoir and Lacoste's faces. Who'd heard what he really said.

He thought she was working with them. Thought. But wasn't sure.

At that moment Charles's laptop came alive. Still wearing gloves, Lacoste hit a key at random and a box asking for a password appeared. No big surprise, but a disappointment. They'd hoped he'd disabled it.

"He must think we'd know it," said Isabelle.

"Or that someone close to him would find it and be able to guess," said Beauvoir.

"Or that we could guess," said Gamache. He looked at Nichol and pointed to the chair in front of the laptop.

Isabelle and Jean-Guy were accomplished on computers, but few knew more about them than Yvette Nichol. While still a new agent, she'd been assigned, as punishment for insubordination, to the data center in the basement of Sûreté headquarters. It was meant to keep her out of trouble. But once there she'd filled the tedium by learning everything there was to know about how their network functioned. About dark sites. About cyber-security and lack of security. About data retrieval.

Gamache had called on her services once before when in a crisis. And now he needed them again.

"Figure out the password."

"You say that like it's easy." But no one was listening to her anymore.

While she did that, Gamache put in a call to the penitentiary warning them to be alert to any threat to Marcus Lauzon, but to be discreet about it. Then he joined Jean-Guy and Isabelle in the living room, where Reine-Marie had lit the fire.

"Tell us about your meeting with General Whitehead."

"'FEDS' stands for Fire Event Detection Suite. It's a new technology created by NASA after the megafires. It predicts where ash will go."

"Why would that be important?" asked Lacoste. "It's good to know, I agree, but still, it's not much use, is it? I guess you could warn the cities and people, but you couldn't stop it, could you?"

"I was confused too and asked General Whitehead. That's when things got weird. He said that FEDS is predictive—"

"We got that," said Lacoste.

"—and he asked what happens if someone can predict the future."

"They're put in the asylum?" asked Isabelle.

"Maybe. But he said if they really can predict it, they can control it."

"Not necessarily," said Lacoste. "Even if you knew for certain what was going to happen, some big event, could you change it? You can't stop an earthquake or even a fire."

"You might not be able to change it, but you might be able to change your own actions," said Gamache. "If you knew a stock was going to go way up, you'd buy it. If you knew the winning lottery numbers, you'd get that ticket. If you knew a train was going to derail, you wouldn't get on it. You'd try to warn people."

"Okay, point taken," said Isabelle. "But how does knowing where smoke from a forest fire is going to go change what you'd do? You couldn't change the jet stream, could you?"

Now she looked worried. What horrific new technology had been created that could change the course of the atmosphere itself?

Gamache shook his head. "I don't know."

He seemed to be saying that a lot lately. Was admitting ignorance really the beginning of wisdom, or prelude to disaster?

"General Whitehead seemed to think that somehow FEDS was an incredibly powerful tool," said Beauvoir. "But I can't see how. Useful, maybe, but powerful?"

"There must be more," said Gamache. "He must've told you more."

"He did. He said he was afraid of what happens when this"—he picked up his glass of water—"runs out. What?"

Gamache was staring at the glass, his mouth partly open, though he did not seem to be breathing.

"Water." Now he looked at them, his two most trusted colleagues. "What happens when water runs out? That's what he said?"

Beauvoir nodded. "What is it?"

"Nothing good," said Armand. "That's the answer."

CHAPTER 18

⌒

"B ert Whitehead knows, or suspects, something," said Armand.

"If he does, the General wasn't going to tell me," Beauvoir said. "He expected you, *patron*."

"I can't cross the border," said Gamache. "I don't want any trail, any way for my movements to be tracked. And he can't come up here for the same reason."

How to meet in person without either of them crossing the border?

He was quiet for a moment. "There is one way."

He sent an invitation to the chair of the Joint Chiefs. Bert Whitehead answered almost immediately. He was obviously expecting a message from the Chief Inspector. Though perhaps not this.

A ticket, Armand? You want me to see a play about someone named Billy Bishop? Whitehead wrote.

So, you know about Napoleon, but not Billy Bishop?

Well, Napoleon was the Emperor of France and I don't think your Mr. Bishop was.

Come to the play and find out, my friend, wrote Armand. *It's a musical. I know you like them.*

Even though they were using the secure messaging app, they were both being cautious. Keeping it light.

Armand stared at the three dots, undulating.

And finally: *You're wrong, Armand. I don't like musicals.*

Armand's brows dropped in surprise. Bert was refusing?

I think you'll like this one, he pounded out. *It's very catchy.* He didn't dare say more.

I understand. I just can't make it.

For God's sake, Bert— But before he could write more, the connection was lost. Bert Whitehead had hung up.

Armand went online, ordered tickets, and sent one to General Whitehead.

He'll show, thought Armand.

Yvette Nichol was struggling with the laptop, unable to get into it.

"Take a break," said Gamache from the door into the study.

"No, not yet."

"Take a break, Agent Nichol," Gamache repeated, making it clear this was not a suggestion.

Without waiting to see if she obeyed, he put on his field coat and called the dogs, and Gracie. Then Gamache, Lacoste, and Beauvoir walked slowly around the village green. The sun had set without them noticing. The wind had picked up.

It was an unpredictable season. Anything could be coming their way.

They walked in silence, breathing in the fresh air, feeling the bracing cold against their cheeks. Each lost to their own thoughts. Behind them they heard the galumphing steps of Yvette Nichol as she ran to catch up.

"I can't—" she began, before the Chief Inspector stopped her.

"You're not alone," he said softly, and held her worried gaze. "None of us is making headway. That's why we're out here. To clear our heads and do something useful." He picked up the slimy orange tennis ball Henri had dropped at his feet and gave it to her.

She made a face, tossed it, then wiped her hands over her jeans.

The dogs, and Gracie, ran after it, joyous.

If this is useful, we're doomed.

And yet she found herself smiling. She looked at Gamache, then over to Beauvoir and Lacoste, all watching the romping animals. All smiling.

Twice around the green, and then they all veered off to the bistro for drinks and an early dinner. Clara, Myrna, and Reine-Marie were already there.

Reine-Marie had met her husband on his return and seen that now familiar expression as he once again strained to understand what she said.

She hugged him and silently hoped that flight had been worth it. And it might have been. She'd also seen the laptop.

Nichol pulled up a chair next to Ruth.

"I see they're down to scraping the bottom of the barrel," said the old poet.

"Are you still alive?" asked Nichol.

"She's lost the will to die," said Gabri, joining them.

"I was talking to the duck," said Nichol.

As they drank their wine and Pepsi and hot chocolate and put in their orders for dinner, Ruth studied Yvette Nichol. Who was studying Gamache. Who was looking at the pitcher of water on the table.

"What're you thinking?" Ruth asked Yvette.

"That he's aged since I last saw him. More lines down his face."

"He claims they're laugh lines," said Ruth.

"Nothing's that funny."

Ruth let out a cackle and touched the young officer's arm. "We've missed you."

"You might've, but they haven't."

Ruth looked at the other Sûreté officers, then back at Nichol. "You wouldn't be here if they didn't want you."

"I came down on my own. They didn't ask."

"But you're still here. Clearly they need you."

"Sure," said Nichol, taking a slab of smoked trout and putting it on pumpernickel. "They need me, but they don't like me."

"Is that important?"

Nichol studied the elderly woman, then looked at the others, so comfortable with each other. "Even you know it is." Then she looked out the mullioned window to the village beyond, and the bright orange ball sitting among the leaves on the green.

"*This rock is Eden*," said Ruth quietly. "*Shipwreck here.*"

"One of yours?"

"Auden."

"My luck to shipwreck on Gilligan's Island."

Ruth wasn't fooled. She'd seen the yearning on that young face. Heard it in her voice. "We all shipwrecked here. Don't look now, but I think you're heading for the shallows."

Ruth cocked her head toward where Chief Inspector Gamache was looking at Yvette. And smiling.

This rock is Eden.

After dinner, Armand and Jean-Guy drove the hour to the theater. There they sat, in the dark, Jean-Guy watching the actors on stage. Armand watching the door. But no one joined them.

When it was over, they drove home. In silence.

Once back, Armand went online again, ordered tickets again, and sent one to Bert Whitehead. Again. Then he went to bed.

Yvette Nichol accepted the Gamaches' offer to stay the night.

After borrowing what she needed from Madame Gamache, she crawled into bed, the cool sheets warming around her small body. She drifted off to the soft murmur of the others, Walton-like, wishing each other good night, and awoke a few hours later to the sound of sleet hitting the windows. It was two thirty in the morning.

Unable to go back to sleep, she went down to the study and worked some more on the laptop, knowing that whatever was in there was vital. Once again unable to make headway, she was about to return to bed when she noticed, through the squalls outside, a light. Up the hill.

At the church.

Putting on boots, a heavy coat, and a pink tuque she found in the closet, Yvette Nichol bent into the wind and sleet and wet snow—and was that freezing rain?—and plodded up to St. Thomas's.

"Chief Inspector?"

He was sitting in a preformed plastic chair in the basement and staring at the wall. Actually, at a map of Québec.

Reaching out, she touched his shoulder, then leaped back when he abruptly stood up and wheeled around, sending the chair flying and bracing for a fight. It took just an instant for him to realize who it was, but it was terrifying to Nichol. She'd seen him in action before, and was always surprised at the rapidity of his reactions and ferocity of his fight instinct.

He dropped his hands to his sides. "What're you doing here?"

"I saw the light."

His face broke into a smile, and he wondered if she knew how that sounded, standing as she was in church. He resisted saying, *Hallelujah*. But only just.

"Couldn't sleep." She'd spoken directly to him, enunciating carefully. Her father was losing his hearing. She recognized the signs.

Without being invited, she stepped forward and looked at the map, then turned to him. "What's so special about this?"

"It belonged to Charles Langlois." While his hearing had improved greatly, clearly that plane trip had set it back. "He hid it."

"Why?"

"We think because of this." Gamache put his finger on the lake. "It's the last place he visited before being killed. It's where we found his laptop."

Now they stood side by side.

"'What happens when the water runs out?'" said Nichol. "Isn't that what your friend in the States said? And you said, 'Nothing good.' But it won't run out. How can it? Look how much we have."

It's what Armand had been doing. Staring at the amount of blue in the map. Indicating water. Freshwater lakes, rivers, streams, reservoirs. The area to the north of the St. Lawrence River was almost more water than land.

So what did Bert Whitehead mean? Armand wondered. That was the first question he would ask the head of the Joint Chiefs of Staff when they met that evening.

He'll show. He must... He must.

The weather wasn't helping. But Gamache would snowshoe to their rendezvous if he had to. He suspected Bert had the answers they needed. Or at least significant parts.

Nichol was right, of course. Unless there was some sort of cosmic, or seismic, catastrophe heading their way, there was no way Canada would run out of water. There were droughts, especially out West, but there was still far more fresh water than almost any other nation enjoyed.

But if it did run out? What then?

What happened to a country that ran out of the most precious of resources? The only thing vital to life on earth, or anywhere. Wasn't that what astronomers looked for in surveys of distant planets? Signs of water. Without it, there would be no sign of life.

After a while Yvette Nichol cocked her head to one side and stepped closer to the map.

"What is it?" asked Gamache. But she was silent, staring at the lake he'd indicated.

"I'm just wondering…" She continued to stare, then turned to him so he could understand what she was saying. "Can I take a photo of the lake?"

"I'd rather you didn't." He himself had taken a close-up of the numbers and symbols on that last lake and sent it to Shona Dorion, asking if she could figure out what they meant. But there was no way for her to tell where they were from.

"Don't you see, *patron?* They're the right length for a password."

His eyes opened wide and he whispered, "Well, I'll be damned."

CHAPTER 19

"Well, fuck me," whispered Jean-Guy, staring at the laptop, as Nichol entered the numbers and symbols. "Excuse my English."

He was already awake when Armand and Nichol arrived home, dripping wet. It was still dark, not yet six in the morning, but he too had seen the light at the church and was preparing to join them when they returned. Fortunately, he'd put on the percolator and lit the woodstove in the kitchen.

Dropping her sodden coat on the wood floor for Armand to pick up, Nichol went straight into the study, sat down, and put in the numbers while the others watched.

Please God, please God, pl—

"*Patron!*"

She was so focused she didn't realize he was standing behind her, gripping the back of the chair.

"What is it?" Reine-Marie asked. Awoken by the sounds downstairs, she'd joined them in her housecoat and slippers.

Henri, Fred, and Gracie bounded in behind her, tails wagging. Had the others had tails, they'd have been wagging too.

"You did it," said Jean-Guy.

"Nichol did it," said Armand. "We had the code all along. It was one of the string of numbers and symbols Charles had written on the map."

Files were flashing up on the screen.

"Damn. They're encrypted. *Merde,*" Nichol whispered.

"All of them?" Gamache asked, looking at the labels Charles Langlois had put on his files.

Lakes. Rivers. Treatment Plants. Water Sheds.

She clicked on the one labeled *Poisoning.*

173

"Look." Sure enough, all they saw was gibberish. "We need the code."

"Leave it," said Gamache. "It's not important."

She turned to glare at him. "Don't you think the *Poisoning* file could be important?"

"No. We've gone beyond that. And I doubt he'd label it so blatantly. It's a ruse, a time waster. Charles was smart. He wanted anyone who found this and broke in to spend precious time on nothing. I'll bet whatever's in there is nonsense, maybe even misdirection. Open this one."

He pointed to *Water Sheds*.

"*Patron*—" Lacoste began.

The commotion downstairs, and the smell of coffee, had dragged her up from a dream about being chased by a huge root that looked like Ruth. A Québécoise trying to pronounce the English "Ruth" would almost always say "Root." It made a sort of warped sense. As much as any dream about an animated tree could.

"Open it," commanded Gamache.

"Why that one?" Jean-Guy asked.

"Because it's misspelled," said Armand.

"'Watershed.' It's right, no?" said Isabelle.

"No," said Jean-Guy. "He labeled it as two words. *Water Shed*. As a biologist Charles would know it's a single word."

"He wants you to notice it," said Reine-Marie.

"Wait," said Jean-Guy as Nichol, huffing her disdain, moved the cursor down.

"What now?"

"Could he have sabotaged his files?" asked Jean-Guy. "Maybe by clicking on it, a virus will be released."

They looked at each other. It was possible.

"I think if he was going to do it, it would have been when we clicked on *Poisoning*," said Armand. "We have no choice. Do it."

A watershed, he knew, was a divide, a place where fresh water changed direction. But it was more than that. It was an expression. A watershed moment was when a decision needed to be made that changed everything. It was a turning point.

They were, he knew, at a watershed.

With a less-than-respectful snort, Yvette Nichol double-clicked on the file.

It opened.

Things were moving quickly now.

Isabelle Lacoste drove to Ottawa through the sleet, with Gamache in the passenger's seat, where he was free to send and receive messages. Or just stare out the window at the worsening weather. And think.

He'd prodded his contact at the Canadian Security Intelligence Service for information on the third set of prints they'd lifted off the laptop. For some reason it was taking time. He asked her to copy Beauvoir and Lacoste on the findings.

He'd also written to Shona Dorion to let her know she did not have to pursue the meaning of the string of numbers and symbols Langlois had written on his map. They now knew it was a passcode. He did not say to what.

He hadn't heard back from her but wasn't worried. Given what the young woman thought of him, he suspected the next thing he'd hear would be some shouted insult at the next news conference. Or when she published the evidence he'd given her, evidence that would almost certainly ruin him.

But he couldn't worry about that now.

The first message he'd sent that morning after seeing the *Water Shed* file wasn't to her. Marked *urgent*, he'd hit send on a secure text to James Woodford's office asking for a meeting ASAP.

While the young journalist hadn't replied, the Prime Minister of Canada had.

A meeting was set up on Parliament Hill for eight thirty a.m.

It was time to talk.

He'd also sent an update to Bert Whitehead and ended it by saying he'd see him that evening. But there was no reply.

He'll show now, thought Armand as he stared out the window at the snow and sleet. *He has to.*

They'd taken Nichol's car, the battered one belonging to her father, since neither it nor the plates would be clocked. Now, on the slippery road, both Gamache and Lacoste were wondering if that had been the very best decision.

"The tires are bald," said Lacoste, working to keep the old car in its lane.

While they slipped and slid their way to the nation's capital, Jean-Guy sat beside Yvette Nichol in the study, both working on their laptops, chasing down what Charles Langlois had left behind.

The *Water Shed* file contained another series of numbers.

"They're IP addresses," said Nichol.

"Yes, I know."

"They go to the dark web." Nichol could not contain her excitement. "To .onion sites."

"Yes, I know."

Most Sûreté investigators were familiar with those sites. Instead of .com or .ca, the dark web masters had created another layer. Actually layers. Like an onion. And now the two investigators found themselves diving into the deepest caverns of the web.

Where the nuts lived.

Now Jean-Guy sat back, his eyes wide. Hidden within those layers he'd found a name. Repeated. *James Woodford.*

"Chief Inspector." Woodford rose and came out from behind his desk, his hand extended.

"Mr. Prime Minister. May I introduce Inspector Isabelle Lacoste. She shares second-in-command duties."

"Inspector. I've heard about you, of course. It's an honor."

"And for me, *Monsieur le Premier Ministre.*"

Armand studied the carpet and barely suppressed a grin. For much of the trip up Lacoste had babbled. Her way of dealing with the strain of driving through sleet that kept trying to tug them off the road. While Gamache had thought about their upcoming meeting, Lacoste had railed against politicians.

Normally an optimist, her one area of cynicism was politics. She'd seen too much, and the recent events had only served to solidify her opinion.

But now, in the presence of James Woodford, she was practically swooning.

It was not that he was especially handsome, nor was it some magnetism. Not a force of personality or some shining aura. It was, Gamache could see, just the opposite. The very lack of pretense made him unique, and accessible. Relatable and likable in a strangely gentle but compelling way.

He seemed completely genuine in being pleased, even humbled, to meet this officer much decorated for her valor.

"I don't suppose I can convince you to move to Ottawa and join my team?" he said to Lacoste.

"Now, sir," said Gamache with a smile. "No poaching."

"God knows I could use good people. I seem to have made a mess of those I've chosen to have around me. Not the best quality in a leader."

He'd had a carafe of coffee and some pastries brought in for them, and they helped themselves before sitting down again.

"Tell me, Chief Inspector, was Marcus Lauzon really behind the poisoning plot?"

Instead of answering directly, Gamache said, "Why do you ask? The courts found him guilty."

"True." Woodford cupped his warm mug in both hands, as though chilled, and looked at Gamache for a moment, trying to decide something. "I haven't actually known the man for a long time, but I struggle to believe it. That might be my own ego. An inability to admit I not only didn't see it, but actually elevated a mass murderer to Deputy PM." He shook his head. "I'm surprised the no-confidence vote in Parliament failed."

It was close, Gamache knew. Woodford had survived by only a few votes.

"Though you're not here to relitigate the Lauzon case." The Prime Minister looked at both officers. "What can I do for you?"

"Can we speak privately?"

Though surprised by this highly unusual request, Woodford only hesitated for a moment before asking his Chief of Staff to leave them. The woman did, though she'd been looking at Gamache as though he was not exactly an ally.

Then the Prime Minister leaned forward. "You have my complete attention, Chief Inspector."

"Holy shit," muttered Beauvoir. He'd eaten through two bagels with cream cheese and smoked salmon without even noticing.

"What?" asked Nichol.

"The crap that's on the web. I've visited some of these sites in the past, researching conspiracies for cases, but these really are nuts."

He thought of the young Sûreté officer who, in all sincerity, had believed the poisoning plot never happened. And that Lauzon was being railroaded by political enemies. That was crazy enough, but these sites Charles Langlois had listed went beyond nutty into demented.

"Yeah? Big surprise."

Despite what Gamache had said, she was still trying to get into the *Poisoning* file. Now she leaned over and read what was on Beauvoir's screen.

"Come on, no one's going to believe that." With a snort of laughter, she pointed to a post calling for an American patriot militia to be formed to protect the border against the imminent Canadian invasion.

"Has syphilis come back?" she asked.

It was right beside a report that Canada was training geese to bring down American planes.

Beauvoir was struggling to believe that people could be that stupid, that gullible. And that was one of the saner posts. Though clearly "sanity" had a whole other definition in this echo chamber.

Picking up on the previous thread, a few claimed Prime Minister Woodford had set the megafires as a first volley from Canada. An intentional attack. The worst since 9/11.

The prelude to an invasion.

Some were outright calling for his assassination. Jean-Guy forwarded that to Gamache.

"Why would we want to invade the States?" asked Nichol. "You'd think it'd be the other way around. We should put penicillin in their water. Would that be considered poison?"

"By this lot, yes. Apparently so is fluoride, which, according to one site, brainwashed people into voting for Obama."

"And made people support those damned equal rights. Reproductive rights. Immigration. Environmental protection. Ruining our lives," said Nichol. "Fucking fluoride."

Jean-Guy slid her a look, hoping to God she was kidding. But it was hard to tell. Yvette Nichol also had layers within layers.

"Before we begin, I have some news," said Gamache.

They'd taken armchairs in the comfortable seating area.

"I can see by your face it's not that you've won the lottery," said Woodford. "Or, better still, that I have."

"*Non.*" Gamache turned to Lacoste.

"We've found the body of Frederick Castonguay," she said.

"Who?"

"Jeanne Caron's executive assistant."

"That young man at the desk outside her office?"

"*Oui,*" said Gamache.

"An accident? No, of course not. You wouldn't be here if it was. He was murdered."

"Shot in the head and buried in a shallow grave," said Lacoste.

Prime Minister Woodford's face had hardened. "An execution?"

"*Oui.*"

"Why?"

"We think Castonguay was looking for something," said Lacoste. "Something Charles Langlois hid."

"Langlois was the biologist who first alerted you to the poison plot."

"*Oui,*" said Gamache.

Woodford considered. "Did Castonguay find it?"

"*Non.* He was murdered before he could," said Lacoste.

"Do you know what it was?"

They'd reached the *moment de vérité.* On the way up, while Isabelle had struggled with the elements and babbled about politicians, Armand had contemplated how much to tell the Prime Minister.

"We do," he said. "It was Charles Langlois's laptop. We've been looking for it ourselves since all this began."

Now Woodford cocked his head, his intelligent eyes locking onto Armand's. "You know because you found it, didn't you?"

"*Oui.*"

"And?"

"If you'll allow me, I'll get to that in a moment. We believe Moretti was behind the murder."

"You 'believe,' but if it's an execution, isn't it obvious, Chief Inspector?"

"Well, sir, we still need evidence. Unfortunately, anyone can put a gun to someone's head and pull the trigger."

"Anyone?" Now Woodford smiled ruefully. "You run in strange circles, Chief Inspector."

"You know what I mean. It looks like a mob hit, but it could be a copycat, or done to implicate Moretti."

Prime Minister Woodford opened his mouth, but before he could say anything, Lacoste spoke.

"*Excusez-moi.*"

Her phone had vibrated with a message, as had Gamache's. He glanced at his, then nodded to Lacoste to take it. She stepped into a quiet corner. Woodford watched her, then turned back to Gamache.

"Where was Castonguay killed? If the Sûreté's involved, I'm assuming it's in Québec somewhere and outside of Montréal."

"True."

The PM waited for more, but Gamache was silent. So, he asked another question: "How did this Castonguay even know to look for the laptop?"

"Turns out he and Charles Langlois knew each other from school and met up again recently."

"Does Jeanne Caron know about the murder of her assistant?"

"I haven't told her."

Which was different, they both knew, than her not knowing. Woodford nodded his understanding.

"Why are you here, Chief Inspector? Not just to tell me about the tragic death of one of my people."

"I have reason to believe the attempt to poison Montréal's water was just the first step. A prelude," said Gamache.

Now Woodford sat back and stared. "If that's the prelude, what in the world is the main event?"

"It's not clear, but it seems to have something to do with water."

"Again? More poisoning?"

"Possibly, but I don't think so."

"Can you explain?"

"No, not really, not yet."

"Come on, Gamache. You can't walk in here and tell me, the Prime Minister, that there might be a catastrophic attack on the population without giving me more. What am I supposed to do with that?"

Gamache noticed movement in his peripheral vision and turned.

Isabelle Lacoste was holding out her phone. "*Désolée, patron.*"

He took it, read the message; then, his face neutral, he handed the phone back to her. "*Merci.*"

"Something's happened," said the Prime Minister, searching their faces.

"We discovered three sets of prints on the laptop. Two were easy to identify: Charles Langlois's and Jeanne Caron's. We just identified the last set. I think what I'm about to say won't come as a surprise. They're yours. Perhaps, sir, you can explain."

The warmth had drained from Gamache's voice.

Now James Woodford cocked his head and smiled. "You aren't thinking I'm the Black Wolf, are you?"

"How do you know that term?"

Woodford looked at Lacoste, then back to Gamache. "Can we speak in private?"

"Absolutely not. How do you know about the Black Wolf?"

"Jeanne Caron told me. She said it was your code for whoever's behind the poisoning plot. I'm assuming you mean Marcus Lauzon."

"You've been in touch with Madame Caron recently, then?"

"Yes." Like Gamache, his eyes, his expression, his entire posture had hardened. The temperature inside the office had plunged. Sleet was possible... "You don't really expect me to be content in my ignorance? I learned after Lauzon was exposed that ignorance is not, in fact, bliss. I wanted to hear directly from her all she knew."

"And what has she told you?"

"Frankly? Nothing useful. Nothing I hadn't already read in reports, including yours. Certainly nothing about another attack. If you know more, you need to tell me. Now."

But Gamache remained focused on his own line of questioning. "How did your prints get on Charles Langlois's laptop? A computer he hid just before he was murdered."

"Are you interrogating me, Chief Inspector?"

"We're having a conversation, a useful and mutual exchange of information, as a defense against ignorance."

Woodford stared at him, making up his mind. "Jeanne Caron and

Charles Langlois came to see me shortly before he was murdered. They had suspicions. To be honest, I never trusted, never liked Madame Caron. She's a walking bag of dirty tricks. Still is, as far as I know. But the biologist seemed to trust her."

"You feigned ignorance when I first mentioned Frederick Castonguay. As Caron's assistant, you must have known him."

Gamache knew that one skill any ambitious politician developed was a memory for faces and names. The PM could not fail to know a bureaucrat that close to his own office. Never mind one mentioned more than once in subsequent investigations.

"I'm sorry about that. It's a habit I learned in the army. To gather and hold information close. To not always be completely transparent." He again studied Gamache. "I suspect we have that in common."

"It would be helpful, sir, if you could bring yourself to be less opaque. Can you tell me about that meeting?"

"Langlois had found some sort of evidence of a possible attack. He first took it to Caron, and after doing some investigating herself, they came to me. Most of it seemed gibberish. Dark web crap. It amounted to some marginal site hinting at a terrorist attack to do with our water. By the way, the same site also claimed Canada was salting the clouds so that acid rain would melt American cities."

"In fact, what he'd found were references to the poisoning of Montréal's drinking water."

"In retrospect, yes."

"And you did nothing?"

Prime Minister Woodford shifted in his chair, recrossing his legs.

"What was I supposed to do, Chief Inspector? Like you, I need evidence before I act, and there was none. Just some vague references to threats. I get them by the truckload every day. We can't react to every one of them. What's that expression? 'Saving our powder.' I told them to come back when they had proof. And now you say something else is planned. But like them, you have no proof."

It was Gamache's turn to shift in his seat. "True. But we do have enough circumstantial evidence to warrant investigation. Including the murder of Frederick Castonguay."

Isabelle, listening and watching, noticed that the Chief Inspector hadn't told the PM about Charles's map. Or his suspicions about the second notebook.

Woodford was shaking his head. "So, in other words, you have nothing. Just, what? A feeling? An inkling?"

"A lifetime of experience. Hard-won. It's not over. Not by a long shot. You saved your powder once, and by that you mean power, and tens of thousands almost died. When exactly do you plan to use it?"

Gamache had crossed a line, and all three knew it. Prime Minister Woodford colored but managed to keep his temper.

"What is it you expect me to do, Chief Inspector?"

"I'm not asking for any action. You're right, until we know what's planned, there's nothing to do."

"Then why are you here?"

"To warn you. To ask you to be vigilant. To see if you've heard any rumblings, any whispers." Gamache took a deep breath and exhaled. "Anything at all. Something's stirring. Something that seems to involve you."

"How so?"

"Some of the posts we found on the dark web are saying you set the forest fires on purpose. They're calling for your assassination."

"God, just what I need. More loons making up shit. And why would I set those fires? They're a disaster. Never mind the environmental catastrophe, but the other issue no one appreciates is the cost of fighting them. And we all know there'll be more, if not this year or next, then eventually." He looked out the window, and the others followed his gaze. Sleet was drumming against it. He brought his attention back to the room. "And now those fucking corporations want me to give them compensation for broken illegal contracts. And the American government's hinting they also want compensation for all the ash." Prime Minister Woodford held up his hands. "Forgive me. I asked for the job. You're not here to listen to my problems."

Gamache smiled. "I'm afraid we're just adding to them. *Pardon*, I need to take this."

He walked a few steps away to take the call, leaving Lacoste and the Prime Minister to stare at each other.

"Tell me, Inspector, do you really believe something else, something worse, is about to happen?"

"I do, sir. I know this must be incredibly frustrating for you, to have us come here but without anything specific."

"No, no. Despite what I said, I do appreciate it. I need to know. Your Chief is right. I made the terrible mistake once of ignoring a warning. I won't do it again."

"That was Inspector Beauvoir," said Gamache, slipping his phone back into his jacket pocket. "He's going through the links on Langlois's laptop, and one constant is a conspiracy theory that's gaining traction."

"What is it now?"

"That Canada is about to attack the US."

That brought the conversation to a standstill.

Prime Minister Woodford stared from one to the other, resting his eyes finally on Gamache.

"So?"

It was not the reaction Armand expected. "So? You aren't surprised?"

Now Woodford laughed. "I'm sorry, but you should sit there for an hour"—he pointed to his desk—"and you'd see that nothing is surprising. My Chief of Staff came to me just yesterday with a site devoted to proving I'm an alien. An extraterrestrial. I kid you not. There are more than twelve thousand followers. Twelve thousand. Now, not all believe I came from some unfriendly planet, but if even one does..." He shook his head. "I can't be worried about the nutcases. I wouldn't get anything done."

"Still—"

"Yes, I know. It's not generally the sane ones who take potshots."

"Not just potshots."

"Not to worry, Chief Inspector. Everything's passed along to the RCMP, even the ludicrous ones."

Politics was not just becoming more polarized, it was far more dangerous, with people on all sides giving themselves permission to act in the most horrific ways. Ways that their grandparents would never recognize or approve of. That they themselves would not have approved of just a few years ago. All in the name of patriotism. A word, a concept, that had become weaponized, even toxic.

"So now, on top of all our environmental troubles, I'm supposed to be organizing an armed attack to take over the United States? Frankly, at this point we couldn't invade Luxembourg and win. That's just between us."

"The people of Luxembourg will never hear it from me," said Gamache.

The Prime Minister smiled wearily. It wasn't yet nine a.m., and he seemed spent.

"The problem isn't whether that's planned," said Gamache, feeling bad that he needed to keep pushing. "It's that more and more people seem to believe it. Apparently, militias are being formed."

"What? Really? To repel our attack? Let them play soldier as long as they don't hurt any of our people."

"Or you. Those sites will also be passed along to the RCMP and our intelligence services, and I'll make sure the FBI and Homeland Security in the US get them. Most of these .onion sites seem to originate in the US, though it's possible that's just a port of convenience."

"Like a flag of convenience for ships, to mask where they actually come from? I haven't heard about internet ports of convenience."

"I just made it up."

Now Woodford really did laugh. "Well, I'd copyright that if I were you. Please tell me you made up the rest of it too."

Gamache shook his head, then looked about to say something.

"What is it, Chief Inspector? Out with it. Our time is short."

"Have you or your intelligence people heard anything out of the US about a thing called FEDS?"

"That's the Fire Event Detection Suite. FEDS. Yes, I know about it, but it's not really an intelligence issue, is it, or a big secret? It's about tracking ash from megafires. Our meteorologists have access to FEDS, but after an initial flutter of excitement they had to admit it didn't have many practical applications. It's not like it can stop or even predict a fire. Though it is useful, I guess, in telling us where the ash will go. To warn the population. But not helpful stopping it."

"Then why are we being warned about it?"

"We are? Warned? About FEDS?" Prime Minister Woodford looked confused. "In those files you found?"

Gamache chose not to tell him the FEDS references came from both

General Whitehead and Marcus Lauzon. Instead, he waited for the PM to continue.

"I can't think why a detection system could be important, but you seem to think it is."

"Can you put me in touch with the Chief Meteorologist?"

"Absolutely. Make sure you have plenty of time. She loves to talk. Apparently she has a new dog. A golden retriever. How do I know that? She sends me photos. Every day. Is there anything else? I'm sorry, but I have a meeting to chair."

He got up, as did Lacoste and Gamache. At the door, Gamache chose to stand right in front of the handle, so the PM couldn't reach it.

"What happens, sir, when the water runs out?"

"I beg your pardon."

"Water. What happens to a country if it runs out?"

"Come on, Chief Inspector, that's a ridiculous question. Something else from those dark web sites? Now our water's drying up? Is that why we need to invade the States?"

He was trying to get at the door handle, but Gamache stood still, refusing to move out of the way, or answer.

Woodford finally gave up. "Common sense will answer that question. Without water there's drought, then famine, then war, then death. The UN just issued a warning about imminent wars for resources in drought-stricken areas of the world. You haven't been watching those disaster movies, Chief Inspector? Spaceships going to distant planets because Earth is dying? Jeez, maybe my home world can welcome the earthlings." It was said without humor. "Why're you asking this?"

Still the Chief Inspector refused to answer, or budge.

"Listen," the Prime Minister exhaled in exasperation. "Canada will never run out of fresh water, if that's what you're worried about. We're one of the lucky ones. What used to be laughed at, our vast forests and waterways, what was considered wilderness and dismissed as less important than manufacturing, has now become precious. Envied. Can we do a better job of protecting our resources? Absolutely. I campaigned on that platform and got huge pushback from corporations. But the fact is, unlike most of the world, we're blessed with more natural resources than we can possibly screw up. So that's one worry you can put out of your mind. We will never have to find out what happens when the water runs out."

Gamache nodded, then put out his hand. "Thank you for your time. I wish we could have brought good news."

"That's okay. No one ever does. But please, next time be more specific."

Woodford shook both their hands and finally managed to open the door. "I'm sorry about lecturing you about my stand on the environment. I'm afraid I'm never far from my soapbox. I think people have stopped inviting me to parties." Now he smiled. "So that's one good thing."

Gamache also smiled. "Thank you for seeing us. Please don't say anything to your colleagues about this just yet."

"About what? I'm more in the dark now than ever. I just hope you get that bastard Moretti."

"And please, be vigilant. Watch yourself."

"*Merci.*" As the door closed, Prime Minister Woodford leaned against it. "Oh, shit," he whispered.

CHAPTER 20

"Do you believe him?" Lacoste asked as they drove back.

The roads were even worse now. The sleet had turned to snow that wanted only one thing: to tug vehicles into a ditch, or a tree, or each other.

Sûreté SUVs were patrolling, and tow trucks were assisting cars that had slid off the road. Flares marked accidents up and down the highway. It was no use stopping to help. The highway cops had it under control. Besides, in trying to stop, they'd almost certainly make it worse.

Lacoste's knuckles were white on the steering wheel, and her lips were compressed as she silently cursed Nichol and her father for the bald tires. And herself for suggesting they take this car and not Clara's. Or Myrna's or—

"Do you?" Gamache asked.

"Believe the Prime Minister? I want to. Does it seem strange to you, *patron*, that the Prime Minister of Canada knows about FEDS? An obscure technology to track ash? A technology he admits is interesting but essentially useless."

"That did occur to me. It also seems odd that he's in daily contact with the Chief Meteorologist."

"Well, we are a nation addicted to the weather. It's our main topic of conversation."

He gave a grunt of laughter. It was true.

"I noticed you didn't tell him about being in touch with General Whitehead."

"*Non.*"

"Or the map."

"*Non.*"

She took her eyes off the road for a second to look at Gamache. "You don't really think we're about to attack the US, do you?"

He gave one quick burst of laughter and looked at her. "No, I don't. Do you?"

She laughed now too, her sharp eyes back on the road. "*Non.* But it might not be an official, overt invasion. Maybe it's by some marginal militia group. Could that be what Moretti's involved in?"

"A sort of Canadian Bay of Pigs?"

"A what?"

"An American misadventure in the '60s, using the Cuban mafia to reclaim Cuba from the communists."

"It's still communist. I take it the plan didn't work."

She'd been to Cuba a few times on vacation. Loved the people, the music, the culture. The level of education and literacy. Not so much the poverty and the fact the citizens were prisoners on their little island.

"Foolish scheme to begin with. A debacle." Still, it got him thinking.

They both knew that the tendrils of organized crime reached deep into legitimate business, corporations willing to fork out billions to further their own needs. On top of that, the mafia had its fangs in the judiciary, the armed forces, powerful interest groups, including the media, not to mention elected officials and the civil service. On both sides of the border.

So that begged the question, why would they need an armed invasion? Didn't they already have enough control?

Talk of an invasion was ridiculous, a smoke screen.

There was something else planned. Canada attacking the US would be like that animated short "Bambi Meets Godzilla." Bambi did not fare well.

Though he now spent a few kilometers wondering what would happen if an invasion was launched. Not by the official armed forces, but some ragtag militia. Or maybe not so ragtag. Trained and organized by the Montréal mafia, in collaboration with the Five Families, and God knew who else they could pull in. Far-right militia? Former special ops? Mercenaries? Commandos. Funded with cartel drug money, prostitution, gambling, arms sales, and by any third parties or countries with an interest in destabilizing the US, even momentarily.

It was a long list.

If he were in charge of the attack, how would he go about it? First, a covert war. Create a common enemy. Subvert the media. Form their own outlets, broadcast media, newspapers, social media platforms, to spread lies. Scare the population into believing their way of life, their very lives, were threatened. Condition them. Groom them. Then, when the moment was right, get rid of any leader likely to oppose them and install a dummy regime, including a charismatic but not overly bright bully sold as a strong leader who could bring order to chaos.

The UN would be powerless, of course. Paralyzed by fear and endless debate and vetoes.

Yes, he thought as they slid down the highway, it could be done. But it would take years of preparation, of groundwork, of placing conspirators in key roles.

Even then it would almost certainly fail. Just one thing needed to go wrong. And there was a fair chance more than one element would immediately go pear-shaped.

Another Bay of Pigs. Equally ill-advised. He could not see any tactician agreeing to lead such a scheme. Not even Napoleon could pull it off.

Napoleon...

Still, even a failed attempt would throw both countries into chaos, even momentarily. Perhaps just long enough for a regime change. And that could lead to—

"A watershed," he muttered.

"What was that, *patron?*"

"Nothing. Just imagining..."

Though what he could not imagine was why Canada would want, or need, to take over the United States. It made more sense the other way around. For the US to invade Canada. Now that would be relatively easy. As the PM implied, Luxembourg could probably do it.

But again, why bother?

No, all this talk of invasion was misdirection. What they were dealing with was something to do with water. And maybe fire. FEDS.

He stared out the window at the first snow of the year and tried to see clearly.

That night Jean-Guy again drove him to the theater. Snow was still falling, but lighter. Just fluffy flurries now. The roads were clear, having been plowed and sanded and salted.

They took Myrna's all-wheel drive vehicle this time.

The volunteer at the door looked perplexed when they handed her their tickets. She'd been on the night before when the same two men had come to the show.

She almost asked, but seeing their grim faces, she decided best to just rip the tickets in half, hand them back, and leave it at that.

"He's not coming, *patron*," whispered Beauvoir, two-thirds of the way through.

Gamache took a deep breath but said nothing. He waited until the end. Until the scattered applause had died and the cast had left the stage. Until the lights had come up and there was the sound of a vacuum cleaner.

Until the usher approached, asking them to leave.

And they did, Jean-Guy walking beside Armand and silently cursing Whitehead.

"Let me call the General," said Jean-Guy over coffee the next morning. They were alone in the kitchen. "Better still, I can go back to DC, see him in person."

"Why?" asked Armand.

"You know why. To convince him to come up, to see you." Beauvoir felt the sting of insult. That Chief Inspector Gamache should sit for two nights running, like some heartsick teen hoping his date showed.

It had broken Jean-Guy's heart to see Gamache walking slowly back to the car. It was humiliating. If nothing else, Beauvoir wanted to give the General a piece of his mind.

"I didn't really expect him to show," admitted Armand.

"Why not?"

"You do know what I was asking him to do," said Armand, getting up.

"But you sent him another ticket for tonight."

"Never give up hope. Isabelle?" he called.

"Ready, *patron*," came the reply from the study. "She'll meet me at headquarters."

"*Bon*." He looked at his watch. Just enough time to get to his own appointment in Montréal.

Snow, not thick but heavy, coated the village. In the early-morning light Three Pines and the surrounding forest sparkled. The snow, fresh and bright, lay on the ground, on the roofs, on the cars. The trees were bowed and bent close to breaking under the weight of it.

All around the village residents were swatting branches with brooms to knock the snow off the limbs before they broke. As they did, the branches sprang back, sending puffs of snow into the air, so that the village looked like a series of very small blizzards.

On his way to the car Armand took hold of a large pine branch that was bowed to the ground and about to break. When he gave it a yank, it detached so quickly it dumped snow all over him.

"How could you not see that coming?" laughed Reine-Marie, using her broom to brush him off.

He smiled and thought, if it was the only thing he failed to see coming, it would be a good day.

A few minutes later Armand and Isabelle were heading into Montréal. Once in the city, Isabelle dropped him off on boulevard René-Lévesque for his meeting, while she continued on to Sûreté headquarters.

Armand stood on the pavement and tipped his head back, looking up at the thirteen saints standing on top of the magnificent Marie-Reine-du-Monde Cathedral.

This was where Reine-Marie had gotten her name. Her mother's water had broken while she took communion there. Because of that drama, the archbishop himself agreed to baptize the baby girl in the cathedral. Overwhelmed and nervous, her godmother, when asked the name of the child, had said "Reine-Marie" instead of "Marie-Reine." Her mother, also nervous, didn't notice until the holy water was already dribbling down her shrieking baby's head.

She decided, since that was the name God had heard, it was best to keep it.

Armand, while not a huge fan of organized religion, had affection for this church for that reason. He'd go there sometimes to get away from the turmoil of the great city. Sitting in a pew, he'd stare at the altar and imagine those events. Both, as it turned out, involved water.

As did his visit there today.

"God bless you," said the guard at the front door when he arrived. And seemed to mean it.

"And you," said Armand, smiling. And meant it.

At the top of the long aisle Armand, out of habit, genuflected. Huge seashell fonts with holy water were on either side. He did not dip his hand in. The only magic water he knew of had been spilled on the altar decades ago.

Armand took a seat in the front pew and noticed that someone had left their hat. Taking it off the hook, he saw it was a Canadiens de Montréal cap. He replaced it, grinning. Few were more religious these days than Habs fans.

He was, from what he could see, alone in the church. But not for long. A few minutes later he heard the heavy door at the entrance softly close. He did not turn.

"Armand. Shall we?"

The two moved to a more discreet pew, off to the right and hidden from the main body of the church. It was their regular meeting place.

The head of the Sûreté's Homicide division turned to the head of the Sûreté's Organized Crime division.

"What's this about, Evelyn?"

"Oh, for God's sake," muttered Beauvoir.

"What?" Nichol leaned over to look at his screen and started laughing. "That's adorable. Play it from the beginning."

Instead, he hit pause. On his screen was the frozen image of a golden retriever doing yoga with its owner.

"So, while I'm trying to track down whatever crisis we're facing, you're googling cute dog videos?"

"I am not. This was sent to me in a message from the Chief Meteorologist. I thought it was an answer to my question about FEDS."

"Maybe the dog's called Feds."

Jean-Guy sighed. Beside him, Henri's majestic ears were pointing so far forward they almost brushed the computer screen as he stared with adoration at the video.

Beauvoir went back to the text message, found Dr. Maybeck's phone number, and called her.

"Yes, Inspector. The Prime Minister has instructed me to cooperate completely. Did you get the video? I think that will be helpful."

"Of the dog doing yoga?"

There was a pause. "Ooops."

"Ooops" was never the thing a cop, a surgeon, or a pilot liked to hear or, worse, say.

"Attached the wrong one. I'll send the one about the Fire Event Detection Suite."

"Great, but in the meantime, can you just tell me about it? Its uses, both obvious and maybe not so obvious."

Whenever there was sensitive information to pass along, Gamache and Tardiff had long since realized, Sûreté HQ was not the place for it. So they came to the basilica, where they were almost guaranteed to be alone.

He'd heard nothing from her since their lunch on Sunday.

Chief Inspector Tardiff looked exhausted. Her hair needed a wash, her clothing was rumpled. Here was a once soignée woman near the breaking point. With energy enough to focus on only one thing. And personal hygiene was not it.

Now she ran her hands through her hair so that it stood on end.

"I read your report of the Castonguay murder in this morning's briefing notes, Armand. You were vague about it being a mafia hit. Thank you for that. I don't need the Super coming down on me, as though it was my fault. It's now obvious that Moretti's keeping things from me."

"What do you need from me?"

"I got a message from him today telling me to find out what the Sûreté knows about the Castonguay murder. You need to give me something. More than what was in your report. What was the kid looking for way up there?"

"We think it was Charles's laptop and maybe a map."

It was safe to let that much out since Moretti must know something was hidden up there. Why else send hitmen with Castonguay, and execute him when it couldn't be found?

Still, he wasn't going to tell Tardiff that they had both. He couldn't risk her telling Moretti.

"Why did Frederick Castonguay think they were there?" asked Tardiff.

"He and Langlois were old friends. Went to school together. Langlois must've told Castonguay to look at that lake."

Tardiff nodded, thinking. "Good, this is good. I can give this to Moretti."

"I'm a little worried that whoever went up there with him actually found it," said Gamache, feeling absolutely no discomfort at misleading his colleague.

Evelyn Tardiff was shaking her head. "*Non*. Moretti would've told me."

"Are you so sure? You just said he's holding information back. Maybe this's part of the test. To see what you'll pass along, when he already knows the answer."

Now she was considering. "Maybe. It would be like him."

"Or maybe whoever went up with Castonguay is playing a lone hand." Gamache watched her closely.

"Who?"

When Gamache didn't answer, she said, "It's possible it was made to look like a mob hit, but wasn't."

"But if it was?"

She turned in the pew to look at him. "Are you saying the New York mob sent their own people? Behind Moretti's back? That would be a declaration of war."

"Is it possible?"

Tardiff thought about it. "A few months ago I'd have said no, but Moretti's ambitious. The Five Families won't want him getting too powerful. With the recent arrests of Gambino associates, others are moving in. The Bonanno family in particular. They see their chance." Now she was essentially talking to herself. "If Moretti was looking to grab more territory, this would be the time. Maybe they want to cut him off at the knees."

With the mafia that was not simply an expression.

"And maybe Moretti knows it," said Gamache. "Could that be the war we're hearing about? The invasion? Not from the Canadian military, but an attempt by Moretti to take over the Five Families before they get him?"

She shook her head. "I can't see it. More likely the other way around. But even that's unlikely. Why would they?"

"Why would the mob want more control?" asked Armand, with a smile.

"You have no idea what the mob wants," she snapped. "Don't forget who you're talking to. You watch *The Godfather* or *Goodfellas* or *Omertà* and think you know. You know shit."

"Then tell me. What's going on? I told you about the laptop and the map. Now you have to give me something."

"Okay, you're right. It's just possible Moretti isn't telling me anything about Castonguay's murder because he doesn't know."

"So you do think the New York crime families came onto Moretti's territory and killed Frederick, without his permission," said Gamache.

She nodded, suddenly exhausted. "I think, judging by Moretti's reaction to the murder, that's possible. And if true, it's trouble. It's never good when the head of a crime family is worried."

"But you have no proof?"

"None."

"Then why are we here?"

"Because I do have something that might interest you."

She brought out her phone and showed him a series of surveillance photos. All of Moretti.

"We know most of his associates, but this person's new. Do you recognize her?"

Chief Inspector Tardiff zoomed in.

In her office at Sûreté headquarters, Isabelle Lacoste stepped forward and extended her hand.

"Madame Caron."

"Inspector."

Unlike some, Jeanne Caron did not appear disappointed that Chief Inspector Gamache himself wasn't there. In fact, she seemed relieved. Her unpleasant history with the head of homicide meant their interactions could be testy. And, as a result, their conversations mis-, or over-, interpreted.

"A former colleague in Ottawa said they saw you and the Chief Inspector in the Parliament Buildings yesterday."

The statement surprised Lacoste, but it was no use lying. "Yes, we were there."

"Why?"

Instead of answering, Isabelle said, "I have news."

"News that needs to be said in person." Caron held the officer's eyes. "I see. Last time the Chief Inspector and I spoke, he mentioned the possibility there was something else, something bigger planned. Have you discovered it?" There was a pause. "*Mais, non*, it's not that, is it? This is something else."

"Please." Lacoste waved her to a chair and sat across from her. "I asked you here because we've found the body of Frederick Castonguay."

There was a stunned silence before Caron asked, "In Parliament?"

At first Gamache thought the woman in the photos meeting with Moretti was Jeanne Caron, but then he looked more closely. "*Non*. I don't know her. Do you?"

"No. I was hoping…"

"May I have a copy of these?"

"*Oui*." She sent them to him. "Is there anything else you can tell me. Anything I can use with Moretti?"

He almost told her about FEDS, but decided to keep his own counsel, for now. Instead, he said, "*Non*, but I promise to update you on the Castonguay case whenever we have developments. Right now we're trying to track down the pilot who took them there."

"*Merci*." She got up.

Armand watched her leave, walking down the long center aisle, past the monumental paintings of missionaries converting grateful "Indians." "Savages" in the wilderness. Though judging by the actions of religions and governments, it was now clear who the savages really were. And that the wilderness wasn't limited to forests.

He looked down at the photos Tardiff had sent. The woman was unfamiliar, but there was no denying that Moretti knew her. And she knew him.

Armand forwarded them to Beauvoir and Lacoste. At the last minute he added Yvette Nichol. *Does this person with Don Moretti look familiar?*

Armand looked again at the paintings. Far from depicting acts of clerical heroism, they actually showed the nascent barbarism of the church in the so-called New World.

In a dry and parched land, where there is no water, Armand thought.

The Psalms, of course, meant it figuratively. Water being faith. But suppose Dom Philippe meant it literally? The Abbot of Saint-Gilbert-Entre-les-Loups had stood on the dock, looked out at the vast lake, and quoted that phrase from the Psalms just before he left the remote monastery. Never to return.

He'd been murdered shortly after, in the small church in Three Pines.

Armand closed his eyes. *In a dry and parched land . . .*

What happens when the water runs out?

"No, not in Parliament," said Isabelle Lacoste. "Frederick was in a shallow grave at a remote lake. Shot in the head. Execution style."

Jeanne Caron's eyes widened and there was the slightest intake of breath.

"He was murdered? By a lake?"

It seemed odd to mention the lake in the same breath as the killing, as though it was equally important.

"*Oui.*"

"The poor little shit. Why did they do this to him?"

"Who?"

"You said execution style. I don't think it was the fellow from the House of Commons food truck, do you?"

"We wondered if you might know."

"For God's sake, it's Moretti again. You know that. But why Frederick?"

"Could he have been working with them?"

"The Montréal mob? Are you kidding?" But then she paused. And finally shook her head. "*Non.* No way."

"Why not?"

"Because he was a coward. Great at filing, terrific at keeping my appointments in order. He was an officious little—" She stopped herself, remembering what had happened to him.

"Shit?" suggested Isabelle. "Why did you call him that?"

"That night, in the church in that little village—"

"Three Pines."

"Whatever. When they murdered my uncle and tried to kill me, Frederick got me meds, but then took off. Didn't even take me to a hospital. He was a coward."

"He could've driven off when he heard the shots, but he waited to see—"

"If I was dead?"

"If you needed help."

"Which I did. So why not take me to hospital? Never mind, you don't know."

But Lacoste did. At least, she knew what it was to lose your nerve. It happened to seasoned cops. To hardened veterans in battle. They suddenly broke. It was too much. They froze, or hid, or ran away. Not through cowardice. These were brave men and women. The fault lay in being asked to be superhuman. For far too long.

It happened to the best and the worst. Equally.

"But you're right. The fact he waited and drove me that far, and didn't leave me at the church or on some godforsaken back road to bleed to death, proves he wasn't working for the mob. They wanted me dead. He saved me, sorta. He was just some scared little shit in over his head. He would never align himself with the mob, and the mob wouldn't want someone so unpredictable."

Lacoste wasn't so sure. "You seemed surprised by the lake."

"I am. As far as I know, he'd never visited a lake in his life. If he didn't have asphalt under his feet, he got nervous. His family?"

"Has been told." Lacoste studied the older woman, who had once held so much power, and was now just another former civil servant living on a pension.

And she made up her mind.

"Chief Inspector Gamache and I went to Ottawa to talk to the Prime

Minister. To warn him. Just like you did, when you went there with Charles Langlois not long before he was killed."

"How do you know about that?"

"Was it supposed to be a secret?"

"No. At least, not now. We needed it to be secret at the time so that Lauzon wouldn't find out. Even then I had my suspicions."

"Did you pass them on to the PM?"

"About his Deputy PM? Not in so many words, but he's a smart man, he probably figured it out. After all, why would the Deputy PM's Chief of Staff go to him, and not Lauzon himself?"

"And Woodford didn't ask about Lauzon?"

"No. And even if he had, we had no proof of anything. It was a mutually frustrating meeting."

Not unlike the one they'd had with the PM, thought Lacoste.

"Still, I think he knew. Woodford's often underestimated," Caron was saying. "I think he likes it that way. And I think it's why the electorate like him. No chaos, no drama. He's like the college prof you always wanted. Someone who'd round your grade up."

It was, thought Lacoste, an interesting character study.

What had made Jeanne Caron so effective as the Deputy PM's Chief of Staff, and chief fixer, was her ability to accurately read people. And, as a result, see their weaknesses, their disappointments, their dreams and fantasies and fragile delusions.

It meant she could manipulate them. And did. And, if necessary, break them. And did. The only one she'd gotten wrong was Gamache, when she thought, more than a decade ago, that she could break him. That mistake, that effort, had repercussions to this day.

"Thank you for telling me in person about Frederick. He was a little shit, but he was my little shit. I liked him." She nodded, and the stuffing seemed to go out of her.

"That's not the only reason I asked you here. Why didn't you tell us about Frederick's friendship with Charles Langlois?"

"It didn't seem to matter. And they weren't really friends. They just met up again recently. Does it matter?"

Lacoste's phone dinged with a message from the Chief. She glanced down. "*Excusez-moi.*"

While Caron watched, slightly annoyed by the interruption, Isabelle scrolled through the photos the Chief had sent. Her brows had drawn together, then she shot off a reply. Hesitating for a moment, she decided to close her phone and put it on the table between them.

"You met Charles on one of your official visits to The Mission in Montréal."

Caron nodded and Isabelle continued.

"With Frederick's help you recruited him as a biologist, to look into your growing suspicion that your boss, Lauzon, was into something even worse than his normal payoffs and intimidation. Something to do with water security and Montréal."

"Yes, yes. I told you that at the time, and it came out in the trials."

"But without consulting you, Charles decided to volunteer at a nonprofit environmental group in Montréal, Action Québec Bleu, whose mandate is water security. Why didn't he tell you about that?"

"I guess because it was just a personal interest. That little group had nothing to do with the attacks. Why're you asking now? That's all in the past."

"As part of his work with AQB, he visited some remote lakes and took water samples."

"So?" But Jeanne Caron's clever mind did not let her down. "Lakes? One in particular?" When Lacoste was silent, she took the next leap. "Was that where Frederick's body was found? He was murdered at a lake Charles Langlois had visited?" It was said almost to herself. "So there must be something important about that lake."

"Your boss was paid tens of millions by major American corporations," said Lacoste, "to give them controlling interest in some Canadian primary industries. Logging. Mining. It was illegal. You helped with the deals and to launder that money."

"Some, true. But I didn't know about the biggest payoffs. The bribes I helped with came from Canadian companies to get lucrative government contracts. I knew nothing about the American ones. Those were worth billions, not millions."

Caron sounded annoyed at being cut out of the big payoffs.

There was, in fact, nothing that connected her to those huge bribes to her boss. What they didn't know at the time of the poisoning plot, had only just discovered, was that those massive payoffs had been laundered through a small, insignificant, easily overlooked, struggling nonprofit.

Action Québec Bleu.

And now there was one more thing that linked AQB to the poison attack and what might be happening next.

Chief Inspector Gamache had just stuffed a twenty-dollar bill into the offering box at the door to Marie-Reine-du-Monde when the message from Isabelle Lacoste arrived.

Woman with Moretti is Margaux Chalifoux, head of AQB.

It wasn't easy to surprise the head of homicide, but this message did just that. He stared at the message from Lacoste, then fired off a reply.

Ask Agent Fontaine to call me, please. Then pick me up at the basilica when you're finished with Caron.

He took a seat in the quiet cathedral, breathing in the musky, slightly cloying fragrance of a century's worth of incense. It smelled of guilt and sin and a promise of forgiveness and a place in heaven, if you ate fish on Fridays.

When the call came in, he gave Agent Fontaine her instructions.

Jeanne Caron put on her coat.

"You said that Frederick was shot in the back of the head. So, it would've been quick. He wouldn't have suffered."

"He didn't suffer."

Caron nodded, reached for the door handle, then turned back. "Thank you for that."

"For what?"

"The lie. I don't know why I even asked. We both know that while his death might've been instant and painless, the lead-up to the shot must have been ... harrowing. I know. I saw it."

For a split second Isabelle thought she was confessing that she'd been at Frederick's execution, then she realized Caron was referring to Gamache's.

Both men would have been kneeling. Hands tied behind their backs. Defenseless. Waiting. Praying perhaps. Heads pushed forward, the guns pressed to the base of their skulls. They'd have been in shock that it should have come to this...

It would have been... harrowing.

"I could save one," said Caron. "But not the other. Poor little shit."

Minutes later, Isabelle pulled the vehicle to the side of the busy street and Gamache jumped in, waving apologies to the drivers honking and gesturing.

"Where to?" she asked.

"Back home. You realizing it's Chalifoux with Moretti is huge," said the Chief. "I've sent Agent Fontaine to volunteer at Action Québec Bleu, undercover."

"Good idea. She's young and new, no one knows her yet. What about Shona Dorion? She's volunteering there too."

"I've sent a message to her to get out of there. It's too dangerous now that we know AQB isn't just implicated in the government bribes, but that the head of the organization is involved with the mob."

He looked down at his phone.

Still no reply from Shona. He shifted uneasily in the passenger's seat. Worried now. She hadn't replied to his earlier message either, about not needing to pursue the other series of numbers on Charles's map, as they now knew it was the password to get into his files.

He wrote a message to Agent Fontaine: *Find Shona Dorion at AQB. Do nothing, just report to me.*

As soon as they arrived home, they were met at the door by Jean-Guy.

"You need to see what we've found." He dragged the two of them into the study before they'd had time to take off their boots and coats. "I didn't want to risk writing or calling."

"I've never seen anything like this," said Nichol, equally excited.

Gamache took Jean-Guy's seat. "What am I looking at?"

"The IP addresses in Charles Langlois's file, the *Water Shed* one, took us to a whole other level in the dark web. Beyond .onion," said Beauvoir. "A new domain. A new territory. The addresses end with 'family.' Dot family."

Armand grew very quiet.

He was no longer in the comfortable home, with the log fire in the living room muttering and the scent of wet wool and wetter dog in the air.

The Chief Inspector was lying on the hot asphalt road, breathing in the smell of melting tar and holding the bloody hand of Charles Langlois, moments after the vehicle had struck the young biologist. Just nicking Gamache himself as they'd left the Montréal café Open Da Night.

The boy was dying. Armand knew it. Charles knew it. And when Armand had begged him for something, anything, useful, Charles Langlois had said, "Family."

The single word, the final word, had come out in a sputter of blood that hit Armand's face.

Family.

Armand had thought Charles meant he was to tell his family what had happened, and he promised to do so. And he did. But instead of providing some comfort, that pledge had created panic in the young man's eyes.

That had been Charles Langlois's last word and final feeling.

Armand had thought the panic was because Charles knew he was about to die. But now he realized he'd been wrong. The young biologist was trying to tell him something. And he'd misunderstood. Charles's panic was that he knew, in his final moments, that he'd failed.

"I understand," Armand whispered. "Finally. I'm sorry it took so long, son."

Not all the .family sites were password-protected.

"They assume anyone who got this far was directed here. That they belong," said Nichol, at her own keyboard, exploring the sites.

Gamache turned to Isabelle. "We need to find out all we can about Margaux Chalifoux."

"I'm on it, *patron*."

Isabelle had interviewed Margaux Chalifoux back in August, and had organized the search of AQB. She herself had conducted the search of Chalifoux's tiny, cluttered home. And found nothing except a map with pins in it in her basement. She'd had that brought in as "evidence," mostly because she felt she had to show something for their efforts. The map had proved useless.

Isabelle now realized she'd missed something vital. She was determined to correct that.

"And tell Agent Fontaine to be careful," said Gamache.

He knew young agents could be cavalier, take chances. Because they were immortal. He was damned if he was going to walk behind another coffin.

Gamache turned back to Jean-Guy. "What is it?"

His brows had drawn together in surprise. "This topic on .family. The subject line."

Worst attack on US soil since 9/11.

"What are they talking about? What attack?" Lacoste also leaned in.

"They mean the wildfires. It's an older post."

It was accompanied by images, some AI-enhanced, some not, of ash-covered streets and homes, cars and people. The wildfire fallout was side by side with images from 9/11.

Though an exaggeration, it was compelling. And a trigger.

"It's what General Whitehead also said, when I met him in DC," said Jean-Guy.

"Bert Whitehead said our wildfires were a deliberate terrorist attack?" Armand was dumbfounded.

"He was quoting what others are saying. I forgot to tell you. Actually, to be honest, *patron*, it seemed such a ridiculous claim I dismissed it. But…"

They turned back to the screen.

"Send these links to General Whitehead over the secure server."

While Beauvoir did that, Nichol said, "Why bother. He's obviously already seen the posts. Those images are beginning to break out onto the regular web. Not just dark sites. Even mainstream media is beginning to pick it up. And they're warning there's more coming. The crazier ones are saying the fires were deliberately set."

"Do they say why?" asked Lacoste.

"No, never. Who cares why?" said Nichol with a snort. "This isn't about reasons or reason. It's all emotion."

Armand opened his mouth to speak, then closed it again. There was nothing intelligent to say. Checking his watch, he turned to the door.

"I need to leave."

"I'll drive you," said Jean-Guy, knowing perfectly well where he was going.

"Me too, *patron*. I can work on this on the drive," said Lacoste. She lowered her voice. "Please don't leave me with her."

She jerked her head to indicate Yvette Nichol, who was shoving popcorn into her mouth, picking at her teeth, and humming three notes over and over as she stared at her screen.

She spat out a shard of popcorn; then, on seeing Beauvoir's face, she rolled her eyes, heaved a long-suffering sigh, and picked it off the floor.

Gamache went in search of Reine-Marie.

He found her in the kitchen. The dogs, and Gracie, were gobbling their dinner, and she was opening a can of ravioli from Monsieur Béliveau's General Store.

"Has it come to that?" he asked.

"I made the mistake of asking our guest what she might like for dinner. This was the answer. We haven't had it since Annie insisted. Remember that?"

For two weeks it was all their eight-year-old daughter would eat, thanks to some ad on television showing a little boy running through a street in Italy.

"Better than when all Daniel would eat was canned spinach, thanks to Popeye," said Armand. "What are you having?"

"I'm going over to the bistro."

"Don't you mean taking refuge there?"

She laughed. "*Sauve qui peut.*" At the door she said, "Do you remember how *Animal House*—"

"*Farm.*"

"*—Farm* ends?"

He thought a moment, then shook his head.

"The pigs and the humans sit down to dinner together. And it's impossible to tell them apart."

What a brilliant, terrifying book, thought Armand as they drove to the meeting.

CHAPTER 21

⁓

Armand stopped just inside the door and exhaled a breath he didn't know he'd been holding.

"Bert."

"Armand." They shook hands.

The General, on seeing Beauvoir, greeted him like an old comrade, though Jean-Guy's greeting was less warm.

On the way there, as he drove and Isabelle worked in the back seat, Jean-Guy had wondered if he should say something. Prepare the Chief for disappointment. Though he knew that probably wasn't necessary.

While Armand never gave up hope, neither did he divorce himself from reality. And the reality was that General Albert Whitehead, the head of the Joint Chiefs of Staff, would not show up. Again.

"I know," said Armand.

"Know what?"

"What you're thinking. And that you're right. General Whitehead probably won't show. But we have to try."

When does "trying" become a waste of precious time? When does hope become delusion?

And then Armand said something completely unexpected: "I'm not sure I would, if I was him."

In the rearview mirror, Jean-Guy saw Isabelle look up.

"Why not?"

"Do you wonder why he hasn't told us all he knows? Because he clearly knows something."

"It must be sensitive information," said Beauvoir. "Classified?"

"I think so. Otherwise he'd have given it to you, or sent it to me."

"In sending him the theater tickets, you're asking him to commit treason," said Lacoste.

"*Oui.*"

A few kilometers passed in darkness, and silence, except for the tap of Isabelle's fingers on her keyboard.

"So no," said Armand, quietly, "I don't expect him to show."

And yet, when they walked through the door, there he was. Not in uniform, of course. Bert Whitehead had his coat folded over his arm and was wearing a plaid flannel shirt and cords. He looked like a lumberjack meeting a university professor.

General Whitehead turned his incisive gaze on Isabelle and offered his hand. "You must be Inspector Lacoste. Armand speaks of you often. And highly."

He held her eyes, and the two recognized each other, if not physically, then as veterans of similar battles. Then he spoke quietly to Armand. "I envy you them. I had two young adjuncts. Once."

Once. Before. And now the eternal "after."

Introductions over, Whitehead glanced around in astonishment. "What is this place?"

"Take your seats please," said the elderly usher. "The show's about to begin. If you can just..."

He reached out with his foot and tried to shove the General's boot back over the thick black line painted across the floor of the ornate theater. Then the usher gave Gamache a stern look.

Without realizing it, the General was standing half in and half out of the United States, while the Chief Inspector was perfectly aware that he was standing half in and half out of Canada.

Whitehead raised an eloquent brow, and while staring, glaring, at Armand, he very slowly moved his foot. As did Gamache. For a moment the two large men, mirroring each other's movements, looked like they were line dancing.

The Canadian head of homicide for the Sûreté du Québec had invited the American Chair of the Joint Chiefs of Staff to the only place he could think of, the only place he knew of, where they could meet in person, anonymously, without crossing a border.

"Welcome to the Haskell Opera House," said Armand.

"An opera house, here? In the middle of nowhere? You brought me all the way from DC for an opera?"

"I brought you here so we could talk, of course. The music is the cherry on top."

"Maraschino," said Jean-Guy and got a laugh from the General, which no one else understood.

"Here" was the village of Stanstead, Québec. And also the small town of Derby Line, Vermont. The Haskell Free Library and Opera House straddled the two communities, and therefore the US-Canada border.

It had been built more than a century earlier, a collaboration between the two communities, the two countries, when borders were disregarded, essentially meaningless. People moved back and forth at will. That all changed with 9/11.

"Your seats, please," said the usher, getting vexed even though they were essentially alone in the theater.

Isabelle and Jean-Guy sat on the Canadian side, while General Whitehead and Chief Inspector Gamache took seats behind them, side by side, on either side of the black line of the international border.

The lights went down, two actors took the stage, one sat at a piano, and they started to sing. The performance of *Billy Bishop Goes to War* began.

The colonial boys are lining up, we're lining up for war...

"Did you get the links we sent?" whispered Armand.

"Yes. We're aware. I was going to tell you about .family, but you've found it on your own. What they're saying on those sites has begun to spread all over the dark web."

Armand looked at him. "They're saying that Canada is about to attack the US. Some say we already have, in the form of the wildfires. These are marginal people on marginal sites. Please tell me you don't take it seriously."

"You look dubious."

"Dubious doesn't begin to cover it."

"Remember January 6."

"Yes, of course." It was the argument everyone used when discussing the power of social media to distort and manipulate. The example was getting old, though no less true.

"So-called patriots stormed the Capitol in an attempt to overthrow the government," Whitehead continued anyway. "To overturn a legitimate election. Here. In the United States." He swept his hand around, though he was actually indicating Canada. Armand did not correct him. "And they almost succeeded. Good, reasonable people, and some idiots, were made to believe a lie, then act in the most unconscionable way. Never, ever underestimate the power of social media, of groupthink, Armand. Or the power of toxic nationalism. Combine the two and you have—" He lifted his hands in exasperation. "Had you told me months earlier such a thing was possible, I'd have been . . . dubious."

Armand was bewildered and disappointed. He had hoped Bert Whitehead had more to say than rehashing the bizarre conspiracy theory about a Canadian invasion that was patently never going to happen. They needed substance, not an unnecessary lesson in human dynamics and misguided patriotism.

> *We were off to fight the Hun, and it looked like lots of fun.*
> *Somehow it didn't seem like war at all, at all, at all.*

General Whitehead stared at the stage; then, raising his formidable brows, he looked at Gamache. "A musical about the First World War?"

"About Billy Bishop. A Canadian pilot. *Oui.*"

"He existed?"

"Yes."

"I'm talking about an attack, Armand. But not the one on the websites you found."

Armand was relieved. He hadn't really thought there was anything to that insanity about Canada invading the US, but as Bert had said, equally unlikely things had happened in the recent past.

"What are we talking about?"

"What happens when the water runs out?"

"You've already asked Jean-Guy that. And I asked our Prime Minister."

"You spoke to James Woodford about this?"

"I did. You look worried."

Bert Whitehead was quiet for a moment. "What did he say?"

"The Prime Minister? What could he say? When I asked if there were plans to attack the US, he thought I was crazy. When I then asked what happens when the water runs out, I thought he was going to call the guards. He did admit that he had had some foreknowledge of the poisoning plot but had dismissed it."

"He was dubious?"

"That's one word for it, yes."

"I think you're doing the same with these latest rumors, Armand. Dismissing them too quickly."

"But you just said we aren't talking about a war between the US and Canada."

"That's not exactly what I said. Wars come in different shapes and sizes today. You know that."

Armand thought for a moment, then leaned forward and said to Isabelle, who was clearly listening, "You said something similar earlier today."

"I did?"

"You suggested what was happening wasn't a prelude to outright battle, but something more covert."

"And I think you're right," Whitehead said to Lacoste. "At least, that's the first thrust."

Armand was staring at his companion. "The first thrust? Are you saying there's a second? An attack actually planned?"

"Not just planned. From what I can see, it's already started."

I'm dreamin' of the trees in Canada, Northern Lights are dancing in my head.

If I die, then let me die in Canada, where there's a chance I'll die in bed.

"Come with me." Gamache rose to his feet. "We need to talk privately. Beauvoir. Lacoste."

"With you, *patron*."

One of the actors in the two-person play was now pretending to be Lady St. Helier, in a meeting with Billy.

> *You've been making rather a mess of it, haven't you. You're a rather rude young man, behaving like cannon fodder. Perfectly acceptable characteristics, in a Canadian.*

There was scattered laughter in the near-empty theater. On stage now, Lady St. Helier announced she'd written a poem in Billy's honor.

Isabelle paused at the exit, to listen.

> *So don't be so naïve, and take that heart off your sleeve,*
> *For a fool and his life will soon be parted.*
> *War's a fact of life today, it will not be wished away,*
> *Forget that fact, and you'll be dead before you started.*

The door swung shut.

Once out of the opera house, they found themselves in the free library. Armand and Bert were sweeping the walls with their hands, looking for the light switch, when the usher appeared. He'd clearly followed them.

"You can't be here. The library's closed. Please return to your seats." He'd turned on the overhead lights and was looking at them like a father at disappointing children.

Armand had hoped not to have to do this, but there was no choice. He brought out his ID, and the usher, fortunately on the Québec side, opened his eyes wide, looked up at the Chief, and nodded.

"*Désolé.* I should have recognized you, Monsieur Gamache."

"I'm glad you didn't. Please keep this between ourselves." Gamache held the man's eyes and the usher nodded.

"*Absolument.*"

"And make sure we're not disturbed, please." He held out a fifty-dollar bill.

"*Ce n'est pas nécessaire, patron, mais merci.*" The usher waved away the offering with a smile, handed Gamache a key, then closed the door. Armand gave the key to Lacoste, who locked the door.

Grabbing some chairs, they sat in a circle. The play could just be heard through the door.

"All right, Bert, what the hell did you mean that the attack had already started? How? Where? We need facts. Evidence. Not rumors. Not guesses."

"What happens, Armand, when the water runs out?"

Armand sighed. "For God's sake, we've been through that."

"Have we?" Whitehead snapped, suddenly annoyed. "Think. Really think."

"This isn't a game, just tell us."

"You have all the information you need, you're just not focusing, not adding it up right."

"Then add it up for me!" Gamache had reached the end of his very long tether. His anger was breaking free. It was something Beauvoir and Lacoste had rarely seen.

Just then Armand's phone buzzed. In his frustration he almost tossed it across the room. But he glanced at it. A brief message from Agent Fontaine.

Shona Dorion still here at AQB.

"Damn," Gamache muttered. Realizing he was perilously close to the edge, he took a deep breath and put the phone back in his pocket. Then changed his mind. He couldn't let his annoyance get the better of him. "*Pardon.*"

Stepping away for a moment, he placed a call. This time she answered.

"I was about to write you," said Shona. "You were wrong."

There was no denying the satisfaction in her voice.

"I don't care. You need to get out of AQB." He didn't tell her about the mob connection they'd discovered. That would almost certainly convince her to stay. "I'm not kidding."

"Screw you. You're not the boss of me. Do you want to know where you fucked up or not?"

Lyrics were sliding under the door between the library and the opera house.

> *Jeffrey made a virtue out of cowardice and fear,*
> *He was the first to go on sick leave and the last to volunteer.*
> *He was running from a fight when they attacked him from the rear.*
> *And he never got out alive, non. He didn't survive.*

Isabelle's brows drew together. It was eerily like her conversation earlier that day with Jeanne Caron, about Frederick Castonguay. Who made a virtue out of cowardice and fear. He never got out of that forest alive. *Non.* He didn't survive.

Off to the side, Gamache was still on the phone.

"All right. Tell me but be quick about it."

"Those numbers and symbols on the map? The ones you told me to ignore because you'd figured out they're passwords?"

"*Oui.* And they are."

He didn't have time to listen to her gloat or to argue with her about AQB. If he had to, he'd issue a warrant for her arrest. It wouldn't stand for long and he'd be sanctioned, of course. But it would get Shona out of Action Québec Bleu.

"Keep your knickers on," she said, and was surprised by the phrase she hadn't heard, or used, in years. It was something her grandmother, who was from Jamaica, used to say to her. It was, Shona knew, a term of endearment. "They probably are passwords, but they're something else too. This Charles was clever. Far more clever than you realized."

Now Gamache was paying attention.

"I contacted some scientist friends, and they sent me to someone in Environment Canada. The numbers are isobars."

"*Quoi?*"

"Isobars, you know? For weather? They measure high and low pressure systems. They predict storms. *Allo?*"

Gamache had lowered the phone and looked over at General Whitehead.

> *So when you fight, stay as calm as the ocean,*
> *And watch what goes on behind your shoulder.*
> *Remember war's not a place for deep emotion,*
> *And maybe you'll get a little older.*

"Leave AQB now," he said, and didn't bother waiting for her reply.

Clicking the phone off, he strode back to the group and stared down at Bert Whitehead.

"Why would a dead biologist write isobars on a map?"

Isobars? Beauvoir and Lacoste exchanged a glance. This was news to them.

"Isobars?" said Whitehead. "As in weather? I don't know."

"I think you do," said Gamache, glaring at him. "You came all this way for a reason, Bert. Out with it."

"I've said more than I probably should."

"All you've done is repeat 'What happens when the water runs out?' Unless there's some sort of supernatural interference, that will never happen here."

"I agree." The General rose to face Gamache. "That's the point. Canada won't." He was staring at Gamache with such intensity, Armand felt in a few more seconds he might melt. "For God's sake, Armand, I'm begging you. Don't make me say it."

Don't make me commit treason.

The world stopped turning, gravity lost its grip. Time was suspended. Nothing existed except those two, staring at each other.

Armand opened his mouth. But instead of speaking, it stayed open. And his eyes widened.

In that instant all those pieces they'd collected over days, weeks, months, those shards of evidence and shreds of ideas, of guesses and fears, shifted. Not so much fell into place, but like in a kaleidoscope, the angle changed. And what had been a jumble of disparate, even contradictory, and often ridiculous pieces suddenly made sense. The chaos resolved into a cohesive picture.

"You see," said the head of the Joint Chiefs of Staff. "I can tell by your expression."

There was, on Armand's face, a look of utter horror.

"What happens when the water runs out?" General Whitehead continued. "What happens when a nation runs out of the one resource necessary for life?"

"They take it from those who have it," said Armand, his voice barely audible. Saying what Whitehead could not. "It's not Canada that's running out."

"No."

"The United States is."

"Yes."

"It's not Canada that will invade the US."

"No."

> *Civilizations come and go, don't you know.*
> *Dancing into oblivion, oblivion.*
> *The birth and death of nations, of civilizations,*
> *Can be viewed down the barrel of a gun.*

CHAPTER 22

———

The United States is going to attack Canada?" said Lacoste. "Come on."
Gamache was studying the General. "What do you know, Bert?"

"I know the necessary first step in any war. And so do you. How do you get young people to sign up and fight? How do you get their parents to let them? How do you motivate them to risk and perhaps lose their lives?"

"You create a common enemy," said Gamache, quietly. "A threat."

"A clear and present danger, yes."

"But why do it?" asked Beauvoir. "Why would anyone want to provoke a war between us?"

"For the water, of course," snapped Whitehead. "Haven't you been paying attention? The US is running out."

Armand Gamache turned to Lacoste. "Call Nichol. Have her find out who's behind the .family posts."

To Beauvoir he said, "Contact the Chief Meteorologist. Send her that sequence of numbers and symbols from Charles Langlois's map."

"The password?"

"They're not just a password, they're an isobar. We need to know what specifically the sequence says. But don't tell her where we got them."

"I wouldn't," said Whitehead, and Beauvoir, his phone out, hesitated and looked at Gamache.

"Why not?" Armand asked.

"Because the isobar your young biologist put on his map must have come from some document he found. One that scared him. Someone in the know had to provide the sequence to whoever's behind this. Who better than a meteorologist?"

"He's right," said Gamache, and Beauvoir clicked off his phone. "Come on, Bert. We need more. What's going to happen?"

"I don't know, not for sure. Not really. Or maybe I just refuse to believe it. Like January 6. We had warning, we saw the posts, we just never . . ." He wiped his hand across his face, then gave a huge exhale. "But this? I suspected something was up when you first asked for help with the poisoning plot. In digging deeper, I found those messages about a possible aggression by Canada. They were so in lockstep and yet so unbelievable. Hardly worth noting. But then they began spreading, appearing outside far-right conspiracy sites. It seemed someone powerful was trying to make Canada appear as our enemy. A threat. But why? And then I remembered the plan."

"Plan?" said Gamache. "There's a plan?"

But Whitehead was focused on his own train of thought. "Someone high up in our government, someone with clearance, must have found it and seen the possibilities. Though, of course, it doesn't have to be our—"

"Wait." Armand put up his hand and the General stopped. "Are you saying there's an American plan? To what? Invade Canada for our water?"

"Of course we have one," snapped Whitehead. "The fact a plan exists isn't the point."

"Really?"

"Don't be so naïve, Armand. What makes you think the most powerful nation on earth wouldn't have contingency plans for everything? Attack from North Korea, Russia, China. Terrorists. Nuclear and conventional attacks. Cyberattacks. We've had war games in case extraterrestrials invade, for God's sake. And now there's global warming. Heating. And with it extreme weather. Cat 5 hurricanes and predictions we'll have to raise our measuring to Cat 6 and even 7. Tornadoes, earthquakes. Forest fires. Floods and, yes, drought. You think we wouldn't be prepared for that? We will do what is necessary to survive. As would you."

Whitehead's own levee had broken and out poured this no-doubt classified information.

"Be prepared?" said Gamache. "You make it sound reasonable, as though you're leading a Boy Scout troop. You hoping to get your 'invading an innocent country' badge, Bert? Oh, wait, you already have that."

All-out war threatened to break out now between the two men. But both got to where they were by choosing their battles carefully. And controlling their emotions. This was not a fight either wanted.

Both stepped back.

"*Désolé*," said Armand, with a tight smile. "That went too far."

"And so might we," General Whitehead admitted. "If someone has their way."

"Do you have any idea who?"

"No. But having a plan and implementing it are two very different things. Is the US going to invade Canada tomorrow? No. No chance. Will we if necessary? I think so. Don't look so shocked. We're both realists, we have to be. What happens when you're low on water but have missiles up the yin-yang? You use one to get the other. What would you do, Armand, if you and your family were dying of thirst and your neighbor had plenty of water?"

"I'd knock on the door and ask for whatever they could spare. I wouldn't organize a home invasion."

"We'd do the same thing. Ask for help, politely. And I'm sure Canada would share. Even open its doors to the first few thousand environmental refugees. The first hundred thousand. Maybe even the first million Americans who came knocking, asking for a cup of your pure spring water. But ten, twenty, a hundred million Americans needing your water? Your food? Your power? Your hospitals and housing?" He shook his head. "No, Armand. We know what would happen."

"Okay, walk me through it."

General Whitehead hesitated. Armand was asking him to go even further. To divulge their invasion plan. To give the enemy forewarning. To commit treason.

Whitehead took a deep breath, then took the plunge.

"We've run the scenarios. It would be little use asking for your help. We would at first, mostly to show the international community we're reasonable. But eventually, as I said, we'd be forced to take what we need. Ninety percent of your population lives within a hundred miles of the border." He looked down at the black line on the floor that, to Armand's tired eyes, seemed to be thinning. "It would not take long."

Armand was quiet. Trying to absorb what was being said. Trying, he knew, to marshal arguments. And he found one.

"But you have the Great Lakes. Why would the US need to take over Canada when it has the largest supply of fresh water in the world right there?"

"And what would Canada do if we started to drain the Great Lakes? It's a shared resource, as you know."

"What could Canada do?" Armand's voice had risen slightly in pitch. "We wouldn't shoot you."

"Not at first, no."

"We'd protest, but we'd be powerless to stop it. We would not attack. What? Did I say something funny?"

Whitehead was smiling. "We've run the scenarios in war games. Not, of course, on the ground, but in computer models. I've played all sides many times. Sometimes I'm in charge of the American response to the crisis. Sometimes I'm Canada. I've been the UK. Once I was the UN. That was boring. I just sat there writing stern letters of protest. The outcome was always the same. Shall I tell you?"

Armand wanted to decline. Wanted to pick up his coat and go home to Reine-Marie and the dogs. And Gracie. To have a drink by the fire and read a book. And not know.

He nodded.

"In our war games, when Canada found out we were taking huge amounts of water from the Great Lakes and other sources, there'd first be a diplomatic response. A polite, then not-so-polite request from your country to stop. When that didn't work, there'd be a trade war. We depend on you for more things than most know. Minerals, for instance. Cement. Imagine if we no longer had cement? But more than that—"

"Oil," said Armand, with some sadness, seeing where this was going.

"Yes."

"If you started to drain the Great Lakes, we'd turn off the tap."

"Bingo." Whitehead tapped the side of his nose, then turned his finger toward Armand, like a pointed gun. "And that would be it. The trigger. Even the threat of it would be enough to provoke an invasion. You'd be framed in our media as the aggressors. As the enemy. Not helping an ally in need. Not sharing your abundant water, and even turning off our supply of oil. Stopping shipment of valuable minerals. We get most of our uranium, aluminum, nickel, potash from Canada. When faced with drought, with abandoned cities, with an energy crisis and food shortages? When looking north and seeing the ready riches just on the other side of the longest undefended border in the world?" Once again General Whitehead looked down at the black line between them. "Don't you think desperate people pushed to the limit would readily, happily even, get behind taking those resources? To survive? People break into homes when they're starving. This would be framed as the same thing. Just a very big home."

Gamache was shaking his head. "I refuse to believe it."

"For God's sake, man, take your head out of your own ass before it's too late."

"If you crossed our border in an armed invasion, Canada would push back. It would be a losing proposition, we could never hold out, but we'd try."

"I know you would. That happened every time in our war games. And you know what happened next? The first image of a Canadian soldier killing an American, and even those against an invasion would come onside. It's human nature. Our nature. You kill one American and a hundred more take their place. It would quickly degenerate into all-out war, all along the border, from New England—"

"The Maritime Provinces."

"To Washington State."

"British Columbia."

"And everywhere in between. They want you to push back. It would justify the invasion."

"Who are 'they'?" demanded Gamache. "You must have some idea."

"I've told you, I don't know." Whitehead was exhausted and exasperated. "I've tried to find out, but..."

Gamache studied the large man in front of him. His friend. His colleague. Was he telling the truth? Did he really not know?

"Guess," said Armand.

"I do wonder..."

Armand held his breath. *Say it, say it. Tell me.* But he saw Whitehead pull back. Though even that was telling. It suggested to Gamache that whoever Whitehead suspected of being behind this was prominent. Perhaps even someone he owed allegiance to.

"Someone's trying to push us into a war with each other," Gamache probed. Pushed. "If you have any idea who it might be, you need to tell me. I need to see that plan."

"I'm sorry, Armand. I can't. Not before I speak to someone."

"The person who's behind it?"

"I hope not. But I need to find out. Then I will give you what you need. I promise."

It sounded so sincere, almost innocent. Armand was tempted to ask for a pinkie swear. Instead, he asked, "Is this really only about water?"

"Isn't that enough? No water, no life. But it doesn't hurt that we'd have access to your vast supply of hydroelectricity."

In Québec, electricity came from the network of huge dams. From water. In Québec water literally meant power.

"But it doesn't stop there," said Armand. "You'd have our oil, minerals. Natural resources are the new currency. Power is measured in liters now. Not missiles. Not GDP."

"Now you're getting it," said Whitehead. "The countries with the most water, the most oil, the most minerals are quickly becoming the most powerful. Canada is climbing to the top of the heap."

"And becoming a target. Like walking around inner-city Montréal with a bag of heroin around our necks."

"Now there's an image, and oddly appropriate. With water comes another sort of power. Political power. And that's a drug. It's driven more than one decent person crazy. Power-mad. If this takeover happens, the person who leads it will become a despot, with all of North America under their control."

"You're talking about your President," said Gamache.

"I didn't say that," General Whitehead snapped.

"But you suspect."

Whitehead said nothing.

"You need to find out who, Bert. And we need proof."

"It's not just the US, Armand. There're people in Canada involved. People who want this to happen. Who'll benefit."

"Moretti," said Beauvoir, who'd been following this closely.

Finally, it was clear why Joseph Moretti was involved. What he'd get out of this unholy alliance. He would provide the muscle for the corrupt politicians and greedy corporations. He would do the assassinations, the murders, the intimidation. The dirty work. He would eliminate anyone standing in their way. He'd open the door for the Americans.

And when it was over, and the new government installed, he'd turn his soldiers loose on them.

Joe Moretti was not content to be the capo di tutti capi of Canada. His addiction demanded more. Always more.

Sitting in the calm of the Haskell Free Library and Opera House, with the soft sound of music drifting under the door, it was near impossible to believe it could happen.

But Armand suspected every country ever invaded had felt the same way. Every group ever targeted, ever rounded up, refused to believe their neighbors could do it.

Every people who found themselves under the thumb of a tyrant must wonder where it began, and how they didn't see it coming. And what moment they missed, when it could have been stopped.

Armand was quiet, hesitating to voice what needed to be asked. "You're the head of the Joint Chiefs, Bert. You control the forces. Would you ... ?"

"Invade Canada? If ordered by my Commander in Chief?"

The two men stared at each other. Armand Gamache was shocked that it had come to this. That he'd had to ask the question, and that Bert Whitehead was considering his answer.

One the hunter, one the hunted,
A life to live, a death confronted.

"Would you, Armand? If I was in your sights, would you fire?"

And for you the bell is ringing,
And for you my bullet's stinging.
Oh, my friend, it's you or I.

"Suppose American forces…" General Whitehead moved his foot slowly, slowly. Inch by inch. Approaching the black line.

Touching it. Penetrating it.

Slowly. A centimeter at a time. Then breaking through the other side. One foot, then the other. Until the head of the American armed forces stood, uninvited, in Canada.

Gamache watched this. A few paces away Beauvoir and Lacoste stepped closer until they were ranged behind their Chief.

Armand had raised his eyes from the violated border, from the boots on the ground, and was staring at the head of the Joint Chiefs. Whitehead was also staring. Daring Armand to retaliate.

There was complete silence. And then, in the face of Gamache's unwavering glare, Whitehead stepped back with a laugh.

But it had been no joke. They had their answer.

"Where would an invasion start from?" Armand asked. "The commando base in Jericho?" Another piece had found its place in an increasingly ugly picture.

"You know about it? That's a shame. I can't confirm, of course." Though he just had. "I've already broken my oath. If anyone finds out, I could be, will be, put in prison. At the very least."

"I would hide you." Armand was not actually kidding. "I would protect you. Just look for three pines planted in a cluster."

Though both knew Bert Whitehead would never leave his country. He was doing this to save it, not betray it. And would take whatever punishment it meted out. Including a firing squad. But he would not run away.

"Are there any scenarios where we repel your attack?" When Whitehead shook his head, Armand gave one curt nod. "I need to know the rest."

"You do know. If armed commandos came across and seized"—he looked around—"this place. Seized all the towns and villages along the border. And on our way to Montréal, Three Pines…"

"We'd fight back."

"You'd lose." The General looked at his friend, his confrère, and the two younger people standing resolute behind him. Whitehead's eyes were beseeching. Begging. "Why not just give up? Would it be so bad to be the fifty-first state?"

Now Armand smiled. "*Animal Farm.*"

"I'm sorry?"

"We'd fight back because in your new country, some would be more equal than others. Any nation that would invade a friendly country is not a friend and certainly cannot be trusted. How long before we were taken from our homes, because you'd need them too, and put on... let me think... reserves? You call them reservations, but it comes to the same thing. Or maybe camps—" He put up his hand to forestall the protest. "You know perfectly well, Bert, how easily the inconceivable becomes a reality. Becomes acceptable. Becomes the norm. Isn't that what we've been talking about? As you said, never underestimate the power of groupthink. *Non.* We would fight. And once we lost, as you pointed out we inevitably would, then a guerilla war would start. A resistance would spring up. We might concede, but we'd never, ever surrender. It would become a mutual nightmare. For generations. Did your war games predict that?"

"Yes," General Whitehead admitted. "But still, if given a choice between generations of conflict or slow death by starvation, I suspect Americans would hop on board the invasion train. Besides, you'd be the bad guys, remember? We're the patient victims with a legitimate grievance, pushed to do something we really didn't want to do, but had no choice. After all, you attacked us first. Or so people would believe. It doesn't matter if it's true or not. All that's needed now for this to work is a common enemy."

"Attack first?" said Lacoste. "Never."

There was silence. Until Armand spoke.

"It's already started, you said." They saw Whitehead nod. "The wildfires. Those dark web sites are already sending out the narrative."

"'The worst attack on American soil since 9/11,'" said the General. "That's how they're framing the wildfires. They're preparing. Grooming the population. Those photos are pretty convincing."

"They're AI-generated," said Lacoste.

"You're still living in a world where truth matters, where facts are important. They aren't anymore. They're fluid, and we're losing facts as fast as we're losing water."

Armand felt the pit of his stomach drop out. For the first time, he could see how this could actually happen. How the common enemy would be created. How Americans, even reasonable ones, would be persuaded to come across the border.

"The frightening thing is, our water crisis isn't manufactured." Whitehead's voice was soft, reasonable. "We really are facing a disaster. The Mississippi is drying up. It's forecast that in a generation Palm Springs and Phoenix will be uninhabitable. Major cities are already in crisis, rationing water. The UN has declared a global emergency, and warning that all-out regional war over water is inevitable. Inevitable. Anyone who thinks we're different from people in Africa, in Asia, in the Middle East is wrong. We're all driven by the same need to survive."

"Your President isn't a warmonger," said Gamache. "Would she really authorize an invasion?"

"If public sentiment swung that way? If Americans were suffering and scared and angry and reelection was in doubt. If powerful lobby groups like the National Association of Realtors—"

Beauvoir's sudden laugh stopped Whitehead.

"What? You expected the NRA? The Realtors' Association spends billions every year lobbying. Can you imagine what happens to their members when cities become uninhabitable? Add to that pastors in churches demonizing Canada and preaching that it's America's God-given right to protect itself—"

"If there was another megafire...," said Lacoste.

"Another aggression," said Beauvoir.

And with that twist of the prism, Gamache saw what Charles Langlois had tried to warn them about all those weeks ago.

But had Charles told him the US was preparing to invade Canada for their water, would he have believed the young biologist as they'd sat over bomboloni at Open Da Night?

No. He'd have dismissed him as a former cokehead with wet brain. As it was, it had taken Armand almost too long to believe there was a plot to poison Montréal's water.

And now this.

"Another fire," he said, working his way forward. Staring into Bert's eyes as he spoke. "We know there will be one, eventually. But... but..." Still he held the stare. "But that's not good enough. This thing has been planned. Carefully. Over years. They wouldn't leave anything to chance. They wouldn't wait, hoping another megafire would drop ash..." He paused, thinking. Thinking. Inching toward the border between the state of happy ignorance and the truth. "They could set a fire, of course. That would be easy enough, with incendiary bombs." Whitehead's eyes were pleading with him. Begging him. To continue? Or to stop? "But how would they know when and where..."

Now his face turned ashen. Even his lips lost color.

"Chief, what is it?" asked Lacoste.

Gamache turned to her and Jean-Guy. "The isobars. The ones Charles left behind. They tell us the flow of air."

"Or ash," said Jean-Guy. "Jesus."

Gamache turned back to Whitehead. "FEDS. That's why it's so important. FEDS can predict where ash from the next megafire will fall."

"It can predict the future," said Lacoste. "And all someone has to do is light the match. Set the forest on fire when the isobars and FEDS line up."

"The lake." Lacoste turned to Gamache. "That's why Charles was so interested in that particular one. It's the first example of what's possible. If it can happen by mistake, it can happen on purpose. That's what the so-called 'second notebook' was saying. Trying to say. Trying to warn us."

But Charles Langlois's notes and notations and drawings and maps had been written for himself, in a sort of shorthand. He'd expected he'd have time to marshal his arguments, his evidence, and make it at least understandable and maybe even convincing. But time ran out. He'd made one last trip into the wilderness. To hide his laptop. Then he'd told Frederick that if something happened to him, to go there. To find it.

But Frederick had hesitated. Waited too long, and then asked the wrong person to accompany him.

"Is your President involved?"

"I don't think so."

"Our Prime Minister?"

"Not that I know of."

Armand Gamache stared at Bert Whitehead and remembered what

Reine-Marie had said, about how *Animal Farm* ended. Eventually, inevitably, the oppressed and the oppressors become indistinguishable. If not all of the oppressed, then enough.

Was Whitehead one of them? Was this meeting and everything Whitehead said part of the plan?

Am I making the same mistake Frederick Castonguay made, trusting the wrong person? Confiding in the wrong person?

Who better to be the Black Wolf than the head of the Joint Chiefs of Staff, the one who controlled the hounds?

Armand had a decision to make. His days were filled with them, many of them life-and-death, but never had he been faced with one with such consequences.

"We need to figure out how to stop this, Bert."

He'd come to his decision. And he really had no choice. If what Whitehead was saying was real, and it seemed to be, he had to trust him.

And if he was the Black Wolf? Well, that die was already cast.

"Agreed. That's what I've been trying to do, but the bad actors aren't just on my side of this border, Armand."

"Agreed. You need to speak to your President, and I need to be clearer with Prime Minister Woodford."

While Beauvoir and Lacoste made for the exit, General Whitehead and Chief Inspector Gamache shook hands over a line that should not be crossed.

Then they parted ways.

"Damn Americans," said Beauvoir as they drove back to Three Pines.

"Why do you say that?" asked Armand.

"You heard what General Whitehead said." He was astonished that the Chief would question his statement. "They plan to attack us, supposedly to defend the homeland."

"It's already happening," said Lacoste. "Those posts. The news reports. Those are the first shots."

"And you don't think Canada would do the same thing?" said Gamache. "Don't kid yourselves. If our lives were threatened? Do you think we'd just watch our children and grandchildren die of thirst, of starvation? We'd cross the border in no time. We'd fight tooth and nail for survival."

I'm dreamin' of the trees in Canada, Northern Lights are dancing in my head.

If I die, then let me die in Canada, where there's a chance I'll die in bed.

Once home, while Isabelle and Jean-Guy joined Nichol in the study to do more digging, Armand grabbed a book from their library, then called Henri, Fred, and Gracie and took them for a walk. Reine-Marie was still in the bistro. He stood outside in the darkness and saw her in the light, talking earnestly with Clara and Myrna and Ruth. With Gabri and Olivier. He tried to guess what they were saying. To read their lips, their bodies. But he couldn't. It was chilly, and he was about to join her, to sit by the fire with a scotch and read, but he changed his mind and, pulling his coat more tightly around him, he whistled and heard the panting behind him. Up the hill they walked in procession to the church.

Half an hour later he sensed a presence and turned. Reine-Marie was sitting at the end of the pew.

"How long have you been there?"

"Not long." She slid over and handed him a scotch and a wedge of lemon meringue pie.

"*Merci.*"

"Can you tell me?"

And he did. When he finished, she put out her hand. He passed her back the glass. She took a swig and gave it back.

"Do you believe it?" she asked.

"Iraq comes to mind," he said.

"Who'd have thought so many reasonable, intelligent people could be convinced to invade a country that had not attacked them?"

"Saddam was a tyrant," said Armand. "A madman who used poison gas on his own citizens. It was not that difficult to convince people that he'd helped the 9/11 conspirators and had weapons of mass destruction."

"But he didn't. There was absolutely no proof."

"There doesn't need to be proof. Fear replaces facts." He fell silent, staring ahead. Following his own train of thought.

It was then that Reine-Marie noticed the book on the pew, with his finger at a certain page. "*Animal Farm?*"

"*Non.*" He held it up.

"*Nineteen Eighty-Four.*" She understood. "Orwell."

Armand opened it and read the section he'd been looking for.

"*The Ministry of Peace concerns itself with war, the Ministry of Truth with lies, the Ministry of Love with torture and the Ministry of Plenty with starvation. These contradictions are not accidental, nor do they result from ordinary hypocrisy: they are deliberate exercises in doublethink.*"

"Can it be stopped?" she asked, quietly.

"Yes."

"You're not a member of the Ministry of Truth, are you?"

He laughed. It felt good. "*Non.* I believe it. But keep that pitchfork handy."

"I'll do better than that. We can post Ruth at the border, then dare the commandos to come across."

"Poor commandos."

They sat quietly, and into that silence the dogs started snoring. And Armand started humming. It was a tune Reine-Marie recognized from a musical they'd seen together recently.

She sang, softly.

> *Friends ain't supposed to die 'til they're old.*
> *And friends ain't supposed to die in pain.*

Driving through the night back to the Burlington airport, Bert Whitehead thought about the meeting and the play.

> *So when you fight, stay as calm as the ocean,*
> *And watch what goes on behind your shoulder.*
> *Remember war's not a place for deep emotion,*
> *And maybe you'll get a little older.*

Mostly the head of the Joint Chiefs of Staff thought about the look in Armand's eyes when he himself had stepped over the border. When he'd crossed the line. Went too far.

That look of determination. Of cold, calm resolve. Almost daring him to go further. And Armand's two aides-de-camp standing firm behind him.

Any invasion might not be the cakewalk the computer models suggested. He'd have to run another scenario. After he reported to the President, that was.

In Three Pines, under the forgiving gaze of the stained-glass boys, Reine-Marie placed her hand on top of Armand's.

> *No one should die alone when he is twenty-one.*
> *And livin' shouldn't make you feel ashamed.*

CHAPTER 23

—⁓—

"What do you want?"

"To apologize." Nichol was whispering into the phone. It was the next morning and the others had left, and left her alone. *Of course.* Still, she needed to be careful. "And—"

"Apologize?" demanded Evelyn Tardiff. She didn't need to whisper. She was in her office at Sûreté headquarters with the door closed. And no assistant out front. *Of course.* "For which part? Spying on me? Leaving me? Betraying me?"

"But you knew that's why Gamache put me in your office. You wanted me to report back to him."

"That doesn't make what you did any better. And now you're with him. You said you were sick, but instead, you deserted me."

"But we're all on the same side, *non?* How can I desert to my own side?"

"You know what I mean."

Nichol did, and she didn't. She understood that she'd lied to her Chief. But then Chief Inspector Tardiff had lied to her.

Earlier that morning, before the sun was even up, the four of them had sat at the long pine table in the Gamaches' kitchen.

A fire was lit in the woodstove at the far end of the room, taking the damp and chill off. The old percolator was bubbling away on the counter, sending coffee vapor into the air.

"No, *patron,* there's no way to find out who's feeding those sites," Nichol had said, in answer to his question. "That's the whole point of them. .onion is deep enough, encrypted and protected. But .family is something else."

"Keep trying."

"Waste of time, but okay."

"There are other lines of inquiry," said the Chief Inspector.

"Thank God for that," muttered Nichol.

"Any luck tracking the plane that flew Castonguay and his killers to the lake?" Gamache asked.

"Not yet," said Beauvoir. "We're scouring the airports and flying clubs. Especially the fish and game clubs. It would help to have some idea of the date."

Lacoste was shaking her head. "He'd been in the ground too long. You saw the report. Dr. Harris just said weeks." She turned to Gamache. "I'm trying to track down the corporations that paid to take over Canadian primary industries. We know it was billions and the money was laundered through Action Québec Bleu. Anything from Agent Fontaine?"

"Not yet."

"From Shona Dorion?"

"Only the isobar information. We'll stop on our way up to Ottawa and take her with us."

"Willingly?" asked Jean-Guy.

"If not…" Lacoste showed him what was on her phone.

"Don't you just hate people who make life difficult?" asked Nichol.

Beauvoir no longer knew when she was kidding. And no longer cared.

"And you, Jean-Guy, need to get up to Archambault and interview Marcus Lauzon again. Get him to admit the payments and tell us who they were from." Armand leaned forward, his eyes intense. "I think that's our best hope, our way in. We just need one of those corporations. One Chief Executive. One comptroller to testify. One witness."

"But they'd never admit it," said Lacoste. "For no other reason than that they're terrified of Moretti. They know what he'll do to them, and their families, if they talk."

"We need to convince them that he's going to kill them anyway. Their only hope is to help us stop this."

"But why would Lauzon give us a name now?" asked Jean-Guy. "He's denied everything so far."

"Why would he warn us about FEDS?" asked Gamache.

It was rhetorical. He really didn't know. What he did know was something no one else had seen: the former Deputy Prime Minister's eyes as he'd stumbled into Armand and whispered his warning about FEDS. Armand knew terror when he saw it, and he'd seen it then, in that split second.

"Lauzon obviously didn't want Tardiff to hear him," said Beauvoir.

"That must be a mind-fuck," said Nichol. "Trying to throw suspicion on her."

"Maybe," admitted Gamache. "You've worked closely with Chief Inspector Tardiff. What do you think of her?"

"You're asking if she can be trusted?" There was silence while Agent Nichol considered. "I would. I do."

Gamache turned to Isabelle. "Agents are still watching Margaux Chalifoux's home?"

"*Oui*," said Lacoste. "They reported a few minutes ago. She isn't up yet."

Gamache looked at his watch, then got up. "I need you to come with me. Jean-Guy?"

"I'll head up to Lauzon."

"What about me?" asked Nichol.

"You stay here."

Of course, thought Nichol with a scowl.

"Keep trying to get into those last .family sites. They must be important if they're so protected."

She heaved a sigh so forceful, her lips fluttered in a raspberry.

"Gamache thinks there's a chance you're working for Moretti," said Nichol.

"And you?"

"No. I know you're trying to stop him. I called because I don't think Gamache will tell you, and you need to know what we've found."

"Go on."

When Yvette Nichol finished, Tardiff said, "So he has the laptop. No, he didn't tell me. Has he found Charles Langlois's map?"

"Yes."

"Fuck. I need that password."

"*Oui, patronne.*" Though there had been a slight hesitation.

"You aren't doubting me, are you? Gamache hasn't gotten into your head."

"*Non, patronne.*" Yvette Nichol hung up and hit send on the password,

234

then sat back in her chair in the Gamaches' study and took a sip of the Gamaches' coffee, then looked at the remains of the Cap'n Crunch cereal with chocolate milk Madame Gamache had made her. And Yvette Nichol wondered why she felt so uncomfortable.

Then she rifled through the desk and found the copy of Charles Langlois's second notebook.

Here was the document that everyone had dismissed, thinking it contained Charles Langlois's initial notes. Thinking it was unimportant, and not, as it turned out, the most important.

That was until Gamache had gone back and reread it and realized their mistake. His mistake. And understood it contained a warning of something much bigger than the poisoning.

And yet, read and reread it as the Chief Inspector might, as the others might, they could not figure out what Charles was warning them about.

Yvette Nichol took the sheafs of worn paper into the kitchen, and sitting in front of the woodstove, she began to read. Once finished, she returned to the study and got the other one. The first one . . . the one they now dismissed, believing it had already coughed up all its secrets.

Many kilometers away, in Montréal, Chief Inspector Tardiff placed a call.

"We need to meet."

"Agreed," said Moretti.

Prime Minister Woodford stared at the three people in his office. His sharp gaze went from Gamache to Lacoste to that intense young woman who was introduced to him as Shona Dorion.

He'd listened to what they had to say. Now he opened his mouth, then closed it again. When the Prime Minister of Canada finally did speak, it was not what anyone expected.

"*Mein Kampf.*"

While Lacoste and Dorion looked at each other, perplexed, Armand Gamache opened his eyes wide in surprise. "My struggle?"

"Yes."

Of all the things a leader might say when told of a possible plan by a foreign power to invade, the title of that book was not one.

"Why are you quoting Hitler, sir?"

Now Dorion mouthed "Hitler?" and Lacoste frowned. Both turned to Gamache, who seemed to know the what but clearly not the why of it.

"His book, *Mein Kampf*—" the PM began.

"I'm familiar with it."

"Then you probably know about the Big Lie."

Oh, shit, thought Lacoste. *He doesn't believe us.* Though she didn't dare say anything.

"Are you calling us liars?" Shona asked and watched as the Prime Minister of Canada turned to her.

When she'd woken up that morning, she'd never expected that this would be part of her day. Her week. Her life. That within hours she would find herself in a private meeting with the PM. That he would be looking at her. At her. Shona Dorion.

Granted, his expression was one of annoyance, but still . . .

Indeed, Shona was trying to catch up with everything that had happened so far that young day.

She'd just showered and dressed, getting ready to go into Action Québec Bleu, when there was a knock on the door. Her phone said it was just after seven. This could not be good. Had she paid the rent? Yes. Had she given her neighbor back her dishes from two nights ago?

Yes.

So who could—

"Ms. Dorion, it's Armand Gamache."

Oh, fuck. Not him.

"Go away, you dirty old man. I told you I'm not putting out again." She grinned, imagining his face turning a bright red. She hoped he wasn't alone.

"I have something for yooooou." The singsong voice of the Chief Inspector came through the door, and despite herself Shona laughed.

"Is it candy?"

"Better. It's a warrant for your arrest unless you open this door in twenty seconds."

His voice had gone from playful at the beginning of the sentence, to neutral, to actually menacing. It was both impressive and more than a little disconcerting.

She opened the door.

"*Merci*," he said and introduced Inspector Lacoste. "May we?"

"Can I stop you?"

His answer was to step inside her tiny, tidy studio apartment in the Petite-Bourgogne *quartier* of Montréal.

"All this to stop me from going into AQB? You do know that because of what I did there you're so much further along. I found out that those numbers on the map are isobars. And I got into Chalifoux's computer and found the money being laundered through Action Québec Bleu. And I'm sure there's more to find. I can do what you cops can't."

"And that is?" Lacoste asked. The bed was so tightly made, there was no give when she sat on it.

"Break the law," said Shona.

"Nice that you think we won't," said Gamache, taking a chair at the table by the compact kitchen and waving her to join him.

Shona stood for a moment, then realized she just looked mulish. "You're in my place."

To her amazement, he got up and moved. She'd lied. It wasn't where she normally sat, though he was now in her actual place.

Gamache was staring at her with such intensity, it almost frightened her. She sat down. "What? What's happened?"

He was trying to decide how much to tell her.

All the way there from Three Pines, he'd been discussing it with Lacoste. Getting her take. But finally, neither of them had an answer. It wasn't that they suspected Shona of working for the other side; it was that information was her fuel, and giving her more could, almost certainly would, propel the young investigative journalist into dangerous waters.

"You've figured out what's happening, what's going to happen," Shona said, leaning toward him. "Come on, Papa, tell me."

Lacoste raised her brows when she called him "Papa." But realized it was said ironically, and maybe, maybe, with just a little nascent affection.

"In exchange for this information, you need to promise not to act on it. Not to post about it until I say so. And to leave AQB. In fact, to pack a bag and come with us now."

"Where to?"

"First Ottawa, and then down to my home in Three Pines."

"Where?"

"Exactly," said Isabelle.

While the two cops stared at her, Shona Dorion had her own decision to make. She hated, loathed, having to make any sort of deal with cops, especially this one. But she also recognized that they were offering her an exclusive on what might be the story of a lifetime. One that could win her a Polk award.

She also recognized that she almost certainly had no choice. Gamache was framing it as her decision, but that had already been made. Unless...

"May I see the warrant?"

Lacoste got up and showed Shona a document on her phone. A warrant for her arrest.

"It's signed by you," she said, turning to Gamache.

"True."

"It's a lie. I've done nothing to be arrested for. This is an abuse of power."

"Absolutely. I have, in signing that warrant, broken the law. Who knew?"

It was said with some amusement, though his eyes remained intense. She tried, tried, not to feel grudging admiration for the man at that moment.

But anything she felt was fleeting.

Armand Gamache had also arrested her mother, probably with as much cause as this warrant. It had led to her death.

"I clearly have no choice."

"Well, you do, but it's not a good one," said Lacoste. "The shit's about to hit the fan, and you're standing right in front of it."

"What do you mean?"

Gamache nodded to Lacoste, who showed Shona the photo sent by Evelyn Tardiff.

"This was taken by Sûreté surveillance two days ago."

Shona squinted at it, then looked up. "That's Moretti. And he's talking to Margaux Chalifoux. Holy shit. The head of AQB's involved with the mob? She's even stupider than I thought."

"She's far from stupid." Lacoste clicked her phone shut. "If AQB is a front, then she's managed to keep it under the radar for years and is almost certainly an accessory to at least three murders, maybe more. This is not someone you want to underestimate."

"But what are they up to? You know."

"You will not post what I'm about to say. Not until I tell you to. And then you need to use your social media to sound the alarm."

"Well, now, there's a problem with that, one you've probably already considered."

"That you don't take direction well?" asked Lacoste, and got a smile.

"That too, though I am willing to make an exception." She looked at Gamache. "You tell me the problem if you're so smart."

"The problem is that you've made a career out of calling out politicians, cops, judges, corporations. You have a small and very loyal following. But it's not enough to sound any serious alarm. Not quickly enough anyway."

"Exactly. All it will do is alert whoever's behind this and put everyone, including myself, in the crosshairs. But—"

"*Oui?*"

"There is someone who could do it. My mentor, Paul."

"You have a mentor?" asked Lacoste.

"And you don't?" Shona's eyes slid to Gamache. "At least mine knows what he's doing and doesn't act without proof."

"Does he have a big enough following?" asked Lacoste.

"Well, he's unemployed, so he has time."

"That wasn't my question," said Lacoste.

"Yes, he has a following."

Lacoste studied the young woman, then turned to Gamache. "You must know other journalists, *patron*, contacts who can get the story out when the time comes."

"I do. We have drinks regularly, as you know, and exchange information." "But?"

"While I trust them, I'm not so sure about their editors and execs."

"My thoughts exactly," said Shona. "One of the first things any tyrant does is control the narrative. And that means controlling the media. My guy's no longer involved."

Gamache was nodding. "His stories no longer need to be vetted and approved. Who is he? Have I met him?"

"I doubt it. He hasn't spent much time in Canada."

"Does he spend time on this planet?" asked Lacoste.

"He swings by occasionally, when the Great Pumpkin allows it."

"Good grief." Isabelle was trying not to like this annoying young woman, but she found herself hoping her daughters might grow up to be like Shona one day.

"Not a word to him until I say," said Gamache.

"Jesus, control issues?"

Isabelle turned to her mentor. "Please tell me we aren't putting all our eggs in this basket case. Any other ideas?"

"None."

Shona Dorion got up and packed a bag.

"No, I'm not calling you liars," Prime Minister James Woodford said a couple of hours later as they stood in his office on Parliament Hill. "Though I'm not sure I believe you. I'm talking about a strategy Hitler had, a theory he described in his book."

"*Mein Kampf*," said Gamache. "A self-aggrandizing polemic written by a man on the threshold of derangement."

"But a compelling read," said Woodford, "for a population longing for hope, for leadership, for a way out of their degradation and misery."

"Unless you happen to have any sort of disability. Or be gay or a Gypsy or Jewish," said Gamache. "My guardian, my adoptive grandmother, was Jewish. Deported from Paris. My father found her close to death in one of the camps and brought her to Montréal. She raised me after my parents died. *Mein Kampf* is a manifesto. A hate-filled, hateful blueprint for how to turn a friend into an enemy."

"The necessary first step in any invasion," said Woodford. "I'm sorry about your parents, about your grandmother. I didn't know."

He wasn't the only one. Shona was staring at the Chief Inspector, surprised by this series of revelations.

"Unfortunately, Hitler was right about this," said Gamache. "If you want to start a war, first you create a Big Lie. And, from there, a common enemy."

Oy Gutt, his grandmother's expression, came to mind. It was a shame they were themselves tied to the Big Truth. So much harder to believe.

"Sir, we need to take this seriously. I think there's still time to stop it, but we need to act."

"And do what? You still have no proof."

"You need to speak to the American President. She must be aware of the chatter. Get a sense of where she stands."

"Are you thinking she might be involved?"

"I don't know. But she needs to know that we are aware that Canada is being re-framed as an enemy of the American people. An enemy with all the resources the US needs, including, especially, water."

"Will you excuse me, please?" Woodford made for the door. "My Chief of Staff needs to hear this."

He returned a few minutes later.

"I don't think you've met everyone here. Manon Payette, this is..." The PM introduced them. "Can you repeat what you just told me, Chief Inspector?"

When Gamache finished, Payette looked at him as though the head of homicide for the Sûreté du Québec was wearing a tinfoil hat.

"No offense, but are you nuts? The Americans are going to invade Canada? Are you sure you haven't stumbled on the plans from the War of 1812, when the Americans last invaded? A war which, by the way, we won."

"Well, that's disputed," said Gamache. "Though we did repel them. And yes, I'm pretty sure their plans have been updated in the last two hundred years."

Just then there was a sharp rap on the door, and before the PM could say anything, it burst opened.

"Mr. Prime Minister, there've been shots fired."

"What? You showed Gamache photographs of us together?" demanded Margaux Chalifoux. "Are you crazy?"

"I had no choice," said Evelyn Tardiff. "He was beginning to suspect me. I had to give him something."

"You gave him me, you dumb fuck! I've spent years setting up this blind, and you blow it? Now we have to sterilize AQB before they raid it, if it hasn't happened already."

She reached for her phone, but Moretti stopped her. "No rush, Margaux." Chalifoux looked puzzled, but replaced her phone.

They were in the Jean-Talon market, in one of the storerooms. It smelled of fish, and innards and broccoli on the turn. The women were breathing through their mouths. Moretti and his soldiers seemed not to notice the stench.

"She did the right thing." Moretti looked at Tardiff. "Your informant in Gamache's circle says they have the biologist's laptop and the map. You're sure of that?"

"And have found .family, *oui*. I confirmed it with the passwords."

"They've gotten further than I'd have liked. Thanks"—he shifted his gaze—"to you."

"Me?" said Chalifoux. "What've I done?"

"It's the sin of omission, Margaux. Charles Langlois worked for you, but you didn't know what he was doing? You didn't realize he was collecting information on us?"

She pressed her lips together. She knew Moretti enough to know any defense was seen as an offense. And that, for Moretti, was a capital crime.

"You went to the lake with Frederick Castonguay. He trusted you because Charles Langlois did. He hadn't yet tumbled to your rule. But then you killed Castonguay before he found the laptop. And now they have it."

It was said in a reasonable, measured voice. Which was terrifying.

She shifted uncomfortably in her chair and was about to defend herself, to tell Moretti that Castonguay only knew the lake was important but had no idea why. When kneeling on the ground, a gun to his head, the young man would have told her everything, anything. But he did not. By then, of course, he had to die anyway.

All this went unsaid.

There was a small commotion outside the storeroom, unintelligible voices raised slightly.

"My informant also tells me that Gamache is speaking to the PM again today," said Tardiff.

"For all the good that'll do," said Chalifoux.

Moretti's look of annoyance was followed by a tense silence, broken by more noise outside. Moretti spoke to one of his soldiers, who left. Then he turned back to Evelyn Tardiff. "I want you to plant stories with your journalist contacts telling them what Gamache is saying."

"The truth?" asked Tardiff. "About water and the Americans?"

"Exactly. I want him portrayed as a delusional old man, a broken-down warhorse who's taken one too many blows to the head. Who needs to be replaced before he does any real damage."

"Look, that won't stop him," said Tardiff. "He doesn't care what others think and eventually he's going to get proof. Why not just kill him?"

"Why not?" demanded Chalifoux. "Because it'll convince everyone that he's telling the truth." She turned to Don Moretti. "Has it occurred to you that for them to get as far as they have, they must be getting help?"

"Actually, it has." He slowly turned to Tardiff, as an owl might on spotting a mouse in a dark field. "Someone here is passing along information."

He nodded to one of his soldiers, who advanced into the room.

Dear God, help me, thought Evelyn Tardiff.

But the large man walked right by her to Margaux Chalifoux.

"Are you crazy?" the head of AQB shouted at Moretti as the soldier gripped her arm and lifted her up like a doll. "She's the informant. Not me."

But Moretti was unmoved. Just then his other soldier returned, whispered in Moretti's ear, and handed him a phone.

Reading the screen, his eyes widened in surprise. He waved Tardiff over. "You need to see this."

What they both saw was a live news report, and under it in red letters, *Shots fired*.

Marcus Lauzon had just arrived in the interview room in the penitentiary when the warden came in.

"Have you heard?"

"Heard what?" Jean-Guy instinctively reached for his phone, but he didn't have it. He'd had to leave it in the guards' room.

Yvette Nichol typed what she'd found in Charles's notebook. The first one. The one everyone had set aside as no longer important.

As soon as the sequence of numbers and letters was in, she hit enter. "Holy shit."

She sent off a secure text to Gamache, Lacoste, and Beauvoir, with the link. As she hit send, her phone lit up.

"Have you heard?" Madame Gamache stood in the doorway into the study, brittle leaves stuck to her heavy sweater and one hanging from her hair. "I'm turning on the television."

In an instant Armand took in every detail of what was happening and instinctively stepped in front of the Prime Minister, who was on his feet and looking stunned.

Members of the RCMP's Parliamentary Protective Service with weapons drawn had poured into the room. Guns out at close quarters was a dangerous situation, Gamache knew. One could go off unexpectedly.

Or even on purpose.

As he moved, Gamache put his hand to his hip, where his holster would be, if he carried one.

Then he turned to Lacoste. But she'd had to surrender her weapon at security since Ottawa wasn't in Sûreté jurisdiction. Shona was standing frozen in place, her eyes wide, staring toward the PM and his Chief of Staff.

"Where?" Gamache demanded of the officer in charge.

"Not here. Washington. DC. The White House. Get him away from the windows," he ordered the agents surrounding the PM. "We're locking down Parliament, just in case."

On hearing that the danger was not close, was not imminent, there was a noticeable relaxation on the part of the Prime Minister.

"Turn on the televisions," he said.

Manon Payette grabbed a remote, and the bank of monitors came to life. Assorted channels appeared, from CBC to Radio-Canada to CNN to the BBC and Al Jazeera. All showed the same image. The familiar exterior of the White House used by journalists in their stand-ups.

With everyone in the PM's office riveted on the news, Gamache took the opportunity to slip out and get his phone, left in the outer office.

He quickly returned before he was missed and sent a text: *Bert, what's happening?*

The PM was also sending messages. No doubt to the President and other world leaders. Desperate for information.

Armand stared down at his screen. Nothing.

He tried again. Then he tried calling.

It rang and rang. Nothing.

If shots were fired in the White House, the head of the Joint Chiefs must be rushing over from the Pentagon. Inundated with reports on the ground.

Unless...

Unless General Whitehead had done exactly what he had done. And that was go first thing in the morning to the leader of his country.

Now Armand lowered his phone and watched the news reports...

CHAPTER 24

⌣

B ert Whitehead had returned the salutes of the Uniformed Division guards on duty at the side entrance to the White House and been escorted along a corridor he'd walked down hundreds of times.

He'd asked to see the President as early as possible and was told she'd be happy to meet with him over breakfast.

President O'Rourke was already at work. She got to her feet, smiling when she saw him. "General."

"Madame President."

"I ordered you bacon and eggs and coffee, of course."

"Wonderful. Thank you."

Tiny and kinetic, with grey hair in a motherly bun, she came around the side of her desk and indicated the small dining room off the Oval Office.

"Ah, I see the food has arrived."

Two navy valets in black slacks, white shirts, black vests, and bow ties were putting plates on the table while a third poured coffee, then retreated to the small pantry.

Whitehead waited for the President to be seated and was just about to do so himself when he stopped.

The head of the Joint Chiefs of Staff knew the sound of a gun being drawn and the look on someone's face when they realized they were about to die.

He saw it now on the President. He reached out and gripped the back of the chair to use as a weapon, hoping he could—

That was as far as Bert Whitehead got.

Jean-Guy Beauvoir leaned against the doorpost into the guards' room and watched the live reports. So far no one knew what had happened inside. Maddeningly, they only had the picture of the exterior of the White House.

Reine-Marie and Yvette Nichol sat side by side on the sofa and watched, wide-eyed. Barely breathing.

Olivier turned on the TV in the bistro, something he only did for Stanley Cup finals when the Canadiens were playing. He'd lost the remote, and now, brushing the dust off it, he turned the screen on. Myrna, Clara, and Ruth watched, along with other patrons, their crêpes getting cold.

All around the country, the world, televisions and computers were turned on, tuned in. Cameras were trained on the exterior of one of the most recognizable buildings in the world as more and more emergency vehicles arrived. Sirens blaring. Lights flashing. Special forces, armed to the hilt, were pouring out of trucks as perimeters were established.

Journalists in every language tried to work out what was happening. Though one thing was known.

Shots had been fired in the White House.

Prime Minister Woodford sat down with a thump and brought his hand to his mouth, as though trying to stifle a word, a shout. His phone lay in his other hand, the screen lighting up as messages poured in, ignored for the moment.

More Parliamentary Protective officers had arrived, this time armed with M4 carbines. They'd secured the perimeter of Parliament Hill in Ottawa, and the officer in charge was trying to get more information. The Minister of Defense for Canada, Giselle Trudel, arrived and was stopped at the office door and frisked.

Gamache was on his phone. No one noticed.

"Anything, *patron*?" Lacoste joined him.

He was quiet, listening. "Get back to me when you have something." Then he hung up. "Nothing. Everyone's scrambling. There was absolutely no chatter about any sort of attack."

"Get me the feed from inside the White House," the PM demanded.

"We're trying, sir," said the head of intelligence.

A technician had arrived and was on a call. "Got it," he said.

Gamache and Lacoste turned and saw the main monitor switch to a camera showing a long marble hallway.

All eyes were on the screen. Even those supposedly guarding the doors and windows turned to watch a heavily armed tactical team moving deeper into the White House.

"The Oval Office," commanded the PM. "We need to find the President."

The technician finally landed on cameras in the Oval Office, where Uniformed Division officers, weapons raised, had burst in. It was empty.

The cameras followed them into the next room.

Three bodies lay on the carpet.

Two were valets.

The other was in full military uniform. A valet was kneeling over him.

A thousand kilometers away Lacoste turned to Gamache and saw his face drain of blood.

"The President? Where's the President?" Woodford shouted at the monitor.

At that moment the valet, blood on his shirt and a gun in his hand, stood and turned to the officers.

"He's armed," several of the guards in the PM's office shouted. Some even pointed toward the screens.

On the monitors they watched as someone stepped between the armed valet and the armed guards.

There was a moment frozen in time.

Lacoste heard Gamache inhale. He'd seen, a split second before Lacoste, who it was.

President O'Rourke had placed herself in front of the valet, her arms wide. Protecting him.

"*Non*," whispered Gamache. "*Arrêtez.*"

But it was too late. *Bam, bam, bam!* Shots went off.

What Gamache was afraid of had happened. He and Lacoste both knew from bitter experience that this was how tragedies occurred. Not on purpose, but because once the brain had committed to an action, it was almost impossible to stop.

Once the message had been sent to pull the trigger, it could not be recalled.

"Oh, God," someone whispered.

Someone else, perhaps the PM, shouted, "No!"

Shona had closed her eyes but opened them again when she heard Gamache exhale.

The senior tactical officer in the White House, grasping the situation, had raised his arm, knocking the rifle of the guard next to him so that the shots hit the ceiling.

The President fell back, obviously thinking the bullets must have struck her, and probably repelled by the deafening noise within inches of her.

The valet she'd been protecting dropped the gun he'd taken off the assassin and grabbed the President. Holding her safe.

Within the small dining room, what looked like complete chaos broke out, but it was, in fact, finely orchestrated by the senior officer.

"Madame President, you need to come with us."

He didn't wait for her agreement before yanking her forward, away from the suspect.

She was immediately surrounded by officers and hurried out of the room. Then he turned his attention to the surviving valet.

"Chief Petty Officer Oscar Flores," said the valet, his arms raised.

"I know who you are. What I don't know is why you did this."

"I didn't." Flores's voice was calm, though his eyes were wide with shock and alarm. "The General..."

Officers were on their knees, ripping General Whitehead's uniform jacket off to reveal his wounds.

"He's still alive."

"These ones are dead," another reported.

"Get moving," said the officer and nodded to one of his soldiers, who shoved Flores forward with his rifle.

At that moment the Secret Service arrived in the Oval Office. All this had taken less than a minute. When they tried to take the President away from the Uniformed Division officers, she stopped them. Pale and trembling, President O'Rourke still managed to take command.

"I'm in good hands. Help General Whitehead. Chief Petty Officer Flores comes with me."

"But Madame Pres—" began the senior officer.

"You heard me. He saved my life. You can question him in my presence."

In the Prime Minister's office there was silence, before Woodford turned to the room and said to no one in particular, "What the fuck just happened?"

Was still happening.

Gamache watched, his expression one of shock and grief, as medics worked to save the life of Bert Whitehead.

Shona, who was watching him, whispered, "Can we talk?"

"Not now."

"Now."

He looked at her, at the intensity in her stare. And nodded.

"Mr. Prime Minister, do you mind ...?"

But the PM was paying no attention to them. Gamache did not have to look at Lacoste, knowing she didn't have to be told to follow them. In the outer office Gamache turned to Shona.

"What is it?"

"Not here. Outside."

The corridor was lined with Mounties armed with automatic rifles at every door.

They were watched closely as they made their way to the exit.

"I'm sorry," said the heavily armed guard at the door. "We're on lockdown. No one in, no one out."

"Understood. *Merci.*"

Sunshine spilled through the windows, so tantalizingly close.

As he stood there, trying to decide where to go, Armand couldn't get the sight, the thought, of Bert Whitehead out of his head. Could he survive those wounds? Was he still alive ...?

War's a fact of life today, it will not be wished away,
Forget that fact, and you'll be dead before you started.

"*Patron?*"

Gamache looked around and saw that Lacoste was standing at a rare unguarded door. It was immediately obvious why no one was on guard. It was a utility closet, with a bucket and mop, a broom and rolls of paper towel.

The three of them squeezed in.

"What—" Gamache began to ask, but Shona was already talking.

"Did you see?"

"See what? The attempt on the President's life? Yes."

"No, before that. When the guards told us there'd been shots fired. Everyone reacted as though the attack was here, in Parliament."

"*Oui.*"

"Except one person. I happened to be looking at the Prime Minister when that happened."

"He wasn't surprised?" asked Lacoste.

"Oh, no, he was like the rest of us. Shocked and afraid. It was that Payette woman, his Chief of Staff. She was looking at him as though she knew something. Something bad."

"We all thought it was bad," said Lacoste.

"No, this was different. She wasn't afraid, at least not in that way. She seemed to know there was no danger. Not here."

At that moment the door was yanked open and an armed special forces officer stood there, her rifle pointed at them.

"Out, get out. Now!"

"But—" Shona began to step forward.

A gun was cocked.

"Shona!" Gamache stepped in front of her and spread his arms wide in obvious submission. As he did, he gave her a look that was impossible to misinterpret.

Her hands went up, as did Lacoste's.

Once out of what must've looked like a hiding place, they were frisked and their IDs taken.

The commando handed Gamache back his Sûreté ID. "What were you doing in there, sir?"

"We needed a private place to talk about what just happened."

"A closet?"

"Well, we didn't know," said Gamache, replacing his ID.

He knew how ridiculous they must've looked, all crammed in there like clowns in a circus.

The guard, no fan of clowns, smiled tightly. The atmosphere still tense. "Come with me."

There was no "please."

She led them to a large, comfortable lounge. Those in Parliament at that early hour were being held in different rooms. Gamache recognized a few members of Parliament and civil servants, as well as a couple of senators. All were gathered around a television.

"Any news?" one of them asked when she saw them enter.

"The President is safe," said Gamache. "That's all I know."

"Thank God for that."

"What the hell happened?" asked another.

"*Désolé.*" He put up his hands to indicate he had nothing more.

They sat in a cluster of comfortable, though worn, armchairs in a far corner, away from the others.

Armand leaned forward. "How do you interpret what you saw?"

"The look on the Chief of Staff's face?" said Shona. "I don't know, but I watch people for a living and that was just strange. Her reaction was different from everyone else in the room."

"Still, some people are slower to react than others," suggested Gamache. "Madame Payette might've been in shock."

"Maybe." But she sounded far from convinced.

"*Patron*, have you checked your messages?"

"Not yet. Is there one in particular?"

"Yes."

He got out his phone and found the message from Agent Nichol. It took him a few minutes to read through what was on the link. Then he looked up into Lacoste's eyes. She too had read it.

"I know," she said, agreeing with something he didn't say. Didn't have to say. The look on his face said it all.

"What?" Shona had perched on the arm of his chair and was straining to see.

He went back and read the document again.

"Holy shit," Shona whispered. "That can't be right. 'Cause if it is..."

"We need to speak to the Prime Minister," said Gamache.

He approached the guard but was barred from leaving.

"Can you at least take a message to Prime Minister Woodford?"

His request was met with stony silence.

"What're we going to do?" asked Shona. "We can't just sit here. Can we send it to the PM?"

Gamache had considered that but decided against it. They needed to control who saw this document. They needed to protect it as long as they could. Besides, it probably would have been lost among all the other messages that must be pouring in.

Gamache's own phone was slammed, jammed with messages. But one caught his eye.

Sherry Caufield had written on the secure server.

She was counterintelligence in the UK, and a famous misanthrope, rarely communicating unless she had something important to say, and even then her messages were terse. Often outright rude. She was tolerated because she was so good.

Under the heading *What do you make of this?* was a link. He clicked on it. Up came President O'Rourke at her desk in the Oval Office. She looked up and smiled as Bert Whitehead arrived.

Gamache sat back in his armchair, as though given a slight shove.

"What is it?" asked Isabelle, leaning over to see.

CHAPTER 25

President O'Rourke got to her feet. "General."

"Madame President."

"I ordered you bacon and eggs and coffee, of course."

"Wonderful. Thank you."

Armand watched as the President, with her customary and often parodied rapid little steps, led the head of the Joint Chiefs of Staff, with his long strides, into a small room off the Oval Office.

"Jesus," whispered Shona, looking furtively around to see if anyone was paying attention. "It's the security tape from the White House. The recording from this morning." She looked at Gamache. "Who are you?"

"Someone with a lot of friends," muttered Lacoste.

On the tape, two navel valets are placing breakfast on the table, while a third pours coffee, then steps back into the pantry.

"Ah, I see the food has arrived."

General Whitehead stands by his chair and watches the valet they now recognized as Chief Petty Officer Flores seat the President; then Flores looks around, a bit confused.

Gamache hit pause.

"Why'd you do that?" demanded Shona.

"Why's Flores hesitating?" asked Lacoste.

Gamache hit play, and saw Flores give a subtle gesture toward his colleague.

"He's expecting the other valet to seat General Whitehead," said Gamache. "But he isn't. The valet is just standing there."

"Flores is sensing something's off," said Lacoste.

As they watched, Flores steps around the table to seat the General himself. His face is set in a neutral expression, though it's clear he's irritated but not yet alarmed.

Gamache again hit pause and took a moment to look at Bert Whitehead. Alive. Unharmed. If he could only freeze this image and stop the bad thing from happening...

Instead, he touched play.

Whitehead, smiling at the President, notices her expression, and his own changes. Gamache rewinds a few seconds, freezing it on the President's face.

"She knows what's about to happen," says Shona.

"She believes she's about to be killed," said Lacoste. She knew that look. Had had it on her own face. And had almost been right.

"Bert sees it," said Armand.

Bert. Shona looks at Gamache, realizing for the first time that he knows this man. Well.

Armand rewound again and hit play.

"*Arrêtez*," said Lacoste, and he did.

"What?" he asked.

"Do you hear it? Play it again."

Gamache did, but try as he might, he still couldn't hear anything strange. The buzzing in his ears, though mild now, was enough to mask any subtle sound. Clearly both Lacoste and Shona heard something, though only Lacoste knew what it was.

"It's a gun being drawn."

It all happened in less time than it took to gasp. For a veteran of combat like Whitehead there was no escaping what this meant. The combination of the look on the President's face and the familiar sound behind him made the conclusion inescapable.

He isn't alone in his alarm. Chief Petty Officer Flores is also alerted. He begins to come around the dining table just as the General reaches for his chair to use as a weapon, but there's no time. The valet behind him shoots.

The force of the bullets lifts Whitehead off his feet. Then he drops. Shot in the chest. President O'Rourke pushes back in her chair, in shock.

Flores, reacting quickly, leaps forward and tackles the first valet. Disarming him. He turns and sees the other valet in the pantry, armed and aiming. And firing.

"He misses?" said Shona. "How can he miss?"

Gamache has again frozen the video.

"He doesn't miss," said Isabelle Lacoste. "He hits his target."

"But he missed the President and even missed Flores. He got the other guy, the one who shot the General. Weren't they in this together?"

"That's who he meant to kill," said Gamache, his face grim. The video advances.

The valet now turns his weapon on Flores, but the Chief Petty Officer has grabbed the gun off the floor and gets off a round. The valet falls.

Flores looks over and sees the President is uninjured, then scrambles to the General, bending over him.

At that moment, the guards arrive. Thinking Flores is the assassin, they're about to shoot when President O'Rourke moves quickly, shielding him with her body.

The three of them watched for another minute before Armand again paused the video.

Then, without a word, he went back, and they watched over and over, the valet aiming and firing. And hitting Whitehead.

What do you make of this? Sherry Caufield had written. It was now clear what "this" was. Not the entire video, but that instant.

"Does it seem to you, *patron . . .*"

"That the shooter wasn't aiming at the President," said Gamache.

"His target was General Whitehead." Isabelle Lacoste turned to Gamache. "Why?"

Gamache thought for a moment, but there was only one possible reason. As disconcerting as it was.

"Because they couldn't allow him to speak to the President."

Isabelle's face opened in sudden realization. "To tell her what we talked about at the Haskell Opera House. Jesus."

"I think so. Every conversation would be recorded. There'd be a record of what he told her, but also what he asked her. About the plan."

"But how would they know? We just met him last night. And it was just us."

While Gamache wrote back to Sherry Caufield in London—*Whitehead was the target. What do you know?*—Isabelle stared behind him at an old oil painting on the wall. It showed skaters on the Rideau Canal. They were in Victorian garb. The rosy-cheeked women in long flowing dresses and fur muffs, the men in heavy coats and hats. All were smiling, enjoying a day out.

She wished she could crawl into the painting and leave all this behind. Instead, she turned back to Gamache.

"What Nichol found. The link. That was what General Whitehead wanted to tell us last night."

"But he needed his President's permission. I think so."

Bert obviously realized the danger this document posed and wanted to warn them. But too late.

"The valet killed his own co-conspirator," said Shona. "Wouldn't you have thought he'd kill the President first?"

"If they wanted to kill President O'Rourke, she'd be dead," said Gamache.

"They want her alive?"

"They need her alive."

"Oh, shit. You think she's involved," said Shona.

He turned and looked at her full-on. "I'm trying not to jump to conclusions. That's the worst thing we can do now. That's how we miss things. These people traffic in untruths and misdirection. We can't afford to be taken in."

"In other words, you have absolutely no idea," said Shona.

"Would not be the first time."

Armand turned to their fellow detainees. Unfortunately, they'd been placed in a room with junior cabinet ministers and low-level functionaries. And a few elderly senators. No one with the clout to get out.

"What the fuck is this?"

Ruth had turned away from the television coverage in the bistro and been checking her messages. Now she showed the others what had appeared.

Clara stared at the phone, its face cracked, not unlike its owner's. Scrolling down, her brows drew together in concern. "We need to show Reine-Marie."

Jean-Guy returned to the interview room.

"What was that about?" Marcus Lauzon asked. "Something happened?"

While his expression was bland, with that slight smugness that was like a caul over his face, the former Deputy PM's tone betrayed his anxiety.

There was little to be gained by not telling him, so Beauvoir did. When he finished, Lauzon heaved an uncharacteristic sigh.

"I'm sorry to hear that. I've met General Whitehead on more than one occasion. This is a loss. But it means you're getting close."

"To what?"

"Well, you obviously already know. You don't need me for that."

"We think we know, but need evidence. You have that evidence. You need to give it to us, before—"

"Before I'm killed too?"

"Yes," he snapped. No use mincing words. "If they could get into the Oval Office, they can get to you here. The only reason you're still alive is that Gamache is protecting you."

"*Non.* The only reason is that I've placed myself in here."

Beauvoir cocked his head. "What do you mean?"

"Why do you think I never talked? Never effectively defended myself?"

Beauvoir was silent, not wanting to get sucked into Lauzon's games, though he knew the answer. It was because there was no effective defense for a guilty man.

"It's because I needed to be found guilty. I needed to be put in here. I wanted Gamache to put me into solitary. I knew if I was let go, I wouldn't get off the courtroom steps."

"Are you trying to tell me that you're innocent and intentionally put yourself in prison?"

"I'm not 'trying' to tell you that, I just did. Can't be clearer. Out there I'd be killed."

"We need to know which heads of multinational corporations bribed you to get control of our resources. Names."

"I'm not the one they bribed."

"Of course you are. We have the trail through Action Québec Bleu into your accounts."

Lauzon actually snorted derision. "God, you really are stupid. What you found is a pittance compared to the billions paid out. And not into any account of mine." He leaned forward. "I'm not the one who can make what they need happen."

Beauvoir stood up. "Goodbye."

"Wait."

Beauvoir did not. He pounded on the door.

"Let's play a game."

The door opened. As he stepped out, Jean-Guy heard Lauzon shout, "The game's called 'Suppose I'm telling the truth.'"

The door closed behind him. Beauvoir was halfway down the hall when his steps slowed.

"Oh, fuck it," he sighed. And turned around.

"Ohhhh," sighed Reine-Marie and closed her eyes. Then she looked up at the others. Ruth, Myrna, Clara were staring at her. Even Rosa looked concerned, something she very rarely did.

"It'll pass," said Myrna. "People are focused on the White House. No one will pay any attention to this."

"And no one who reads this will believe it," said Gabri.

"It isn't the first time people have tried to make Armand out to be incompetent," said Clara.

"Ridiculously easy to do," said Ruth, and Rosa nodded agreement.

"Except, this time—" Nichol began.

"I think you have work to do," Reine-Marie interrupted her.

The last thing she needed was for Nichol to complete that sentence: *This time the posts are true.*

That Armand really did believe the US was being groomed to take over Canada, by force, if necessary.

It sounded crazy. Delusional. Except to those few who understood the global water crisis, and what the future held for drought-stricken nations. Including their neighbor to the south.

"Wait," Beauvoir shouted.

Lauzon was being led away. The guard kept going, despite Beauvoir's call.

Now he repeated, louder: "Wait!"

This time the guard paused, then turned. "What?"

"I need to speak to him."

"You just did."

The guard had his hand gripping Lauzon's thin arm. It did not look right. And neither did the expression on Lauzon's face. It looked to Beauvoir as though the man was about to cry.

"Bring him back to the interview room." When the guard hesitated, Beauvoir approached. For a not-very-large man, he had the ability to look menacing. A bundle of tightly wired threat about to come unraveled.

The guard escorted Lauzon back.

Beauvoir made a note of his name, then followed the former politician into the room. When the door closed, Lauzon exhaled.

"Okay, I'll play," said Beauvoir. "Suppose you're telling the truth about what?"

"That I am not the one behind, or even involved, in all this. I've been set up. Just for a moment, Inspector, entertain that possibility."

"So, if not you, then who?"

"Think. Who could have placed those documents in my desk? Who had access to my accounts and my diary? Who could have set up those meetings with Joe Moretti in Sainte-Émiline and made sure I was photographed? And made sure Gamache saw them?"

Beauvoir remained silent. But he was now in the game. It didn't take much to arrive at the answer.

"Jeanne Caron."

Lauzon nodded. "My Chief of Staff, my longtime assistant and confidante."

"*And a man's foes shall be they of his own household,*" muttered Jean-Guy.

"What was that?" Lauzon asked.

"Matthew 10:36. Something the Chief Inspector learned from his first boss in the Sûreté and passes on to all his agents."

"I wish he'd told me."

"Jeanne Caron," Beauvoir whispered.

"I'm a shit, I know that. I've bribed and bullied and threatened. I've done terrible things. Broken all sorts of laws. But I'm nothing compared to her."

"Why's everyone staring at us?"

Shona tilted her head toward the crowd in the lounge.

Sure enough, one by one, almost everyone had turned toward them, then quickly looked away.

"Are we suddenly naked?" Shona actually looked down at her fully clothed body.

"I think this's why." Armand showed them his phone. Reine-Marie had sent him a message.

"Oh, shit," said Isabelle. "Someone's posted that we believe the US is about to invade Canada."

"Not 'we.' You." Shona looked at Gamache, then took out her phone.

"There're calls for your resignation, *patron*," said Lacoste, now on her own phone. "Saying this proves you're incompetent. That you're delusional and dangerous."

"Really? The posts I'm reading have a different take," said Shona.

The two Sûreté officers turned to her, hopeful despite themselves.

"They say you're just plain loony. Too many knocks to the head." She looked at him. "They're not wrong. Unfortunately, in this case, you're actually telling the truth. But why would they put this out there? Why admit it?" She opened her eyes wide. "Ooooh, I see what they're doing. The clever fucks."

Armand was nodding. The fact he was being portrayed as incompetent, perhaps even crazy, wasn't necessarily new or worrisome. What was new was that they were using the truth against them. Turning it into something ludicrous. Laughable.

So that when he did sound the alarm, no one would believe it.

"They've grabbed the narrative," said Shona. "And twisted it."

"The Ministry of Truth," said Gamache. "This time actually telling the truth."

"Ah," said Shona with a small appreciative laugh. "*Nineteen Eighty-Four.*"

"This must've been put out in a hurry," said Lacoste. "They might not have covered their tracks as thoroughly as before. We might be able to trace it back."

Gamache and Lacoste exchanged glances, then he sent off a message to Yvette Nichol.

If Nichol was sending information to Chief Inspector Tardiff, as he believed she was, and if Tardiff really was working for Moretti, as he was afraid she was, they were well and truly in the *merde*. This would just hurry it along.

There was little to lose at this stage if Nichol and Tardiff were working against them, and a whole lot to gain if Nichol and Tardiff were on their side.

"It's time for you to contact your mentor," Gamache said to Shona. "That Paul fellow."

"Paul Workman."

Gamache stared at her. "Paul Workman's your mentor?"

"You sound surprised."

"Surprised doesn't begin to cover it," said Isabelle. "He's the most senior, most respected journalist in Canada. One of the top foreign correspondents internationally. He's covered wars and catastrophes, crisis after crisis—"

"God, you sound like you have a crush on the guy," said Shona. She was not far wrong. Even Gamache looked a bit smitten.

"Until his network, CTV, closed his London bureau and let him go in a journalistic bloodbath," said Gamache. "It was a travesty."

It left millions of Canadians at the mercy of the reporting, the perceptions, and the interpretations of other nations. Including, especially, the American networks.

Paul Workman. This might actually work.

Gamache told her what he needed.

Just then a message from Jean-Guy appeared on the secure app.

"Lauzon says Jeanne Caron's either the Black Wolf or knows who is."

Gamache's mind raced. How much had he told her?

"Didn't he suggest the PM was the Black Wolf not long ago?" said Lacoste, reading the message. "Who's next? You? He's messing with us."

Gamache took a deep breath. He hoped so. Because if either Woodford or Caron was behind all this, they were in deep trouble.

He put his phone away and looked around. "We have to get out of here."

CHAPTER 26

A gent Fontaine looked around the office.

She was not alone. A few of the Action Québec Bleu volunteers were also standing there, staring.

"What happened here?" asked one. "Did someone break in?"

"Why would anyone do that?" asked another.

"Why would anyone do this?" said the first, sweeping his arm around.

"This" was rifle their desks, rip maps off the walls, take their computers.

Fontaine had gone directly to Margaux Chalifoux's office. It was empty. Not a piece of paper, not a pen, not a paperclip was left.

"Oh, fuck."

She took a photo and sent it to Inspector Lacoste, her direct superior. Then she contacted the agents assigned to watch Chalifoux.

Is she still at home?

Hasn't left.

Fontaine lowered her phone and considered. Chalifoux should have been in already.

Check.

Two minutes later came the reply. *No answer at the door. No activity at windows.*

She forwarded the information to Inspector Lacoste, who replied immediately:

Break down the door.

No warrant.

Break down the door!

Fontaine relayed the order and waited. It didn't take long.

No one there.

Now it was Armand's turn to stare at the painting of the skaters on the Rideau, the canal that wound through Ottawa.

The painting had been done well over a century ago, but except for the clothing, it could have been painted last winter. Skaters still glided for miles along the frozen waterway. Some civil servants even skated to work.

He smiled. The painting brought back one of his most vivid memories of his parents. They'd come here on a bitterly cold day in February for a tour of the Parliament Buildings, but first, his mother explained, they were going skating. She knelt at Armand's feet and did up his laces, pulling them tight. She smiled up at him as she patted the double-knotted bow.

"*Ça va?*"

"*Oui.*" He'd never skated before, but he'd watched his heroes, the Canadiens de Montréal, play hockey. It looked easy enough.

He gripped his mother's hands and she heaved him upright.

His father took one hand, his mother the other, as he stood wobbling between them. Then they'd ventured onto the ice together until first one, then the other, had let go.

When he realized he was unmoored, he had a moment of terror. And then... off he'd glided, half tripping. His arms out to keep his balance. A wide smile on his rosy-cheeked face. What exhilaration. What freedom, what—

Even now, half a century later, he could feel the shock as he realized he was airborne, then falling. He could still feel the jarring as he hit the ice, and taste the blood as he bit his lip. But mostly what he remembered was the burning of his tears. They'd welled up partly from shock, partly from pain. Mostly from embarrassment.

And then his parents had hauled him to his feet, laughing. And sent him off again. To fall again. But each time he went further and further. And understood that falling wasn't embarrassing, it was natural. Expected. It was okay to fall. Which he did many more times. Not just on the ice, but when learning to ride his bike. When learning to ski. When climbing the apple tree at home.

He knew his parents would always be there to—

"*Patron?*"

He turned. "*Désolé.* Just thinking."

He saw a look pass between Isabelle and Shona and wondered if his eyes were bloodshot.

Looking down at his phone, he composed a message.

Can we meet? I need your advice.

He considered, then amended the message.

Can we meet? I need your help.

His finger hovered over the send button; then he touched it and saw the message to Jeanne Caron disappear. And felt, just for a moment, his feet go out from under him.

"You're a fool," said Jeanne Caron.

"They'll never find her," said Moretti. "Even better if they do. It'll be a warning to the CEOs, the judges, the cops, those fucking politicians. This is how we deal with anyone who betrays us."

"Jesus, you sound like a mob boss."

Don Moretti stared at her, then laughed. He didn't like her any more than she liked him. But she was amusing. And useful. For now.

Caron studied him for a moment. "It's one thing to kill Chalifoux, but you ordered incaprettamento? You'd better start praying they never find her. The New York mob will kill you for this, and incaprettamento will look humane."

The corte de florero came to mind.

"They can't. They need me."

Sadly, that much was true. For now.

They were strolling through the forest on mont Royal, kicking the decaying leaves ahead of them. Moretti's soldiers, in front and behind them, were trying to look like locals out for a stroll. And failing. Miserably.

Yeah, you blend.

They came to the lookout and stopped. A few tourists were milling around, trying to figure out the landmarks, though the infamous Olympic Stadium was all too obvious.

"The Olympics could no more have a deficit," declared the Mayor of Montréal in 1976, "than a man can have a baby."

For the rest of his life, he was portrayed in cartoons as heavily pregnant.

Caron's phone pinged and she glanced down. "A message from Gamache. He wants to meet."

"What's that about?"

"He says he needs my help." She replied to the message: *Yes, where and when?*

"I'm not surprised. Have you seen the feeds?" said Moretti.

Tardiff had done well to get it out so quickly, and so effectively. The posts were going viral. Thousands, soon millions, would read that the revered head of the Sûreté's Homicide division believed the US was about to invade Canada. He'd have been better off claiming he'd seen little green men in the woods.

Armand Gamache was fast becoming a laughingstock.

Caron had to admit it had been an unexpected stroke of genius from a man more accustomed to a sledgehammer than a stiletto.

But the thrust had been effective. Gamache's credibility was bleeding out all over social media.

Jeanne Caron had worried for a while now that her sudden decision to save Gamache in the water-treatment plant had been a rare mistake. She'd done it because the poisoning plot had clearly failed. The perpetrators exposed.

In saving him, she'd saved herself. And allowed the second part of the plan, the real plan, to also survive. It had been a risk that looked, when Gamache realized there was more to come, as though it would not pay off. But now...

I need your help.

Now her phone vibrated with his reply. *In Parliament now, needs to be later. Someplace private. Haskell Opera House? 4 p.m.?*

"Don't fuck this up," said Moretti.

"Like you fucked up the whole Frederick Castonguay fiasco? The kid's dead, his body found, and they have the laptop. And now this attack in the White House. It's sloppy. If Whitehead had been able to tell her how far they'd gotten and made his request—"

"Well, he didn't. Once again God is smiling on us."

Caron shook her head. She knew that Moretti went to church every

Sunday. His wife and mother more often. *He'd better pray there is no God*, she thought, *because if there is, there won't be a lot of smiling when Joe Moretti stands at the pearly gates.*

Caron couldn't wait for the moment when this shit-head would meet his maker. That day was coming, it was close. But for now, Joe Moretti still had his uses. Mostly as a distraction.

Gamache had stood right beside the Black Wolf and never realized it.

"You wanted to see me, Chief Inspector?"

An older man was standing beside Inspector Lacoste.

"We haven't met," Gamache put out his hand. "Armand Gamache."

"Yes, I know. Douglas Walls." They shook.

"I need your help, Senator."

"Really?" The bushy grey eyebrows rose. It might have been a while since anyone sought his help. "Is what they say true? You actually think the Americans are about to invade us?"

He tried to keep a straight face as he asked.

"Well, not 'about to.' I think it's already happening. I really hate to use the word, but I do think there's a conspiracy."

"You're right. Probably best for someone just labeled nuts not to start babbling about conspiracies."

"I didn't realize I was babbling."

"Well, at least you're not drooling. Why me?"

"You're the oldest person here."

Walls looked around, then smiled. "That's true. You need an *éminence grise*? Isn't that what senators are supposed to be? The wise counsel. But every time I hear that expression, my mind goes to Marguerite d'Youville and her Grey Nuns. *Les Soeurs grises.*"

The senator couldn't see Shona standing behind him, pretending to shoot herself.

Gamache opened his mouth to head off a history lesson, but the senator got there first.

"Did you know, Chief Inspector, that the name 'Grey Nuns' is a misnomer? They never wore grey, and at the time, back in the 1700s, 'grise' meant drunk. The Drunk Sisters."

He laughed, though his eyes were sharp and clear and held Gamache's.

"Then the Senate, being filled with *éminences grises*—" said Gamache.

"Bunch of drunks."

"So much for sober second thought." Which was how John A. Macdonald, Canada's first Prime Minister, described the Senate. Though he himself was rarely sober.

"Given what's happening..." Senator Walls looked behind him at the television. A crawl across the bottom said that the President was safe but that the head of the Joint Chiefs had been critically injured when he took the shots meant for her. "How could my age possibly matter?"

When Gamache explained what he needed, there was a pause. Then Senator Walls turned his back on Gamache and returned to the group, shaking his head.

After whispering to the cabinet secretaries, Chiefs of Staff, functionaries, and politicians, they all looked back at Gamache, amused.

"This isn't going to work. They're laughing at you," said Shona.

Though a few looked sad. Sorry that a fine career like the Chief Inspector's should end in such ignominy. Even Shona Dorion was beginning to feel bad for him.

A few minutes later, while Armand was trying to get an update on Bert Whitehead's condition, there was the sound of something shattering. He looked over and saw that Senator Walls had dropped his coffee mug.

The senator's face went slack. Reaching out a veined hand, he tried to grab the arm of a chair before he sank to his knees. And fell over.

A cabinet minister ran to the door and pounded while others knelt beside the prone man, loosening the senator's tie, feeling for a pulse.

When the door opened and the guard saw what was happening, he rushed over.

And Gamache and the others slipped out.

CHAPTER 27

Shona Dorion found herself being marched down the wide hallway, almost suspended between the two Sûreté officers gripping her arms.

Only one Parliamentary Protective officer challenged them.

"An intruder," said Gamache, his voice brusque.

"Fucking white fascists," she shouted, trying to twist out of their grip. "Nazis!" Then, as an afterthought, "*Mein Kampf!*"

She felt Gamache squeeze her arm slightly, in warning.

The Mountie stepped away.

It was both a relief, for their purposes, and an indictment. No one questioned the arrest of a young Black woman. Her anger was enough proof of guilt.

This had been Shona's idea.

Gamache had explained his plan, including how to get them out of there. "But we need to get more than five feet down the hall."

With armed guards all over the Parliament Buildings, that seemed impossible.

That was when Shona had proposed this, knowing from experience what would happen.

Gamache and Lacoste had listened, then looked at each other. It was Lacoste who, recognizing the truth of it, said, "It could work."

"It will work," said Shona.

"It better work," said Gamache.

A few minutes later Senator Walls had his "stroke."

Evelyn Tardiff always knew where Joe Moretti was. As soon as the technology had become available, she'd put covert tracking on his phone and that of his chief bodyguard. A man rarely more than five feet away from his boss.

Now she stood in the forest and watched Moretti and Jeanne Caron talking. This was the first time she'd seen the two together. She lowered her lens, in surprise. Though it now seemed obvious. Of course Jeanne Caron, that piece of shit, would be behind this.

Lifting her camera again, she could see through the long-distance lens that this was not a friendly chat.

She snapped a series of photos.

Unfortunately for the head of the Sûreté's Organized Crime division, Don Moretti had stationed others around the site of this meeting.

Evelyn Tardiff was, in effect, about to be hunted to extinction.

They always knew that the last few feet, if they made it that far, would be the most difficult.

The door to the PM's outer office was closed and guarded by two heavily armed RCMP officers.

Shona could feel Gamache and Lacoste not so much tense as brace.

They'd gone over and over what would happen and what each of them must do.

As the Chief Inspector had walked them through his plan, then had them repeat it, two things surprised the young journalist: The audacity of it. And the fact he seemed to trust her to do her part.

And now they stood in front of the first barrier. The fact they'd gotten that far was a shock, but they still had two inches of solid oak, and two solid guards in full combat gear between themselves and the next goal.

"Chief Inspector Armand Gamache. We need to see the Prime Minister." His voice wasn't just authoritative, it was commanding. "Immediately."

There was a long pause as the guard studied them. Gamache silently prayed that these two recognized him but were not yet aware of the social media posts about his mental state.

"We were with the PM when the attack on the White House happened," he continued. "We have vital information, and someone"—he looked at Shona—"he needs to hear."

The moments elongated, stretching their nerves to breaking. Gamache could feel Shona trembling.

"For God's sake," he snapped. "This's a matter of national security. Come with us if you have to."

One of the guards stepped forward, and for an instant Gamache thought he was about to arrest them. Instead, he frisked all three.

"No phone?" he said to Shona, who just glared.

"We already checked," said Lacoste. "She doesn't have one."

The guard frisked Shona again, then held up the two phones he'd confiscated. "These will be at the entrance to the building when you leave."

"Understood," said Gamache. He'd anticipated this. Even depended on it.

The guards stepped aside.

"What've you got?"

Jean-Guy had just arrived back in Three Pines. As much as he desperately wanted to go to Ottawa to help the others, he knew with that assassination attempt and the lockdown of Parliament, there was no way he could get to them.

Besides, he had to get back here.

When Nichol didn't answer, he stepped forward and turned the screen toward him. As he did, he noticed that Agent Nichol was just staring ahead. Shocked.

"What's he doing here?" came a voice from outside the study.

Reine-Marie was standing stock-still in the living room. Dead in her tracks. She'd seen Jean-Guy's parked car from the kitchen window and headed to the study, anxious for an update. But didn't make it to her son-in-law.

She stood staring at Marcus Lauzon. It was as though she'd been hit in the face by a two-by-four. Here was the man who'd put her son into prison, and back into addiction, and knowingly pushed him to the brink of suicide.

The man standing not two feet away would have essentially murdered Daniel if his parents hadn't intervened.

She'd had nightmares about this. About coming face-to-face with Marcus Lauzon.

"Madame Gamache," Lauzon began, before Jean-Guy grabbed his arm and yanked him into the study.

Jean-Guy looked at his mother-in-law, a woman he loved as much as his own mother, perhaps more. And saw an accusation of betrayal there.

"*Désolé*" was all he could think to say before closing the door.

Nichol had turned to him, her face ashen.

"She is working for Moretti." Nichol's voice was barely audible. "I traced back those posts mocking Gamache about the American plan. The stories originate from Chief Inspector Tardiff's encrypted address. They're being spread by journalists she regularly uses."

"Oh, shit," said Beauvoir, sitting down and reading the screen. "No one's going to believe it now."

"Who do you mean?" asked Marcus Lauzon, approaching the screen. "Who's 'she'?"

"Who's he?" asked Nichol, turning to the new person. Then she recognized him. "Wait, aren't you supposed to be dead?"

"Almost," said Beauvoir. "I think they were about to kill him. I had to bring him with me."

"Not sure he's much safer here." Just before the door had closed, she'd seen Madame Gamache's face. And fists.

"Who're you talking about?" Lauzon leaned closer to the computer. "Evelyn Tardiff? The head of Organized Crime for the Sûreté?"

"How do you know her?"

"Well, she had Sunday lunch here with me. But I knew her long before that. Or of her, at least. She's working for CSIS."

"The intelligence service?" said Beauvoir.

"Yes. You think she's working for Moretti? She's not. She's one of ours. That's another reason I couldn't defend myself. I couldn't risk it becoming public."

"What becoming public?" Beauvoir was struggling to take this in.

"Who the high-level informant within the Moretti organization is. Evelyn Tardiff was recruited by CSIS years ago to infiltrate the mob when she was just an agent."

"You knew?"

"I was the Deputy Premier. There's a lot I knew. Know. Tardiff has been invaluable, giving CSIS a heads-up about drugs and arms smuggling, human trafficking. Information about the activities of the New York mob. But not about the poison plot or whatever's happening next. Because Moretti doesn't know. He's just the enforcer."

"I knew it, I knew it, I knew it!" said Nichol.

"But if that's true," said Jean-Guy, "why would she put out these posts about Gamache and the American plans to take over Canada? Making it sound crazy."

"Because she had no choice. If she hadn't, Moretti and Caron would have known. *Non*, she had to."

"But she's done irreparable damage," said Beauvoir. "No one's going to believe us now."

"There's more, *patron*," said Nichol. "Did you check your email?"

"No. Didn't have time. Why?"

"This. I found this IP address in Charles Langlois's first notebook."

"You mean his second."

"*Non*. I mean his first. He found this early on and didn't realize its significance. Neither did you. You were all so focused on the second notebook, you didn't bother to go back and reread the first."

Beauvoir clicked on the link she'd sent.

Here was the plan that General Whitehead had alluded to. The one that might have killed him.

They were through the first door, but the next, the last before Prime Minister Woodford's office, was even more heavily guarded.

Gamache and Lacoste released Shona. That ruse had run its course.

On seeing them, the senior officer stepped forward, her hand out, palm flat in their faces in the universal sign to halt.

"This is now a restricted area. We're on lockdown. That applies to you too, Chief Inspector. I need you to go back to your holding room."

Her voice was calm, but there was no mistaking the seriousness of what she was saying. She would be obeyed.

There was no way they could push their way through. They'd never make it. They'd be tackled and arrested. At best.

At worst…

If their bodies couldn't get through the door, maybe something else could.

Armand Gamache gave her a small, almost apologetic smile as one officer to another, then raised his voice. "WPR!"

"What're you doing?" the senior officer demanded.

"WPR!" Gamache shouted again, this time at the top of his lungs.

"Stop it!" commanded the officer and nodded to her colleague, who approached Gamache, carbine pointed. Shona backed away, even as Lacoste moved to intercept the armed guard.

"War—" That was as far as Gamache got before the door was flung open.

"What the hell's happening out here?" the Minister of Defense demanded.

"W." Pause. "P." Pause. "R." Gamache's voice was low now, little more than a whisper. He aimed each letter past the guards, past the baffled cabinet minister, to the man standing in the middle of his office.

Everything hung in the balance. And then the PM nodded.

"Let them in."

Shona felt her legs turn to jelly.

"A message just came in from Chief Inspector Tardiff," Nichol said, clicking on it.

There were no words, just a series of photographs.

"Proof," said Lauzon, looking over her shoulder. "Caron was finally sloppy."

"Or overconfident," said Beauvoir. Or just confident.

On Nichol's screen were the pictures taken of Jeanne Caron meeting with Moretti. It was not anything that a defense attorney could characterize as haphazard. They were clearly deep in conversation. Still, while damning, it was not actually illegal.

This was not proof enough to arrest, to convict. But it did make it clear to them, finally, that Jeanne Caron was deep in the conspiracy.

"That's on mont Royal," said Jean-Guy. "The lookout."

"There's one more. Just came—" Nichol fell silent.

"*Merde*," whispered Beauvoir.

The photo showed Moretti's soldiers, weapons drawn, bearing down on Tardiff through the forest.

"What is War Plan Red, sir?"

"I don't know how you got through the lockdown—" Prime Minister Woodford gave his security detail a stern look.

"You can thank Canada's not-so-latent racism," said Shona.

The senior ministers and armed officers turned to the young woman, and Isabelle Lacoste vowed that the first thing she'd do, if they got out of this, was introduce her children to Shona.

"What is War Plan Red?" While still cordial, there was steel in Gamache's tone.

He glanced over to the cabinet ministers. Robert Ferguson, the Minister of Public Safety, had joined Giselle Trudel, the Minister of Defense, in the PM's office. Both immediately dropped their eyes to the carpet.

Tragically, the posts they'd all just read were right, and the Chief Inspector had lost his mind. Now he was babbling about some war plan.

Prime Minister Woodford turned to Isabelle Lacoste and Shona Dorion. His voice gentle now, kindly even. "I see he's somehow convinced you that his fantasies are real. This has gone from pathetic to dangerous. Monsieur Gamache—"

"Chief Inspector Gamache," said Shona.

"—is making no sense. You need to distance yourself from him in every way before he causes you harm. I beg you."

"When we were here earlier, you seemed to agree with us," said Lacoste.

"No. I asked you for proof. Instead of that, you come marching in here raving about some war plan that sounds like a Saturday morning cartoon. We have bigger problems." He waved toward the TV screens, which showed armed activity around the White House. "I don't have time to spend on your delusions."

But Gamache was studying the Prime Minister. "You know what 'WPR' means."

"Wasn't that a sitcom?" said Ferguson, who was responsible for Canada's intelligence service. "With Loni Anderson?"

"That's *WKRP*," said Giselle Trudel, the Minister of Defense.

"It's a public radio station in Wisconsin," said the head of the Parliamentary Protective Service, reading from his phone. "WPR."

"Dear God," said Shona. "If Luxembourg does invade, we're screwed."

Gamache only had eyes for the Prime Minister. "It's the name the Americans have given to their plan to invade Canada, as you know perfectly well, sir."

Giselle Trudel sighed. "Oh, God, this is heartbreaking."

"General Whitehead was at the White House this morning to ask the President for permission to release to me classified information on the plan."

"This is ridiculous," said Ferguson. "Can't we get him out of here?"

"The General was gunned down to stop him," Gamache persevered.

"All right!" Woodford finally snapped. "Enough! You're unwell. You need help." His voice dropped again, cajoling now, trying to reason with a madman. "That was an assassination attempt on the President. The General was injured saving her life. We all saw it."

"I met with General Whitehead last night. He admitted there was a plan."

Gamache was composed, despite huge temptation to shout.

When you fight, stay as calm as the ocean,
And watch what's going on behind your shoulder.
War's not a place for deep emotion,
And maybe you'll get a little older.

"That's another lie," said the Minister of Defense. "He's probably dead and can't deny it. You're slandering a hero, though I don't know why."

"He's sick," said the Minister of Public Safety. "He needs help."

"He needs medication," said the Minister of Defense.

"This needs to stop," said the Prime Minister.

The head of the security detail stepped forward, expecting the PM to order them to escort Gamache and the others out the door. But instead—

"You're right," said Woodford with a huge sigh. "War Plan Red is the American strategy for invading Canada. Making this nation the fifty-first state."

There was dead silence as everyone in the room—politicians, the PM's

Chief of Staff, the security—turned to Prime Minister Woodford, astonished. He might as well have admitted he was indeed an alien.

"You're humoring him, right?" said Ferguson. "You're not serious."

Though it was eminently clear that he was.

"Wait a minute," said Giselle Trudel. "There is such a thing? I'm the Minister of Defense. Why don't I know about it?"

Shona was on the verge of saying something, but a look from Lacoste stopped her.

"Because it was only ever an exercise and was torn up in the 1930s," said Woodford. "What you found, God knows in what archive, Chief Inspector, is an anachronism, a footnote. An oddity. War Plan Red no longer exists."

"You're wrong there, sir," said Gamache. "It was never torn up. It's been updated by every American President since it was first conceived in 1919. It's also known as the Atlantic Strategic War Plan."

"No, no," said Trudel, on her phone. "I just googled it. The Prime Minister's right. It was scrapped in 1939, when war in Europe broke out."

Gamache looked tired now. "Do you really think you're going to find the American invasion plans on Google? Of course it says it was canceled. What else are they going to say? That they have an active and updated strategy to cross five thousand miles of undefended border and take over their friendly neighbor to the north?"

Gamache had moved a few steps to his left, dragging all eyes with him. Except Lacoste's. She was following their own plan and had stepped to the right, so that she was standing beside Manon Payette, the PM's Chief of Staff.

"We need to talk," Lacoste whispered.

"No, we don't."

"Yes. We do. And you know why."

"I don't. But"—she hesitated—"I want to hear what you think you know." Payette began to move toward a door.

"*Non.* Not yet. Wait for it ..."

"Planned," the Prime Minister was saying, losing all patience and what little sympathy he might once have had for the Chief Inspector. "Not 'plan,' 'plan-duh.' Duh." He leaned right into Gamache's face. "Duh."

"Okay," whispered Lacoste. "Now."

The intent of Woodford's words, the last two sounds, were so insulting to the Chief Inspector that even the head of the Parliamentary Protective Service looked over.

Everyone was now riveted on the two men. No one noticed the two women slip into a side office.

CHAPTER 28

Jean-Guy could see the Champlain Bridge into Montréal just up ahead.

Agent Nichol was beside him. Stern, silent, staring out the window. Her small hands in fists. Lauzon was in the back seat. Beauvoir didn't dare leave him in Three Pines with Reine-Marie, her friends, a collection of knives, and a duck capable of God knew what.

If the mafia knew about Rosa, she'd be a made duck in no time.

He'd alerted the Montréal police, who were already crawling all over mont Royal. But the park, in the middle of the city, was vast, made up of three peaks covering almost seven hundred forested acres. Most of it left to go wild.

It would take days, if ever, to find . . . well, a body.

"If you knew about War Plan Red," demanded Shona Dorion, "why didn't you admit it earlier when we first asked?"

As soon as she spoke, she saw her mistake. Though Gamache's expression hadn't changed, she knew she might have just blown everything. She'd deviated from their own plan and pulled the PM's attention away from Gamache. To her. And, by consequence, to the two missing women.

But Woodford never took his eyes off Gamache, even as he answered her question.

"Because it's not important. It would just muddy the waters. It's a bizarre footnote in our shared history with the United States, nothing more. Let it go," he pleaded with the Chief. "Can't you see you're so disoriented you no longer know the difference between past and present?"

"Then why did you let us in?" Gamache pushed. "If this's such a waste of time, why are you still talking to me? I saw your face. The initials 'WPR' scared you."

"What scared me was having a lunatic at the door. Better to let you in, to help save at least part of your reputation. You were making a fool of yourself. Worse, you're in danger of doing serious damage to our international relations. I've already had a call from the American Ambassador asking, demanding, to meet thanks to the social media shitstorm you and your conspiracies have created."

The PM had once again worked himself into a rage.

"I'm not asking you, sir, if the Atlantic Strategic War Plan still exists. I'm telling you. And it's being acted on even now." His words created a void, a vacuum. The air was sucked out of the opulent room as those around them listened to the thoughtful, measured madman. "War has changed. Assaults come at us from all sorts of fronts, from social media attacks, to cyberattacks, to trade wars. To drones and artillery and age-old full-frontal offensives. But the reasons are as old as the hills."

"And those are?" asked the Minister of Defense, to the PM's obvious annoyance.

"The world is changing. Our very climate is changing. Look at the wild-fires, the hurricanes, the floods, the melting ice pack, the droughts and famines. The reasons for all that can be debated, I suppose, but the effects are undeniable, as are the consequences."

"And those are?" asked the Minister of Public Safety.

"Oh, for Christ's sake," snapped the PM. "Don't encourage the man."

Gamache never took his eyes off Woodford. "Nations go to war over resources. It might look like something else, but at the root of most conflicts is that one country, one territory, one leader wants what the other has. Wants, or needs. And today the most precious resource, the real currency, the real power, is water."

There was a noticeable shift in the room. A watershed. The balance had changed toward Gamache. They were listening to him now.

"The loss of fresh, clean, drinkable water is the single greatest threat to survival worldwide. It's not a one-off crisis, it's an existential threat. Parts of Canada are vulnerable, as we know, but to the south it's even worse. The US is losing vast amounts of water every day. Lakes and rivers are drying up. Infrastructure is crumbling, and with it the pipes that carry water. The loss to leakage is huge. Cities are becoming uninhabitable as temperatures rise and water disappears. And when that happens, there will be millions of environmental refugees. And where will they head?"

He stared at the Prime Minister. But it was Giselle Trudel, the Minister of Defense, who spoke. Though it was a partial answer, as though she was afraid to go all the way.

"Not south."

"*Non.*" Gamache turned to her briefly, before returning to Woodford. "North. They'll be coming here."

"Okay, what do you know?" demanded Isabelle Lacoste.

The two women were standing in the PM's private bathroom.

"I don't know what you mean," said Payette.

"We saw the look you gave the Prime Minister when word of the shootings happened."

"Of course I looked at him. He's the leader of the nation. We all look to him in times of crisis."

"Stop with the sound bites. The look you gave him wasn't fear, it wasn't a plea for guidance. You knew something. Know something. Suspect something."

Manon Payette pressed her lips together.

"All right," said Lacoste. "Let me ask you this. Why did the Prime Minister leave his office to go get you?"

"Because I'm his Chief of Staff," she snapped. Impatient. Imperious. Self-important. And defensive.

"Yes, but why leave?"

"What do you mean?"

"Isn't that what the intercom is for? Isn't that what text is for? So the leader of the nation doesn't need to leave his office to search for his Chief of Staff."

Lacoste had her. Cornered. The only way out was through the truth.

The Montréal cops found Chief Inspector Tardiff's ID in the woods.

There's blood, the captain texted, *but no body.*

Beauvoir pulled over. They'd arrived at mont Royal and were about to join the search. Instead, Jean-Guy sat in the vehicle. Thinking.

Where would Moretti's people take Evelyn Tardiff to execute her?

"Come on," demanded Nichol, reaching for the door handle. "We can't just sit here."

"Stay where you are. We're not just sitting here," snapped Beauvoir. "I'm thinking. I suggest you do too. You spent the last while eavesdropping on conversations with Moretti. Where would he take Tardiff?"

"The Jean-Talon market?"

"Are you asking me?"

"I don't know, I don't know—"

"Stop it! Deep breaths. Think. The market's too public. They're probably on mont Royal somewhere." Beauvoir brought up a map of the huge park. "She was taken from here." He placed a finger on the map. "Probably unconscious, given the blood." He glanced at Nichol and saw she had taken command of herself. Barely. He understood her anxiety. Had they been talking about Armand or Isabelle, he'd be near hysterical.

"The caves," Nichol suddenly said. "I remember reading in a message that Moretti had become obsessed with the caves."

"What caves? There're caves on mont Royal?"

"Jesus," said Lauzon, springing forward so that his head was between them. "The ones they found in the Saint-Léonard *quartier* of Montréal, you mean?"

"That's right," said Nichol. "It's not far from where the Morettis live. He said it would be a perfect place to put a . . ."

"*Merde*," said Beauvoir.

The three stared at each other. Those caves were twenty minutes away. If they left mont Royal, there was no turning back. If they were wrong . . . The only comfort, cold as it was, was that it was probably already too late.

Keep searching, he texted the Montréal police captain. *We're trying another area.* Then he put the siren on and swung back onto the road, his foot heavy on the gas.

Not *like this, not like this, dear God, please.*

Not yet.

Not like this . . .

Her legs were heavy, the muscles burning. Her back was spasming from the effort of arching. Then, without warning, her legs dropped an inch. And as they did, the rope around her ankles pulled taut and her head was pushed back as the rope around her neck tightened.

And she gagged.

With a huge effort, Evelyn arched her back again and brought her legs back up, loosening the garrote slightly.

Not like this . . .

Oh, God, please. Help me.

Out of the corner of his eye Gamache noticed Lacoste had returned to the room with the Chief of Staff. Isabelle was looking stern. Payette was looking sick.

Lacoste nodded toward Gamache. So it was true. The PM's Chief of Staff had confirmed their suspicions.

Shona saw it too and slowly slid her hand into her pocket. Preparing . . .

If the guards saw her, they wouldn't care. They'd searched her and found nothing. But they were wrong.

Gamache had counted on the guards being in full combat gear. Which included Kevlar.

"When they approach to frisk us, which they will," he'd told Shona, "you need to palm your phone and slide it into the pocket of their vest so that when they search you, they don't find anything. Then take it back."

Shona had looked at him, astonished and angered. "You assume because I'm a Black woman I know how to pick pockets?"

"No, I assume you'll do as I tell you. The Kevlar vest is designed to stop a bullet. And because it does that, it'll also stop the guard from feeling anything you do. You could put a Volkswagen in the pocket and they'd never notice."

She'd smiled at that and felt her tension lower. "Okay. I'll try."

"You'll do more than that. You'll succeed. You must."

And she had.

Now the time to act was near. She could sense it.

Shona brought the phone out and waited, waited...They were almost there...

Beauvoir had never been to the network of caves beneath the parc Pie-XII, and never hoped to. The first cave had been discovered decades ago, but a huge second cavern, essentially a network of passageways, was only recently found.

He'd read about it and seen photos and watched with some dismay as Honoré had become pretty much obsessed with the caves. He'd begged his father to take him there. But just the news reports were enough to send Jean-Guy to the verge of a panic attack.

Where the Chief was terrified of heights, Beauvoir's terror was holes. And what they'd discovered in the middle of Montréal was an epic hole.

He hoped Honoré would forget and move on to another obsession. He kept feeding the boy stories about mummies, and spaceships, and dinosaurs, but no, Honoré kept at it, showing his father photos of archeologists and cave explorers actually kayaking through the narrow passages with sheer rock walls. He'd even gotten his little sister, Idola, hooked. Her face lit up when Honoré showed her the videos.

His father's face did something else entirely.

"You okay, Papa?"

Jean-Guy had gone pale and felt lightheaded. "Just fine."

"Can we go for my birthday? *S'il te plaaaaaît?*"

And now Beauvoir stood at the entrance. It would have to be a cave...

Do we have to go? I never really liked Tardiff. And it's probably too late—

"Done."

Don Moretti read the text and saw the photo. And for a brief moment he almost felt regret. They'd known each other for so long. Even, briefly, been lovers.

Then he forwarded the photo to Jeanne Caron with the subject line *This is how we treat traitors.*

Caron had been waiting for the message, though hadn't expected a photograph.

She'd thought she might be repulsed, disgusted. But instead, she found herself almost aroused.

There on her phone was the picture of Evelyn Tardiff, the head of Organized Crime for the Sûreté, lying on her stomach, hog-tied. The rope expertly placed around her neck and ankles, so that as she struggled, she strangled.

In the photo Tardiff was obviously still alive, her eyes wide with terror. Her body showing the effort, the strain, of keeping her legs raised and back arched.

Death would be slow. Excruciating.

It was the mob execution for the worst offenders.

Incaprettamento.

The first cave, the only one open to the public, was closed for the season, the entrance locked. For a moment Beauvoir thought that maybe they wouldn't have to...

But the lock had been broken and the door stood ajar.

"This must be it," said Nichol, excited.

Beauvoir drew his gun and was disconcerted to see Nichol was also armed. He never really thought of her as a full-fledged agent.

"They might still be in there," said Lauzon, his eyes wide. "Maybe I should wait in the car."

"Maybe you should walk in front of us," snarled Beauvoir. He didn't mean it, but he was not in the best of moods, and the look on the former Deputy Prime Minister's face was very satisfying.

Jean-Guy took a deep breath. *Oh, fuck it.* Cautiously opening the door, he peeked inside.

"You've had a remarkable career, Chief Inspector. Thank you for your service." The Prime Minister stepped toward the door. "But the time has come for you to go home. Sit on the porch with your wife. Play with your grandchildren. Tend your roses. You've done enough. It's time to rest. Let us take care of this."

His voice was cajoling, as though speaking to a sick child. Or someone standing on a ledge.

But Gamache held his ground and Woodford's smile faded.

"Not this again. Please, Monsieur Gamache. If you don't leave, I'll have to have you removed. You're making of fool of yourself. You'll be forever remembered as the boy who cried wolf."

He all but leered at Gamache.

Still he stood there. He could see Shona behind the PM, her phone in her hand. She'd done it. Smuggled it in. Until that moment he hadn't known for sure. This was a vital part of their own plan.

Everyone else in the room was watching the two men and ignoring the young woman whose actions were far more dangerous.

"I'm warning you." Woodford nodded to his head of security, who raised his carbine and cross-checked the Chief Inspector, shoving him toward the door.

The cabinet ministers looked surprised and uncomfortable at this sudden act of aggression. But neither said or did anything.

Gamache was given another shove, harder this time, so that he stumbled but regained his balance.

"I want their weapons confiscated. And"—Woodford turned to his Minister of Public Safety—"take their Sûreté IDs."

"But we have no authority—"

"This is a matter of national security. Do it."

Without meeting Gamache's glare, Ferguson slid his hand into the Chief's breast pocket and took out the ID. Only after he looked at it did he meet Gamache's eyes.

"Give it to me," said Woodford, and the Minister did.

Lacoste's was also collected.

"The Chief Inspector wasn't armed when he arrived," the head of the RCMP security detail reported. "Inspector Lacoste surrendered her weapon at the door."

"Good. Keep it." Prime Minister Woodford turned back to Gamache. "If you breathe a word of War Plan Red, Chief Inspector, I will have you arrested."

"On what charge?"

"Does it matter?" Woodford spoke so quietly only the two of them heard. Or so he thought. "You'll do as I say, or they"—he glanced at Lacoste and Shona—"go down too. Do you understand?"

"Perfectly. Now understand this. Our loyalty is not to you. It's not my job to mindlessly do your bidding."

"You have no job anymore, Monsieur Gamache."

At another nod from the PM, Gamache was again shoved, this time right through the door.

Once in the outer office Armand said slowly and clearly, "War Plan Red. Come clean about War Plan Red, Mr. Prime Minister."

"I'm warning you." Woodford's eyes narrowed, and his cheeks burned. "Don't. Don't make me do it."

But it was too late. Armand Gamache might not be armed with a gun, but he had a much more powerful weapon at his disposal.

He raised his voice so that it was loud but not raucous. Not out of control. This was the voice of a person in complete command of themselves.

"War Plan Red, sir. Tell us the truth."

"Be quiet! Stop it." The PM waved at the RCMP guards. "Stop him. Arrest him."

The guards were momentarily off-balance. The Chief Inspector was not only highly respected; he was also, as far as they could tell, not breaking any law.

"The man's mad. Do it." Prime Minister Woodford jabbed his finger at his head of security, who approached Gamache.

Then the Prime Minister noticed what Shona Dorion was doing.

"She's recording! Get her phone."

"I'm a journalist," Shona shouted. "Covering the story. I'm a journalist. I'm a jour—"

The phone was ripped from her hand, and the head of the RCMP detail raised the butt of her carbine. Shona cringed and brought up her arm to ward off the blow.

Lacoste moved quickly and stepped in front of Shona, just as the rifle descended, hitting Lacoste on the side of her head.

She dropped.

Gamache moved toward her but only got one step before being hit in the solar plexus by the butt of the same rifle. He fell to his knees, gasping.

Fighting to regain his breath, he crawled toward Isabelle. When he reached her, he looked up, right at the PM, and rasped, "Stop this! Tell the truth about War Plan Red. I'm begging you."

Instead, Woodford gestured toward the guards. Hands grabbed and dragged the three of them into an adjoining office. The door slammed shut. They were locked in.

"Isabelle?" Armand stumbled over to her.

"I'm okay." She touched the side of her head and her hand came away bloody. Blood was streaming down her neck. "Looks worse than it is."

Gamache turned to Shona, his voice still gravelly. "You okay?"

She nodded, though her eyes were wide.

"Tell me you did it," said Lacoste.

It took Shona a moment to understand what she was asking.

"I did."

"Oh, thank God," said Gamache, and Shona felt a wave of relief, a kind of well-being.

She'd done it.

Gamache had anticipated Woodford's reaction to War Plan Red, knowing the PM would not want those three words to escape his office. He certainly would not want the rest of the world to hear them. Woodford's entire plan depended on keeping that plan secret.

Gamache's plan was to get the word out. The three words out. Into the public. As well as showing people who Woodford really was.

While Shona recorded and streamed what was happening, Gamache would raise his voice and say, clearly, for all to hear, "War Plan Red."

Its purpose was twofold: to get the word out, but also to provoke an aggressive overreaction on the part of the Prime Minister, all captured on Shona's phone.

That was their plan, such as it was.

What Gamache had not anticipated was that Woodford would also order his guards to attack a journalist. Take her phone, yes. That he'd seen. But to physically threaten her?

He thought the target would only be him. Seeing that guard lift her rifle at Shona had shocked him, and terrified her.

Lacoste took the hit. And now took the handkerchief he offered. "Well, that was something."

He was pressing his lips together, thinking. Nodding. He looked at the door. What happened next would decide things for them. *How bad would this get?*

His attention was drawn to Shona's rapid breathing. "You need to sit down."

When she did, with unusual compliance, Isabelle put her hand on her back and gently pressed her forward. "Place your head between your knees. Breathe."

Shona turned to look up at them. "Isn't this the crash position?"

Armand gave one grunt of amusement. "We're going to be fine."

"Yeah, I have Ruth's latest collection of poetry. I know what 'FINE' stands for."

Gamache turned back to Isabelle, the handkerchief still pressed to her head.

"Payette?"

"*Oui.* The Chief of Staff admitted that when the PM left his office to get her, he also made a phone call."

"To the White House?" asked Shona, her voice muffled by her legs.

"She doesn't know, but when the shots were fired, she began to put things together. She already had suspicions."

"How?"

"She'd seen some documents. Ones Woodford had kept from her."

"Did she agree to do it?" It was the vital question.

"She wasn't happy. But she agreed. You?"

"Ferguson palmed it," said Gamache. "What he does with it is another matter."

"At least he didn't give it to the PM," said Isabelle. "So, the Prime Minister is behind all this."

Gamache nodded. When they'd arrived, they weren't sure how deep into it the PM was, if at all. Which was why all this was necessary.

"We still have no proof," said Gamache.

"The video?" said Shona, sitting up now and feeling less like she was about to throw up and pass out. Maybe one or the other, but not both. "Won't that be enough?"

"*Non,*" said Lacoste. "All it proves is that he lost his temper. There'll be blowback, but he'll manage it."

"He threatened a journalist and had two senior Sûreté officers beaten," said Shona. "He can't survive that, politically, can he?"

"It can be explained away," said Gamache, "as a strong leader in a time of stress pushed to do something drastic to stop a lunatic—"

"You," said Shona.

"—from seriously damaging international relations and maybe even provoking a conflict."

"Would anyone believe that?" asked Shona.

"Millions believe Canada is training geese to down planes," Lacoste reminded her.

"*Napoleon is always right*," said Gamache.

"We're fucked, aren't we. Still, the geese ... maybe not such a bad plan ..."

"We need evidence," said Gamache. "The video will help, but we need more."

"We have the link to War Plan Red," said Shona. "The one your person found. I sent it to Paul. If anything happens to us, he'll release that."

"*Oui.* But it's from a site known to contain wild conspiracies," said Gamache. "*Non.* Not enough."

"Do you think Prime Minister Woodford realizes we know he's the one behind what's happening?"

"He does now," said Lacoste.

"That was always the risk," said Gamache.

They were deep inside the Parliament Buildings, and the wolf was at the door. They had to find a way out.

He turned to Isabelle. "Does it seem to you—"

"—that the guard pulled her blows? *Oui.* She knew exactly what she was doing. It could have been much worse."

And would almost certainly be. Woodford could not let them leave. Ever.

In his Toronto office, Paul Workman, the former Chief Foreign Correspondent for CTV News and the most respected journalist in Canada, watched the videos. They'd come in from two difference sources, two separate phones. One was from his protégée, Shona Dorion. She'd warned him something was coming, but had not said it was this explosive.

The other, incredibly, appeared to be from the phone belonging to Manon Payette, Prime Minister Woodford's Chief of Staff.

They hadn't just been recording the events, they'd been streaming it to him. Which was very bad news for the PM. Woodford must've thought in taking away Shona's phone he'd contained the damage. Instead, he'd only managed to make it worse.

The image of a Prime Minister using violence to stop a journalist from reporting an event was shocking. Damning.

As a seasoned journalist who'd covered wars and insurrections, riots and natural disasters, few things surprised him. But what he saw on those two feeds from Parliament left him shaken. Made worse because he'd voted for James Woodford. Had thought him a decent person, a man of integrity. But the mask hadn't just slipped, it had fallen and shattered.

He posted the raw video on his site. In doing so he placed his formidable reputation on the line. His social media was trusted by journalists and opinion makers worldwide.

Then Workman sat back and watched the views and shares tick up. And up. As the confrontation in the PM's office went viral.

The PM's face was thunderous.

Messages were pouring in. All red-flagged. All asking what the hell he was thinking. What the hell he was doing.

Cabinet ministers, party executives, donors, even other world leaders were forwarding social media posts containing links to videos on Paul Workman's site. And reposted. And reposted.

Giselle Trudel, the Minister of Defense, was about to click on one when the television screens covering one wall changed. The Canadian networks had moved from the exterior of the White House to the interior of the Prime Minister's office. And up came the video.

"Fuck me," moaned the PM.

There for everyone to see was Chief Inspector Gamache shouting "War Plan Red," and the PM ordering his security to violently stop a journalist from videoing it.

The feed continued even after the phone was taken from Dorion. Now, from a different angle, they saw first Inspector Lacoste, then Gamache drop to the floor, hit with the butt of a rifle, on orders from the PM.

Then the senior Sûreté officer, on the ground, begged the Prime Minister to come clean about the plan.

For a moment those in the office were silent, shocked. Not that it had happened, they'd all seen it in person, but that it should be broadcast. And that there was clearly a second phone that had recorded the shameful events.

Woodford looked around. "Where's Payette? Get her in here!"

"I'll find her," said Ferguson.

As he left the office, the Minister of Public Safety glanced down at the slip of paper Chief Inspector Gamache had placed into his ID.

Whether it was meant for him specifically, Robert Ferguson didn't know, but it was put there deliberately by Gamache for someone to find. He must have gone to the PM's office knowing what would happen. Knowing he was ending his career.

Knowing his ID would be confiscated. And so, in a *beau risque*, he'd written out this message and placed it where someone would find it.

Someone, Gamache was gambling, with integrity.

As he left the room, the Minister of Public Safety crumpled the paper and was about to drop it into the wastepaper basket. But, changing his mind, he put it into his pocket. And left.

The Minister of Defense watched her cabinet colleague.

Giselle Trudel had had her doubts about him for a while now, no longer believing Robert Ferguson could be trusted. She'd said as much to the PM, but he hadn't believed her.

But since the poisoning plot, and the revelations about Marcus Lauzon, her concerns had ratcheted up.

More than once her own Chief of Staff had come to her worried that files had been compromised. And that could only be done by another minister. Or the PM.

And now this mess.

Still, Trudel was a Woodford loyalist. She knew that leaders had secrets, things that were confidential, classified.

"What're we going to do with Gamache and the others?" she asked him.

"Let me worry about that. I'm calling a full cabinet meeting in half an hour. Be there."

"Of course."

Once out the door, she turned to go to her office, then changed her mind.

"They'll be fine, they'll be fine," Reine-Marie repeated as she and her friends watched first Isabelle, then Armand collapse to the floor of the Prime Minister's office.

"They'll be fine," Clara and Myrna, Gabri and Olivier agreed, their eyes wide with disbelief.

"Though I don't think Woodford will be," said Gabri. "And I voted for the shit."

Ruth reached out a scrawny hand and gripped Reine-Marie's.

"He'll be fine," she whispered. "Now that the images are out there, they can't do anything to harm them."

Reine-Marie squeezed the old poet's hand. "*Merci.*" Then she got up and called Isabelle's husband. And after that, Annie and Daniel.

"They'll be fine," she told them.

Evelyn Tardiff was barely conscious. Her breathing came in rasps as she dragged air through her slowly collapsing windpipe.

As her head was pulled back, she could see she was not alone. She had a companion in the caves. The body of Margaux Chalifoux was not two feet away.

It wasn't enough that Moretti had her put there; she had to stare right into Chalifoux's face, frozen and contorted in pain and horror as her own noose had tightened.

That would be her, soon.

Evelyn Tardiff, the head of Organized Crime for the Sûreté du Québec, was about to die. And nobody would find her. She'd rot there.

Her legs dropped again, and her windpipe closed. She struggled, but that only made it worse, tightening the noose further. She gurgled. And then... nothing.

No more air. No more air. No more air.

The only consolation was that she'd no longer have to stare into those dead eyes of Margaux Chalifoux.

CHAPTER 29

Beauvoir, Nichol, and Lauzon made their way forward.

The deepest caverns were not just dark, they were pitch black. No light penetrated. No cell phone signal. They'd had to risk putting on the flashlights of their phones to see where they were going. Beauvoir watched his beam shake and wondered if the others realized he was trembling.

The walls were closing in. Crushing him. He felt lightheaded as the panic came in waves. He worried he was about to pass out.

He was, he knew, a liability. An armed liability. If something happened, he couldn't help.

"*Patron.*" He felt a hand on his arm and saw Yvette Nichol looking at him. "Let me take the lead. She's my boss. I need to be the one to find her."

Beauvoir nodded, and while he was willing to accept what she said, he knew it wasn't the truth. Nichol did it to save him and his jangled nerves.

"Careful," she whispered a few minutes later. "There's a drop-off. This section's flooded."

He heard a small splash and a sharp intake of breath. The water was bitterly cold and waist-deep on her.

Then it was his turn. He slipped into the water and gasped. But the biting cold acted as a sort of slap, bringing him out of his panic at least enough to regain some control.

A current was dragging them forward. Getting stronger. They had to fight to stay upright.

Nichol turned a sharp corner and put up her hand to stop the others. Switching off her flashlight, she whispered, "There's a light up ahead."

"Maybe I should stay here," whispered Lauzon.

Beauvoir considered, then agreed. If there was a confrontation, there was little the former politician could do. And maybe he could escape and at least tell someone where they were.

Beauvoir retook the lead and felt Nichol's small hand on his shoulder, keeping close, as they edged forward.

The tunnel was closing in for real now. The way ahead getting tighter and tighter. His shoulders rubbed the walls, and he kept his eyes focused on the dim light ahead. Deep breath in. Deep breath out.

"Oh, God," Nichol whispered.

On a ledge jutting out from the wall were two bodies. Trussed up. A phone with its flashlight on was propped against the wall. Since there was no cell phone coverage, it wouldn't be live. It was recording the murders. A snuff film.

Sick fucks.

He scanned the area. They appeared to be alone.

Nichol surged forward before Beauvoir could stop her. She'd been so focused on Chief Inspector Tardiff, she'd missed what he'd seen at the very last moment. The movement in the shadows.

Beauvoir shoved Nichol aside and fired, just as the shadow fired.

Both missed, their bullets ricocheting off the stone, the sound echoing down the long passageway. There was, along with the echo, the sound of surging water, as both Beauvoir and the shadow plowed toward each other.

And then the other man was upon him. Jean-Guy lost his footing, and the current swept his feet out from under him, carrying both downstream until their bodies struck a wall and were pinned there. It was totally dark now. Jean-Guy had lost his gun and his phone and was lashing out with his fists, hoping to strike flesh and bone.

Then his face was shoved underwater. Jean-Guy felt pressure on his head. A boot was crushing his cheekbone against the cave floor. He thrashed and fought, but the boot was too firm. He was losing consciousness.

Dear God, I'm going to die.

Then, as suddenly as it had appeared, the pressure was gone. Beauvoir bobbed up, and through his coughing and sputtering, he heard the sound of fighting close by.

Nichol. She must have jumped the man. But she wouldn't have a hope...

There was another shot, but hardly any echo. The bullet had found its soft target.

Nichol... Yvette...

Hands grabbed him again, and again Beauvoir lashed out. Fighting for his life.

"*Non, non*, stop!"

It wasn't Nichol, it was Lauzon.

Marcus Lauzon had come back. Marcus Lauzon had saved them.

The door opened and Giselle Trudel stepped into the room.

It was not the cabinet minister Armand had been expecting. He watched her, warily.

"We need to go in with you, ma'am," said the guard.

"No, you don't. You and I both know these people are not threats."

There was a pause, a reluctant nod, and the officer withdrew.

"Do you need a doctor?" Advancing into the room, she turned to Inspector Lacoste, whose hair was matted with blood. "Are you all right?"

"'All right' is not how I'd describe our situation. Would you?"

"I'm sorry." Trudel hesitated, then chose her words carefully. "I think you put something into your ID, Chief Inspector. A piece of paper."

Gamache was silent, studying the woman.

"Ferguson palmed it."

"Why are you here, Madame Trudel?" he asked.

"I want to know what it was you passed to him."

"Do you plan to beat it out of me?"

"God, no." She looked horrified. "Ferguson was about to throw it away, then changed his mind. I suspect by now it's ash." Her intelligent eyes were studying him. "You need to tell me what it said. Quickly. Before they come for you."

There was a beat as Gamache weighed the options. Then spoke. "It was an IP address and password."

"You came here knowing your ID would be taken?" He nodded. "You wanted it taken. You did all that on purpose."

"It served many purposes, but yes."

While his voice was steady, his mind was racing, trying to work out what this could mean. He saw Shona watching him, worried. This was not how it was supposed to go. Their plan wasn't so much unfolding as unraveling.

"It was your bad luck Ferguson was the one who found it," said Trudel.

"Did Prime Minister Woodford see it?" His tone gave away none of his anxiety. Only Lacoste, standing beside him, could see his right hand closing into a loose fist.

"No."

The fist relaxed.

Trudel turned to Shona. "You smuggled your phone into the meeting and live-streamed?"

"So it's out there?" said Shona, excited. "Paul got it out?"

"Workman? Yes. It's going viral, of course."

While Shona laughed with relief, both Armand and Isabelle simply exhaled. One huge part accomplished.

"Did you really have to do that?" Giselle Trudel continued. "You've ruined the career, probably the life, of a decent man who made a mistake."

"'Mistake,'" said Shona. "Is that what you call it? And yes, I really had to do it. I'm a journalist. We witness, and we tell the world what we see. Until, that is, we're stopped by a tyrant."

"What we see is not always the whole picture. The Prime Minister isn't a tyrant. He made a mistake when he ordered the guard to assault you. But you aren't exactly blameless." She turned to Gamache. "You set him up. It was a psychological and emotional sting operation. He'd just seen his friend and colleague, the American President, narrowly escape assassination. He was on edge and you pushed him over."

"Are you practicing for the news conference?" Gamache asked.

"No. I'm simply telling you what I know to be the truth. Now it's your turn. I want to see that IP address."

Since the Rubicon was already crossed, Gamache walked over to the desk and wrote it out, along with the password. Then handed it to the cabinet minister.

"What will happen if I put it into my phone? Will this be treason? Will I be fired?"

"Treason? No. Fired? Almost certainly."

"Where does it take me?"

All three continued to stare at her but said nothing.

"Is War Plan Red for real? Are the Americans really planning to annex Canada?"

"Annex?" said Shona. "I guess that's one way of looking at it."

"But they'd never get away with it," said Trudel.

"You think not?" said Lacoste. "Who'll stop them? You? You couldn't even stop your own people from doing this." She held out the bloody tissues.

The Minister opened her mouth, but no answer came out. Then she looked back down at the paper. And, making up her mind, she put in the internet address.

"Are you kidding me?" she said, staring at the site that had appeared. "I knew about .onion. We monitor it. But I was told that's as deep as the dark web goes."

She hesitated just a moment before taking the final irrevocable leap into the darkness. Into .family. Then she typed in the code. And there it was.

What she read was not some rusty old battle plan using bullets and bombs and young men sent to slaughter. And abandoned in 1939. Here was a long-range, detailed blueprint for the takeover of one country by another. Years in the making, fine-tuning, adjusting as technology and society changed. As the narrative changed over the decades. As the needs and threats changed.

It talked of AI and journalistic "dark arts," used to both manufacture consent and undermine any protest. It was a slow drip, drip, drip until that final drop that started the flood.

It was never meant to be acted upon. It was, as Bert Whitehead said, a contingency. An exercise even. Taken as seriously as the alien-invasion exercise.

But then someone had found it and seen the potential, the opportunity buried in the looming climate crisis. In the catastrophic and inevitable loss of fresh water.

Someone saw the possibilities. And War Plan Red was secretly updated and quietly put into action.

It was all mapped out in the document the young biologist Charles Langlois had found. Though it was possible, even probable, he never really believed it. .family, after all, was littered with lunatics.

His hesitation had cost him his life. As had his decision to show it to the wrong person.

The ground war, should one be necessary, was also mapped out. It would be short and brutal. And once Canada ceded, as it eventually must, would come the final step. The silencing of all dissent.

And those few who continued to resist? According to the plan, their homes and workplaces and families would be targeted by angry mobs of "patriots."

The Minister sat down. She'd have missed the chair if Lacoste hadn't moved it for her.

Evelyn Tardiff was still alive, but unconscious.

A few feet away they found the body of Margaux Chalifoux. Trussed up and cold.

All three had to look away from her face.

"We need to bring her with us," said Nichol, indicating Chalifoux's body.

"No, she stays here."

"But we can't just leave her," said Lauzon.

"And if we bring her?" said Beauvoir. "What then?"

They couldn't very well take her to the morgue. There'd be questions as they lugged this contorted body down to the basement. And the mob definitely had informants in the morgue.

No, they had to leave Chalifoux. They'd come back for her once this was over.

Beauvoir and Nichol supported the semiconscious Tardiff as they made their way out of the cave.

Once back in the sunshine, Nichol tried to get reception on her phone. But she'd dropped it into the cold water and stepped on it. It wasn't working. Beauvoir had lost his phone in the fight with the mob enforcer. And of course neither Tardiff nor Lauzon had one.

They'd grabbed the phone that had recorded the attempted murder but could not unlock it.

"Caron," Tardiff rasped. "She's behind this."

"We got your pictures," said Nichol, holding her tight. "We know."

Then Tardiff's blurry eyes focused on Lauzon. "What's he doing here?"

"It's okay," said Beauvoir. "He's with us. Do you need a hospital?"

"*Non, non.*" There was a deep cut on her forehead and a bloody slash around her throat where the rope had cut in. Her voice was gravelly, and her breathing came in gasps, but it was improving.

"We need to get away before Moretti realizes what's happened," said Lauzon, dragging Beauvoir forward.

"We'll go to headquarters," said Nichol as they made their way to the car.

"*Non,*" said Tardiff. "It's the first place they'll look, and who knows who's compromised."

"I need to find a phone," said Jean-Guy.

They stopped at the first convenience store they came to. But there was no answer from Gamache or Lacoste. Jean-Guy left a message, then ran back to the car.

"South. Go south."

To Three Pines. Where else would a boy on a bicycle go when the straight road splayed?

The Minister of Defense for Canada finally reached the last page of War Plan Red, where the shiny new combined nation was described. A country and peoples enjoying security and prosperity unknown in the last half century. A once deeply divided nation, on the verge of another catastrophic civil war, had at the last minute turned its ire outward. Northward. And was finally united.

The document described a new North America. A place of cohesion, under one flag. A country envied by the rest of the world, where there was peace and plenty. Where abundant water flowed south. And, with it, wealth beyond the dreams of avarice, and power beyond even Alexander's and Napoleon's fantasies, for whoever would lead the luminous new land.

Along with a return to water security and stability and a life of plenty, there'd be a return to common values. Christian values.

Happy days.

Giselle Trudel looked up from her phone. "Dear God, it might work. Enough people might buy into this bullshit. The Prime Minister needs to see this. He needs to be told."

She made for the door, but Isabelle Lacoste stopped her.

"He knows. Why do you think he denied War Plan Red exists, then had us isolated?"

"We've been through this. The Prime Minister has no idea what the US plans to do. Is doing. He might know that this plan exists, but not that it has been updated and implemented. He needs proof, and this is it."

"That's not it," said Lacoste. "That's a document anyone could have created and put on a dark web site populated by marginal conspiracy theorists."

"Are you so sure that isn't what's happened?"

"People have died to get us WPR," said Lacoste. "This is no lunatic fantasy."

"And it's not just the US," said Gamache. "Surely the document makes it clear. This didn't start with the Americans. It started right here in Canada. The leader, the architect, is Canadian. We've already signed over vast amounts of our forestry and mining and fisheries to the Americans. Someone powerful in this country had to do that."

"Yes. It was Lauzon. Remember him? A narcissistic shit-head if there ever was one. And he's in prison. This"—she held up the phone with the document—"is out of date. Whatever was once planned has been stopped."

"*Non*. Not stopped. It isn't Lauzon," said Gamache. "He's been set up. We're meant to think it's him."

"Are you really saying Lauzon's innocent?"

"Well, innocent," said Gamache. "I would never use that word to describe him, but yes, Marcus Lauzon was not behind the poisoning, nor is he behind the takeover. He's the scapegoat."

"Why did Prime Minister Woodford leave our meeting this morning after we told him about Whitehead's visit to the President?" asked Lacoste.

The Minister was briefly lost in what seemed a non sequitur. "I have a feeling you're going to tell me."

"He said it was to get Manon Payette, his Chief of Staff, but I spoke to her," said Lacoste. "She admitted he went into a private room and made a call."

The Minister paled. "You think it was to the President? To warn her about what Whitehead was about to ask?"

"To someone in the White House," said Gamache. "There was no need for him to leave to get his Chief of Staff."

"I took Payette aside and pushed her," said Lacoste. "She admitted nothing, but neither did she deny it. I asked her, begged her, to stream what was about to happen. She was uncomfortable and didn't commit—"

"She did," said the Minister. "That video of the PM was from more than one angle, one phone. The PM has sent people to find her."

"Payette's disappeared?" asked Gamache.

"Yes."

"I hope she knows a good hiding place," said Gamache. "What is it?"

The Minister was looking perplexed. "I find it hard to believe she'd help you, of all people."

"Why do you say that?" asked Gamache.

"You obviously don't know who she is."

"Manon Payette."

"Like many Québécoise whose first name is Marie, she goes by her middle name, Manon. And Payette's her mother's last name. She didn't want anyone to know who she is. Didn't want preferential treatment. She was my Chief of Staff, but after the poison scandal, Woodford transferred her to his office, where he could offer her some protection."

"From whom? Who is she?" asked Isabelle.

"Marie Lauzon."

"*Merde*. Marcus Lauzon's daughter." Isabelle turned to Gamache. "The one you arrested for manslaughter years ago. Her father got her off and never forgave you. Tried to ruin you."

"Not just me." Armand wondered if they knew what Lauzon had done to Daniel.

His eyes narrowed as he quickly tried to see what this might mean. It was clearly not good news. But just how bad would it prove to be?

Though one thing was not debatable.

"We need to get out of here," he said.

"Agreed. If you're right, they'll need to silence you too. I suspect the only reason they haven't is because of that video. But something will happen to you, it has to."

The Minister now seemed to believe them about Woodford. She looked at all three, and something dawned on her. "Huh. You knew when you arrived there was a chance you'd be the first victims of a covert war."

"Not the first. The first was a young biologist murdered on a street in Montréal," said Gamache. "But yes, we discussed that possibility."

Giselle Trudel went to the door and asked the head guard to join them.

Shona looked at Lacoste, who was looking at Gamache, who was staring at the Minister of Defense, who turned to the guard.

"Arrest them."

CHAPTER 30

⌒

The car crested the hill, then began its slow descent into Three Pines, passing the bench with its inscription.

Surprised by Joy.

Then, below that, the Marilynne Robinson paraphrase: *May you be a brave man in a brave country.*

It was as though the bench were a gatekeeper, etching the words into itself as enchantments. With its tattooed incantations, it stood guard over this tiny Québec village not found on any map.

As their vehicle rounded the village green and passed the three immense pines, Jean-Guy hoped and prayed they would not be followed and found. Not just for their sake, but for the sakes of everyone who'd found refuge there from a world not always kind. Who'd been surprised by joy when they realized Three Pines wasn't just a haven, it was home.

As he parked, he knew the biggest hurdle was going to be convincing Reine-Marie to let Marcus Lauzon into her home. Though, as it turned out, that was not a problem.

"I'm sorry, Minister, but from what I've seen these people have done nothing wrong."

The RCMP guard in full gear had closed the door behind her, and now cradled her carbine across her chest. She looked uncomfortable.

It was not easy to refuse a direct order.

"I said arrest them, Captain Pinsent," demanded the Minister of Defense. "This is a matter of public security! You saw what they did."

"I saw her"—the officer nodded toward Shona—"behaving like a journalist, which she is. And I saw him raising his voice. If everyone who

shouted in Parliament was arrested, the place would be empty. And she"—
now she turned to Lacoste—"took a hit. From my rifle. And for that I am
sorry, and ashamed."

"It could have been far worse," said Isabelle. "You pulled your blow."

"It should never have happened. No, Minister. Enough. I will not arrest
them."

The RCMP officer raised her head in defiance.

The Minister of Defense glared at her, then turned to Shona, who
bumped into the Chief Inspector as she backed away. Her eyes were wide
with fear.

"It's a shame you weren't able to record that," the Minister said to
Shona, smiling.

"What?" said Shona.

"What's happening?" asked Captain Pinsent, looking from one to the
other.

"You passed the decency test," said the Minister. "We need to get them
out of here. What do you suggest?"

"Me?" said Captain Pinsent, trying to catch up with what just happened.
"A minute ago you wanted me to arrest them, now you want me to help
them escape? Refusing to arrest them is one thing, aiding and abetting an
escape is another."

"You said yourself, we're not criminals. We haven't been arrested. We're
detained against our will, illegally," said Gamache. "It's not a question of
abetting. We're free to leave."

"Even if that's true, sir, we're on lockdown. I can't even leave." She
looked at them all before landing on Trudel. "Madame Minister, you need
to tell me what's happening."

"I'm sorry, there isn't time."

"You need to trust us," said Gamache.

She was the commander of the unit, in a leadership position. It would
have taken her years to get there. The Chief Inspector was aware they were
asking her to throw all that away. To not just lose her job, but perhaps even
be prosecuted.

She was also aware of that.

The moment stretched on.

"I know who you are," she finally said. Not to Gamache, but to Isabelle Lacoste. "I've followed your career. Do you promise that you're not planning any harm?"

It seemed both a hugely naïve and perfectly appropriate question.

"I promise."

"Okay. Okay." She seemed to be convincing herself.

"Pinsent's your name?" said Gamache. The RCMP officer nodded. "Captain Pinsent, we need our phones, and Inspector Lacoste needs her firearm."

There was silence. That last request might've been an ask too far, but after considering, Pinsent nodded.

"I can escort you to the front door. We'll probably make it that far without being questioned. Most of those on duty are my people."

"'Most'? 'Probably'?" said Shona. "What happens if we are stopped?"

The officers exchanged a look.

"We'll need a distraction," said Lacoste. "Nothing alarming, just something to draw attention away. Give us a chance to get to the door, at least."

"I'll do it," said the Minister of Defense. "I can fake a heart attack or stroke."

"I doubt they'd fall for that twice," said Lacoste.

"Twice? You mean Senator Walls—?"

"I'm sure he'll make a full and speedy recovery," said Gamache. "No. I'll lead them away. They'll follow me. They'll be curious, but not alarmed. Besides, I know my way around these buildings."

Isabelle stared at him, trying to decide if that was true.

"Where will we rendezvous?" she asked.

Gamache thought. "Under the first bridge across the canal."

That was where his parents had told him to go should he get separated from them. They would find him. They promised.

"*D'accord*," said Lacoste.

The Minister of Defense looked at her phone. "Shit, I'm supposed to be in a cabinet meeting. It's about to start."

"Go," said Gamache.

"If you need help..."

"You've done your part."

"Okay, but I'm sure I could do a convincing heart attack. I'm not that far off."

"Perhaps another time," said Armand. "*Merci.*"

She opened the door and peered out. "There're two assistants at their desks and two RCMP guards."

"My people," said Captain Pinsent. "I'll reassign them."

"And I'll get rid of the assistants," said the Minister.

They both left. Less than a minute later Captain Pinsent returned. "Follow me."

Once in the anteroom, Gamache looked at the door into the PM's office. He was tempted to go in and rifle the desk, knowing Woodford would be in the cabinet meeting. But there was no time for that.

He reached for the door into the main hallway, but Pinsent stopped him.

"There're other guards out there, not under my command."

Gamache nodded. "I understand." He looked at Lacoste and Shona. "You know what to do."

"Meet you under the bridge," said Shona.

Isabelle held Armand's eyes and nodded. Knowing he meant more than the rendezvous, should all this go terribly wrong.

"When you leave, head to the right," said Pinsent.

"Aye, aye, Captain," said Gamache. He saw Lacoste's eyes open in genuine amusement. And she saw his genuine delight. Who knew the phrase would finally come in handy?

With that, he opened the door and strolled out as though he owned the place. As though he not only belonged but was in charge.

About twenty paces on he turned and saw the guards looking at him, perplexed. Then one of them called, "Stop there, please, sir."

He did not.

Reine-Marie ran out onto the porch to meet them, followed by Clara, Myrna, and Ruth.

"Jean-Guy, where's Armand? Is he all right? Is Isabelle?"

She barely noticed the others. She did see Marcus Lauzon but found she didn't care anymore. All she cared about were Armand and Isabelle.

Jean-Guy approached his mother-in-law. Her tone, her face, her whole being spoke of far more than anxiety. There was outright fear, verging on panic.

"Why wouldn't they be? They're in Parliament meeting with the Prime Minister."

"Haven't you seen?" asked Clara.

"Seen what?" asked Nichol.

Isabelle and Shona moved swiftly but without breaking into a run, following Captain Pinsent down the wide corridor.

The entrance was up ahead, heavily guarded. Any moment now the alarm would be sounded as the guards who followed Gamache realized what he was doing.

They had to get out before that happened.

Once at the entrance the RCMP officers saluted Pinsent.

"I need their phones," she said after returning the salute. "And Inspector Lacoste's firearm. They're being allowed to leave."

"Our orders are to let no one out."

"Orders I gave you," she said. "And now they've changed. The phones and the firearm. Now."

The guard retreated to the office, leaving his four colleagues watching them, their rifles at the ready.

Why was it taking so long? Lacoste wondered. What was that RCMP officer doing in there? Making a call? Confirming the orders? Had they realized the prisoners had escaped? Were escaping? Were standing right there?

Just as Pinsent stepped toward the office, the officer came out holding two phones.

"These are yours."

"We need Chief Inspector Gamache's too," said Captain Pinsent. "He's in the cabinet meeting and will take the west exit. And the firearm? Where is it?"

Time was ticking. Ticking.

"I don't have them, Captain."

"Where are they?"

"Prime Minister Woodford's Chief of Staff signed them out."

"You gave her a gun?" demanded Lacoste, and looked at Pinsent. Who looked equally disconcerted.

"She said the PM wanted them," explained the RCMP officer, nervous now.

"We'll have a talk when this is over," snapped Captain Pinsent. "In the meantime, open up."

By now the guard was so anxious, having obviously made his superior angry, he did as he was told.

The guards' boots picked up speed as they began to suspect something was off.

"Monsieur Gamache? Chief Inspector? *Arrêtez.*"

"*Un moment,*" he called, his voice from farther away than they would have liked. "I'm looking for the toilettes."

"That isn't the way. Please turn back, sir."

But now there was silence, except for the disconcerting sound of the Chief Inspector's footfalls getting farther and farther away.

Now the guards, still not worried enough to sound the alarm but getting closer as the Chief got farther away, picked up their pace.

Soon his steps could no longer be heard.

They finally came to a more remote bathroom. The senior officer motioned the junior to enter. He returned a moment later.

"He's not here."

"Damn!"

The doors opened. Isabelle and Shona stepped into the bright sunshine and crisp autumn air.

Captain Pinsent had decided to stay behind. To leave with them would be desertion, and she was not willing to go that far.

"You'll be detained," said Lacoste. *Or worse,* she thought.

"I know." *Or worse,* she thought. "You'd better make it worth it."

"*Merci,*" said Isabelle, and marveled again how quickly friendships were formed in battle. And this was a battle.

As the door closed behind them and Captain Pinsent headed to her fate, Isabelle looked around, getting her bearings. Parliament Hill was deserted, the police cordon in effect. The tall, emblematic Peace Tower loomed behind them, and ahead was the eternal flame.

"This way," said Shona, walking swiftly to their left.

"How do you know?"

"My mother brought me here once. We skated on the canal, and she said if I was ever lost, I should meet her under the bridge."

Isabelle followed. She knew perfectly well what had happened to Shona's mother, and that the journalist blamed Gamache. And that once this was over, there'd be a reckoning.

They could see the bridge. It seemed a long way off.

"What does it mean that Manon Payette has your gun?"

"Not Manon Payette, Marie Lauzon."

"Right. Shouldn't we—" Shona looked behind her.

"Go back? *Non.* We wouldn't get ten feet, and that wouldn't help him."

They needed to get their part done and trust he'd join them soon. First, though, they had to get under that bridge and regroup, before all hell broke loose. And it was about to.

CHAPTER 31

"They'll be all right," said Jean-Guy, staring at the screen. "They'll be fine." He sounded as though he was trying to convince himself. He was as shocked as everyone by the images of the Prime Minister of Canada effectively ordering a journalist detained and two Sûreté officers beaten. And not just any officers. His friends. His family.

Beauvoir tried to tamp down his rage.

When you fight, stay as calm as the ocean . . .

"FINE you say?" said Ruth. "Well, that sure describes someone in that video. Fucked up, insecure, neurotic, and egotistical." She turned to Rosa. "I wish we hadn't voted for the bastard."

Rosa nodded. Though she had soiled her ballot.

Nichol stared at them, unsure if she loved or loathed the elderly woman. And her duck.

Myrna and Clara had tended to Chief Inspector Tardiff's wounds, putting salve and disinfectant on the rope burns and offering her painkillers. Which she rejected.

"I need a clear head," Evelyn rasped, wondering if her voice would ever stop sounding like Fats Waller. Her whole body ached. The wounds on her neck, where the rope had torn her skin, stung, but they also acted as a welcome counterirritant, to take her mind off her throbbing head.

But she was alive. Alive. Alive . . .

As the three of them rejoined the others, they heard Reine-Marie say to Jean-Guy, "You really think they'll be okay?"

"I do. The RCMP officer pulled back at the last moment. She made it look worse than it is. And with the video out for everyone to see, there's no way Woodford can do anything more."

What worried him, and obviously worried the others, was that by now this video was an hour old. Who knew what had happened on Parliament Hill in the meantime.

What was happening now.

In the background the television was providing updates from Washington. The President was safe. A Chief Petty Officer was being questioned, but it appeared the assassins were dead.

There was no word on General Whitehead's condition.

The National Guard had taken control of the capital, and a state of emergency existed. Rumors were rife that this was the first of a series of planned attacks, hitting at the very heart of American democracy.

The rhetoric was ramping up, even from seasoned reporters and anchors.

Myrna switched to a Canadian station, where there was a shot of Parliament Hill, while commentators analyzed what had been posted on Paul Workman's site.

"Look." Clara showed them a feed from a popular social media site. The video had been changed, edited to make it appear Gamache and Lacoste were attacking the PM and the guards were simply defending him.

"No one will believe it," Beauvoir said. "The original is out there. What is it?"

"They're saying that the first video is doctored," said Clara, "and that this is what really happened."

The edited video from Ottawa was beginning to appear on the major networks in Canada and the US, with analysts now saying that the new video made more sense.

"More sense?" demanded Myrna. "To who?"

There was a tinge of hysteria in the air, the airwaves, now.

"They're beating plowshares into swords," said Ruth. "What's happening to the world? I don't understand."

"Believe me now?" said Marcus Lauzon. "There's your wolf."

Frozen on the laptop screen was the face of Prime Minister Woodford, distorted. A wild creature unmasked.

The alarm had been sounded.

Not a siren. This was an alert sent only to the men and women guarding

Parliament and its perimeter. The three detainees had escaped and needed to be found.

Two of them had left the building and were at large. One was almost certainly still in Parliament. All efforts needed to be focused on recapturing him. There was reason to believe Chief Inspector Gamache was armed and planned to harm the PM.

He should be considered dangerous and stopped at all costs.

Armand pressed himself against the wall, squeezing his large body between two tall filing cabinets. The stomp of boots on concrete was getting closer. Closer.

He held his breath. All senses heightened, tingling.

And then the guards were upon him. He tensed, prepared. Then they raced right by. He waited a few moments, exhaled, and continued on.

He had no idea where he was going.

He'd taken the back stairs down, down, figuring they would lead into some warren of a basement. Which they did.

As he'd led the guards away, he'd searched his memory for anything he knew about the layout of Parliament. Despite what he'd told Isabelle, he actually had very little knowledge of the building beyond what he'd seen over the years when coming to meetings.

Unfortunately, none had been held in the sub-basement.

All he could remember now was what he'd learned fifty years ago on the tour of Parliament with his parents.

The guide had explained that everyone had expected, in the 1850s, that Queen Victoria would choose Kingston, or maybe Toronto or Montréal, as the capital of the soon-to-be sovereign nation of Canada. The three cities vied for it, competed, wined and dined the Queen's representatives. Lobbied, cajoled, and bribed.

And then, when the time came, she chose ... Ottawa. Ottawa??

Angry city leaders claimed she'd thrown a dart at a map and hit what was, at the time, essentially a cow town.

In fact, as their tour guide had explained, it came to light later that the decision was strategic and, as it turned out, prescient.

Queen Victoria, or more likely her advisers, had chosen Ottawa because it was farther from the US border. Should the Americans invade, the PM and other leaders would have more time to organize resistance.

While an invasion in the late 1800s did not seem likely, neither was it altogether unlikely. Even 150 years ago, the danger was obvious, if not imminent.

What Queen Victoria could never have foreseen, or believed, was that the threat would come from inside the border. From inside Parliament.

But all that was useless at the moment. What Armand needed was a way out.

He had absolutely no idea of the building's layout. Just that wings had been added over the years. Common sense told him there must be some underground connection, where equipment and documents could be moved without clattering around the main corridors.

His goal at first was to keep the guards following him until he was sure Lacoste and Shona were out. By now that must have happened. The alarm must have been sounded. He was no longer being followed, he was now being hunted.

He needed to get out too.

The sub-basement of the old building was as worn and musky as he'd expected. There were the mechanical rooms, the storerooms; file cabinets lined corridors, filled with God knew what sensitive material.

What he hadn't found, and now needed, was a passageway that would take him to the next building over. That was his plan, such as it was. Once there he could escape and head to the bridge.

Now, as the guards closed in again, he resisted the temptation to duck into one of the storerooms and hide. To curl into a corner, as small as he could make himself, and close his eyes. That was a childish impulse, an illusion of safety. If they decided to search it, he'd be trapped with no way out.

His only hope was to get to the next building.

The RCMP guards were approaching. Slower this time, sure they'd passed him by. He could hear them opening and closing doors.

Had his hearing been better, had the cicadas all left, he'd have heard another, more subtle sound. Much closer.

The same one that, earlier that endless day, had alerted General

Whitehead. But even had Armand heard the cocking of a gun behind him, it would have been, as it was for the General, too late.

"All right, out with it," Beauvoir demanded of Lauzon. "What do you know?"

Everyone else had left. Beauvoir, Nichol, Lauzon, and Tardiff sat in a circle, leaning toward each other. A conclave.

"I know that your Black Wolf is the Prime Minister," said Lauzon. "I've known all along."

"Then why didn't you say anything?" asked Beauvoir.

"I had no hard evidence, and I assumed, no, I hoped that someone would at least take the time to look deeper. Honestly, any imbecile could see that the Prime Minister must be behind it. Who else could have possibly organized all this? Who else has the ear of the American President? I was set up, and my only hope of staying alive was to keep my mouth shut."

Now that Lauzon said it, it did seem all too obvious.

"The PM calls the shots, with Jeanne Caron his covert number two," said Evelyn Tardiff.

"That's it. She's the only one in a position to set me up so perfectly. She does the dirty work, as always, while Woodford remains in the shadows."

"For Christ's sake, we know all that, but it's the Prime Minister!" said Beauvoir. "We need more than the word of a convicted traitor."

Seeing the look on Lauzon's tired face, Jean-Guy stopped and took a deep breath, pulling himself together. When he spoke again, his voice was almost gentle. "*Désolé*, Monsieur Lauzon. I went too far. But we need hard evidence, and we need it now."

"Give me the gun." Armand held his hand out.

While he hadn't heard the weapon being pulled, he had sensed a presence and turned quickly, just as a hand grasped his jacket and yanked him backward.

Even as he fought to stay on his feet, instinct told him it wasn't one of the RCMP officers. They'd have made themselves known in ways that would have been unmistakable and unpleasant.

This was different. Though also unpleasant.

The guards patrolling the corridor had passed by, and now he found himself in an indent in the stone wall, hidden behind one of the tall filing cabinets. With a gun pointed at his chest.

"Please"—his voice a whisper—"Madame Lauzon."

"So, you know who I am?"

"I didn't recognize you," he admitted. "It's been, what? Twenty years?"

"Twenty-two, as you know perfectly well."

It was true. He knew to the day how long it had been since he'd arrested her for manslaughter, a charge her politician father had had dropped. And the high-stakes match with Marcus Lauzon had begun.

He looked down at the weapon still pointed at him. "That's dangerous. Please give it to me."

"Are you going to hurt me?"

That shocked him. "Why would I do that?"

"My father always told me to stay well away from you. To be careful whenever I went home to Québec. That you had it in for both of us and had the weight of the entire Sûreté behind you."

"He was wrong." Armand noticed that in her other hand she was gripping some files. "Why are you still here? You could've gotten out long ago."

"I was about to, but then I heard that you'd escaped, so I waited for you."

"Here? In the basement?"

"Where else would you go? If you were going to escape, it wouldn't be through the front door." She looked around. "Where're the others?"

"They escaped out the front door."

"Come on."

"Really." *At least, I hope . . .*

"How?" She thought about it. "They must've had help. One of the guards?"

Armand considered, then nodded. Everyone would know soon enough. "Captain Pinsent. We can't stand here forever. Do you really plan to pull the trigger?"

"I will if I have to. You've caused my father, my family, enough pain.

318

He's a good man, you know. Far better than you realize. I needed to find out where you really stand."

"I think you know where I stand and have all along." He glanced down at the gun, which had not moved. "Just as you know what you did all those years ago. I wasn't the one on the wrong side of the law then, and I'm not now."

She looked about to argue, but instead exhaled, suddenly tired. "I need you to read this."

She held out the files.

"I will, but first..."

She hesitated, then handed over the gun. He'd recognized it right away as Sûreté issue and knew it must be Isabelle's. He quickly took out the magazine.

"We'll be unarmed," she said.

"True. I have no intention of shooting fellow officers, or anyone else. Having a gun escalates violence, it doesn't prevent it. How did you get this?"

"I asked for it at the front door. Told them the PM wanted it as evidence. I also have..."

She handed him his phone.

He noticed, without surprise, that there was no reception down there.

"We need to get out." He tucked the weapon into his belt and the phone into his pocket.

"*Non.*"

"*Non?*"

"You need to read this first." Once again she offered him the slender dossier. "I got it while the cabinet meeting was on."

"I'll read it once we're out."

"Now, read it now. It won't take long. We're not leaving until you do. It's important. I think you'll be surprised."

He looked at his watch. It was one o'clock.

"What?" she said. "You have a lunch date?"

Not exactly that, but he did have an appointment with Jeanne Caron at the Haskell Opera House in three hours. But that was not going to happen unless he got out of Parliament. And he needed Marie Lauzon for that.

He took the file. The light was dim, and he'd lost his reading glasses when he'd hit the ground after the blow. But slowly his eyes adjusted.

It was just two pages. When he finished, he reread it to be sure he understood. Then he looked up at Marie Lauzon.

"You know what that says?" she asked.

"I'm not sure..."

"I think you are."

"Do you know for sure that this"—he held up the file—"is legitimate? Not doctored. Not put there for us to find?"

What she'd found was essentially a skeleton. The structure, the core of what was planned. What was plotted. While complex, covering years and eventualities, this slender document acted as a clear schematic. Appropriately, Gamache thought, in bullet point.

It was beyond damning, if true. It named names. It outlined roles.

"It's real. We need to get to Prime Minister Woodford."

"Are you insane?" he asked.

"Are you a coward?"

"I'm a realist. There's no way we're getting to Woodford."

"Not just getting to him, we need to bring him with us."

He looked back down at the document in his hand. It was more dangerous than any weapon he'd ever held or beheld.

If they got caught, it would be destroyed, and they'd be killed. They'd have to be. There was no doubt now.

He raised his eyes to hers and wondered if she realized the full import of this slender document. What it was saying without actually saying it.

But that didn't matter. Not now, not yet. All that mattered was getting it out.

He thought about taking a photo of the document, but if they were caught and his phone hacked, they'd know he and Marie Lauzon had the file. They'd be forced to give it up. He wasn't sure how long either of them would stand up to torture.

Besides, even if he was able to send the photos of the documents to Jean-Guy and Isabelle, they would never be considered proof. Only the original would be accepted.

"Let's go," she said.

"Wait. Wait." He was speaking to himself. "Wait..."

There might be a way. Not to get to Woodford—that would almost certainly fail, and they'd be caught in the attempt. And if they couldn't get out, neither could the document. But there was something else they could do. He thought.

Think. Think it through. He stared at the file folder. *Think.*

The plan had been updated in the past year. It was detailed, and yet, finally, like many invasions, it came down to weather. Something the conspirators could not actually control. All they could do was wait for the right conditions.

He remembered the numbers on Charles Langlois's map. The isobars.

"Come on." There was urgency in her voice. "Waiting isn't going to help. Let's go!"

"Wait... wait..." He almost had it. There was one other thing, something he needed to—

And then it was there. FEDS.

She was pulling at his sleeve. Still he stared. And then he finally spoke.

"Where's the corridor to the other building?"

"When the time comes, we won't take it. There's an unused tunnel that houses the electric cables and old pipes. We'll take that. Later. First we need to get to the Prime Minister. Come on."

"I'll go with you to get him, but you need to show me the way to the tunnel."

"In case I'm caught?"

"If you are, so am I. We can't take this with us." He held up the file. "We need to hide it, and the tunnel seems the best place. Then I need to get far enough up to send a couple of messages."

"How long do we wait?" whispered Shona.

It was dank and cold beneath the stone bridge. They'd been there for twenty minutes, and there was no sign of Gamache.

"Longer." Isabelle knew if he didn't show soon, they'd have to leave. And leave him behind. It was no use all of them getting caught. Already they'd evaded one patrol, but eventually someone would look closer. Someone would find them.

The alarm had obviously been sounded. She wondered how Captain Pinsent was doing. Mostly she wondered about Armand.

Pulling out her phone, she wrote Jean-Guy and was about to hit send when Shona touched her arm.

"Gamache just wrote."

Lacoste grabbed Shona's phone. Thank God. But why would the Chief write Shona and not her? Was it a trick? Was he being forced? Or maybe it wasn't from him at all.

But the short text contained their private code to identify themselves.

I'm FINE, the message began. It was him. And on his own phone. Which meant he'd run into Marie Lauzon. Or vice versa. And somehow he'd recovered his phone and, she hoped, her gun.

When she read it, Isabelle understood why he'd sent it to Shona. He almost certainly had very little time, maybe just enough for the one message. And it really was for the young journalist.

"I don't understand why he wants me to do it," said Shona.

"But can you?"

"Yes."

"Then hurry."

Minutes later Jeanne Caron studied the email she'd just received from the senior meteorologist and muttered, "Jesus."

She thought for a moment.

Then she wrote a text. But didn't yet send it.

This was happening much faster than expected, certainly sooner than was ideal. But ideal had passed them by when the poisoning plot had been discovered and stopped.

If that had worked, they'd be in the transition phase now, that netherworld between complete chaos and utter control. The War Measures Act would have been declared and in place for a few months. Any protests would have been quashed, the protesters rounded up. Most Canadians would not only have accepted the draconian measures but welcomed them, as a bulwark against anarchy. They'd be getting used to living in, essentially, a police state. They'd happily trade freedom for safety. History had taught those in power that frightened people always did. Which made fear of an attack a far more effective weapon than any actual attack. And less messy.

While Canadians welcomed the strong hand of a single leader, in the United States there'd be moves to demonize the nation to the north. The messages in the media, social or otherwise, would declare that Canada was moving into a dangerous dictatorship. A nationalistic, fascist, protectionist state that had closed its border and was jealously guarding its resources. And had no intention of sharing.

And they would not be wrong.

Something would have to be done to bring Canada to heel and get the resources that the United States so desperately needed. And that would belong to them, if not for some arbitrary line on a map.

How bad, really, would it be to move that line? To remove that line?

That was the ideal.

Since the poisoning plot had been discovered, Marcus Lauzon arrested, and the War Measures Act made unnecessary, they'd had to pivot. And they had. It proved more difficult to paint Canada as a threat, especially since few Americans gave the benign nation to the north a first, never mind second, thought. But the narrative was taking hold, thanks to wildfires and sophisticated messaging.

Caron studied the new forecast sent by her contact at Environment Canada. She'd been assured that, so far, no one else had seen it.

According to his message, within the next twenty-four hours, a high-pressure system would collide with low pressure, whipping up strong northerly winds.

To be sure she understood what was about to happen, her meteorologist had sent an illustration. The lines on the map undulated. They went as far west as Chicago and swooped south, embracing Boston, and New York, and ... Washington.

Thanks to the new technology of FEDS, they now knew that thick ash would fall all over those cities, as it had a few years earlier. Only worse. Should a wildfire happen to ignite during this window of time.

The scientist assured her these conditions were unlikely to happen again for many years.

Jeanne Caron considered the options.

According to Darwin's *On the Origin of Species*, it wasn't actually the fittest that would survive. The species that survived was the one that best adapted to the changing environment.

And the environment was changing.

And Jeanne Caron was adapting.

She composed a message, then hit send.

And with that she lit the spark that would become a wildfire that would change North America and the world forever. Other drought-stricken nations would watch what happened next and see what was possible. And permissible.

As the environment changed, so would borders. They were, after all, only lines on a map. And a map was flammable.

"Oh, fuck."

"What is it now?" demanded Beauvoir.

"Look." Nichol turned her laptop around.

"Jesus," he whispered and looked from the screen to Lauzon, then Tardiff. "What?"

They both leaned in and studied the illustration. And if they were in any doubts, the text put those to rest.

"Can your contact be trusted?" Tardiff asked.

"She's the assistant to a senior meteorologist," said Nichol.

"Not a climate scientist herself?" asked Lauzon. "How does she know?"

"She sees all the reports even before he does."

"The isobars," said Beauvoir. "They're lining up again. Even worse. Who else will see this?"

"Eventually everyone at Environment Canada, and pilots, of course. Control towers. MétéoMédia and the Weather Network, as well as—"

"Got it," snapped Beauvoir. "We have to stop the information from getting out."

Nichol shot off a quick text to her contact and waited for a reply.

"But really, would anyone care?" asked Lauzon. "It shows a trough of high pressure, but would anyone see the danger?"

"After the megafires, I suspect every meteorologist in North America will be paying attention and know what this could mean," said Beauvoir.

"But there's no real danger, is there?" said Tardiff.

"Exactly," said Lauzon. "If there were forest fires burning in that area, we'd be in trouble, but there aren't." He looked at their worried faces. "Are there?"

"How're we going to do this?" Marie Lauzon asked Gamache.

"I have no idea. You're the one who wants to get the Prime Minister."

"But you're the cop."

"A cop, not a kidnapper."

They were standing in the stairwell closest to the PM's office. Fortunately, as ignorant as Armand was of the layout of Parliament, Marie Lauzon was knowledgeable. She'd played there as a child and explored every nook and cranny.

Marie looked at the time. "The cabinet meeting will be over in a few minutes. The Prime Minister keeps them to one hour sharp. He'll be heading back to his office soon."

"Is there an alarm he can press?"

"Yes. Under his desk."

Gamache nodded. No surprise.

"And the office has cameras, of course."

"*Oui.*"

So even if they could slip in and wait for him, they'd be clocked.

"How much coffee does he drink?"

Madame Lauzon was about to protest this ridiculous question, but stopped herself, realizing there must be a reason for it. And then she had it.

"A lot."

"And he must have—"

"A private bathroom. That doesn't, of course, have cameras." For the first time since he'd met her twenty-two years earlier as a scowling, frightened, angry, and entitled teenager who'd just killed a boy on a bike, he saw Marie Lauzon smile.

"And after an hour in the meeting, drinking even more coffee—" said Armand.

"The first thing he'll do is use his bathroom. There's a door into it from the corridor so the cleaners don't have to go through his office. It's kept locked, of course. And yes, I have the code."

Gamache paused at the door to write a message.

Marie Lauzon glanced at it. "The Chief Petty Officer? That valet fellow from the White House? What's that about?"

Armand hit send, without replying.

"Come on," hissed Marie Lauzon. "What're you doing now? Christ, tell me you're not doing Wordle?"

Gamache wasn't. He was composing one more message. One last message. Just a few words. Once sent he tucked the phone back in his pocket and took a deep breath.

Ready.

Minutes later Armand was standing in the Prime Minister's private bathroom, watching the door handle turn. *Please let it be Woodford.*

Then it stopped.

Come on. Come on.

"Are you kidding me?" the Prime Minister's voice came through the door. "They still haven't found Gamache? Where the hell is he?"

"I'm getting an update, sir." It was the head of the PM's security detail. "He's definitely still in the building."

"Well, find him, for Chrissake."

"And we're looking for Marie Lauzon." On hearing that voice, Gamache's brow dropped. But after reading the document, he knew he shouldn't have been surprised.

It was Giselle Trudel, the Minister of Defense. Their supposed ally. Whose side was she really on?

"Focus on Gamache. We can deal with Marie later. She's not a threat."

The door handle turned another millimeter.

Come on. Come on.

"Captain Pinsent admits to helping the other two escape," said the head of the RCMP security detail.

Gamache closed his eyes in relief. Confirmation. *They're out.*

"What the hell is happening?" the PM said. "It's impossible to know who to trust anymore."

Truer words, thought Gamache as he watched the door finally open.

James Woodford stepped in, closed the door behind him, turned, looked in the mirror, and came very close to needing a new pair of slacks.

Jeanne Caron read the reply.

The planes would be loaded with the incendiary bombs and ready to take off to the northern lake on her word. The fires would be so intense, whipped up by the forecast winds, they'd put all previous conflagrations to shame.

They'd burn for weeks, marching south, eating millions of hectares along the way, consuming every community in its path and sending the remains of ancient forests into the atmosphere. The plume would once again bypass Canadian cities to descend on the United States, killing Americans by the thousands.

Word would get out that their friendly neighbor to the north was doing nothing to fight the blazes. There would even be some evidence, carefully managed, to show the fires had been intentionally set. As an attack.

The scope of Canada's duplicity would slowly become clear.

It would not be a Big Lie.

This time it would be the awful truth.

Canadians, in turn, would be told that the bombs that started the fires were supplied by the US.

And that too would be the truth.

The incendiary bombs had been smuggled in using trucks supplied by Joe Moretti. Caron had made sure they were not stopped at the border.

The American government, propelled by grieving and outraged citizens and the media, would be compelled to act. To send troops into Canada. Perhaps on the pretext of fighting the fires, perhaps not. By then they would need no excuse—the images on the news would see to that.

And the troops would never leave.

It was all mapped out in the now grotesque War Plan Red. A document conceived in 1919, going dormant in 1939, then resurrected as a contingency, little more than an almost laughable exercise.

Until a visionary had seen the opportunities presented by the looming water crisis.

All crises presented opportunities to those bold enough to grab them. Few were. Which made the prize all the greater for those who did.

All it would take now was the spark. And Caron had provided that.

She texted her counterparts in the United States to be ready with their own payload of incendiary news releases. Already locked and loaded.

A second, terse message came in from Gamache, this one for Isabelle.

"I don't understand," said Shona, reading it. "Why does he want us to go to an airport?"

"I don't know." Isabelle put the phone away and peered around the stone pillar of the old bridge to see if anyone was approaching. "I'm thinking the reason will be obvious once we get there."

"Just us? Shouldn't we call for backup or whatever you call it?"

Lacoste turned to her. "From who?"

Shona was about to answer. *The Sûreté. The RCMP. The Armed Forces, for God's sake.* Instead, she was silent.

Who? Who could they trust?

No one.

"We need to get out of here," said Lacoste.

"Shouldn't we wait for him?"

"*Non.*"

As they ran to the car, Isabelle Lacoste could not believe she was leaving the Chief behind. But she had to go, and Armand had to stay, to cope as best he could.

"There's no fire there now," said Beauvoir. They'd moved up to the church basement and were staring at the map on the wall. "Which means they'll need to start one. The conditions are too perfect to ignore."

Nichol turned to Marcus Lauzon. "How would they do it?"

"You're asking me? I have no idea."

"Come on, you sat in on cabinet meetings," said Beauvoir.

"We talked about putting them out, not starting them. But—"

"What is it?"

"We fight forest fires with water bombers, among other things."

"*Oui.* So?"

"So if I was going to start one? I'd do the same thing, only instead of dropping water, I'd drop incendiary bombs."

"Shit." Beauvoir's mind was moving quickly. "They'll need planes. Which means the collaboration of the Air Force."

"CFB Bagotville," said Lauzon. Canadian Forces Base Bagotville.

"*Oui.*" Beauvoir thumped his fist against the map, squishing the large base north of Québec City.

"That'll play right into Woodford's narrative," Lauzon said. "The one he wants spread by American media. That the fires have been deliberately set by Canada as an attack."

"And they'd be right," said Tardiff.

Nichol almost protested, pointing out that it made no sense. No one would believe that Canada was going to attack the US using ash, for God's sake. It was ridiculous. But she realized it didn't have to make sense.

The less rational, the better. The point was not to engage brains but emotions. And emotions could be manipulated ridiculously easily.

Besides, the real point wasn't to defeat the Americans—that was impossible. The point was to provoke a counterattack. Give the Americans a pretext for invading Canada. And winning.

"So what do we do? Who do we tell?" Nichol demanded. "We at least have a pretty good idea where the fire will be started."

They now looked at the remote lake. Where Charles had visited, and Frederick had died. If it was where the bombers would end their mission, then the start was the Air Force base in Bagotville. But Beauvoir could hardly send a message to the commander there. She might very well be among those involved in what amounted to a coup.

"Wait," said Evelyn Tardiff. "Moretti sent trucks to Mirabel. I didn't know why, but—"

"Of course they'd move the planes," said Beauvoir, exasperated with himself for not seeing it. "Where there'd be fewer witnesses."

They shifted their gaze to Mirabel. The civilian airport north of Montréal, long considered a white elephant and all but abandoned, could easily handle those bombers.

Beauvoir made for the door. "We're going."

"We who?" said Nichol, looking around. "Just us? Are you kidding? This sounds half-assed, like kids putting on a play. Mom can do the costumes and we can use Uncle Ned's barn..."

Despite herself, Chief Inspector Tardiff gave one snort of laughter. Yvette was not wrong. But neither was Beauvoir.

"What can we do against bombers?" Nichol was now saying. "We need to get more support."

"From where?" asked Tardiff. "Who can we trust?"

Nichol had no answer.

"I'll stay here," said Lauzon. "I won't be any use in a fight."

"You were earlier today," said Beauvoir.

"Damn," sighed the former Deputy Prime Minister. "I knew that would come back to bite me on the ass."

Jean-Guy's face had been so grim for so long, smiling almost hurt. "You saved our lives. I'm not sure I ever thanked you."

"No need."

"But there is." Beauvoir patted his jacket pockets and found what he was looking for. "I got this from the warden at the prison. I believe it's yours." He held out a phone. "I'm sorry, sir, for all you've been through and my part in it. You were wrongly convicted. I know that now."

Lauzon took the phone. "Thank you, but we both know I'm not exactly the innocent type. I've done a lot I'm ashamed of, including to the Gamaches."

"No one is as bad as the worst thing they've done." Beauvoir surprised even himself with that statement. He wondered where it came from, then realized it was, of course, Gamache.

Jean-Guy did not remember that the Chief was himself quoting a death row nun.

"Can I send just one message?" The man, once the second most powerful person in the nation, now looked small, and vulnerable, and very emotional. "To my daughter. I won't tell her where we're going, I just want her to know..."

Beauvoir, who also had a daughter he loved more than life, said, "Of course."

While Lauzon sent the message, Beauvoir returned to the map and circled a town. He didn't dare send a text, but if the Chief should make it home, he'd know where they went.

Mirabel.

While Jean-Guy and the others headed out, Isabelle and Shona were also racing north.

CHAPTER 32

"Move your hands off to the side. Don't say anything, Mr. Prime Minister."

James Woodford did, then looked at the gun in Gamache's belt. "Are you going to kill me?"

"No. I'm taking you out of here."

"You're kidnapping me?"

"Such a strong word." Gamache flushed the toilet. "I'm escaping you."

It was, Armand realized, not the actual use of the word. But that did not seem to matter, the meaning was clear.

Holding Woodford's arm in a firm grip, he opened the door to the hallway a crack before shutting it again.

He'd already gotten a sense of the rhythm of the patrolling guards. There was a time when both guards had their backs to the hallway. That was how he'd managed to punch the four-digit code in, unlocking the bathroom door.

It would be, should be, easier to head back across since Marie Lauzon was keeping the door to the stairs ajar. As long as the PM didn't resist or, worse, scream.

"You have nothing to fear from me unless you try to warn the guards. Do you understand?"

Woodford nodded, his eyes wide. "You're going to kill me, aren't you?"

"Mr. Prime Minister?" came a voice from the office. "Everything all right?"

"I'm here to stop the killing, not to do more. And for that I need you alive. Answer her. Just say 'fine.'"

"Fine."

Gamache turned on the taps and checked the hall again; he waited a beat, then turned off the taps and shoved the PM out the door. Three strides took them across the hall.

The door was closed. He leaned against the crash bar. It didn't open. He tried again. It was locked. Marie had locked them out. He looked to his left. The guards were about to reach the end of the long hallway. They'd turn any moment.

His grip on Woodford tightened. He reached for the crash bar one last time. If it didn't open, he'd have to take off down the corridor, dragging the PM along. They would not get far. With the gun in his belt and the PM in his grip, there'd be no reason the guards wouldn't assume he meant the Prime Minister harm and act accordingly.

That would be his assumption, if he were them.

All these things flashed through Gamache's mind as he reached for the door, but this time, without prompting, it opened.

He plunged through, dragging the PM with him. The door clicked shut.

"What the—" he said before Marie Lauzon spoke.

"Sorry, I was testing to see if it could be locked."

"It can," snapped Gamache.

"Marie?" said Woodford. "For Chrissake, what're you doing here? Why're you doing this?"

"Are you telling me, sir, you really don't know?"

"Come on," said Gamache. "Explain later. We need to hurry."

Woodford looked about to refuse.

"Don't make me carry you, sir," said Gamache. "I'm not as young as I once was and I might drop you."

Woodford looked at the steep concrete stairs and allowed himself to be rushed down them. Once at the bottom, Marie took them to the right along what looked like a dead end, but it proved to have a door.

She yanked it open and stooped to grab the dossier they'd left there.

But it was gone.

She turned, panicked now, and saw Gamache staring straight ahead, his body tense, his face set.

"Are you looking for this?" A heavily armed special forces officer held the manila file. "You aren't the only one who knows their way around these buildings, *madame.*"

Jean-Guy and Nichol approached the Mirabel airfield. Slowly, slowly. Weapons drawn.

They'd parked a kilometer away and jogged forward, leaving behind Chief Inspector Tardiff, who was still recovering, and Marcus Lauzon. They were to be the last line of defense. Should Jean-Guy and Nichol fail, those two could at least try to get the word out. Before they too were killed.

Beauvoir had asked Reine-Marie's permission to give Chief Inspector Tardiff Armand's Sûreté-issue Glock, which was locked securely away. The head of Organized Crime now held it and watched as her colleagues disappeared into the thick forest.

Jean-Guy held up his fist for Nichol to stop. She bumped into him, never clear on signals. He could see trucks. Activity on the airfield. There were planes, but not bombers. Which surprised him.

Had they made a mistake?

But it seemed not. The trucks had *Moretti* on the side.

"Look," whispered Nichol.

Don Moretti himself was directing the operation.

Nichol was looking at Inspector Beauvoir. Her eyes were wide. He wondered if she'd ever fired her weapon at another human. Probably not.

That was about to change.

It was ten past four, and Jeanne Caron was turning full circle, staring in some surprise at the Haskell Opera House.

She'd heard of it and knew that Gamache had met General Whitehead here just the evening before, though why he also wanted to meet her there, she couldn't guess.

I need your help.

That's what his message said.

Gamache was acting in ways that were unpredictable. And that was always disconcerting. But then maybe their social media campaign against him hadn't been that far off. Too many blows to the head had unhinged the once formidable senior officer. Though that made him even more dangerous.

Also, he was late. Which didn't surprise her. She doubted he'd show up at all, given what she'd seen on the video from Parliament.

Moretti's people were spread throughout the woods, and some were posted inside the building, with orders to let Chief Inspector Gamache pass, should he appear. Moretti himself wasn't there. He was directing operations at the airport.

Mirabel.

Now there was a *coup de grâce*. A stroke of genius.

This ends now. As soon as she gave the word, a sniper on the balcony would take out Gamache. Should he show up.

But before that happened, she needed to find out all he knew.

Taking a seat, she looked down at the thick black line at her feet and wondered what it was for. Then her gaze moved around the beautifully maintained old building, a tribute to a very special relationship between two sovereign nations. A relationship that had also, despite the occasional disagreement, been beautifully maintained.

This starts now. As soon as she gave the word, the planes would take off. Mirabel—she almost laughed.

She took out her phone and sent a text: *Pret?*

Ready?

Isabelle Lacoste and Shona Dorion parked five hundred meters from the airport and slowly made their way forward.

They could see activity on the airfield. Trucks and planes.

And people moving between them with long trollies.

"What're you doing?" Lacoste whispered. Shona had brought out her phone.

"You have your weapon, I have mine."

"For God's sake, you're not live-streaming this?"

"Not to everyone, just sending it to Paul. He'll know what to do with it."

It was, Isabelle had to admit, a good idea. Whatever happened to them, the world would know. Though she hoped her secret crush, the journalist

Paul Workman, had a good place to hide. They'd be coming after him next.

Workman was having lunch at the Queen Mother Café on Queen Street in Toronto with the head of Reuters North America. She'd flown up from Washington as soon as she'd seen Paul's feed from Parliament.

The two old friends and comrades had covered conflicts all over the world together, rising to the top of their profession. Now the Reuters woman needed to hear everything Workman knew.

"The events in your Parliament, hard on the heels of the attack in the White House, smell like a concerted attack on both our 'houses,'" she said.

"Did you look up War Plan Red?" he asked.

"Of course. It was put aside in 1939. I don't know what that cop was yelling about."

"There's more to it. It's been quietly updated over successive Presidencies." Workman pulled a napkin over and wrote .family, then a series of numbers and symbols. He shoved it toward her. "Follow that, then put in War Plan Red."

"There's no such thing as .family. The deepest the web goes is .onion." She looked at Workman, then down at the napkin. "Even if this domain exists, we both know whatever is down there is highly suspect."

"True. But where else would you hide a truth except among a bunch of lies?"

"Look, the narrative has changed since this morning. Even legitimate news outlets are airing the new version from your Parliament, showing that the PM was physically threatened. They say that the video you sent out was doctored to show your PM in the worst light—"

"Doctored by me. Yes, I know what they're saying. Do you believe that?"

"No. That's why I'm here. People who know you trust you."

"And the world trusts Reuters," said Workman.

The saying among reputable journalists was "Reuters for writers." If the news service reported something, it was true.

"I'm willing to stake my reputation and that of the agency on this," she continued. "But I need proof."

"You need the original files," he said.

336

As they made their way back to his home office, he checked a new flagged message.

"What is it?"

Workman had stopped dead on the sidewalk and was staring at his phone. Then he quickly hit record.

"Oh, thank God you came."

Jeanne Caron turned abruptly on hearing his voice.

"You look surprised to see me," said Armand, striding down the aisle.

Beauvoir and Nichol advanced.

Jean-Guy quickly took in the placement of everyone, and everything, on the airfield. There were two large men with assault rifles guarding the perimeter. The rest, those unloading the trucks, didn't appear armed, but Beauvoir suspected they probably were. Best to assume.

The guards didn't look overly vigilant. Probably convinced no one would know they were there.

One seemed much more concerned about some horsefly or wasp buzzing around him.

Beauvoir made his way toward the other guard. Tucking his gun into his holster, he picked up a large rock.

The guard, one of Moretti's soldiers, was watching the progress of the unloading and loading. Had he been looking outward, as he should have been, not inward, he might have seen the blow coming.

Beauvoir dragged the unconscious man into the woods, cuffed him, and picked up his rifle. Crouching down, he looked across the airstrip. There was no sign now of the second guard.

Nichol had done her job.

Lacoste crept forward, then paused and looked behind her.

"Are you getting this?"

"If you mean a nice shot of your ass, then yes."

The Reuters reporter smiled. They were now in Workman's office, watching the live streaming on his laptop.

Oddly, that was always her worry. Not just that she'd be killed while covering a war or natural disaster—that would be bad enough—but that the last photo of her would be of her ass, since the photographer with her was always "bringing up the rear."

"What's so funny?" Paul asked, his censure obvious.

"Nothing." Though she suspected Paul and all other male reporters were even more vain and had the same fear. That the last photo of them would be deeply unflattering. And would be the one that won a Polk.

Isabelle Lacoste turned back toward the activity in front of them.

The planes were almost loaded. It was now past four in the afternoon. Would they take off or wait until morning?

If she'd filled in the blanks correctly, those canisters contained some sort of firebomb. Napalm or the like. Against a night sky the resulting fire would look like Armageddon.

If she was calling the shots, she'd make sure those planes got off the ground and dropped their bombs in time for the six o'clock news.

"Isabelle?"

The tone of Shona's voice froze Isabelle's blood.

"Oh, shit," said Workman.

His Reuters colleague was staring at the screen, no longer smiling.

The Sûreté inspector had been struck hard and fallen to the ground.

The phone streaming the images also dropped. Then went dark.

"Is that...," began the Reuters journalist.

Workman was already on it, going back a few seconds. As the phone slipped from Shona's hand, it hit the ground, bounced, and a moment before it went off, a face appeared.

"Robert Ferguson."

"Your Minister of Public Safety."

"After seeing that video from Parliament," Caron said, getting up and moving to greet Gamache, "I'm surprised you made it. How did you get out?"

"I had help. Seems not all the RCMP guards are willing to just follow orders."

"Thank God for that."

She noticed movement behind Gamache, on one of the balconies. A sniper was steadying their rifle. Waiting for her signal.

Armand seemed oblivious. Clearly whatever instincts he once possessed had been blunted.

"We haven't much time," he said. "Fortunately, we got Woodford out. We also found this. It's pretty damning."

He held up the dossier.

"What do you mean you got Woodford out?" she demanded. "You kidnapped the Prime Minister?"

He offered her the file. "Here."

She took it. "Where did this come from?"

"The office of the Minister of Defense."

Jeanne Caron was silent as she looked down at the file, but did not open it.

"I think you already know what it says," he continued, quietly. "Since you wrote it."

"I did no such thing. What're you saying?"

"Why're you objecting, if you don't even know what's in it? It might be good things. Or it might be the outline for the revised and updated War Plan Red."

The two stared at each other.

"You're a fool, Armand." She stepped away and nodded toward the balcony and waited for the sharpshooter to take the shot.

Nothing happened.

"Jeanne Caron?"

She turned.

A man, familiar, though she couldn't quite place him, was walking toward her from the far door. He was in uniform.

"I'm arresting you under the Homeland Security Act on charges of terrorism."

"What the hell is this?" she demanded, turning back to Gamache, whose face was neutral.

Not yet panicked, she waited for the shots that would drop Gamache and now this other man.

None came.

She turned back to the man, and now recognized him. It was the valet from the Oval Office that morning.

They had to move quickly now.

Nichol closed in from one side, Beauvoir from the other.

His targets were Moretti's people moving the containers to the planes. Nichol had only one goal: Don Moretti himself.

She got there first, coming up behind the mafia boss, who clearly felt he was perfectly safe.

She placed her gun at the base of his skull. "Joseph Moretti. Agent Nichol of the Sûreté du Québec. You're under arrest."

"What the fuck?" He whipped around and reached out for her.

She pulled the trigger.

All activity on the airstrip stopped, the moment frozen in time. Then, quick like lightning, everyone turned and looked toward where the shot had been fired.

Everyone except Beauvoir. He'd been trained well enough, by the best, to just keep going.

"Don't look back," Gamache had always warned them. "You need to keep your eyes on the target. That must be your priority. Keep moving forward, no matter what happens."

And Beauvoir did. That moment's pause gave him time to reach the first man and drop him with a sideswipe. Then he turned and fired, just as another pulled a gun and was about to shoot.

The man dropped. But now two others closed in on Jean-Guy. He could never get both.

"*Arrêtez!*" It was Nichol's voice, commanding.

And then another sound. A man screaming in pain; then his voice, strangled but recognizable: "Stop."

It was Moretti. He was kneeling on the ground and bleeding from a bullet wound to his shoulder. Nichol had him in a headlock and was pressing her fingers into his wound. He was writhing.

"Do as he says," she commanded, "or—" Without hesitation she dug her fingers in deeper and he screamed.

There was a hesitation, then they dropped their weapons.

Beauvoir scooped them up.

"Open it." He pointed to a canister.

The man looked to Moretti, who gasped in pain and nodded.

First one, then another, then another, until all the drums had been opened.

"What?" said Nichol, still holding up a now semiconscious Moretti. "Napalm?"

"Sand."

"Can't be."

"All of them. Just sand."

Moretti, eyes closed, managed a chuckle. "Damn Caron. She's fucked us all."

Beauvoir stared in disbelief at the sand. It was the wrong airfield. They were in the wrong place. The bombs were somewhere else.

"You're American," shouted Jeanne Caron. "You have no jurisdiction here."

She backed away and bumped into Gamache, who didn't move, except to point to the floor. And a thick black line.

He was on one side, and she on the other.

"I'm Chief Petty Officer Oscar Flores. You've crossed illegally into the United States, ma'am. I can and will arrest you."

Once again Jeanne Caron looked around, searching the balcony, the stage, the entrances and exits for Moretti's people. And there were men and women standing there. In Canadian uniforms on one side and American uniforms on the other.

She turned to Gamache, who looked anything but triumphant.

But she did. There was malevolence in her eyes, in her voice.

"You really are a fool. This won't hold. I'll be out in days, if not hours. And then there'll be no mercy. When they're finished firebombing the forests, we'll turn on your little village and obliterate it. As punishment, and a warning to anyone who also thinks they can stop us. All you've done is made it worse."

Gamache ignored Caron and turned to Flores. "General Whitehead?"

The officer shook his head.

As he left, Armand glanced toward the empty stage.

So don't be so naïve, and take that heart off your sleeve,
For a fool and his life will soon be parted.
War's a fact of life today, it will not be wished away,
Forget that fact, and you'll be dead before you started.

Stepping into the cool late-afternoon air, Armand could smell the earthy forest, the sweet pines.

This needed to end. And it would, before the sun set. One way or another. He desperately wanted to head north to the airfield, but knew by the time he got there, it would all be over.

Whatever the outcome, his place was back home.

I'm dreamin' of the trees in Canada, Northern Lights are dancing in my head.
If I die, then let me die in Canada, where there's a chance I'll die in bed.

CHAPTER 33

⌒

A rmand stared at the map and the red circle.
Mirabel.

Mirabel.

The wrong airport. They'd headed to the wrong one.

And it was his fault. He'd chosen to tell only one of them where to go. Where the firebombs would be. The airport named in the dossier Marie Lauzon found in the files of the Minister of Defense.

He hoped and prayed Isabelle was on her way there. He didn't dare write to distract her. Or alert anyone.

He checked his phone again. Still nothing from either Isabelle or Jean-Guy. He paced, then stopped. And listened, cocking his head.

The remaining cicadas were now playing an especially nasty trick on him. It was as though the few that were left were seeking revenge, determined to do as much damage as possible before leaving.

Now they sounded less like screaming insects and more like the drone of bombers approaching.

He walked to the door and, opening it, looked into the late-afternoon sky. The sun was low on the horizon, and he thought he could just make out Venus rising.

A careful man, he stood there a few moments, to make sure Venus wasn't, in fact, moving. Toward the village.

But it was stable.

Armand closed the door and looked at his phone again.

A message had come in from Bert Whitehead's wife. He climbed the stairs, and in the demi-darkness of the church, he called her.

The blow that dropped Isabelle Lacoste had not been pulled at the last minute. This one struck her hard in the abdomen, breaking a rib and winding her.

She lay on the ground, gasping for breath, inhaling dirt and leaves. Tasting blood and trying to cough but without enough air in her lungs to do more than wheeze.

"How did you know to come here?" demanded Ferguson.

When Isabelle said nothing, the Minister of Public Safety nodded, and the soldier kicked her, hard.

Isabelle threw up.

"Stop it," shouted Shona. "I'll tell you."

"*Non,*" groaned Isabelle.

"It was Gamache," said Shona, kneeling beside Isabelle and trying to protect her. "He told us to come here."

"How did he know?"

"I don't know, I don't know," said Shona. "All I know is that he sent a text. I can show you."

Shona reached for her phone and looked at Ferguson for permission to turn it on. He nodded.

"It's back," said Workman.

"Are you recording?"

"Of course I'm recording!" Still, he double-checked.

"Where are they?" the Reuters woman asked.

Workman studied what little they could see of the background. But it looked like everywhere else in Northern Québec. Trees. Just trees. And a single bird in the sky.

"I don't know."

"No, no," said Shona, replacing the phone on the ground. "*Merde.* It wasn't to me. Of course it wasn't. I'm sorry, I'm not thinking straight." Her voice was high and panicked. "He sent it to her. All he wrote was *Mont-Laurier.*"

* * *

344

The two journalists looked at each other. Then leaped on their phones to find an airport in Mont-Laurier, Québec.

"Got it," they said in unison.

"We need to call the closest Sûreté detachment," said Workman, looking it up.

"Stop, wait. They might be in on it."

"And if they are, alerting them will make it worse?" said Workman, his phone to his ear now. "*Oui? Bonjour.*"

He quickly explained who he was and what was happening, and what they needed to do.

"*Non, non!*" he shouted, then lowered the phone. "They hung up on me."

"We need to get the planes in the air. Now."

"Yessir."

Ferguson turned to the two women. "Get up. You're coming with me. Hurry up!"

Shona helped Isabelle to her feet, and with slow steps they followed the Minister, prodded by the soldiers behind them.

Two CF-18 jets were at the end of the runway, with technicians making final checks on their payload of bombs.

At least twenty heavily armed military personnel were scattered around the area, taking up defensive positions. Trained soldiers, Canadian soldiers, not mercenaries, not Moretti's band of thugs.

Sitting off to the side was a military helicopter. That was how the Minister got there so quickly.

"Get in."

A soldier cross-checked Shona, shoving her toward the helicopter. The force of it made her stumble and fall, dropping Lacoste in the process. The soldier cocked his rifle and pointed, on the verge of shooting.

"No," commanded Ferguson. "We drop them into the fire. Get their phones. No evidence, no remains. Nothing that can be traced back here. To us."

"Oh, God," whispered Workman.

Shona's phone was still working. He was still recording what would now be their murders.

He turned to his Reuters colleague, who, like him, had seen terrible things. And this was right up there with the worst. Normally they came upon atrocities after the fact. Mass graves. Evidence of executions.

Neither had actually watched, helpless, as it happened. And, in Paul's case, to someone he cared about.

Robert Ferguson climbed in and nodded to the pilot.

"You know where to go." Then he turned to the officer in charge, standing on the tarmac. "As soon as we're airborne, send off the planes. We'll follow."

"Yessir."

The door slammed shut, and the Minister tapped the pilot's shoulder. He gave a thumbs-up and the blades began to turn slowly.

Shona lay on the floor. Unable to accept that this was really happening.

Someone would save them at the last minute.

The helicopter would not be allowed to take off.

But the rotors picked up speed, their thud, thud, thud mimicking, mocking, the pounding of her heart.

She was about to plead, to beg for her life. But the words died on her lips. It was useless. She was going to die. Nothing now would stop that. She was damned if her last act was begging. Still, a small "Please" escaped. Unheard over the rotors.

Shona looked around the cabin. There must be something she could use, to fight back.

Something. Anything. But there was nothing.

The helicopter lifted off, wavered for a moment, then tipped forward. On its way.

Isabelle lay on the metal floor. Shona reached out and held her hand.

Out the window, she could see the mauve of the early-evening sky and the forest below. Its canopy of autumn leaves, red and yellow and amber, undulated with the current created by the rotors making it look as though the woods were alive.

Then the helicopter banked sharply.

CHAPTER 34

A rmand checked his phone again.

It had been too long since he'd heard from Isabelle or Shona. He had, though, had a call from Jean-Guy.

"We're at Mirabel. It's the wrong airport, *patron*," Jean-Guy shouted into the phone. "Moretti's here. We've got him, but there're no bombs."

But of course Gamache already knew that.

He tried to calm Jean-Guy, reassure him. "Not wrong. You got Moretti. You couldn't have known that he was being used as a decoy."

"So where are the planes? The bombs. What's going to happen now? For God's sake, *patron*. Where are they if not Mirabel? And where's Isabelle?"

Where was Isabelle? Why hadn't she checked in?

"Clean up there, then come home."

Come home.

That had been an hour ago.

The sun was setting, Venus was rising, and Armand was standing on the porch of the church. Looking at the peaceful village below. And the three tall pines that signaled safety.

A car passed and he waved, but in the twilight, he wasn't sure if they saw. Then he made his way into the church and took his place in the pew. And waited.

His phone vibrated and he glanced down at the message.

Still he waited.

Some malady is coming upon us. We wait. We wait.

Before long Marcus Lauzon slipped into the pew beside him. The last of the light through the bodies of the stained-glass boys bathed the men in warm amber and red and yellow.

"We went to the wrong airfield, Armand."

"I know."

In the silence Armand heard the drone of an aircraft in the distance. This time he wasn't fooled.

"You have a remarkable daughter," he said. "She saved the day, you know."

"Really?" Lauzon turned to him. "How so?"

"In Parliament, she managed to find and smuggle out a file that outlines the entire plan." Gamache placed it on the pew between them. "It was in the office of the Minister of Defense but was written by Jeanne Caron for her boss."

"Her boss being Woodford." He shook his head. "I've known Jeanne since she was a child, you know. I paid for her university. So bright. And yet even then . . ." He looked down at the file. "That's the whole plan? But why would Giselle Trudel keep a hard copy of a document that damning? Still, we're lucky she did. Does it implicate Woodford? Is it the smoking gun?"

"I think you should read it, sir." Armand pushed it a centimeter toward the former politician.

Lauzon picked it up, then paused. "Do you hear that?"

"You hear it too?" said Armand, rising.

"Something's coming."

The two men stepped out of the front door of the church. From the small porch they could see a light just above the horizon.

"It's Venus," said Lauzon.

"Venus doesn't make a sound. Before it's too late, I want you to know the other things your daughter did. She ordered Captain Pinsent released from custody, freeing her to help us escape with the file, but also with . . ."

Armand nodded down the hill, to a shadowy figure standing next to the three pines on the village green. Jean-Guy Beauvoir was on one side of him and Chief Inspector Tardiff on the other.

"My God," whispered Lauzon. "It's Woodford. You got him. Your Black Wolf."

"Yes. We got him."

Two others were approaching.

Lauzon squinted, peering into the darkness. "Is that you, Marie?"

His voice, hopeful, faded as the elongated light from the church door stretched toward and finally revealed who was approaching.

Not Marie Lauzon.

"I'm Reine-Marie Gamache," said the voice out of the darkness.

"*Oui.* I know who you are."

"But you don't know me," said the large man beside her. "I'm Daniel Gamache."

Armand could sense a change in Lauzon. A stiffening. A sudden alertness.

"You're under arrest." Reine-Marie's voice was strong and clear.

"What is this? I don't understand."

"It's a citizen's arrest, Monsieur Lauzon," said Armand.

He looked beyond the man at his side, to Reine-Marie. To Daniel. Who had waited so long for justice. That he and his mother should be the ones to deal it out was more powerful than any arrest Armand had ever made. More poetic than anything Shakespeare, Auden, Atwood, and Zardo could ever capture.

If the head of homicide had his way, every murderer would be arrested by citizens whose loved ones had been stolen from them.

Now the three figures on the village green separated themselves from the pines and walked up the hill. Led by Prime Minister Woodford.

"What?" demanded Lauzon. "You're arresting me? You think I'm behind it?" He turned to Gamache, pleading. "For God's sake, man, it's him." He waved toward James Woodford, who was now standing between Reine-Marie and Daniel at the bottom of the stairs. "He's fooled you. Don't you see what he's done, what he's capable of? Circles within circles. Nothing left to chance. For Chrissake, before it's too late. Stop him!"

Lauzon was wild now, with panic. With rage. The approaching aircraft stopped and hovered overhead, its floodlight catching his eyes. Here was not just a wild creature, but a rabid one.

Armand gripped his arm and held him fast. Then, while Beauvoir recorded it, Daniel read the former Deputy Prime Minister his rights.

The helicopter landed and Shona got out, falling to the ground with relief. Then she got up and helped Isabelle. Behind them came Captain Pinsent, gripping the arm of her prisoner, the Minister of Public Safety.

It was over.

CHAPTER 35

A s Armand bit into the cannoli, cream squeezed out of the pastry onto his fingers.

Reine-Marie shook her head in amusement as he licked it off. "I can see where Florence gets it from." Their granddaughter loved being brought to Open Da Night by her grandfather.

They'd been joined by their son and daughter, Daniel and Annie, along with Jean-Guy and Isabelle. Evelyn Tardiff and Yvette Nichol, who seemed to be a couple, were also there for this very informal debrief two days later.

The door opened and Shona arrived, followed by a very familiar face. Paul Workman had come from Toronto. He and his protégée had been promised the exclusive.

They dragged over another round table and a couple of chairs.

So far, what had happened hadn't gotten out. Prime Minister Woodford had assembled a hastily put-together committee, made up of all parties, to begin the task of investigating what had happened. And quickly assessing the fallout.

The PM had also prevailed on his people, and those in Washington, to allow the police and intelligence services to quietly finish their job before making anything public.

They didn't want any of the conspirators to go to ground. Or South America.

But Armand trusted everyone at the table, including the journalists. Should anything go wrong, and there was a possibility it still could, the best protection wasn't force but truth.

Transparency.

"How did you know?" Workman asked, placing his iPhone next to Shona's. Both recording.

"That it was Lauzon all along?" asked Armand.

"No. We've read the document." Shona nodded to the file on the table, sitting innocently among the demitasses of espresso and the plates of cannoli and bomboloni.

She looked haggard. She woke up screaming every night, and was followed every hour of every day by the image of being tossed out of the helicopter into the fire below. It was a waking, walking nightmare. Made worse by the fear that it might still happen. If they didn't get this right. Shona had told no one about those dreams. But she didn't have to. They knew.

The Sûreté officers recognized the signs. That terror that clung like a caul. It was called post-traumatic stress by doctors who had no idea what they were talking about. There was nothing "post" about it. The trauma was still present, ever present. Evergreen. A perpetual, perennial horror, relived every day and through the night.

It might lessen, but it never left.

"The document makes it clear that they meant to set up Woodford and the American President," Shona continued.

"Did Marie Lauzon realize what the file was saying?" Paul Workman asked.

"That if it wasn't Woodford, the Black Wolf was almost certainly her father after all?" asked Beauvoir.

"No, I don't think she did," said Gamache. "At least not consciously."

It was one of the more difficult things he'd had to do. Tell Marie that they'd once again arrested her father, using the dossier she'd found containing the plans. And this time the evidence against him, including Jeanne Caron's and the Minister of Public Safety's testimonies, would stick.

"It's obvious that once Woodford was either arrested or killed, Marcus Lauzon would be released from a wrongful conviction," said Gamache, wiping the last of the cream off his hands. "That was why we had to get him out of Parliament. It seemed the most likely course was to murder him so he couldn't defend himself."

"Since Marcus Lauzon would be one of the few now beyond suspicion, he'd be placed at the head of the emergency government," said Isabelle.

Her ribs were bound, and she was on painkillers and bomboloni.

"And Giselle Trudel?" asked Reine-Marie. "How does she fit in? This file was in her office, after all."

"Robert Ferguson's admitted he put it there," said Jean-Guy. "Trudel had no idea. It was a perfect hiding place. People rarely go into paper files anymore."

"But why did they even keep it?" Shona asked. "It seems foolish."

"Electronic files can be hacked," Nichol pointed out. "Hard copies are easier to control."

Both Workman and Shona looked dubious, though the conspirators, who'd been so careful, had obviously made that one fatal mistake.

"I feel awful for Lauzon's daughter," said Isabelle. "Without her we'd never have survived."

She herself had been barely aware of what was happening on the helicopter. It was only later she learned what Ferguson had planned for them. And that Captain Pinsent had been in the copilot's seat. And the pilot was also on their side.

After Marie Lauzon had had Pinsent released, the Captain had rounded up her squad and waited in the tunnel for Marie and Armand to show up with Prime Minister Woodford. While she waited, she'd read the file they'd hidden there.

It had been a shock.

It had become clear to the senior RCMP officer, as the strange day had progressed, that something was very wrong. But she never, ever expected this. A deliberate firebombing of the forests by elements within their own government and military. In order to provoke an action by the United States. And setting up the Prime Minister to take the blame.

Pinsent had gone to the airfield named in the report, leaving her lieutenant behind in the tunnel to wait for Gamache and Marie Lauzon.

Once out, Gamache had driven south to his rendezvous with Jeanne Caron in the Haskell Opera House, while Pinsent had assembled a team of trusted colleagues within both the RCMP and Canadian Armed Forces and headed to Mont-Laurier.

"How did you get Chief Petty Officer Flores to the opera house to arrest Caron?" asked Shona. "You couldn't have had his contact information."

"True. I wrote Bert's number two and told him what was needed, and asked that Flores be sent."

Jean-Guy smiled. There were many ways, he now knew, to be a poet. Not all of them rhymed.

Captain Pinsent had been invited to join them at Open Da Night, but was in Ottawa answering questions about her own actions. Defying orders and allowing prisoners to escape. No matter the happy outcome, it was still, to the RCMP, disturbing.

Armand had also been summoned and was heading there the next day to be grilled.

But nothing those on the quickly struck Parliamentary committee did to him could be worse than being dragged over the coals by Jean-Guy. Nothing would be worse than seeing the look in those eyes. Not anger but hurt when Jean-Guy realized Armand had withheld information and deliberately allowed him to go to the wrong airport.

Armand and Jean-Guy had sat in the bistro by the muttering fire, exhausted. Their limbs and lids heavy.

Marcus Lauzon had been sent back to prison. The Prime Minister had been sent back home to Ottawa. The Americans had been alerted. The conspirators were hearing knocks on their doors. Woken up with warrants.

But there was one more thing that had to be done before the two comrades could finally go to bed.

They were alone in the bistro. It was, in fact, closed, but Gabri had left them the key. Most of the lights around the village green were out and the villagers snug and safe in their homes.

"You could have told me." Jean-Guy's words came out black and blue with hurt.

"You're right. I'm sorry. I made a split-second decision not to. By then I'd grasped that Lauzon was, in fact, behind all this. I couldn't take the chance that he'd see the message and realize that we'd found the file and knew about Mont-Laurier. About him."

Armand watched Jean-Guy as he spoke, to see if his own words might act as a balm. They did not.

"Why not? Why couldn't you take the chance on me? Trust me?"

Now the anger appeared. It bubbled to the surface and poured out of Jean-Guy in his expression. In the balled-up fists thrust into his lap. In the hunched shoulders of a wounded animal protecting its core.

Armand shook his head and heaved an exhausted sigh with the effort to remember his thinking. His reasoning. It wasn't even that. It was instinct. Jean-Guy was standing beside the man responsible for all this. A man so cunning he'd seen and foreseen every twist and turn.

A creature who'd not only been one step ahead of them the entire time, from the moment that note had been slipped into Armand's jacket pocket months ago, but who'd also been behind them, inching them in the direction he wanted them to go.

Toward Woodford.

Marcus Lauzon had been everywhere. In their heads, infecting their instincts and reason. Influencing their every thought. Choreographing their every step. Manipulating them.

Manipulating him. Armand now realized that.

He could not risk Lauzon seeing, sensing, even the slightest change in Jean-Guy. For all he knew, the Black Wolf was still playing them. Even now. The thought terrified him.

He held his suddenly cold hands toward the fire dying in the bistro grate.

Their only chance, Armand had felt, was to do the unexpected. Marcus Lauzon obviously knew him well. Well enough to know he would always, always trust Jean-Guy Beauvoir. Would always, always tell him everything.

And so, in a double sin of omission and commission, he'd withheld vital information and fed him false information. Only if Jean-Guy believed him to be an ally would Marcus Lauzon feel safe. And maybe, maybe lower his defenses.

As Inspector Beauvoir's commanding officer, as the head of homicide for the Sûreté, Chief Inspector Gamache did not need to explain his decisions to a subordinate. But as Jean-Guy's father-in-law, as his friend, he did. Especially since his decisions had put the man beside him in danger.

He'd have felt the same way, had Jean-Guy done that to him. Rationally, he'd understand, but the head and the heart did not always align.

Armand quietly explained why he'd done it. When he'd finished, Jean-Guy nodded. Then he stood up to leave and Armand felt his heart sink.

He too got to his feet. They faced each other. Two tired warriors.

Then Jean-Guy reached out and pulled the larger, older man forward. And held him, tight. So that their chests pressed against each other and Armand could feel Jean-Guy's heart. Beating in rhythm with his own.

Then the two comrades slowly made their way across the village green, pausing to look at the three tall pines. The code that told them they were safe. They were home.

And then they joined their wives in bed. And slept soundly for the first time in months.

"No, I mean how did you know there was more going on after the poisoning plot," pressed Workman. "Everyone thought that was the end of it."

"We have a problem," said Lacoste, and everyone at the table turned to her.

"What?" said Chief Inspector Tardiff. "Again?"

"Still?" said Nichol.

"*Non, non, désolée.* That was the message the Chief Inspector sent Jean-Guy and me." She turned to Armand. "You'd gone back over Charles Langlois's two notebooks and realized we had them in the wrong order. The one we thought was second, that held his conclusions and the key to the poisoning, was actually the first."

"The stepping stone to the real plot," said Beauvoir. "Only we couldn't figure out what it was, just that something else, something bigger, was going to happen."

"So we had to dig deeper," said Lacoste. "Go back over what Charles left behind. Go back to the map and pore over the notebooks."

"And we had to find the laptop," said Jean-Guy.

"So you knew something was up," said Workman. "How did you figure out what?"

"Yvette here realized the numbers and symbols Charles had written on the lake were passwords," said Isabelle. "They took us to .family and eventually to War Plan Red."

Yvette. She called me Yvette. Not Nichol. Yvette. She looked around and realized she was part of the circle.

Workman shook his head. "Hard to believe War Plan Red actually exists."

"Agreed," said Gamache. "After the shock of the First World War, the US decided it needed plans, defenses, should it happen again. So it created various plans. Each with a different color. They were collectively called the Rainbow Plans."

"War Plan Black for war with Germany," said Nichol. "War Plan Grey for Central America. War Plan Orange for war with Japan. There were others."

"Marcus Lauzon, as Deputy PM, had access to the classified files," said Evelyn Tardiff. "He knew that WPR had been resurrected as military exercises. Updated constantly, but never, as General Whitehead said, meant to be put into action. But Lauzon saw the potential."

"He saw how fragile water security was becoming," said Reine-Marie.

"And how desperate the Americans might become," agreed Isabelle. "All they needed was a shove in the right direction."

"Toward Canada," said Jean-Guy.

He was shocked by how easy it had been to turn Canada into an enemy. There were still millions who considered the megafires a deliberate assault. Once that perception was planted, it was almost impossible to refute. The Ministry of Truth at work.

Jean-Guy had just read *Nineteen Eighty-Four*, after first finishing *Animal Farm*.

Now he was reading the biography of Maurice "The Rocket" Richard. A hockey legend who had nothing to do with any of this.

"But how do we know that this thing"—Workman tapped the file—"is real? Maybe it was planted. It all seems too easy."

"Robert Ferguson has admitted it's real," said Isabelle. "Besides, everything in it was proven true."

"War Plan Red. Sounds ridiculous," said Nichol, shaking her head. "And we all thought you were nuts."

Armand had dropped his eyes to the document. He'd been silent through

357

this. Partly remembering the steps to get there. Mostly remembering the missteps.

"I really thought it was Woodford," said Lacoste. "That makes the most sense."

"That's what Lauzon said to me. That only Woodford had the power and contacts to organize all this," said Jean-Guy. "I have to admit it's one of the things that convinced me I'd been wrong about Lauzon. And then, when he saved us in the caves—"

"If he's behind all this, why would he save you?" Workman interrupted.

"He needed you alive," Beauvoir said to Evelyn Tardiff. "To tell us what you knew about Joe Moretti and Mirabel. He needed us to go to the wrong airport."

"It was Lauzon who told us about the caves and got us to go there, re-member," said Nichol. "He wanted us to save you." She took Evelyn's hand. "And really, thank God he did."

"What is it?" Jean-Guy asked. He'd noticed that Armand was still staring at the document.

Now the Chief raised his eyes. Though he said nothing, Jean-Guy could read that look.

Oh, merde, he thought. *We have a problem.*

As they left the café, Armand paused on the terrace and looked at the spot where Charles Langlois, the young biologist, had been mown down and died, as Armand held his bloody hand.

This was where it all began. And Armand knew now, it wasn't over yet.

"What is it, *patron?*" asked Beauvoir.

"Workman was right. This is too easy."

"You consider what happened easy?" asked Isabelle, still in pain from the beating. She watched Shona walking with her mentor down the street. The young journalist's torment all too obvious.

"I'm sorry," said Armand. "I didn't mean that. But Workman was right. Shona also said it. We should never have been able to find this." He held up the document, then looked at Isabelle. "And we should never have been able to escape. They wanted us to. Why let Captain Pinsent go? I was so relieved to be out, and with the proof, I never really thought about it."

"They made a mistake, that's all. Were overconfident." Though even as he said it, Jean-Guy heard the desperation in his voice.

He was tired and sore and desperate to get back to Maurice "The Rocket" Richard. To lose himself in the glory days of Les Habs, and not worry about the present or the future.

But in his heart, he knew the truth. "We were wrong."

"I think so. I think we were set up. I think they relied on my willingness, perhaps even eagerness, to distrust Marcus Lauzon. My desire to believe he's the Black Wolf."

"But if he's not?" said Isabelle. When he didn't answer, she said it out loud. "It's the Prime Minister? It's Woodford after all?"

Armand looked down at the document he held. The document he was always supposed to hold. And use.

To arrest, yet again, the wrong person.

He met their eyes. "I think so."

The next day Inspectors Beauvoir and Lacoste accompanied Chief Inspector Gamache to Ottawa, to answer questions about the role Marcus Lauzon had played in the attempted coup.

And Armand did. He looked the members of Parliament and senators in the face and lied. Over and over.

A week later they flew to Washington, where Armand was an honorary pallbearer at the state funeral of General Albert Whitehead.

After the private reception with the family, Armand and Reine-Marie, along with Jean-Guy and Isabelle, sat in the dim bar in the basement of the Hay-Adams hotel.

"To a man who had the courage to feed the grey wolf," said Armand.

They lifted their Shirley Temples, with two cherries.

The next day Chief Inspector Gamache appeared before the private House committee that had been struck to investigate what had happened and to uncover just how deep the corruption went.

Once again Chief Inspector Gamache was grilled.

Once again he lied. Over and over.

Explaining that, yes, Marcus Lauzon was behind the plot and that as far as they knew, the American President was blameless, though others high up in the administration must have been involved.

No, he didn't know who. And neither did Prime Minister Woodford. And Lauzon wasn't talking. He was in solitary.

Gamache chose not to tell the former Deputy Prime Minister that they now knew he'd been telling the truth. That he'd been, once again, wrongly arrested. By Gamache. Armand couldn't risk it getting out. Woodford had to believe they'd fallen for it.

Instead, the head of homicide for the Sûreté chose to keep a person he knew was not guilty in a hellhole of a prison. In a hellhole of despair.

It was the only way to put the PM at ease, and the best way to see that Marcus Lauzon would one day die of old age, in bed, instead of bleeding out on some disinfected tile floor. Still, Armand had prevailed on two of the men he'd arrested for especially gruesome murders, who were also in the prison within a prison, to watch over Marcus Lauzon.

In exchange, the head of homicide had agreed to watch over the convicts' families, especially their children.

With Lauzon as safe as possible, Gamache and his people rushed to gather evidence against the Prime Minister before it was buried too deep.

They moved at a near-panicked pace, while appearing as calm as the ocean. All the while looking over their shoulders. Knowing they were being watched.

But they were not moving fast enough. In frustration Gamache and his people saw each promising lead evaporate. Evidence was disappearing, being destroyed, just before they got to it. It was a race against time. A race Armand feared they were losing.

Armand and Reine-Marie flew to the UK, apparently to go to his reunion at Cambridge, but actually to quietly meet Sherry Caufield. Over tea and scones in a small shop in the Suffolk village of Eye, Armand asked the head of UK counterintelligence to do her own investigation, since she might find what they could not.

Turned out, Caufield had never believed the official story and was relieved to know that Gamache didn't either. Unasked, unobserved, she'd already started digging deeper.

"Lauzon could never have put all that together," she said. "You're doing that wrong."

"I'm sorry," said Reine-Marie.

"You put the clotted cream on the scone first, then the strawberry jam. Not the other way around."

Caufield seemed as incensed about the scone issue as the plot to provoke mass murder and a regional war.

"*Désolée*," said Reine-Marie and, turning to Armand, she grimaced.

"Lauzon's slimy, but more interested in immediate gains. He has no patience. This plot took patience and a master tactician with all the necessary contacts and access. You're doing that wrong."

"I'm sorry?" said Armand.

"You put the milk in first, then pour the tea." The head of British Intelligence huffed, indignant.

"If she calls us colonials, I'm leaving," muttered Reine-Marie. Though, choosing her battles, she put the clotted cream onto her next scone first.

And in his next cup of tea, Armand poured the milk first.

"So it is Woodford." He realized as he said it that up until that moment, he'd clung onto a thread of hope that Marcus Lauzon was, in fact, guilty.

"It is." Sherry Caufield leaned forward and dropped her voice. "You need to stop him, Armand. If he gets control of North America, we'll all be fucked."

They'd hoped that the danger was past. But they were wrong. While the forests were not deliberately set on fire, the internet was. Conspiracy theories were gaining ground, fueling wilder and wilder claims. More fear, more fuel, more converts.

Clearly the truth was not effective, so Chief Inspector Gamache did the only thing possible. He lied. And lied. And dug and dug. And lied some more when interviewed, when asked. And hoped the lies would buy them time.

CHAPTER 36

⌒

The break came not from Sherry Caufield, but much closer to home.

"*Patron?*" said Isabelle Lacoste, knocking on his open office door and stepping in. It was late one Friday afternoon in February. "My husband and kids are going to his family in Québec City, for the Carnaval. I begged off."

He looked up from the reports he'd been reading and indicated a chair.

"*Non*, I won't sit, *merci*. I was wondering if I could come down to Three Pines for a few days. Bring my skis and a stack of books. I thought I'd start with *Nineteen Eighty-Four*."

He took off his glasses and looked at her closely before saying, "Wonderful. In fact, I think Annie and the kids are also going to Carnaval this week. I'll join you and see if Jean-Guy wants to come down too."

"That would be fun." Though it was clear she did not mean fun.

She too had lied.

It was far too cold over the weekend to consider cross-country or downhill skiing, and only the village children dared go outside, bundled up until they could barely walk. They put on their skates and glided around the pond, with their hockey sticks and soft puck. Checking each other into the soft snowdrifts. When even they got too cold, they ran into the bistro for hot chocolate with melting marshmallows.

The days were bright, the sun almost blinding. The nights were crisp and clear, the sky strewn with stars. Every window in the village was etched with frost, while every chimney had a trail of smoke.

Their footsteps, as they walked briskly to the bistro, or the bookstore, or Clara's for dinner, squeaked on the hardened snow, and their breath froze in their nostrils and sinuses, bringing tears to their eyes.

Most of the time the three of them joined Reine-Marie by the fire in the living room, reading and chatting and trying to avoid eye contact with Ruth and Rosa. Giving every appearance of relaxation, while inside their insides were churning.

Finally, Monday dawned overcast, with flurries. And much milder.

"Downhill or cross-country?" Jean-Guy asked over an apparently lazy breakfast of omelets, English muffins, and crab apple jelly made from the orchard out back.

"I think cross-country, don't you?" said Isabelle.

"Perfect."

"Have fun," said Reine-Marie. "I'm going over to Clara's. She's finished a new painting and invited me to see it. Her solo show's coming up next month."

"It's called *Just before something happens*," said Armand, and saw Isabelle nod. Something was just about to happen.

Finally.

A kilometer into the trail through the quiet woods, their thin skis in the tracks made by previous treks, they paused. Armand had unzipped his coat partway, having worked up a sweat.

"Water?" Jean-Guy offered. Snow had accumulated on his tuque, and Armand had an idea what the younger man would look like as an elderly man.

"I have my own, *merci*," said the Chief, and looked around. "This way."

Now they broke trail through the deep snow. It was hard work, and when, ten minutes later, they arrived at the hermit's empty cabin, all three opened their thick coats and took off their hats, their hair plastered to their heads with perspiration.

Sticking their skis in a snowbank, they knocked their boots against the veranda posts and went inside.

It was cold, like a fridge. And dusty. There were cobwebs and mouse droppings. And yet, and yet, it still felt like a home. A place that had been happy once.

They sat at the wooden table, and Armand brought out the thermos of hot chocolate and three cups. Now the cold was penetrating again. He wrapped his flannel scarf around his neck and turned to Isabelle.

"What have you got?" For it had been clear since Friday, when she'd invited herself down, that she had something. But they couldn't risk talking about it until they were definitely alone.

They'd left their phones at home and had been careful what they'd said all weekend.

Isabelle unzipped a large pocket in her parka and placed a printout on the table.

"You remember my search of Margaux Chalifoux's home? When we first suspected something wasn't right with Action Québec Bleu?"

"Back when this all began, last August? Yes, of course," said Beauvoir. "You found nothing."

"I thought there was nothing, but I was going back over my notes again and this time I spotted something. I remembered that map in her basement. The one with all the pins."

The two men leaned forward but said nothing.

"I had the map brought to headquarters and the pins put back in. Chalifoux said they corresponded to where the various researchers had been. Each volunteer represented by a colored pin."

She looked at her colleagues, her friends. They were listening, closely.

"I went to look for the map in our evidence locker and it was gone."

Beauvoir leaned back, and Armand rotated his shoulders, in an effort to alleviate the tension.

Still they said nothing.

"I didn't look further, and didn't ask about it, of course."

Armand gave a small nod of approval. Evidence didn't just disappear. Someone had taken the map. Someone didn't want them to find it.

"Fortunately, while in Chalifoux's basement, I took a picture of the map to re-create where the pins were placed."

She nodded down at the paper.

"What are we looking at?" asked Jean-Guy.

"Not the pins. Those really do show where the researchers went. It's this." Isabelle placed her finger on the map.

Mont-Laurier was lightly circled in pencil. With a number under it.

"I don't understand how this gets us closer," said Beauvoir. "We already know about Mont-Laurier."

"True. But the number. Look at the number."

Armand's brow cleared and his face had opened in astonishment. "Is it a dossier number?"

"It is. And not just any dossier number. This is the approval for an American pulp-and-paper conglomerate to clear-cut the forests around Mont-Laurier and set up a pulp mill."

"Holy shit," said Jean-Guy. "That breaks all our laws protecting resources, never mind the environment."

"They must be the ones who extended the airstrip," said Gamache.

"That's my thinking too. And to do that, they'd need to bring up lots of 'workers' and tons of 'chemicals,' supposedly for the pulp mill," said Isabelle.

"Never mind equipment and planes," said Jean-Guy.

"Do we know who signed off on this?" Gamache asked.

"I don't, but Sherry Caufield does. I sent her the information. The file had been erased, but nothing disappears completely. She was able to track it down. Woodford didn't sign the document, of course, but it was sent to his private, confidential email. He knew about it."

It was his only mistake. And it was a big one.

"Yes?" said James Woodford.

The Prime Minister was in his office on Parliament Hill. Since news of the coup attempt, and his part in ending it, he had enjoyed unprecedented popularity, and not just in Canada. He was hailed worldwide as a hero.

A new entente was struck with the President of the United States. The two nations had never been closer.

There was talk of a Nobel Peace Prize.

Prime Minister Woodford looked up from his paperwork, expecting to see his new Chief of Staff, and was surprised to instead see Captain Pinsent of the RCMP. She was holding what looked like a warrant.

Clara Morrow's solo show at the Musée d'art contemporain de Montréal had, as its centerpiece, one giant oil painting. Leading up to it, marching down the hall, was a series of portraits. Most of them of unknown people. At least, unknown to the general public, with two exceptions.

The portrait most people went straight to was of James Woodford, whose happy, content expression as he sat at his desk was just, just, just about to change. Hundreds of patrons posed for selfies in front of the now disgraced PM, Clara having perfectly captured that split second before his world collapsed.

The other recognizable face was that of the poet Ruth Zardo, who looked quizzical, while the duck on her lap looked on the verge of solving the mysteries of the universe. That brought smiles to the faces of all the patrons, who also lined up to pose in front of it, trying to mimic the duck's expression.

But the portrait that most people ended up in front of belonged to someone they'd never met. And yet it was so compelling some stood in front of it for half an hour or more and returned several times. Just to visit with her.

It was Reine-Marie. She was anxious, worried . . . as most people seemed to be these days.

But that was just, just about to change. Someone she loved was just, just, just coming into view.

Some stood in front of the canvas and wept, with relief. Hope was taking the edge off their own stresses and fears. Reine-Marie's face let them know that if things could change for the worse, they could also change for the better.

They would change for the better. They were changing for the better.

But the huge painting that all this led up to, the one at the very end, the last one Clara painted, was of a single snowflake, glittering in perfection. A moment before it began to melt.

The tragedy wasn't its disappearance. The gift was that it existed at all.

What a perfect, beautiful world, where snowflakes existed. Even for a moment.

CHAPTER 37

$\sim$

It was now mid-August, a year almost to the day since it had all started, and they could finally talk openly about what had happened.

Marcus Lauzon had been released from prison, and while the former Deputy Prime Minister had clearly broken some serious laws, the prosecutors, with the agreement of the courts, decided he had paid the price. He'd returned home to Québec, where every morning he went across the road to his cheese shop, put on his red-and-white striped apron, and served his friends and neighbors. His main preoccupation being whether his favorite cheese from Isle-aux-Grues would arrive in time to share with family and friends, over a nice crisp Chablis.

Though he still harbored fantasies about bringing down Gamache, he knew he would never act on them. They were simply a companion, lashed to him.

And every night he woke up screaming. Terrified that he was still in that hellhole.

Woodford had been arrested, though the covert investigation into the possible role of President O'Rourke was ongoing. Despite their suspicions, her party had kept her on the ballot for the next election.

Armand had invited Shona Dorion and Paul Workman to Three Pines, along with Jean-Guy and Isabelle.

This was not Shona's first visit to the village. She'd been invited down many times, often when Isabelle was also there. Never when the grandchildren were visiting, though Isabelle had made good on her pledge to herself and had introduced her own children to Shona.

Aunt Shona, as she was now known.

Her night terrors had become fewer. The shrieking less intense. But it still woke everyone in the Gamache house and sent a chill into their marrow. Isabelle or Reine-Marie would rush into her room and sit with the young woman until it passed, and Shona fell into a deep exhausted sleep.

Shona also visited Myrna in her bookshop. They'd sit in front of the woodstove with mugs of strong sweet tea, as the journalist talked, and the former psychologist listened. And listened. And told her she was not crazy or going crazy. That her reaction to what had happened was the most normal, the healthiest thing possible.

Exactly what Myrna had done for Isabelle. For Jean-Guy. For Armand.

Now, as they strolled around the village green, with the prancing dogs, and Gracie, the three Sûreté officers walked the two journalists through what had happened.

"You got us onto the right track," said Armand.

"We did?" said Paul. "How?"

"You asked two simple questions: Why did the conspirators keep a document that dangerous? And how did we know it wasn't faked?"

"It was?"

"Yes. We should never have been able to find it. They wanted us to."

Later that day the full story, the real story, appeared online under Shona Dorion's and Paul Workman's bylines. Its conclusion, something that should have been obvious to leaders for decades, was that the only real war, the one they should be fighting, wasn't against each other, but against climate change. They needed to stop the catastrophe, not react to it.

Shona Dorion and Paul Workman would go on to win a Polk award for their reporting.

The next morning, while everyone else was still in bed, Armand and Reine-Marie took their coffees into the back garden.

They strolled past the gnarled old apple trees. Some of the fruit had fallen, though some had sailed over the clearly-not-high-enough fence.

"Duck," shouted Reine-Marie as another rotting apple whizzed by their heads.

They were just grateful it wasn't the actual duck.

Ignoring the cackles from the other side, they walked past the perennial borders, past the phlox and bee balm, past the plump bobbing hydrangeas, to the very end, where their private world ended and the rest of the world began.

Pausing there, they looked back at their home. It was a rare quiet moment.

Armand exhaled. His hearing was completely restored. In fact, it seemed more acute than ever. He stood in the early-morning sunshine, listening to the birds. The rustle of squirrels and chipmunks. The breeze through the—

"Duck!"

He did, and the apple just grazed his head.

"*Arrêtez*, Ruth!" he called.

"Wasn't me. It was Rosa." And it might've been. That was one odd duck.

Back on the terrace, they sat in the sun and sipped their coffees.

"What're you thinking?" Reine-Marie asked.

"What happens when there's one bad apple. You?"

When she was silent, he turned to look at her. Then, allowing her her thoughts and space, he closed his eyes and listened to all the subtle sounds around him. He believed he could now even hear the sunshine.

Who knew, he thought, *that it sounded like children singing Gregorian chants?*

"I was thinking...," she began, finding her way forward, finding the words. Again she paused. He opened his eyes and looked at her. And waited. She turned to him. "I imagine you've already thought of this, but do we still have a problem?"

"What do you mean?"

Most of the conspirators had been rounded up and were busy informing on each other. Including Joe Moretti, who had thrown everyone he could think of under the bus, even his own widowed mother.

Sherry Caufield had handed over the trove of proof she and her people had uncovered against judges, politicians, senior bureaucrats, industrialists, media moguls and self-styled journalists, military leaders and cops. On both sides of the border.

The depth of the planning, the involvement of so many, was shocking.

"I mean that one day they'll have to come, won't they?" She held his eyes, and he knew who she meant.

If something wasn't done soon, the Americans would run out of water.

One day their crops would fail completely, the once rich earth turned to dust.

"*In a dry and parched land, where there is no water,*" quoted Armand. When Reine-Marie tilted her head, he said, "It's something Dom Philippe said as he left the monastery of Saint-Gilbert-Entre-les-Loups. And yes," he took her hand, "they'll come. Unless something changes, they'll have to. But not today."

Today the sunshine sang.

ACKNOWLEDGMENTS

⁓

As I'm sure you've noticed by now, my friend, *The Black Wolf* is unusual on a number of levels. The first, and most obvious, is that the plot, as you'll know by now if you've read it, is hauntingly similar to real life.

I wrote the book, as I said in the author's note, a year before all the talk from the American President about making Canada the fifty-first state. I worried that my leaning on that plot point would be unbelievable, but it turns out is far too believable.

The other thing that is unusual is that *The Black Wolf* is the second half of a whole. A sibling to *The Grey Wolf.* At the end of that book I took a chance and ended it with the words, "We have a problem." It was not actually, "The End."

The challenge after twenty books with the same characters and same location is not writing the same book. Over and over.

I know, because I read the emails, that some readers want me to set each book totally in Three Pines. To have the villagers front and center. And in many of the books they are. But that is not always possible. I made the decision early on that for the longevity of the series, for its credibility, and for my own creative health I needed to set every few books away from the village.

I do understand this desire to live in Three Pines. I share it. I created the village as a place of refuge. Where we would find companionship and comfort and acceptance. And safety.

Perhaps slightly ironically now, Three Pines is an old Canadian code created to tell Americans fleeing tyranny when they are across the border and safe. In the book, Armand tells Whitehead that he will protect him when the battle for the fifty-first state begins.

Just look for three pines, he tells his American friend.

I love writing the scenes in Three Pines. In the bistro, the bookstore. Those conversations among intimate friends. The love they have for each other. Loved for who they really are, not who they might pretend to be to the outside world.

I love that Armand has found a harbor there, a haven. A place to exhale.

But sometimes we need to leave, so that the haven does not unintentionally become a prison.

When we return, it is all the sweeter.

When I was a child, I was terribly shy. Unsure of myself. Afraid of many things including other children. Afraid of being excluded, and so I chose to exclude myself, to step away and spend time alone. So, I would not be hurt. One of the exceptions was my grandfather. We'd go for walks through public gardens. He'd take my hand, and we'd talk. Though often he'd just recite poetry. It got so that poetry and conversation were one and the same to me. There was nothing unusual, nothing intimidating about it. Even if I didn't understand it, I understood the intention.

One of his favorites was by Sir Walter Scott (my grandfather was a product of his generation). Before long, listening to Papa, I had memorized:

> *Breathes there the man, with soul so dead,*
> *Who never to himself hath said,*
> *This is my own, my native land!*
> *Whose heart hath ne'er within him burn'd,*
> *As home his footsteps he hath turn'd,*
> *From wandering on a foreign strand!*

Home. After yearning for home for much of my life, I found it in a village in Québec, with Michael, with the dogs. With the miracle of new-found friends. And now, in Three Pines. With you.

Three Pines is a state of mind. A place we carry with us always and live in when we see the chance for the clever, often cutting, remark, but choose kindness. When we are forgiving, as we sometimes need to be forgiven. When we choose decency, and acceptance. When we have integrity and the courage to stand up for what we know to be right. Even at some personal cost.

It's now twenty years since *Still Life*, the first Gamache, was published. Twenty years since you first wandered into Three Pines and met all the villagers. In the introduction to that book, I wrote about the years I spent without friends, and the aching loneliness that brought me to my knees. And that the great gift wasn't having a book published, but that I had so many people to thank.

That remains true today.

Thank you to Lise. To Del. To Rocky. To Linda and Isabelle. To Normand and Peter and Bow. To Mellissa and Paul. To Shelagh. Thank you to Danny and Lucy and Ben. To Kirk and Walter and Guy. Thank you to Joan. To Jack and Jane, to Wendy, to Oscar and Brendan, Don and Erin and John. To David and Linda. Thank you Sukie and Bonnie, Hillary and Patsy and Kathleeney and Allida and JuJubee and Ann and Judy and Cheryl, Rita and Bob, Will and David and Jon. Thank you to Pascale and Jean, to Samatha and Nathalie, to Sally and Eliza and Cynthia and Victor and Chris and Zoe. To Sara and Janet and everyone at the Three Pines café. To Tara, Matthew, and Thom at Virgin Hill.

Thank you to Jill, who looked after Hunny with such love and tenderness, and now looks after Muggins and Charlie when I am away.

Thank you to Ann Cleeves and Ann-Marie MacDonald and Alisa Palmer. To all my writer friends, including Rhys Bowen and too many to thank, but you know who you are.

Thank you to my family, for all your patience and support. To Rob, Audi, Sarah, Ryan, Rhett, Waylon, Adam, Lindsay, Nora, Amelia, Kim, Laura, Lucy, and Oliver, to Mary and Brian and Charlie. I love you.

Thank you to my wonderful publishers! Many of whom have become close personal friends. Kelley Ragland, Jen Enderlin, Andy Martin. Thank you Sarah Melnyk, Paul Hochman, Allison Ziegler, Tom Thompson, David Rotstein, Jon Yaged, Louise Loiselle, Jo Dickinson, Jamie Broadhurst. Thank you, Steven Barclay. Thank you to the magnificent Raymond Cloutier, my friend and neighbor, who voices the French audiobooks, and to Jean Brassard for becoming the Québécois voice of the English audiobooks.

A book is both an individual effort—a year sitting alone, working and worrying. And a collaborative effort. This is in your hands because all those people also believe in Three Pines.

Thank you to my agent, David Gernert, and his great team including Rebecca Gardner, Ellen Goodson Coughtrey, Will Roberts.

Thank you to John MacLachlan Gray who, in collaboration with the actor Eric Peterson, created *Billy Bishop Goes to War* and allowed me to quote from that great work of Canadian stagecraft.

Thank you to all the booksellers, librarians, and readers who quickly adjusted expectations, and embraced the new all-Canadian tour for *The Black Wolf.* I am grateful.

Thank you. For coming to Three Pines with me. For following Armand, wherever the need takes him.

Thank you to Canada, to Québec, and specifically the village of Knowlton/Lac Brome for keeping a place at the table for me and so many others who long for a safe place.

Yes, I know. A list like that can be boring, unless you happen to be on it. And maddening if you happen to have been left out. (Sincere apologies if I have failed to thank you. I hope you can forgive me. It is a function of my memory and not my gratitude.)

And finally, a special thank-you to my Golden Girls, Muggins and Charlie, for bringing such unexpected joy into our home, along with all sorts of other things including sticks and dirt and . . . what's that smell? Is that really mud?

I wake up in the night and feel Charlie's breath on my face, and Muggins's body curled up against mine. And I know I am not alone.

The Black Wolf is about choices. About creeping threats disguised as friends. About the courage it takes to be a dissenting voice, to stand up and step forward.

But finally, at its heart, like all the Three Pines books, it's about the power of friendship. And love. And the great comfort of coming home.